W9-BIM-160

BESTSELLING AUTHOR COLLECTION

In our Bestselling Author Collection, Harlequin Books is proud to offer classic novels from today's superstars of women's fiction. These authors have captured the hearts of millions of readers around the world and earned their place on the *New York Times, USA TODAY* and other bestseller lists with every release.

As a bonus, each volume also includes a full-length novel from a rising star of series romance. Bestselling authors in their own right, these talented writers have captured the qualities Harlequin is famous for—heart-racing passion, edge-of-your-seat entertainment and a satisfying happily-ever-after.

Don't miss any of the books in the collection!

BESTSELLING AUTHOR COLLECTION

BLUE SAGE

New York Times and *USA TODAY* Bestselling Author

ANNE STUART

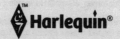

TORONTO NEW YORK LONDON
AMSTERDAM PARIS SYDNEY HAMBURG
STOCKHOLM ATHENS TOKYO MILAN MADRID
PRAGUE WARSAW BUDAPEST AUCKLAND

Recycling programs for this product may not exist in your area.

ISBN-13: 978-0-373-68873-9

BLUE SAGE

Copyright © 2010 by Harlequin Books S.A.

The publisher acknowledges the copyright holders of the individual works as follows:

BLUE SAGE
Copyright © 1987 by Anne Kristine Stuart Ohlrogge

HER BACHELOR CHALLENGE
Copyright © 2002 by Cathy Gillen Thacker

BLUE SAGE

New York Times and *USA TODAY* Bestselling Author

Anne Stuart

ANNE STUART

loves Japanese rock and roll, wearable art, Spike, her two kids, Clairefontaine paper, quilting, her delicious husband of thirty-four years, fellow writers, her three cats, telling stories and living in Vermont. She's not too crazy about politics and diets and a winter that never ends, but then, life's always a trade-off.

Visit her at www.Anne-Stuart.com.

CONTENTS

To Walkin' Jim Stoltz,
whose songs and whose life are an inspiration

CHAPTER ONE

He didn't have to go searching for the volume of fifteen-year-old newspapers and the issues covering that Fourth of July. It was always out, always available for those who wanted to read about it once more, just in case anyone had forgotten the details. Even in the carefully bound edition the newsprint was showing signs of wear. Too many hands had touched it, smoothing the old print. The pictures were faded and grainy, the aging black-and-white print draining the horror from the blood-splattered tableau. He stared at the open page, inwardly reciting the words he'd committed to memory years before.

Vet Goes Berserk—Kills Sixteen in Montana
Morey's Falls, Montana. July 5. Charles Tanner, Sr., a forty-two-year-old unemployed Congressional Medal of Honor winner, killed sixteen people and wounded one before turning the gun on himself during Fourth of July celebrations in the tiny town northwest of Billings. The lone survivor is a sixteen-year-old girl, listed in satisfactory condition.

That was all there was. Later editions of the papers had more information, longer articles, details about the victims, and all of those articles were kept, neatly and carefully, a testimony to the past. But he still liked this one the best. Short, simple, direct. With a quiet sigh of satisfaction he closed the heavy volume and turned to face the new day.

TANNER REACHED THE EDGE of the high mountain meadow with a feeling in his gut that was part relief, part dread. He was almost there. Within a few hours he'd be down in the flat, dusty little town of Morey's Falls, back amid humanity in all its twisted glory. He'd been walking since someone had dropped him off in the middle of Wyoming. It had been ten days since he'd seen another human, and he'd gladly go a hundred days more before he did. He wasn't ready to face what he'd find down in that depressed Montana town.

But if he wasn't ready now, when would he be? He'd come here for a reason. He'd put it off for most of his adult life, ever since his father had taken a rifle and blown away a good part of the town's population. Now, almost fifteen years later, it was time for him to face up to it.

Not that it had been his decision, Tanner thought, slipping the pack from his back and propping it against the tree. If it had been up to him he'd have kept walking, keeping as far away from Morey's Falls, Montana as he could. Not that he was safe anywhere else. The news of Charles Tanner's crime had spread over the western half of the country. Almost anyone over thirty remembered him, remembered the unprovoked bloodbath that had left no family untouched in that small village. And his son bore the same name.

But it wasn't up to him. Alfred was dying. Alfred, the indestructible, as old as time, as strong as the land, as wise as eternity wasn't going to be around much longer. That last stroke had almost finished him, but he was holding on until he could settle the ranch. And that ranch in the mountains of New Mexico, the ranch they had run together since Tanner was a half-wild eighteen-year old, would go to someone else if he didn't stop walking.

Not that there was anything wrong with walking, Alfred used to say in that gravelly voice that had once been pure Cockney. Whiskey and wind and dust had stripped the Britishness from his voice, stripped the softness from his face, leaving him the texture and substance of rawhide. Hell, he used to say, Tanner could walk from the East Coast to the West, up the Continental Divide, the length of the Grand Canyon, or any one of the thousands of miles of trails he'd walked, if he chose. But that was the problem. He walked because he had to, not because he wanted to. And there was no way Alfred could leave the neat, prosperous ranch and thirty of the best quarter horses west of the Mississippi to someone who might get itchy feet again when the going got rough.

So Tanner was walking once more. Leaving Alfred back there with tubes and machines keeping him going, helping him steal a few more months from a greedy eternity, determined to give Tanner the time to come to terms with his past.

And that's what he was going to do. Morey's Falls

lay just over the next rise. The shack and twenty scrubby acres that had once belonged to his father were still there, waiting for him, the son and heir. The townspeople were there, too. Fifteen years after losing a goodly portion of their population to his father's madness, the townspeople were waiting. Somehow he doubted he was going to get a hero's welcome.

He flexed his taut shoulder muscles, stretching his long arms over his head. The pack weighed a good forty-nine pounds, and every one of those pounds seemed tattooed into his back. The thought of a real bed had been obsessing him for the last few nights. One with pillows and clean white sheets. A hot meal came second on the list, and with luck he'd wind up with both that night—comfort and something other than that dehydrated trail grub that took up more than its share of space in the heavy pack.

Whiskey and a cigarette wouldn't be bad, either. Now that he was closing in on civilization he could feel the old familiar craving. When he was out on the trail he never wanted to smoke. Somehow it would have been a crime against nature. But all he had to do was get within a couple of miles of flush toilets and he started longing for tobacco. Alfred always used to lecture him on how dangerous smoking was as he went through three packs a day himself. But it hadn't been cigarettes that had gotten Alfred.

Tanner could give them up, live a clean, healthy life, and still die in a car accident in his early fifties, just like his mother had. There were no guarantees in this life—you might as well take your pleasure where you could find it.

He dropped down beside the metal-frame back-pack leaning against the tree and stared out over the high, flat meadow. There were wildflowers dotting the fields, columbine and Indian paintbrush and field daisies. And there on the soft wind he could smell the thick scent of sage, not the purple stuff that grew down around Texas, but a lavender-blue color, enriching the air, teasing his nostrils with promises made to be broken.

He sighed, rolling up his sleeves in the hot noonday sun. Maybe he should spend the night in that flowered meadow, to give himself one more day of peace before he faced his past. The silence and serenity flowed around him, broken only by the distant call of a golden eagle wheeling and soaring overhead, by the rustle of the wind in the aspens, of the sound of horses' hooves on the thick green grass.

He held himself very still. His instincts had failed him. Usually he knew when someone else was around, whether it was four-legged or human. He was so attuned to being alone that he could almost smell another living creature. But he hadn't heard her coming.

It was most definitely a woman. She didn't see him, and wouldn't unless she was looking. She was out in the middle of the field, riding bareback on a big, stodgy-looking bay. And it wasn't just the horse's back that was bare.

Her faded flannel shirt was spread out over the horse's rump, she wore no hat, and her thick chestnut hair was hanging in a braid down her narrow back. She was wearing nothing but a pair of old jeans—even her feet were bare—and her face was turned up to the hot sun, basking in it, as the horse picked its dainty way across the field.

Tanner held himself motionless. He could do that—he'd had to more than once when he'd stumbled across a mother grizzly with her young cub, or when he'd run smack into a cougar that was bigger than it had any right to be. He knew how to stop, to blend with the landscape as well as any chameleon. He sat there, watching the girl and barely breathing.

She wasn't a girl, he decided, for all her innocent enjoyment of the hot summer sun. Even as he sat there watching her he could tell that her body, lean and spare though it was, held the grace of maturity. Her breasts were small and well-shaped, her arms were rounded with muscle, not softness, and her back was straight, strong, determined. Her legs hugged the barrel of the horse, and a sudden wave of sheer, healthy lust swept over him. He wanted those legs hugging him.

He let it go, noting it with acceptance and amusement. He wasn't surprised. It had been months since he'd had a woman, and being presented with the sight he was seeing would be bound to have a normal effect on his body. He would have worried if he hadn't wanted her.

The horse ambled on, in tune with its mistress, picking its way carefully across the high meadow. At one point she lay back on the broad rump, letting the sun bake into her flesh, and it was all Tanner could do not to protest. He didn't want all that skin burned and blistered by the sun. She should put her shirt back on, he thought critically, not moving. But he hoped to hell she wouldn't.

The sun was bright, glaring into his eyes in the midday, midsummer heat, and he squinted after her retreating figure. Blackflies were buzzing around his neck, and he swatted at one lazily, secure in the knowledge that she wouldn't see him. The bay flicked his tail, arching his neck slightly. The horse knew he was there, but his rider was still sweetly oblivious. He'd better not swat any more flies, not unless he wanted her to take off like a bat out of hell. As long as she was willing to ride around like that, he was willing to look. It would probably be his last moment of peace and pleasure for a long time.

He'd been up since dawn, which was somewhere around five a.m. at the end of June in that part of the country. He'd washed in an icy mountain stream and set out on the final leg of his journey. He'd probably walked a good ten miles over mountain trails until he reached the meadow, and the hot sun was making him unaccountably sleepy. He didn't want to nap, he wanted to watch the woman on the stocky bay. He'd close his eyes just for a moment, just to rest them from the sun's merciless glare, and then...

He felt the shadow cover him. He didn't move, his eyelids didn't flicker, he didn't signal his sudden alertness by anything more than an imperceptible tightening of his muscles. It wasn't an angry grizzly staring him down, and it wasn't a crowd of vengeful townspeople. He heard the soft whirrup of the horse, sensed the gentle equine nibbling at his heavy walking boots, and slowly he opened his eyes.

She'd put her shirt on, damn it. He would have liked to have seen her up close, with all that sun-kissed flesh. He blinked his eyes sleepily, yawned and plastered his most innocent smile on his face before meeting her gaze.

She wasn't a beauty, that much was clear. Her warm brown gaze was a little too direct, her mouth a little too generous, her jaw slightly too determined. And she was older than he'd thought. There were lines fanning out from those soft eyes, lines bracketing her mouth. Lines of unhappiness? Lines of pain?

She was looking at him with a mixture of curiosity, friendliness and a very noticeable unease. He knew just what she was thinking. She was wondering how long he'd been there, how long he'd been asleep. The shirt was buttoned up tight, the sleeves rolled down, but he could see the freckles across her nose and the light peachy blush across her cheekbones.

"Howdy," he said, giving her the full effect of his lazy smile. He knew perfectly well what that smile did to susceptible ladies, and he used it to its maximum effect. The woman on the horse blinked in surprise, and her grip on the reins tightened.

"Where'd you come from?" Her voice was a rich, warm contralto with a faintly husky note. Like whiskey and honey, he thought. For a moment he toyed with the fantasy of pulling her off the horse, into his arms, of unfastening that tightly buttoned shirt and freeing her warm skin to the sun and to his hands.

"Over the mountain," he said, dismissing the brief, erotic thought with a moment's regret.

She frowned, and the lines deepened around her eyes. "There's nothing over there," she said.

"Sure there is. There's Wyoming and Colorado and New Mexico," he said. "I started walking just outside of Casper."

"I beg your pardon?"

"Walking," he said patiently. "You know, shank's mare." He slapped his long legs.

"How long have you been sitting there?"

Here it was, he thought. The million-dollar question. He was tempted to grin up at her, but he knew better. He gave her his most guileless look. "I don't know. I must have fallen asleep," he said.

He could see the tightness of her shoulders relax, and her smile lost its faint hint of frost. "I saw you when I rode into the clearing," she said, testing the lie on her tongue like someone savoring a strange fruit. "I thought for a moment you might be dead. You gave me quite a turn."

I'll just bet I did. "Not me," he said aloud. "Just taking a well-deserved rest."

"Where are you headed?"

"A little town called Morey's Falls. Ever heard of it?" He knew perfectly well she had to have come from there. He remembered his mother's disparaging comments well enough to know it was the only thing resembling civilization within a hundred miles. He might have walked out of nowhere but she could have only come a few miles.

"That's were I'm from. It's a couple of miles down the mountain." Signs of curiosity were showing on her face. "What in the world would you want with Morey's Falls? No one ever goes there. People are too busy leaving."

"I inherited some land a while back," he said easily. "I figured it was time to check it out."

Her wide brow creased slightly, as if she was trying to place him. "Were you thinking of settling there?"

"I doubt it. I might sell the place."

"I don't think you'll find much of a market for your land. Morey's Falls is pretty remote and there aren't many ways to make a living."

So what else is new, he thought to himself. His mother had told him it was the darkest, deadest hole in the universe. Up here in this wild mountain meadow it was hard to believe it was so desolate just a few miles down. But he couldn't see Charles Tanner in a peaceful setting like this one.

He shrugged. "That's okay. I just want to see what it's like. What the town's like." He rose, slowly, stretching his full length. He could feel her eyes run over him, and while her expression remained unchanged, he knew her brain was clicking along. He would have given ten years to have read her mind.

She grimaced. "You're curious about the massacre," she said flatly.

He didn't deny it. "Is that what you call it?"

"Among other things," she said. "I wish to God people could just forget about it."

"It's been a long time."

"Fifteen years," she said. "Maybe once the monument is unveiled…"

"Monument?"

"A big granite monolith in the town square. They're dedicating it on the Fourth of July." She didn't sound pleased with the idea.

"Then I got here just in time," Tanner said softly.

"If you like that sort of thing."

"It'll be interesting," he said. "Very interesting."

She sat there on her placid bay, looking at him. "I'd better get going," she said finally. "I've got bread rising."

Belatedly he checked out the hands holding the reins. Strong, brown hands, with long fingers and short, sensible nails. And a thin gold band on her left hand. Only a married woman would be able to spend a Tuesday morning riding up in the hills. He wondered if her husband knew she took off her shirt when she thought no one was looking. He wondered if her husband knew he was going to have to be very careful with Tanner around.

"Nice meeting you, ma'am," he said.

"Ellie," she said. "Eleanor Lundquist, but everyone calls me Ellie." She held out her strong right hand, the one without the ring, and he took it, holding it not for a second longer than was proper, giving it only the acceptable amount of pressure. He was in no hurry. He hadn't even made up his mind whether she'd be worth the trouble. He'd learned to avoid angry husbands whenever he could. He didn't need to rush into things.

He took a step back, looking up into her clear brown eyes. "My name's Tanner," he said.

All the color drained from her face, her big brown eyes widened, and her generous mouth dropped open. Without a word she wheeled the horse around and took off across the open meadow, racing across the thick grass as if the devil himself were after her.

Tanner watched her go. So it was going to be like that, was it? Well, things had never been easy, and he no longer expected them to be. He looked at her disappearing back, and a grim, determined smile lit his face. Ellie Lundquist had just sealed her fate. He was damned if he was going to let a woman run like that at the sound of his name.

He picked up the pack and slid it over his shoulders, scarcely noticing the weight. He should have remembered. It was the seventeenth of June. Charles Tanner had opened fire on the town square on the Fourth of July, fifteen years earlier. So they were setting a monument up to mark the spot? Maybe he could be guest of honor.

His lips curled in contempt. He hoped to hell Alfred knew what he was doing, sending him up here. If it had been up to Tanner he could have spent the rest of his life avoiding the huge state of Montana. And from Ellie Lundquist's reaction, it looked as if the townspeople would have appreciated the same thing.

It was too late now. He couldn't turn around and walk back over the mountains, all the way back to Santa Fe. He'd promised Alfred. And while he had no objections to lying when it suited him, he never broke a promise. The town of Morey's Falls was just going to have to accept him, for as long as he chose to stay there. Ellie Lundquist was going to have to accept him. Because he had absolutely no intention of taking no for an answer.

He looked in the direction she'd ridden, anger still simmering in his gut. If he was any judge of the matter, that headlong, terrified flight might be the closest thing to a welcome he'd get. He took a deep breath, steeling himself. And then he headed after her, his long legs eating up the distance, heading down the mountain to his father's hometown.

CHAPTER TWO

Ellie's heart was pounding so hard it hurt, slamming against her ribs, twisting inside her so that everything felt tight and strangled. Her hands were gripping Mazey's reins as if they were her only hold on life, her legs trembled as they gripped the horse's heaving sides, and the two of them raced down the rough mountain trail at a dangerous speed.

It wasn't until Mazey slipped and was barely able to right herself that Ellie calmed enough to pull back, to slow their terrified descent. It would do no one any good if they fell on the loose shale, breaking their legs, breaking their necks. Mazey was an old lady; she deserved better than an ignominious death on a mountainside.

He wouldn't be able to catch up with them, even with those long legs of his. They were safe enough, and they'd be back in town long before he made it there. She could warn people....

What in the world was she thinking of? Warn people of what? What made her think the man up in the meadow had any connection with Charles Tanner?

But of course he did. Morey's Falls was too small a town, and Tanners had lived there since its founding in the late eighteen hundreds. Charles Tanner's grandparents and parents were buried in the small hillside cemetery just outside of town. Charles Tanner himself even had a small corner, away from everyone else, away from the graves of the people he'd killed.

He'd had a wife and a son. They'd left long before the massacre, even before Ellie had been born. She would have thought they'd change their name and never come anywhere near Morey's Falls again.

But the man sitting there in the shade of the aspen didn't look like a man who was going to change his name to suit anybody. Despite that easy smile of his, he didn't look like the kind of man who gave a damn whether he was welcome or not.

She could still feel the cold sweat of unreasoning fear drying on her back as the sun baked down. She didn't trust that easy smile, those guileless eyes for one moment. For all his feigned innocence he'd probably been watching her as she'd ridden across the field with her shirt off. For eight years she'd been going up to that isolated field, swimming in the creek on the edge of the meadow, certain that no one would be around to stare at her. It was the only place where she'd felt free, the only place where she wasn't weighted down by expectations and the past. Now that freedom had been ripped away from her, and by Charles Tanner's son.

She had no doubt at all that was who he was. She'd never been a strong believer in coincidence, and if that was all it was, he would have shrugged it off with a laugh and said, "No relation, of course."

But he'd looked her squarely in the eye and said,

"My name's Tanner." Calm, cool, defiant. Good God, why did he have to show up now?

And why did he have to look like that? He was much too handsome for his or anybody else's good. His dark-blond hair was too long, his mouth was too sexy, and those bedroom eyes were too blue and too masked. For all their lazy seductiveness, there was a coldness, a distrust lurking behind their innocent gaze.

He had one of those lean, compact bodies that was stronger than it looked. He wasn't more than six feet tall, with long legs, muscular forearms and wiry shoulders beneath the faded flannel shirt. Which reminded her of her own flannel shirt, or lack thereof, and she felt the color flame into her face. It was a hell of a way to begin a relationship.

And that's what it was going to be, whether she liked the idea or not. Tanner wasn't going to stroll through town and leave. He was there for a reason, and any reason involving Charles Tanner's son would most likely end up involving her.

She needed to get back to the house, to the inadequate shower in the old claw-footed tub, to the proper clothes and proper underwear and layers of protection from the outlaws of this world. Was Charles Tanner's madness hereditary?

She was no longer hot, she was cold as ice. Fifteen years earlier Charles Tanner had taken a gun and opened fire on the town square, shooting anyone that moved, shooting them with the marksman's skill he'd learned in the army. The first person he'd shot had been Nils-Jacob Lundquist. The second had been a sixteen-year-old girl. The third had been the girl's father. And so it had gone on, until sixteen people were left dead and dying, the only survivor the sixteen-year-old girl, lying hidden beneath Nils-Jacob and her father's bodies, her knee shattered by Charles's bullet.

She reached down and rubbed her knee. It always troubled her when she was tense, and God knows, Tanner's appearance was enough to ruffle a saint. And that was just what the town of Morey's Falls thought of her. Eleanor Johnson Lundquist, the martyr of Morey's Falls. Every family had lost someone that day, every family now thought they owned a piece of Ellie. Somehow her surviving made it not so bad for all of them. She wasn't quite sure how it made it for her.

Fifteen years later she was still there, still trying to live for other people. She probably always would, she thought wearily, pushing her hair away from her damp face. If only she hadn't married the judge. But it had seemed the logical thing to do at the time. She'd been in and out of hospitals, mostly in, for more than a year, the money had run out, her gentle father had left nothing but debts, and she had nowhere to turn. The townspeople had collected money for her, but in that remote little town there was never much to spare. Sixteen funerals had dug deep into everyone's pockets.

And there was Judge Lundquist, on the far side of sixty, a widower with his only child the victim of a madman. He offered a home, he offered security, he offered a father's love and protection and name. It would take months and thousands of dollars to adopt her. It took a couple of days and a license that was cheap by comparison to marry her.

Everyone approved. The martyr of Morey's Falls would be well-provided for by the richest man in town. And she'd remain that way, an untouched survivor of a bloody massacre, never to be defiled again.

Ellie bit into her lip. What in the world had made her start thinking of that? The judge had been kindness himself, generous with himself and his money, pampering her and protecting her and asking nothing in return. Except her company, year after year after year in that dark old house.

So here she was, almost thirty-one years old, a wealthy widow, the town pet, still in that dark old house, still alone, still untouched. At this rate she'd probably end her days just as she was now.

It wasn't that she hadn't had offers. Offers she was getting desperate enough to consider. There was Bernie Appleton, who ran the dry-cleaning business. He was sixty, with three grandchildren and a large dark house of his own. There was Lonnie Olafson, the editor of the local paper. Poor Lonnie. No, he wouldn't do at all. And then there was Fred Parsons. He had two teenage boys, a grain business on the edge of bankruptcy and a tumbledown ranch on the edge of town. All decent, worthy marriage prospects.

They all respected her. If it were up to them she'd stay pure.

Now if someone like Tanner were around…

But someone like Tanner was around. And he was very definitely the last thing she needed. Behind that sexy smile, behind those bedroom eyes was a coldness that chilled her to the bone. No, she didn't need a man like Tanner. Not at all.

She tried to think back, to remember his father. She hadn't seen much of him—Charles Tanner had been a recluse, living alone in that rundown shack off Town Road 5, skulking around, watching, smoking those incessant cigarettes, waiting. The only one who ever got close to him was Doc Barlow, and even he wasn't welcome. Charles had been a small man, much shorter than his son, with pale, furtive eyes and an air of despair around him. Apart from the dirty-blond hair, there was no resemblance to his son as far as Ellie could recall. Maybe that would work in Tanner's favor.

She'd gone back a few years before to the newspaper accounts that Lonnie always kept handy in his office for the few tourists he sometimes got. At that point she couldn't recall what Charles had looked like, and for some reason it became terribly important to remember. The newspapers only had two photographs of him. One of Charles, motionless in death, the high-powered rifle at his feet. And one of him in uniform, young, innocent, never knowing how life and history would twist him into a killing machine.

She'd cried when she'd seen the pictures. And then she'd walked away and never looked at them again. If only the entire town could forget the past. She hated the idea of the memorial, hated the macabre dredging up of memories, and she had only gone along with the plans in the hope that this event would be the last of it. The granite monolith was already in place—in a few weeks they'd dedicate it, and then maybe they could forget that Charles Tanner had ever existed.

If only his son would get out of town. He wouldn't be made welcome, that much was sure. If he had any sensitivity at all they'd drive him back to where he came from so fast his head would spin.

But she didn't pin any great hopes on it. Tanner would leave when he was good and ready. It wouldn't matter to him if he was hated. He must have had negative reactions to that name of his before. It wouldn't matter to him that he was rejected. With that face and body of his he wouldn't have had too many women turning him down, but he didn't strike her as the type to have close friends. And it wouldn't matter to him that his presence would tear the town apart a little bit more. He'd do what he came for, and leave when he was finished.

He'd have his partisans, even though everyone else hated him. Doc was unflinchingly fair with everyone. He'd been Charles's friend and tried to help him. He'd be Tanner's friend too. There was old Maude, who'd befriend him out of fairness and deviltry and reasons of her own.

And then there was the martyr of Morey's Falls. She was just as fair-minded as Doc and Maude were. It wasn't Tanner's fault his father had gone crazy. Somehow people would have to accept that, much as they'd appreciate being presented with a scapegoat. And she would have to set an example.

That example would put her in close proximity to Charles Tanner's son. A man far too sexy for his own good, and surely the best-looking thing to set foot in Morey's Falls for many a year. Trouble, she thought again, sighing. Mazey looked back, nodding her head in seeming agreement. Trouble indeed.

ELLIE LUNDQUIST WAS LONG GONE by the time Tanner made it to the outskirts of Morey's Falls. He'd had more than enough opportunity to think about her during the hour and half it took him to make it down from the high ground into the flat grasslands below. He'd been so busy thinking about her that he'd almost forgotten why he was there. Looking at the bleak, dusty little western town ahead, he thought about Ellie Lundquist and her possible sunburn. Had she gone racing through the town shouting "Tanner is coming!" like a latter-day Paul Revere?

Somehow he didn't think so. Despite her initial, insulting panic, he doubted she'd give in to it. She might not even live anywhere near this dreary little town. She and her husband probably lived in one of those stifling little developments over the other side. He'd have to make it his business to find out where.

But that could wait. For now he had other things to do.

Morey's Falls was like most remote western towns— a big, wide main street, a small square of green grass in the center, a couple of residential side streets, a bank, two gas stations and a number of fly-specked businesses that looked as though they were on the edge of bankruptcy. The big old houses on the street behind Main looked dark and deserted, the depressing reminders of a once prosperous past.

Charles hadn't lived in town. He'd owned some twenty acres to the west of the town limits, had even tried to make a living from them for a few years. Once Marbella left, taking her baby son, he hadn't made much of an effort. But the land was still there, waiting.

First things first. He was damned hungry. A hot meal would help. It was a shame there was no motel—he wondered where all the reporters had stayed when they'd flocked around like buzzards. Serve 'em right if they'd had to camp out in their cars. There'd been reporters chasing after Marbella and Charles's son. At eighteen he'd decked one of them, smashed another's camera before he'd taken off. At least Marbella was with Alfred then. Alfred had taken care of her, as he had since he'd picked her up in a honky-tonk five years earlier where she'd been spending too much time with the wrong kind of man and the wrong kind of bottles.

Alfred had put a stop to that. Tanner had always wondered why she hadn't agreed to marry him sooner. He'd been good to her, better than anyone she'd ever known. He suspected that was part of the problem. She was so used to being abused, to being belittled and used and discarded that she'd become convinced she was as worthless as she'd been told she was. All Alfred's tender care couldn't prove her wrong.

This damned town, he thought, moving down the deserted streets. No one had helped her when she was stuck out at the useless ranch with a man already half-crazy. Her parents had turned their backs on her for marrying the wrong man, and she'd had no one to turn to when Charles started sitting in the corner for days on end, eating nothing, drinking nothing, saying nothing until Marbella would be ready to scream. It wasn't any wonder she went looking for someone to talk to, no wonder she found herself heading for the bars when Charles didn't notice.

She'd been ready to leave for good when she'd found herself pregnant. For the baby's sake she'd held out a couple more years, all alone out there. The car broke down and there was no money to fix it, Charles shot their mangy cattle one by one so they wouldn't starve. It was the night he got the gun out, the rifle he'd used years later on the townspeople, that Marbella had run, taking her two-year-old and racing into the night with nothing more than the clothes on their backs.

But someone had helped. Someone had given her enough money to get as far away from there as she could. Doc Barlow had come up with a thousand dollars, and Tanner now had that same amount tucked in a belt, next to his skin. He always paid his debts, and Barlow's was long overdue.

Pete's Fireside Café was closed. Tanner looked around him, mouth thinning in frustration, when he saw the open door across the street. MOREY'S FALLS GAZETTE, it read in gold lettering on the window. All the news that's fit to print.

The man sitting at the desk wasn't much older than he was. At least he couldn't have been working here when Charles Tanner had staged his bloody attack. Tanner stepped into the room, setting his heavy pack down on the floor, and met the man's welcoming smile.

"I was beginning to think this was a ghost town," Tanner said.

"It sure seems like it sometime," the man behind the desk said. "We don't see many strangers around here. Something I can do for you?"

"When's the diner open?"

"Who knows? Essie went home with the back miseries and Pete's gone hunting. If Essie gets better she'll be back for the supper crowd. Otherwise it won't be till tomorrow morning, and you'll have to make do with Davidson's Market. At least you won't starve." He leaned back in his ancient swivel chair. "You walk here?"

"Yes."

The man was undaunted. "On business? If you do, I can help you. I know as much about Morey's Falls as any living resident. My family's owned this paper for generations, and there isn't anything I either don't know or can't find out. So what can I do for you?"

"I'm looking for Town Road 5."

"Out past the edge of town. Though I can't imagine what you'd want out there. The road doesn't go anywhere. There's nothing out there but a broken-down ranch and empty acres."

"Thanks," Tanner said, turning to go.

"Listen, you won't find anything out there," the man said, leaping out of his chair and heading for the door. "If you want, I can give you a ride out. My name's Lonnie Olafson." He held out his hand, a friendly puppy dog of a man with thinning blond hair and a nervous, eager smile.

Tanner looked down at the outstretched hand. If Lonnie really knew everything about this town, he'd be a good place to start. Even if he hadn't worked on the paper at the time of the massacre, he'd probably remember it. His father would have covered it—maybe he could meet him.

"How long have you been working here?" he countered.

Lonnie kept his hand out. "I've been editor for the last fifteen years. Ever since my father died in the massacre."

No help from this quarter, Tanner thought glumly. "I

think I'll just head out there on my own," he said, still ignoring the hand. Lonnie wouldn't thank him for shaking it, once he knew who Tanner was.

That moment was about to come. "Listen, it's no trouble," Lonnie said. "I'll just close the office. We're always ready to welcome strangers. We don't see them very often, Mr....?"

Tanner just looked at him. "I don't think you're ready to welcome me," he said, his voice deep and raspy. "And the name's Tanner."

Lonnie Olafson didn't move. He blinked, looked startled and flinched, as if someone had thrown an invisible pie in his face. He didn't move as Tanner walked from the office, the heavy pack over his arm. He just stood there, staring after Tanner, his face a complete blank.

Davidson's Market was open, with a couple of desultory shoppers and three bored old men leaning against the sparsely stocked shelves and gossiping. At least it had a state liquor license. He bought a pack of Camels, a bottle of whiskey, a loaf of bread, a pound of bacon and a dozen eggs. He ignored the polite questions, the curious glances, the friendly suspicion that followed him around the tiny store. He was paying for his purchases with a crumpled wad of bills when he heard her name. It was all he could do not to look up.

"I hear Ellie's gonna go on a cruise," one withered old man said, his eyes trained on Tanner's figure.

"So she says," the skinny lady behind the cash register replied, her own eyes just as avidly surveying the newcomer. "She won't go. Something'll come up, someone'll need her, and she'll stay. She's got roots, has

Ellie. She's not one of your jet-setters. She knows where she belongs."

"Think she and Fred will make a match of it?" the old man continued.

"Don't know. It's not as if she's got any better choices. There ain't a single man under fifty in this town besides poor Lonnie." She let her dark, raisinlike eyes sweep over Tanner's dusty figure. "How about you, stranger? Are you single?"

He dropped the bills on the scarred wooden counter. "Got any matches?" he said, ignoring her question.

The woman shrugged, putting down a couple of books beside his money. "Just being sociable, mister. We don't see strangers too often around here."

That was the fourth or fifth time he'd heard that. He was getting sick of the curious eyes, the friendliness that he knew was going to fade into hatred and distrust. "I'm not a stranger," he said flatly. "I'm Charles Tanner." And gathering up his purchases, he walked out of the store.

CHAPTER THREE

Ellie shook three aspirin tablets from the bottle over the old metal sink, poured herself a glass of acrid-tasting water and swallowed the pills. Only for a moment did she long for something stronger to wipe out the ache in her knee, not just to dull it. But she'd spent too many years wiping out pain, years that she'd spent placid, accepting, immured in this house and this town. It was only after the judge had died that she'd taken a long, hard look at herself, at the gentle haze she'd kept surrounding her. She'd flushed the Demerol down the toilet and gritted her teeth, prepared to endure. And endure she had, with hot baths and aspirin and determination, anything to break the emotional and physical dependency that had ruled her life for too long.

She was almost free. Once the memorial was dedicated, then she could leave. The judge had left her more money than she'd ever need—he'd been a careful man and hadn't suffered from the latest hard times. She had enough to live on, particularly if she got a job, and still could leave the majority of it behind. She could set up some sort of trust, leave the house to the town, and take off. It wasn't too late to go to college. Somewhere near a city, she thought, with a place for the horses. Sur-

rounded by masses of people who, if they ever heard
of Charles Tanner's bloodbath, had long ago consigned
him to the company of nightmare figures like Richard
Speck and Charles Manson.

And she'd never go back. Not even to visit her
father's grave, not even to visit the judge's mausoleum.
Every week she made her pilgrimage, with half the
town following her, taking flowers to the victims. She'd
brought enough flowers to last them through eternity.
She didn't think her father would care. She no longer
had to please the judge.

Her thick hair was a cold, wet bun at the back of her
neck. The hot bath hadn't helped her knee much, and
it hadn't helped her restless, anxious state of mind at
all. Tanner must have arrived in town by now. The
judge's huge old house was only one block back from
Main Street, only a few hundred yards from the town
park. If they'd decided to lynch Tanner on the site of
his father's crime she would have heard them.

Morbid thought, she chided herself. No one was
going to lynch a stranger just because he bore the wrong
name. And the wrong genes. These people were civil-
ized.

Still, things had been tense during the last few
months. Ellie had blamed it on the memorial, on the
milestone anniversary rapidly approaching. A day didn't
pass without someone mentioning the massacre. Though
to be honest, a day hadn't passed in fifteen years without
someone mentioning it. But in recent months an edge
had crept back, a paranoia spread through the town,
making people lock their doors, cast furtive glances over
their shoulders and keep to their homes after dark.

Two more weeks, Ellie promised herself. Then it would all be over, and she could make plans to leave.

She moved slowly through the huge dark house, the gold-headed cane clutched tightly in her hand. She couldn't rid herself of the suspicion that things weren't going to be that easy. And the unexpected appearance of Charles Tanner's son was going to complicate matters even more.

She sank down in the straight chair and reached for the telephone. It was the only phone in the house, stuck in the middle of the hallway and not conducive to leisurely conversations. She'd always planned to have a phone jack put in her bedroom, or one in the slightly more comfortable living room, or maybe even one in the kitchen. But she never had.

Richard Barlow didn't believe in employing an answering service or a receptionist. He was a doctor of the old school, one who believed in house calls and tender loving care. He answered on the first ring, his gruff, friendly voice momentarily wiping out Ellie's fears. He'd been the one to help her get off the painkillers, he'd held her hand through the long nights and never told a soul, not even his daughter Ginger, who was the closest to a best friend Ellie possessed. He was the one person she could turn to in times of need. Something told her that right now was one.

"Doc?" she said. "I need your help."

TANNER COULD FEEL the eyes burning into the back of his neck. It didn't matter that he was long out of sight—those angry eyes followed him.

They'd gathered in a little crowd at the end of the

main street, watching him as he walked out of town toward the dead-end road that held what remained of his father's ranch. He didn't look back, didn't quicken his even, long-legged pace, didn't exhibit any signs of nervousness or even awareness of the hostile presence behind him. But he was more than aware of them. Part of him was begging someone to start something. A sheer, healthy rage was filling him. It had started with Ellie Lundquist, and each successive citizen of Morey's Falls had added to it, until he was spoiling for a fight.

But they had only watched, in sullen, distrustful silence, as he headed out Town Road 5. He just hoped he'd find what he was looking for.

It wouldn't be a big deal if he didn't. He'd spent a good part of his adult life camping in the wilderness— he could easily spend another night or two until he located what remained of the Tanner family homestead. He certainly couldn't expect help from anyone.

He heard the truck from a long ways away. Lonnie Olafson had said this was a dead-end road—no one would be driving out this way unless they were looking for trouble. Or looking for him. Right now maybe the two were synonymous.

The truck was coming up on him, slowing down. At least it wasn't going to run him off the road, Tanner thought grimly. Hell, he wasn't used to being so damned paranoid. He still couldn't rid himself of the suspicion that the pickup was full of gun-toting vigilantes.

He wouldn't be able to run, and when you were in that kind of trouble the worst thing you could do was to show fear. He stopped as the truck pulled up beside him, turned and faced the occupant with a deliberately blank expression on his face.

It was a middle-aged man, with a shock of thick gray hair, clear glasses and surprisingly kind eyes. *He must not know who I am,* Tanner thought cynically. *Word doesn't travel as fast in small towns as I thought it would.*

"Need a ride, son?"

Not your son, Tanner thought. *Someone else's.* He eyed him steadily. "I don't have far to go."

"That pack looks mighty heavy."

"I'm used to it."

The man sat there behind the wheel, looking at him. "I'm sure you are," he said. "But it'd be a sight easier if I gave you a lift."

"I don't do things the easy way."

To his surprise the man laughed. "I imagine you don't. But your father's place is overgrown, and you'll have a hell of a time finding it if you don't know exactly where to look. Since you haven't been here in over thirty years, I don't think you're going to remember too well."

He didn't allow any sign of surprise to cross his face. "I can manage."

"Listen, Tanner," the man said, his voice growing severe. "That's what they call you, isn't it?"

"Among other things."

He sighed. "You're going to have enough enemies around here. Don't push away people who want to be your friend."

"Why would you want to be my friend?" His voice was distant, cool, suspicious.

"Because I was your father's friend. I'm Richard Barlow." And he held out his hand.

Tanner considered it for a long moment. He didn't like to shake hands with people. It was giving a part of himself, and most of the time he had it thrown back in his face when they knew who he was.

But Doc Barlow knew exactly who he was. He'd been the one to help Marbella and her infant son escape. If anyone was his friend, Doc was.

Tanner slipped the heavy pack from his back and dumped it in the back of the pickup. By the time he reached the passenger side of the truck Doc had dropped his hand, but his expression was still determinedly welcoming. He smiled as Tanner slid in beside him.

"That's better. We'll get you settled into the old place and then see about some dinner." He put the truck in gear and started down the road. "My daughter makes the best pot roast you've ever tasted."

"I bought something for dinner."

"It'll keep. Ginger would skin me alive if I didn't bring you back tonight. The moment Ellie called she started racing around the house...."

"Ellie called?"

Doc cast him a sidelong glance. "Sure did. Told me you were in town and needed some friends. If anyone can see that you have a decent time of it, Ellie can. People listen to Ellie, people respect her. If you've got her on your side then half the battle is won."

Tanner leaned back in the seat, reaching for the cigarettes he'd tucked into his breast pocket. "I didn't know I had her on my side," he said, lighting one and blowing the smoke out in a long, steady stream.

"Those things'll kill you," Doc murmured in token

protest. "Give me one." He lit it, taking a deep, appreciative drag. "Don't tell my daughter. I gave these things up when my blood pressure hit two hundred, but you never get over wanting them."

"Tell me about it," Tanner drawled. "I've spent the last five years giving them up." He stared out at the scrubby landscape. So Ellie Lundquist was on his side, was she? She sure had a funny way of showing it.

Doc was concentrating on the roadway, sparing only a brief glance at Tanner's averted profile. "You don't look much like him," he said. "You look more like your ma."

Tanner considered that. "Did you know him well?" He kept his voice level, incurious.

"We were best friends. We went through everything together, childhood, high school, even the army. He got his Congressional Medal of Honor saving my life."

Tanner turned to look at him. "He killed seventeen people in the war for your sake?"

"Yes," said Doc. "Helluva thing to live with, isn't it?"

"Apparently Charles thought so," Tanner said evenly. "What about you?"

Doc grimaced. "I did a little better than your pa. But then, I was unconscious. I didn't pull the trigger, I didn't watch seventeen people die. Your father did. It's a hard thing to come to terms with. Your father was one of the gentlest people I ever knew. I guess it was just too much for him."

"I guess," Tanner murmured, stubbing his cigarette out in the ashtray and crumbling the filter until nothing but shreds remained.

Doc was watching him. "Your father used to do that. We were taught that in the army. You don't leave any trace behind."

"You don't want to leave any trace behind when you're in the wilderness, either," Tanner said.

"No, I guess not." The road had gotten narrower, turning from rutted paving to rough gravel. Weeds were sprouting out of the middle of it, and the pines and aspens were growing closer and closer to the sides of the road. Doc pulled off, putting the truck in park. "We're here," he said unnecessarily.

Tanner looked around him. The long, low building was set back in the woods. He would have found it, but it might have taken a while. He stared at it for a long, silent moment, trying to imagine his mother trapped out here, young, pregnant, alone with a man who was slowly going crazy. He shivered in the warm summer air.

"At least it's still got a roof," he said, climbing out of the pickup.

"There's a spring out back that's probably still good. It's been a wet year so far." Doc was trailing along behind him. He wasn't much above middle height, and his waist was spreading. If Doc was his father's age he couldn't be more than in his mid-fifties. Somehow he looked older.

Tanner just stood there, staring at the dilapidated shack. He didn't want to go in there, he didn't want to settle into a place that had witnessed his father's descent into madness.

He gave himself a mental shake. That was exactly what he'd come to do. To find out the answers to his past. If he could come to terms with that, with who and what his father had been, then maybe he wouldn't have to keep walking, keep running away.

"Looks cozy," he said in a lazy drawl. "I appreciate the ride." It was a dismissal, but Doc was having none of it.

"My pleasure. We'll just get things cleared up a little bit, find you some sort of light and make up a bed for you, and then we'll head on back to town for some of my daughter's pot roast."

"I don't think so."

"Listen, Tanner," Doc said, irritation breaking through. "I can't go back there alone and face three angry women. Have pity on me, boy."

"Three angry women?"

"Maude Gilles is the nosiest old woman in creation. The moment she heard you were coming she up and invited herself to dinner. And Ellie's bringing dessert. She wants to make you feel welcome."

Tanner didn't allow the smug expression to move past his eyes. He'd let her make him feel welcome, all right. "What about her husband?"

"Ellie's? The judge has been dead for over three years."

"Pity," Tanner said briefly.

"Not really. That girl hasn't had a moment to call her own since the massacre...." His voice faded away guiltily.

"Why not?"

"Guess you two didn't have much time to talk when she met you up in the hills," Doc said, evading the issue.

"She told you about that?"

"Ellie tells me everything. Come on, son. Let's get this place opened up. We may be evicting cougars."

They didn't evict anything larger than a barn swallow. Sometime over the past fifteen years various creatures had inhabited the place. Raccoons had chewed through the leather chair seats, mice had settled in the sagging mattress, birds had nested in the corner over the fieldstone fireplace. The windows and door were long gone, and more than a decade of rough Montana weather had made its mark.

But once it was cleaned out it wouldn't be any worse than a dozen trail camps he'd spent the night in. And it was a good distance from the town of Morey's Falls.

One last time Tanner considered sending Doc away. He didn't like being backed into a corner, even if it was by someone who professed himself to be a friend. He wanted some time alone, in this barren place that still held the memory of his parents, a place that had seen his first two years.

But he remembered Ellie. With the freckles and the sunburned skin and that determined friendliness that had faded into uncontrollable panic. She'd have that friendliness back at full strength now, and she wouldn't let it slip again. Not until he showed her exactly what she had to fear from him.

Tanner glanced around the cabin. His pack was propped against the rough-hewn wall, candles and matches were on the table, the pine floor had been swept clean by a shredded broom that must have belonged to his father. The cabin could wait. He wanted to see Ellie again.

ELLIE SAT ALL ALONE at her kitchen table. Even in the middle of the day the high-ceilinged room was dark and gloomy. Tonight, as the early evening shadows began to lengthen, it was eerie and depressing. She didn't want to get up to turn on a light. She'd be leaving soon enough, maneuvering herself out the door with her cane in one hand and the strawberry torte in the other. For now all she wanted to do was sit there and nurse her last cup of coffee and stop herself putting on makeup.

She never wore makeup, although she had three drawers full of it, most of it untouched. Any salesman found her an easy mark. She had three sets of encyclopedias, two vacuum cleaners and enough Tupperware to hold a year's supply of food for Morey's Falls. She could have used some color on her face. Maybe just a little mascara and eyeliner, to make her ordinary brown eyes more dramatic.

But she knew better than to put any on. Maude was coming to Doc's for dinner, and the old lady didn't miss a trick. She'd take one look at Ellie and demand to know what was going on. Tanner's saturnine presence wouldn't have any effect on Maude's unruly tongue, and Ellie didn't want to give her any ammunition. She didn't want anything embarrassing to happen tonight. She needed to prove to herself and to Tanner that she could be friendly, supportive and helpful. She was bitterly ashamed of her panicky flight down the mountain. She expected better things of herself. She had to take a stand, and that stand included having dinner with the man, making polite, friendly conversation when she'd rather stay right where she was.

She was too honest with herself not to admit that

Tanner unnerved her. And it wasn't just because of his ancestry. He unnerved her with his sexy mouth, his long, lean body, his sleepy eyes and that husky drawl of his. If he were plain John Smith from Colorado he'd be trouble. Charles Tanner, Jr. was sheer disaster.

The grandfather clock in the hallway chimed seven. Doc should be back by now, with Tanner firmly in tow. Unless he'd refused to come. He might, if he knew she was going to be there. She wouldn't blame him for not wanting to see her again. Her precipitous flight had been nothing less than insulting, though the word was that he hadn't been treated much better in the town itself. If he had any sense he'd have kept on going, straight out of town.

But sense had nothing to do with it. Tanner was there to stay, and it didn't matter how many lives came crashing down because of it.

She rose, balancing the cane in one hand and hoisting the strawberry torte with the other. Maybe she'd arrive late enough to go straight in to dinner. Maybe he'd barely notice her. Ginger was desperate for a new man, and Tanner would fill the bill admirably. She'd probably monopolize him, give him no chance to even look in Ellie's direction, and garrulous old Maude would fill any gaps. If he did turn those blue eyes on her she'd be completely unmoved, cool and friendly, as if he were as harmless as Lonnie Olafson.

Hold on to that thought, she ordered herself, stepping out onto the front porch and closing the door behind her. She never bothered to lock it—she doubted a key still existed. Even living alone, she knew perfectly well no one in Morey's Falls would harm her.

At least, not until today. The population had increased by one, and that one man was dangerous. Dangerous to her peace of mind, if nothing else. Maybe she'd better find the key.

CHAPTER FOUR

"So you're Tanner," the woman said, eyeing him up and down as if he were a choice piece of beef.

Tanner was used to that kind of look—he'd seen it ever since he'd reached puberty, and had learned to take advantage of it. Doc Barlow's daughter Ginger was standing in the warm, brightly lit kitchen of their modest ranch house, a faded cotton apron clinging to her voluptuous figure, cabbage roses dotting her generous breasts. Her hair was blond—that streaky kind of look that was supposed to come from the sun but actually came from hours spent in a beauty parlor. He was surprised Morey's Falls boasted such a place. Maybe she'd done it herself.

She knew a thing or two about makeup, too. Her lips were a pale, luscious peach, her eyelids mauve, her blue eyes frankly challenging. If he'd been a piece of fruit in the grocery store she would have pinched him. Hell, she looked as if she still might.

"I'm Tanner," he agreed, letting his own assessing gaze drift over her. It was always nice to know he could find female companionship if he wanted it. She was a lot more his style than Ellie Lundquist. Maybe he'd forget his half-formed plan and settle for Doc's daughter.

"Nice to see a new man in town," she drawled.

"I don't think you'll find too many people who'd agree with you on that."

"Pshaw," Ginger said, dismissing the entire population of Morey's Falls.

"Stop your drooling, girl!" a sharp voice admonished. "Concentrate on the pot roast and leave the poor boy alone!"

Tanner turned to survey the newcomer, keeping his face impassive. Doc had followed him in the back door, and quickly stepped forward to make introductions. "That's my daughter Ginger," he said, casting a fond glance in her direction. "And that mean old lady standing in the doorway is Maude Gilles."

"I may be old," Maude announced, "but I sure as hell ain't mean, and I'll smack the first man who says so."

"I just said so," Doc announced smugly.

Maude glared up at him, her raisin-dark eyes glinting in cheerful malice. "Hell, I'm used to you, Doc. Tell the boy I'm harmless."

"I wouldn't say that."

Tanner moved across the room, forestalling the cheerful argument. He was in no mood for banter, even the lighthearted kind Doc and Maude were indulging in. He wanted silence, he wanted peace and he wanted a drink quite badly.

Maude was looking up at him. She was ancient, with creased, leathery skin wrinkling around her features. Her hair was snowy white, worn in tight braids, her dark eyes were younger than they had any right to be, and her mouth curved in a welcoming smile, revealing a magnificent set of overlarge dentures. She couldn't

have been more than five feet tall, and her trim, un-
bowed body was dressed in jeans and a Native American ceremonial ribbon shirt. Long beaded earrings
hung from her sagging earlobes, and her hands looked
strong.

She met his gaze fearlessly, and the malice was
gone from her eyes, replaced with a softness that was
somehow jarring. "Welcome home, boy," she said
gently.

He wanted to believe that her welcome was sincere,
but his defenses were too strong, too deeply ingrained.
"My name's Tanner," he said, for what must have been
the tenth time that day. "I haven't been a boy since I was
eighteen years old. And this sure as hell isn't my home."

"No offense meant," Maude said in her rusty voice.
"To me, even Doc's a boy. And I know it's not your
home. But you got roots here, roots that go deep. Your
great-grandaddy was a buffalo hunter on the high
plains, your grandparents made the mistake of trying
to farm here. Your blood kin is buried here, and that
makes it some part of home. You know that, too, or you
wouldn't have come back."

"I forgot to tell you," Doc said easily. "Maude thinks
she's a witch. She likes to tell you why you do things
and what's going to happen. That is, when she's not
interfering with my patients."

"I'm not a witch, I'm a medicine woman, like
my mother before me," Maude announced with
great dignity. "She was Nez Percé, niece of Chief
Joseph himself, and he passed on her gifts. I can
heal better with herbs than you can with your damned
penicillin...."

Apparently it was an old argument, one that the two combatants knew by heart. "I know some medicine you both agree on," Ginger interrupted smoothly. "Tanner, you look like a man who appreciates a glass of whiskey. Get my father to stop arguing and make us all a drink."

Yup, Ginger was his kind of woman, all right, Tanner thought, following Doc into the cozy, unpretentious living room. Maybe he'd see if she'd drive him home instead of Doc. He could do with a little recreation about now, and the thought of Ellie Lundquist was fading into the background.

One problem, though. Ginger reminded him of someone, and for the life of him he couldn't figure out who. The memory teased at the back of his brain, nagging at him as he accepted the blessedly dark glass of whiskey and settled into one of the overstuffed easy chairs that rested in front of the empty fireplace. He wouldn't rest easy until he figured out who it was. Who was he kidding?—he wouldn't rest easy until he was back in New Mexico, away from the determined kindness of strangers.

"Your father wasn't a bad man," Maude announced in her cracked voice, and Tanner's head shot up in shock at the bald pronouncement. "He just went through more than any man ought to have to bear, and it turned him. You mustn't blame him for what happened."

He took a deep, delaying sip of the whiskey, thankful Doc had only put in a token cube of ice. "I don't imagine that's a popular view."

"Hell, no," said Maude. "People have been blaming Charles Tanner for everything from the economy to falling farm prices. They seem to think if your daddy hadn't been around life would be peachy. Everyone here tonight knows that just ain't true, even if it's hard to accept."

"I don't know, Maude," Doc said. "People lost a lot of kin, a lot of friends. That kind of thing is pretty hard to live with. Think how different things would be for most of us. For people like Lonnie Olafson. For Ellie."

"Poor Lonnie," Maude said, her chuckle as dry as dead leaves. "I don't know as anything would have made much difference. The boy's a born loser. He's got the reverse Midas touch—everything he puts his hand to fails. The newspaper won't last much longer at the rate he's going. He's gone through his father's inheritance and all his property's mortgaged up to the hilt. The massacre helped him. Harald was all set to bring in a new managing editor the day of the massacre, and then Lonnie would have been left with nothing. Besides, you know he always hated his father. If anything, poor Lonnie was one of the few whose life it improved."

"Why do you call him Poor Lonnie?" Tanner asked. This was what he'd come for, this was what he needed to know: whom his father had touched in his moment of random violence, and what had brought it all about.

"That's what we've always called him." Ginger was lounging in the kitchen doorway. She'd dispensed with her flowered apron, and the clinging hot-pink jersey dress did wonders for her already impressive dimensions. Tanner just watched her. "Lonnie never could do a thing right. When his daddy took him hunting, he shot himself in the foot. When he went to Boy Scout camp he set one of the cabins on fire. When Doc took him fishing he sank a fishhook into his cheek. He's just a complete and utter screwup," she announced with an impartial lack of charity. "Ellie's the only female who ever took pity on him, but then, Ellie's got enough goodness to spare for all the poor losers."

Tanner shifted in his seat, stretching out his long legs in front of him. So Ellie took on losers, did she? Doubtless she thought Charles Tanner's son fitted that category. Well, he was damned if he was going to be someone's pet charity.

"Even Ellie gave up on him," Maude pointed out. "Of course, she was married at the time. The judge was open-minded, but I think even he would have drawn the line at Poor Lonnie."

For some reason their harping on that adjective was getting on Tanner's nerves. "I met him down at the newspaper office," he said, his voice a slow, deep drawl. "He seemed pleasant enough."

"Lonnie's a little too pleasant if you ask me," Maude said, ignoring the fact that no one had. "The boy wants gumption. A little ambition, a little meanness might do wonders. He sure as hell doesn't take after his father."

"Heredity is an interesting concept," Tanner said slowly. "I haven't decided how much I hold with it."

If he wanted to make them uncomfortable he failed. Maude cocked her head to one side, looking for all the world like a brown wren. "You certainly aren't much like your daddy, either in looks or in manner. Charles was one of those quiet men. A dreamer, who didn't really belong in this world. If he'd been left alone he would have spent his days out at the ranch his parents left him, scraping by. Instead he was thrown into hell where he saw and did things no man should have to see or do. It warped him."

"Interesting theory," Tanner said, taking another sip of his whiskey.

Maude glared at him. "You worried you might take after him? I don't think so. You're a fighter—I could tell that the moment I laid eyes on you. You're tough, too. Hard as nails when you have to be. Your daddy could have used some toughening up. Then it all wouldn't have hit him so hard."

"Let's not rehash the past," Ginger protested. "Can't we spend one evening without mentioning Charles Tanner's name?"

"Not when his son's just arrived in town for the first time in…what is it? Thirty-some years?"

"Thirty-two years," Tanner supplied. "I was almost two when we left."

"All right, all right. We'll talk about it," Ginger said. "We'll talk about it, we'll say everything we need to say, and then we'll drop the subject. I don't want Ellie to have to hear about it all over again."

Why not? Tanner was tempted to ask, but he kept his mouth shut. Ginger was wearing one of those oriental, musky sort of scents. It mixed oddly with the aroma of pot roast that clung to her, but it wasn't unpleasant. He wondered what kind of scent the missing Ellie would wear, and when she was going to show up. He was hungry. And he was curious. She couldn't have been as elusive, as appealing as his senses told him she was. In this down-to-earth living room with the smell of pot roast in the air and a ripe and clearly eager woman to his left, she'd seem as ordinary as she had to be.

"Don't you go selling Ellie short," Maude said sternly. "She can take anything and turn the other cheek.

Nothing's going to get that girl down. She's quality, through and through."

"And what does that make me, Maude?" Ginger drawled, a combative light in her blue eyes.

"Honey, you've been through every man in the county. Why your daddy hasn't given you the good hiding you deserve is beyond me."

"It didn't do any good," Doc observed cheerfully enough. "Ginger's always known what she's wanted. Maybe if her ma had lived longer…"

"It wouldn't have made any difference," Ginger said calmly. "Ellie's mother died young, too, and you don't see her holiness spoiling her reputation. What can I say? I'm just a healthy woman." And the smile she bestowed on Tanner was nothing short of a leer.

"Wonder what's keeping Ellie," Maude said, voicing Tanner's thoughts.

"She probably didn't allow enough time. She never does," Doc said. "We'll wait, have another drink, and she'll turn up sooner or later." He swiveled in the big leather chair, fixing his bespectacled eyes on Tanner. "What'd you think of Ellie, son?"

"She seemed nice enough," Tanner said dismissively.

Doc just looked at him, and Tanner had the impression that he wasn't fooled. "Yes, that's Ellie. Very nice," he said, and there was a faint undercurrent of disapproval in his voice. "So what are your plans? You gonna fix up the old place? The land's no good for farming, no good for ranching, set back in the woods like that. No good for much of anything, when it comes right down to it."

"I don't have any plans." He drained his whiskey,

allowing himself a brief, pleasurable shudder. "I just wanted to see where it all happened. Maybe talk with the families, some of the survivors."

There was a brief, uncomfortable silence in the room. Finally Maude spoke up. "I don't know as how any of the families will want to talk to you. The grudge they bear goes awful deep. The loss of sixteen people in a town this size makes a pretty big hole."

"And as for survivors," Ginger spoke up, "there weren't any. Your father was a marksman—he knew how to hit a target."

It was Tanner's turn to be shocked. In the years since it happened he'd managed to repress the details. If he was going to get through the next week or so he was going to have to reacquaint himself with Charles Tanner's massacre. Maybe Lonnie's newspaper office would help.

"That's not true," Doc corrected Ginger. "One survived, and you know it as well as I do."

Tanner rose, crossed the room and helped himself to another drink without asking. "What happened to him?" he asked, and the sense of uneasiness grew into a long, tension-filled silence.

The silence was broken by the sound of the kitchen door opening. "Ginger? Doc? Sorry I'm late."

He already knew that luscious, rich contralto. Even without seeing her he knew that Ginger's obvious charms were of no importance. He stood, motionless, waiting, listening to the uneven sound of her footsteps, to the peculiar tapping sound as she approached the living-room doorway.

They must have looked like crooks caught in the

act, he thought with the last trace of humor in him. Waiting for her, apprehension on all their faces. She paused inside the doorway, a bright, unaffected smile on her face as she surveyed them. These were people she loved, he thought. People she'd grown up with, people she cared about. And he was in the midst of them, the outsider, the skeleton at the feast.

Her warm brown eyes looked fearlessly into his. The last time he'd seen her she'd been racing away like a bat out of hell. She smiled at him, her generous mouth curved in rueful apology, and she moved toward him across the room, with the other three people silent witnesses.

"Hi, Tanner," she said in that honeyed voice of hers. "I'm sorry I was such an idiot earlier today. Forgive me?" And she held out her hand.

He looked at her. Her thick chestnut hair was in a tight bun at the back of her head, her dress was nondescript and did nothing for her. He was holding a drink in his right hand—he could have just nodded politely. He didn't want to shake her hand—he was half afraid to.

He looked down, at the elegant cane with its chased gold head. She'd limped across the room, a barely perceptible dragging of her right leg. And he knew what had happened to the one person who survived his father's attack.

She was still waiting. Carefully he set the drink on a table, controlling the urge to down it in one gulp. Reaching out, he took her slim, strong hand in his.

SHE'D ALMOST FORGOTTEN what he looked like. No, that wasn't true. She'd assimilated his looks, his seductive eyes and sexy grin and long, lean body before she'd known who he was. Now, knowing he was Charles Tanner's son, she had to look at him through fresh eyes, as if seeing him for the first time. She didn't like what she saw.

He was too good-looking, with that faint air of someone who knows it and uses it. His hand was rough, callused, strong and dry and warm around hers. He was trying to look innocent and friendly, but she didn't believe it. He didn't like the fact that she'd run away from him, he didn't like this town or anyone in it. She had the impression he didn't like much of anything, no matter how much charm he tried to spread.

Well, he didn't have to play games for her. He didn't have to flirt with her, smile at her, be anything but what he was. She'd already wronged him with her blind panic. She wouldn't do so again.

"Would you fix me one of those?" she inquired. "More water than whiskey—I never could hold the stuff."

He released her, turning to fill her request without saying a word. She wanted to hear him speak again, wanted to hear those slow, deep tones. He turned back, handing her the pale-amber drink, and for a moment he let his green eyes drift downward, over her breasts in a deliberate glance that brought back her afternoon's ride.

She almost clasped her arms around her chest, almost spilled her drink, almost turned and ran to Doc for protection. But she stood her ground. That lingering gaze was a deliberate affront, and the worst thing she could do was react to it. Instead she smiled, a faint, dismissive smile.

"Thanks for the drink."

"My pleasure," he said in that slow, delicious voice of his. And she knew he wasn't talking about the drink.

She could sense the rekindled tension in the room. Doc was looking troubled, his bushy eyebrows frowning behind his horn-rimmed glasses. Ginger's expression was speculative. She'd always been too damned observant—she'd know something was going on between them, and knowing Ginger, she wouldn't rest until she'd wormed it out of Ellie. She'd probably think it was hysterically funny, the thought of prim Ellie Lundquist riding around half-naked. The two of them would laugh over it. For some reason, Ellie hadn't been able to laugh yet.

"So what do you think of Tanner?" Maude demanded, never at a loss for words. "Think he'll stir up a parcel of trouble?"

Ellie allowed herself a brief glance at Tanner's impassive features. "I imagine he will."

"Should be mighty interesting," Maude cackled.

Tanner was no longer looking at her; his gaze was directed at Maude. But she could still feel his awareness in every pore of her body, and that tingling, nervous sensation she'd been fighting all day was back at full strength. Maybe she wouldn't tell Ginger the details of how they had met.

"Mighty interesting," Ellie echoed faintly. "I can hardly wait."

CHAPTER FIVE

Ellie had been through more pleasant meals. To be sure, Ginger made the best pot roast in Morey's Falls. And Tanner, once he set his mind to it, proved to be an entertaining dinner guest, full of lazy, fascinating stories of the wilderness. He'd walked just about everywhere, he said. The Appalachian Trail, the Continental Divide, the Grand Canyon, even, one monumental year and a half, from Virginia to Oregon. If she could just have sat back and listened to the rich, slow voice and the world he conjured up she could have had one of the best times of her life.

But every time she began to relax, to fall beneath his spell, she'd glance over at him and find those disturbing eyes on her. She didn't trust his eyes. They were too calculating, with their heavy-lidded, deliberate sensuality and their chilly blue depths.

For some reason she didn't much care for Ginger's attitude, either. Ellie knew her well enough to recognize when Ginger was on the make, and Tanner had brought out her old friend's unquenchable predatory instincts. Tanner knew it, too. When he wasn't looking at Ellie with that disturbing expression in the back of his eyes, he was smiling and flirting with Ginger. Ellie didn't know which bothered her more.

He drank a lot of whiskey. She watched him, more covertly than he watched her, watched the amount of liquor he put away without showing it, the edgy, nervous grace of him. She watched him charm Maude, who was old enough to know better, tease Ginger, who'd never had any sense as far as men were concerned, and even treat Doc with a sort of mock deference that held just the right note of respect and assertion of equality. With Ellie, all he did was look.

She had to admit it was the most effective thing he could have done. Flirting she knew how to handle, how to defuse it and turn it into harmless friendship. But she couldn't handle something as ephemeral as subtle glances, she couldn't handle that distant politeness that was a lie.

He was a manipulator, she thought, watching him. He knew just how to play each of them, to get the response he wanted, and the other three were falling for it. She was falling for it, too, fascinated despite herself. The thought gave her a little chill down her sunburned back. With defenses that strong he must have something to hide. Maybe it came from a lifetime of running, no, walking—walking away.

She didn't trust him. But then, he didn't trust any of them, either. If he did, he wouldn't be quite so charming; he'd allow that mask to slip a little.

He was telling the others about the time he came across a mother grizzly and her cub, and how he'd had to walk backward, slowly, carefully, not even daring to breathe, while the mother just stared at him fiercely. "My mistake," he drawled, his voice unslurred by all the Jack Daniel's he'd swallowed. "I wasn't paying proper attention. Usually you can smell a bear before you see him. But it was damned cold that August, I hadn't seen a living soul in thirteen days, and I hadn't been too attracted to the icy streams around there. Probably Ol' Griz smelled me before I smelled her."

Doc laughed, pouring himself another glass of the bourbon that had somehow made its way to the dinner table. The dessert dishes had been cleared away long ago, and they had relaxed in their chairs.

"There's a heap of powerful medicine in that bear, boy," she observed sagely, having matched the men drink for drink. "Don't you go being disrespectful."

"I'm very respectful of grizzlies, Maude," Tanner said. "And I like to keep a respectful distance."

"Well, if you haven't bathed in thirteen days I'm sure they'd like you to keep a respectful distance, too," Ginger said, her blue eyes alight with amusement and something more.

Tanner laughed, a slow, easy laugh, and his eyes once more drifted toward Ellie. "What do you think, Mrs. Lundquist?" he drawled. "Are you one for respectful distances?"

She'd just about never been called Mrs. Lundquist. When she heard that name she thought of the judge's first wife, with her matronly bosom, her blue hair and her unbending pride. She wrinkled her nose in dismay. "I'm not one for being called anything but Ellie," she said, observing Ginger's look of displeasure. "I'm also one for early nights." She pushed her chair back from the table. "I think I'll head home now. Thanks for everything, Doc. Ginger, you put my cooking to shame." She rose, grasping the cane in her right hand, feeling the cool, smooth gold of its head with a reassuring gesture.

Everyone else had risen. Tanner was watching her still, a speculative expression on his face. He probably thought she was running away. Well, she'd like to, but Eleanor Johnson Lundquist, though she might be weak in many ways, wasn't a coward. She met that gaze fearlessly. "Can I give you a ride out to your place, Tanner?"

She'd startled everyone. Tanner recovered first, but then, he was used to hiding his emotions.

Ginger wasn't. "I thought I'd drive him," she said, and there was just a hint of irritation in her voice.

"No," Doc broke in, looking more troubled than Ellie would have expected. "I drove him here, I'll take him back."

"Well, I sure as hell ain't going to offer," Maude announced. "I don't even drive."

"I can always walk," Tanner suggested with the faint trace of a smile. "I'm used to it."

Ellie stood patiently, waiting. She wasn't going to say anything more, press him in any way. He'd come with her if he wanted to, or he'd choose another place and time. Sooner or later those speculative looks were going to evolve into something a little more physical, and she wanted to scotch it before it started.

His eyes met hers again, and she met that gaze fearlessly. "Why don't I go with Ellie?" he said finally. "After all, she has to go out anyway."

"It's no trouble…" Ginger began.

"I don't mind…" Doc said.

"Fine," Ellie said. "If you're ready?"

He followed her out into the cool night air. She always limped more when someone was watching her, and Tanner had the gift of making her feel as if she was on permanent display in a museum. She tried to hurry down the cement walkway to her huge black car, and stumbled slightly.

She hadn't realized he was so close. His hand caught her elbow from behind, steadying her, keeping her from falling in an ignominious heap in front of Doc's modest ranch house. Thank God. It had been years since she'd been lame enough to fall. She had no doubt at all that Maude and Doc and Ginger were standing in the picture window, staring out at them. It would have been a lovely sight.

"Thanks," she said briefly, not even glancing back.

His hand left her. He moved ahead, silent as a forest creature, and opened the door of her Buick. The keys buzzed in the ignition. It had been the judge's car, too new for her to turn in, but she hated the big, unwieldy thing. Its only advantage was the automatic transmission, so she'd held on to it, more out of apathy than anything else.

She slid onto the leather seat and started the car. "You always leave your keys in?" he inquired as he joined her.

"Always," she replied, pulling out into the empty street. "There's no crime in Morey's Falls."

"At least there's been none in fifteen years," he amended for her.

She glanced over at him, but the meager light from the dashboard wasn't enough to illuminate his expression, and Morey's Falls was too small to go in for streetlights. "Not in fifteen years," she agreed.

He slid down in the seat beside her and pulled out a pack of cigarettes. No one had ever smoked in the judge's car. He'd given up smoking when he was sixty, and like most converts, had been rabid about the non-believers. Out of deference to his memory she'd always kept people from smoking in what she still thought of as his car, and she opened her mouth to say something.

She shut it again, listening to the flare of the wooden match, watching as it lit Tanner's face. He looked wary and a little brutal in the flickering flame. Was she out of her mind, driving off into nowhere with the son of a killer?

She was being unforgivably paranoid. "Those things are lousy for you," she observed, striving for a note of normalcy.

"So they tell me." His voice was crisp and cool, inviting no further conversation.

Another long, uncomfortable silence as she drove past the cluster of houses that marked the end of town. "How much did you drink tonight?" The moment the words were out of her mouth she could have bitten her tongue in horror. She wasn't used to having to watch what she said.

His laugh was short and sharp. "Too much. Do I show it?"

"Not at all. That's why I was curious. I'm sorry, that was horribly rude."

"Yes, it was," he agreed. "Are you trying to reform me, Ellie?"

"I wouldn't think of it."

"That's good. Because it's a lost cause."

She glanced over at his shadowed profile. "Some women would take that as a challenge."

"But not you?"

"Not me," she said firmly. "I'm already responsible for too many souls as it is. You'll have to reform yourself." They were heading out Route 5 now, the road getting narrower and narrower, and the moonless night growing darker and darker.

"Maybe," he said. "If I ever find a good enough reason." He was speaking more to himself than to her, and she had the good sense not to respond.

"Why are you here?" she asked finally. "I would have thought this was the last place you'd want to be."

"Why?"

"Because sometimes it's the last place *I* want to be," she said frankly.

"Why don't you leave?"

She shrugged. "Sooner or later I will. That doesn't answer my question. Why are you here?"

"Maybe I don't want to answer your question."

She thought about it. "Do you have a reason not to, or is it just general cussedness?"

He laughed then, sounding surprised and oddly good-natured. "Just general cussedness. I'm here to find out what happened to my father."

"Didn't you read the papers?"

"You know better than that, Ellie," he said. "The papers give you facts, if you're lucky. I need reasons."

She pulled up in front of the clearing and put the car in park, keeping the motor running. "I don't know if you'll find them."

"I don't know, either. I just know I've got to try." In the darkness the words were softly spoken, intimate, a part of him opening up to her.

Just as quickly he slammed it shut again. He slid over

on the wide bench seat, and before she knew it he'd reached out and touched her breast, a gentle, feather-light stroke that shocked and aroused her.

"How's the sunburn?" he murmured.

He smelled of cigarettes and whiskey and warm male flesh. What would happen if the martyr of Morey's Falls tarnished her halo? she thought for a brief, dangerous moment.

She backed away, up against the door, away from him. His arms were long, he could still reach her easily, but he didn't choose to. He just sat there, looking at her in the dark.

"You are the most brazen man I have ever met," she said finally, her voice a little breathless.

He grinned then, a slow, easy smile that made her toes curl. "But then, I don't think you've met too many men, have you, Ellie?" And before she could say anything he slid back along the seat, out of the car, closing the door quietly behind him. "Thanks for the lift."

She sat there for a long moment. He saw too damned much for her peace of mind. She rolled down the window. "Anytime," she said calmly. "Do you want me to wait until you get a light going?"

"I can see in the dark," he said. "Unless you want to come in and complete your little welcome wagon act?"

"Good night, Tanner." She managed a satisfying spurt of gravel as she sped away from the clearing.

He watched her go with a speculative expression on his face. He'd bet she was damned proud of herself. Hell, she had every right to be. He'd done everything he could to put her on edge, and she'd done nothing but give him that faint, damnable smile all evening long. And he couldn't see that well in the dark. He would have loved to have seen her expression when he'd touched her breast. He'd felt her tremble, a little shiver of reaction that was infinitely satisfying. He'd been tempted to push it, then and there, and see how far he got.

But he'd thought better of it. The chase was half the fun. If he'd blown it, it would have made it that much harder in the long run.

So Ellie Lundquist was the one survivor of his father's madness. He'd come up with the impression that she was the town pet, a mascot to be stroked and cosseted, the martyr who belonged to everyone.

She was going to belong to him. Sooner or later there was no longer going to be such a vast discrepancy between the innocent and the profane. Ellie Lundquist was going to descend to his level, whether she liked it or not. Maybe she'd learn something in the bargain. And maybe she'd be able to leave the place she felt so tied to. He was doing a noble thing, he mocked himself. All for her own good.

"Sometimes, Tanner, old boy," he said in a quiet, deadly voice, "you make me sick."

Was that how his father had started? Talking to himself in the quiet stillness of a moonless night? He'd better watch it.

Hell, he'd had too much to drink, too much to think about. What he needed was a decent night's sleep on something that approximated a bed. Tomorrow he'd pull himself together.

It was more habit than anything else that made him

decide to take one last walk around the cabin before he settled down for the night. The kerosene lamp lit the one-room building with a warm glow, shedding a little light out the broken windows. He walked slowly, finishing the last cigarette in the pack, watching the ground more out of habit than interest. There wouldn't be cougar or bear tracks this close to civilization. He didn't have to be that careful.

But it was instinct that made him do it, and sharp eyesight that caught the tiny bit of white paper. He knelt down, brushing at it with his hand.

It was the remains of a cigarette filter. It had been crumpled, shredded, almost obliterated, just as Tanner had always done with his cigarette butts. But he hadn't been smoking out there. And it wasn't his brand.

It was the brand his father had smoked, and it was crumpled the way his father used to crumple them. Tanner sat back on his heels and shivered in the warm night air.

DAMN THE MAN, Ellie thought as she drove, too fast, down Route 5. He was too observant, too sassy, too brazen, and too much trouble. Welcome wagon act, indeed! Trust Tanner to twist things around. All she'd wanted to do was be friendly, to make up for her earlier panic, to show him that everyone didn't hate him, didn't condemn him. If that made it a welcome wagon act then she had nothing to be ashamed of. Damn him!

Of course, he knew perfectly well her motives weren't that pure. She'd been her usual calm, friendly, sisterly self, the way she always was. It was the manner she'd used for years to keep predatory men at bay. God knows, Tanner was the most predatory male she'd seen in a long time. Maybe in her entire life. He needed to be kept at arm's length. She'd been so determined to be calm and friendly, and he'd almost managed to rile her. Almost, nothing! He *had* riled her. At least she could hope that she hadn't showed it.

What she needed to do was help Ginger. She knew her old friend well enough to recognize the predatory female of the species. The two of them would make a perfect pair, and if Ellie had any sense at all she'd do a little discreet matchmaking.

She deliberately loosened her death grip on the steering wheel. Well, maybe that wasn't such a good idea. Besides, how long was Tanner going to be around? It couldn't be that long, given the hostility of the town. What she needed to do, instead of trying to provide a social life for the man, was to help him in his quest. He wanted reasons, he wanted answers. She could help him find those reasons and those answers.

She knew better than anyone else who'd suffered at Charles Tanner's hands. She knew the people who'd known Tanner's father, the people who could shed some light on it. She knew where the bodies were buried, figuratively and literally.

Her course was clear. She'd drive back out to that depressing, tumbledown cabin tomorrow morning and offer her assistance in his quest. With her to speed things along he might very well be gone by the Fourth of July. For everyone's sake she could only hope so.

The massive Victorian house the judge had left her was a blaze of lights. She squashed the tiny feeling of guilt that assailed her. Most people in this economically strapped town couldn't afford to leave their lights blazing. But Ellie lived alone, and not for anything in the world would she enter that huge old structure with only a light or two burning.

Tonight was worse than usual. The sky was overcast, blanketing even the stars, and the blackness around her was thick and inky. If she turned on every light in the entire house it wouldn't keep the darkness at bay.

She pulled into the driveway and turned off the car. As she opened the door the telltale buzzer sounded, reminding her she'd left the keys in the ignition. Maybe Tanner was right, maybe she was a little too trusting. She pulled out the keys and headed into the house.

CHAPTER SIX

Civilization woke Tanner with a vengeance. His head was pounding, his mouth tasted like an armadillo, and his brain was still reeling with the worst nightmares he'd had in almost fifteen years. He sat up on the sagging cot, groaning, staring around him in bleary-eyed disapproval. Why was he hanging around here, in a place full of miserable memories? What the hell did he need the best horse-breeding ranch in New Mexico for, anyway? Maybe he should just take off, head for Canada. He'd always wanted to take the Yukon trail up to Alaska.

He reached for the crumpled pack of cigarettes, then remembered he'd smoked the last one. Cursing, he pulled himself out of bed and headed for the doorless front entrance. Served him right, he thought, stumbling barefoot over the gravel and twigs. He shouldn't be smoking at all.

The spring was still flowing, pure and clear. He washed his face in the icy water, then shook his head back, trying to clear the excesses of the night before. It had been nobody's fault but his own. He'd had too much to drink at Doc Barlow's, and then finding that shredded cigarette butt had sentenced him to a night of chain-smoking and large swigs from his own bottle. He'd probably finished that, too—he couldn't remember. If he hadn't, he had every intention of pouring it out. If he was going to stay on here for even another twenty-four hours he was going to have to do it stone-cold sober.

And he was going to stay on, he knew it full well. He wasn't staying for the horse ranch, or even for Alfred's sake, however much he owed the old man. No, he was staying on for himself, for the hope of a future that would be, if not free from the past, at least at peace with it.

He heard the scrunch of the tires on the gravel outside almost an hour later, but he didn't bother to look out. A small, smug smile lit his face as he tipped back the rickety chair and waited for Ellie Lundquist to walk in the door.

His self-satisfied smirk faltered somewhat as he heard the uneven sound of her footsteps, but he refused to let it bother him. He sat there, waiting, a trap ready to be sprung.

Ellie stopped in the doorway, and the sunlight silhouetted her lean figure. She was wearing jeans again, and her hair wasn't in that tight knot she'd worn the night before. Probably she was supposed to be down-to-earth and disarming, he thought cynically. It would take more than that to disarm him.

"You're up," she said, her low, husky voice a continual surprise to him. "I was afraid I came out too early."

"I've been up for hours," he lied. "Want some coffee?"

She stepped over the threshhold, her eyes narrowed as they adjusted to the dim light. "All the comforts of home."

He reached forward and poured her a tin cup of the thick brew. "You'll have to drink it black. I don't come equipped with cream and sugar."

"Black will be fine." She took a tentative sip without shuddering. He had to admire her self-control. His coffee could strip the paint off a tractor.

"Have a seat," he offered magnanimously. "And then you can tell me what you want." He was sitting in the only chair in the shack—so that left the narrow, sagging cot. Maybe she'd opt for the floor.

But Ellie Lundquist was made of sterner stuff. After all, she'd drunk his coffee without flinching. She perched on the side of the bed, cradling the cup of poisonous-tasting brew as if seeking warmth. It was going to be a hot day—she didn't need that warmth.

She was doing a good job of looking at him, too, he thought lazily, taking another gulp of his coffee and waiting patiently. He was wearing jeans and nothing else. She was keeping that even, friendly gaze on his face, but she'd let it drift down his tanned chest as if it held no more interest than the familiar landscape. He didn't believe it.

"Actually," she said, taking another drink of his coffee without flinching, "I was wondering what you want."

He smiled, a brief, lazy smile, fantasizing for a moment how she'd react if he walked over to that narrow, rumpled bed and showed her exactly what he wanted. "I told you last night," he said, not moving. "I want to find out about my father."

"Well," she said, sitting back on his bed, "I'm here to help you."

"Are you?"

If he'd wanted to daunt her he failed. "Yes. I've got a car, you don't. I've lived in Morey's Falls all my life. I know more about this place than anyone else, with the possible exception of Maude. I can help you find the answers you want."

"Why would you want to do that?" He drained his coffee cup and set it down on the scarred wooden table, barely controlling his own reflexive shudder. "More of your welcome wagon act?"

Her eyes met his. "You want the truth?"

"That's always preferable."

She rose, moving across the room to the empty window frames, her limp barely perceptible. "I'll help you because I want you to leave," she said flatly. "I think you'll stir up a lot of pain and trouble, and the sooner you're gone the better. So I'm here—" she turned to face him then "—to speed you on your way."

"Better than tar and feathers," he said. "What if I decide I like it here? If I want to stay around, to start a family?"

"You won't," she said.

"You sound pretty sure of that."

"No one would stay here if they didn't have to."

"Do you have to?" He rose, stretching in the low-ceilinged cabin. He felt her eyes drift down for a moment, then jerk back upward to his face.

"For now," she said. "Do you want my help or not?"

He reached for his clean flannel shirt and pulled it on, buttoning it and rolling up the sleeves with graceful economy of movement. "I'm in your hands. Where do we start?"

He could see the tension leave her shoulders. Had she relaxed because he had accepted her help? Or because he'd put on his shirt? Maybe a little of both. For all her seeming coolness he could tell for a fact she wasn't used to half-dressed men. Maybe the judge had insisted on making love in the dark.

"We start with the newspaper office."

"I've been there. I don't think Poor Lonnie's going to welcome me with open arms."

"I talked with him this morning. He'll be waiting for us," she replied.

"Pretty sure of yourself, weren't you? How'd you get him to cooperate?"

"Lonnie and I are old friends." Her husky voice had just the faintest tinge of repressiveness.

"Okay," he said. "We need to stop on the way for cigarettes."

"I should refuse."

"You should stop being a pain in the neck," he said, following her out into the early-morning sunshine. "Does anybody ever come out here?" He kept his voice casual as he slid into the passenger seat and began pulling on his running shoes.

She had a strange expression on her face, one he couldn't quite fathom, as she climbed in beside him and started the big car. "Why do you ask? Does it look like someone's been staying here?"

"Nope. I was just curious." *Curious about a cigarette butt that could have been mine, but wasn't,* he thought. But there was no need to tell Ellie Lundquist about that.

"No one comes out here," she said. "They think it's haunted."

"By my father?" he asked, unmoved. "Or his victims?"

"It depends on who you ask. It's also near the site of another massacre. The U.S. government wiped out an entire Native American village—men, women and children. The area doesn't have a happy history."

"It doesn't sound like it. And I suppose some people think it was the ghosts of the Natives that drove my father nuts?"

"How'd you guess?"

"I hope that's not a popular belief. It's not the answer I'm looking for."

She glanced over at him. "You can't afford to be too picky. I don't know if you'll like any of the answers you're going to get. If you don't want to hear them, go back home."

"Don't rush me, Ellie. I'll leave when I'm finished here, and not before."

She stamped on the accelerator and the car jerked forward. "We'll just have to see that you finish quickly," she said grimly.

"What's the rush? Don't you like me?"

"I don't like being toyed with." There was an edge to her voice he couldn't miss. "And I don't like needless suffering. This town has been through enough. You have every right to try to understand what happened, but you have no right to make things worse for these poor people. They've suffered enough."

"At the hands of the Tanner family?" he supplied in a silky, dangerous voice.

"I didn't say that...."

"And what about you? Haven't you suffered? With

that pathetic limp and that kindly behavior I bet you're the town saint. A perfect contrast to the bad penny showing up."

If he'd hoped to shock her he'd succeeded. "Is it everyone you hate, or just me?" she said quietly.

"Don't flatter yourself. You're just one of a faceless pack. My father's blameless victims, suffering nobly at the hands of evil incarnate."

"If you believe that, why are you here?"

"I want to see if it's true. I want to see if things are black and white, or if there's a little gray thrown in."

"You're hoping to find some justification for your father opening fire on a Fourth of July celebration?" Ellie scoffed. "Don't count on it."

"Not justification. Reasons."

"We'll find your reasons," she said. "Then will you leave?"

She was paying more attention to him than to the road. He smiled, an innocent smile that wouldn't have fooled her for a moment. "Then I'll leave," he agreed.

SHE HAD A KNOT in her stomach the size of a fist. First there'd been a sleepless night. Then the anxiety of driving out Route 5 to offer her help to that graceless savage. She'd had to drink coffee that tasted like kerosene, watch him parade around half-naked and then put up with him baiting her while they drove into town.

If she weren't so desperate to get him out of Morey's Falls, out of Montana, she'd have kicked him out of her car. A small, craven part of her wanted to abdicate. If Tanner wouldn't leave, she would. She could fill up the tank of the Buick and start driving, not stopping until she got to civilization and people who had never heard of Charles Tanner.

But she wouldn't do that. She'd stick it out. Just two and a half weeks, and then she'd leave. If she could help keep things relatively placid during her last days there, then she'd be able to leave in peace. Tanner could go back to wherever he came from, and the townspeople could get on with their lives. Two and a half weeks.

She pulled up the car in front of Addie's Quickstop just outside of town. She had no idea whether Addie Pritchard had heard about Tanner's arrival, and she didn't really care. "Get your cigarettes," she said in a sour voice.

He didn't say a word, he just smiled that wicked smile of his that never reached his eyes and slid out of the car. She sat there, watching him go, tapping her fingers on the steering wheel. Addie wouldn't refuse to serve him, would she? Addie was a great, cheerful mountain of a woman, an impartial friend to all. That friendliness probably wouldn't extend to Tanner, but Ellie couldn't see her being vindictive.

Or could she? It was taking Tanner a long time to buy something as simple as a pack of cigarettes. Addie kept a gun beneath the cash register to ward off intruders. Maybe she'd decided to dispense a little rough justice to the nearest thing to Charles Tanner that was left on this earth.

Ellie slammed open the car door and rushed up the front steps of the little store, forgetting her cane, forgetting her lame leg. Tanner was standing at the counter, seemingly at ease, and the glance he threw in her direction was no more than mildly curious.

Ellie stopped running, sauntered into the store and picked up the first thing she could find. "I…I forgot. I needed something," she said breathlessly.

"Did you?"

She nodded, placing the box on the counter beside Tanner's carton of cigarettes. "Where's Addie?"

"Haven't seen her yet. You sure you need that?" He nodded his head toward her hastily grabbed purchase.

She looked down at the bright-pink box of perfume. "One Night of Love Musk Oil, Guaranteed to Make Any Man Your Slave," the box proclaimed. It was a brand Ginger Barlow favored, and it smelled like insect repellent to Ellie. The scantily-dressed couple on the garish package left little to the imagination, and Ellie could feel the color flood her face. She looked up, into Tanner's amused gaze, and considered brazening it out. Considered, then rejected the idea. Addie wasn't known for her discretion, and Ellie Lundquist buying One Night of Love Musk Oil would shock Morey's Falls past redemption.

"No," she said, picking the box up again. "I don't need it. I just wanted to make sure you were all right."

She could see the faint expression of shock wipe the humor from his face. He clearly wasn't used to having anyone watch out for him. *Score one for her.* She'd finally managed to throw him off balance, at least a little bit.

"Sorry." Addie bustled into the room, her broad moon face red and panting. "I was on the phone. How are you, Ellie? Haven't seen you in weeks."

"Just fine, Addie," she said. "How's yourself?"

"Can't complain. What the hell have you got in your hand, missy?"

Trust Addie to be indiscreet. So far she hadn't done more than give Tanner a cursory glance, and Ellie felt herself relax. "I picked it up by mistake," she said with a grin, putting the box back on the shelf. "I don't need it."

"More's the pity," Addie said, turning her attention to her other customer. Her eyes widened for a moment, and her huge bulk quivered.

Tanner had stiffened, waiting for God knows what. He didn't know about the gun Addie kept, and Ellie primed herself, ready to leap.

Addie leaned forward, putting her meaty fists on the scratched Formica counter. "Well, well, well," she said, and there was no anger in her voice. "Look who we have here."

Tanner didn't say a word, and the wary posture remained the same. "Who do you have here?" he asked.

Suddenly Addie smiled, a beam of welcome wreathing her broad, red face. "Marbella's boy," she said firmly. "Your ma and I grew up together. We were best friends all our lives, until she had the good sense to get the hell out of here, away from the crazy man she married. You look just like her."

Some of the tension left his shoulders. "So I've been told. But I've got my father's coloring."

Damn the man, Ellie wailed inwardly. Couldn't he just let things be?

Addie nodded. "You do. It can't be helped. You're his son as well as Marbella's, and there's no changing that. Your ma was a fine lady, son. As fine a one as I've ever known. You ever need anything, you just let Addie know." She cast a glance in Ellie's direction. "You with Ellie?"

"Yes." The sound of his answer gave her a strange feeling in the pit of her stomach.

Addie grinned. "Maybe you better buy that perfume after all, Ellie. Hell, take it on the house."

"Watch your mouth, Addie," Ellie said cheerfully, ignoring the fresh wave of color in her face. "Let Tanner buy his cigarettes, and we'll head on out. Lonnie's going to let us look at the old newspaper accounts."

"Poor Lonnie," Addie said absently, taking Tanner's money and ringing up the cigarettes. "You come back when you have more time, boy, and we can talk about your ma. I still miss her."

Tanner gave her a smile of peculiar sweetness, the kind of smile, Ellie thought, that a woman would die for. Addie wasn't immune to it.

"I miss her, too," he said simply. "Thanks, Addie."

"Take care of Ellie," Addie admonished.

Tanner cast her a swift, curious glance, and for a moment the faint glimmer of a smile reached his blue eyes. "I'll try, Addie. I'll try."

Her face was flaming again when she reached the car. She paused by the driver's door, waiting, as he sauntered after her.

"You know," he drawled, "life would be a lot easier on you if you learned not to blush."

"No, it wouldn't," she said frankly. "I'd just be hiding my emotions away behind a mask, like you do. I don't want to be you, Tanner. I don't want to wear a mask with everyone. If I'm going to get embarrassed I don't mind people knowing it."

His eyes narrowed against the bright sunlight. "I get amateur psychology along with the welcome wagon?"

"Sorry," she said, not contrite. "Do you want to drive?"

"Why should I?" He paused in the act of opening the car door.

"I don't know. Men usually like to drive," she said irritably.

"And you know so much about men," he added.

"Why do you keep saying things like that? I haven't been living in a convent. There are plenty of men around here. You forget, I'm a widow."

"I don't forget. No, I don't want to drive. I don't need to prove my masculinity by ferrying the little woman around."

"What about proving you're a gentleman by sparing my bad leg?" she snapped back, then regretted it. She didn't want to remind him of what his father had done to her. He was living with enough on his shoulders.

Tanner didn't look the slightest bit chastened. "Is that what people do? Make allowances for you, coddle you, keep you from having to stand on your own two feet? In the twenty-four hours I've known you I've seen you can do just about anything if you forget you're supposed to be lame. I'm not about to encourage your notion of yourself as the wounded martyr. Drive your own damned car." He pulled the door open and slid into the passenger seat, and slamming the door shut behind him.

She stood there, white with shock and fury. She knew if she opened her mouth she'd start shrieking with rage, she knew if she moved she'd start beating on the car with her fists. She counted to ten, once, twice, willing herself to calm down.

Finally some of the anger faded. She hadn't been that angry since… Heavens, she didn't know when she'd been that angry. If Tanner was able to ruffle her famous equanimity, how was he going to affect people with a shorter fuse?

Wounded martyr, was she? The damnable thing about it was he'd hit upon her role very accurately. That's exactly how people saw her, and out of lassitude she'd fulfilled their expectations. Now, in one day Tanner had seen through it, and her. Maybe she did need some of his formidable defenses. He was far too observant, seeing things, hinting at things he couldn't possibly know. If she was going to survive his unwelcome visit, survive the next two and a half weeks, she was going to have to become more adept at hiding.

She took a few deep, calming breaths and opened the car door. Tanner didn't say a word when she started the car, didn't say a word as she pulled away from Addie's Quickstop. He just kept looking at her, his eyes narrowed and far too knowing.

She drove slowly and steadily, heading toward town. They were almost there when she finally trusted her voice enough to say something.

"You know," she said conversationally, "you're a real bastard."

He smiled at her with that oddly sweet smile. "Ellie," he said softly, "I only wish I were."

CHAPTER SEVEN

"How about some coffee?" Lonnie Olafson was standing in the door of the *Morey's Falls Gazette*, his blue-striped oxford shirt rolled up at the elbows, his khaki pants properly creased, his Nikes scuffed, his sandy hair drooping boyishly across his high forehead. If his blue gaze behind the pale-rimmed glasses held a trace of reserve, the hand he held out was steady.

Tanner had avoided shaking hands with him the day before. This time he didn't have much choice in the matter. Ellie was watching him like a hawk, that generous mouth of hers pursed in disapproval. He could feel other eyes at his back, watching him. Hostile eyes. Half the town had turned out to see him walk into Lonnie's newspaper office. He couldn't believe that so many people had nothing to do at ten o'clock on a Wednesday morning. They were there to get a good look at Tanner's son, and if Lonnie was reluctantly welcoming, the rest of them weren't.

"Coffee would be wonderful," Ellie said, coming up beside him and threading her arm through his, drawing him into the building, away from the prying eyes. There was nothing sexual in her touch, and yet it was somehow more acceptable than the limp grasp of Lonnie's hand. The instant they were inside she released her hold, and for a half a moment he was tempted to reach out and grab her arm once more. Not for sexual stimulation, but for some odd, ultimately demoralizing form of comfort. He resisted that temptation, noting with interest Lonnie's proprietary glare.

"None for me," Tanner said, unwilling to accept anything more than he had to.

"Don't be ridiculous. That stuff you had this morning didn't even deserve to be called coffee," Ellie said. "Lonnie makes the best coffee in town, and anyone would be a fool to turn down a cup of it."

"I don't need…"

"Lighten up, Tanner," Ellie said, clearly enjoying herself. Getting sassy, was she, Tanner thought. *She must feel safer with an audience.* "You're here for help. Accept it."

Lonnie was watching all this with a faintly troubled expression. "What'll it be?"

Later, Tanner promised himself. "Two coffees. Black."

"But Ellie drinks it with cream and sugar," Lonnie protested.

"Make mine black, Lonnie," Ellie said. "Tanner thinks I'm already full of too much sweetness and light."

The troubled look deepened on Lonnie's high forehead. "Two black coffees," he said. "Go on into the back room. I've laid out the papers for that period. You realize there's a few days gap. When my father…died it took a little while to get things back in order. Even so, we still have the most extensive coverage of the, er, uh, incident."

"Incident?" Tanner echoed with a snort of derisive laughter. "There's no need to be tactful on my account. Call it anything you damn well please. Slaughter, murder, whatever."

"Massacre," Ellie said firmly, undaunted. "That term seems to cover the situation pretty well. Got anything to eat, Lonnie? I'm starving."

A faint smile lit Lonnie's face. "I expect half the women in town will find some excuse or other to come in here and get a look at Tanner. At least a few of them will be bringing donuts and pastries."

"I hope Nilda Tompkins is one of them. She may be the nosiest woman this side of the Mississippi but she makes the best muffins around."

"I'll keep any visitors in the front room. You and Tanner take your time in the morgue."

"Fitting name," Tanner said, following Ellie's tall, straight figure into the back. She'd left her gold-headed cane in the back of the car, and her limp was almost imperceptible, confirming Tanner's suspicions. She limped when she remembered she was crippled. When something occupied her mind, her walk was almost completely normal.

The morgue of the Morey's Falls Gazette had clearly not been brought into the digital age and he found it as depressing as its name. Stacks and stacks of yellowing news sheet covered the shelves of the small, dark room. There was one window, a narrow one set high on a stained wall, and the small patch of sunlight filtering through shed more light on the scarred table than the flickering fluorescent fixture overhead. Tanner moved over to a chair, staring down at the grainy textured photograph of his father's face in the open volume spread out for his perusal, keeping his own expression carefully blank.

"Do you want me to leave you alone?" Ellie's husky voice broke through his abstraction. He looked up, into that direct, warm gaze, and felt a tightening somewhere in his gut.

"Suit yourself," he said evenly, dropping into one of the chairs and pulling the yellowed paper toward him. "It makes no difference to me."

"Then I'll stay."

He almost forgot she was there. During the next three hours he sat in the old oak chair, the words sinking into his brain, playing out pictures of pain and anguish and devastation. He read about Nils-Jacob Lundquist, the youngest victim, the sixteen-year-old son of the widowed Judge Lundquist. He read about Harald Olafson and his new assistant editor, about middle-aged ranchers and young mothers, about farmers and grandfathers and college students wiped out in a blaze of gunfire.

At least Charles Tanner had been a marksman. No one died a lingering, painful death. He knew how to hit a target, hit it neatly and cleanly before turning the gun on himself. His only mistake was sixteen-year-old Eleanor Johnson.

There were pictures of Ellie, pictures from younger days, with a faded-looking man in the background. For a moment Tanner wondered if that were the judge, then realized the man was Ellie's father, another victim of the massacre. The photos were too grainy—newsprint reproductions of old snapshots, and he couldn't get any sense of her before she'd been shot. She looked like any other young girl, on the edge of womanhood, the blurred face innocent and smiling.

He found an interview with Judge Lundquist, accompanied by the old man's picture. The judge spoke thoughtfully of the need for healing in the town, the sorrow of his own loss, the devastation that would take years to recover from. Tanner looked down into the heavy, jowly features, the stern eyes and conservative mouth, and disliked him on sight. He tried to imagine Ellie in bed with him, tried and failed. If that was the limit of Ellie's sexual experience she was in for quite a shock.

"There's a lot more stuff at the local library." Ellie's rich voice startled him for a moment. "We have most of the national accounts of the massacre. *Time*, *Life*, *Newsweek*, all that sort of thing. If you want I can get a key. I'm on the library board and they pretty much let me do what I want."

"When's the library usually open?"

"Every other Tuesday from ten till three. You just missed it."

He leaned back in the chair, balancing on the back legs, and folded his long hands in front of him. "I'd forgotten what a small town can be like. Have you read all this stuff?"

She hesitated for only a moment. "A number of times. About three years ago I reread everything we had in town about it. We had reporters nosing around again, asking questions, and I realized I'd forgotten almost everything. I'd even forgotten what Charles Tanner looked like."

"I can guess why the reporters showed up again.

There must have been another mass murder, right?"
He toyed briefly with the flimsy paper in front of him.

"Exactly. Every time some crazy man takes a gun
and blows away a fast-food restaurant or a post office
they dredge up all the other…"

"Incidents," Tanner supplied with a cynical twist of
his mouth that couldn't be called a smile. "They kept
trying to track me down, get my opinion. After I broke
a few cameras and a few noses they stopped coming
around."

"Maybe I should have learned karate," Ellie said. "I
guess I'm too polite. I don't know how to say no."

Tanner turned the full force of his attention on her.
He could see that look in her eyes, knowing she'd said
the wrong thing, waiting for him to turn it around into
some sort of come-on that she'd have to deflect. He
only smiled faintly, determined to keep her off balance.

"Okay," he said. "I've read the accounts, and I
remember enough from the national media. Charles
Tanner got up the morning of July Fourth, put on his
army uniform, picked up his rifle and several handguns
and drove his old pickup into town. There was a Fourth
of July celebration in the middle of town, on the site of
a proposed new bank, and half the town was there. He
opened fire, shooting for about a minute and a half, and
then turned the gun on himself. Is that essentially it?"

Ellie looked a little dazed. "A minute and a half?"
she echoed. "That short a time? It seemed to last an
eternity."

"What happened to you?"

She swallowed. He could see this was costing her
something emotionally, could see that serene exterior

raveling around the edges. Anyone with compassion would back off. Right now his supply of compassion was running extremely low.

"I was one of the first ones hit. I was talking with Nils-Jacob when Charles Tanner started shooting. I went down, Nils-Jacob fell on top of me, and no one realized I'd only been wounded. I just lay there until the shooting stopped."

"And?"

"What do you want from me, Tanner?" she demanded, her voice raw with pain. "You want gory details and lots of blood? Sorry, I can't help you on that score. I've managed to blot out most of what happened that day. I know the facts, the time sequence, the death count, everything. But I don't remember the emotions, and I don't want to. You'll have to get that from someone else."

He looked at her for a long moment. "What I'm more interested in," he said, his voice low and soothing, "is why no one noticed something was going on. A man walking around in an outdated army uniform and a high-powered rifle shouldn't be an everyday occurrence."

"The gun was a new touch. Your...Charles Tanner often wore his uniform. He'd come into town, not say a word to anyone, cash his disability check and buy some groceries and go back home. Everyone just thought he was a harmless eccentric."

"No one had any idea he was over the edge?"

"He kept away from everyone. I suppose people had their suspicions. Odd things began to happen a couple of years before the massacre. Someone began peering in people's windows. No one was sure who it was, but they thought it might be Charles. Then animals started being killed. Cattle, horses, old hunting dogs were found dead. Someone began daubing blood on people's porches. No one knew for sure who it was, but Charles Tanner was the obvious culprit."

"And no one did anything?" Tanner's voice was cold, emotionless.

"No one had proof. This is a close-knit community—they don't go for help to outsiders. They would have had to have gone to the state or maybe the VA for help, and no one wanted to do that."

"They paid for it, didn't they?"

She stared at him, that clear-eyed gaze troubled. "I guess they did. For what it's worth, Doc had called in help two days before the massacre. Someone was coming from the VA after the holiday weekend to talk with Charles."

"A little late," said Tanner.

"A little late," Ellie agreed. They sat there in silence for a long moment.

"Did they ever build the bank?"

"What?" She was startled for a moment. "Oh. No, the backers pulled out. I guess they thought Morey's Falls wasn't the best possible spot for a new bank. They turned the empty lot into a park."

"Oh, yes," he said. "I'd forgotten. There's some sort of memorial."

She looked even more uncomfortable. "They're erecting a granite marker, with the names of all the victims carved in it. They're planning a big dedication on the Fourth of July."

"They? Aren't you a part of all this? The town survivor?"

"For what it's worth, I tried to stop the town council

from doing it. I think we've spent too much time in the past. No one listened."

"Couldn't you have made a fuss?"

She met his eyes defiantly. "I told you, I'm not good at saying no, particularly to people I care about. The judge left the money for the memorial, and I have to be the one to unveil it. I don't like it, but I'm writing the check and writing my speech."

He said nothing for a moment. "And that's when you want me gone. Before this touching little ceremony."

"Tanner," she said wearily, "don't make it worse."

He stifled the brief surge of compassion. "I could hardly do that, could I? It's about as bad as it could be. I thought I was living with ghosts. It's nothing compared to this town."

"You're probably right." She was looking away from him, refusing to meet his gaze.

He pushed his chair back from the table. "All right," he said. "If you want me out of here in two and a half weeks we can't afford to waste time. Let's go."

"Where to?"

"The Charles Tanner Massacre Memorial Park."

"Don't call it that."

"What do you call it then?"

"The park. For pity's sake, just call it the park," Ellie said.

"Okay, Ellie. Let's go for a walk in the park." God, he was regretting this. Regretting that he'd ever set foot in the state of Montana, regretting that he'd allowed himself to involve Ellie Lundquist in all this. He should have sent her on her way that morning and gone about this at his own pace.

Ellie was complicating matters. He was reacting to her, responding to her in ways he didn't like. She was the essence of martyred saint, while he was the son of evil incarnate as far as this town was concerned. He had no business with her, no business at all, and if he had a shred of decency in his body he'd leave her alone.

Lonnie had reappeared in the open doorway. He'd checked on them periodically during the last three hours—Tanner had felt those eyes on the back of his neck each time he'd paused in the door. "All finished in here?"

"For now," Tanner said, rising and stretching his long arms over his head. "I appreciate your help."

Ellie had moved out of the room ahead of him. Lonnie smiled faintly. "Anytime. Anything you want to know, just ask. I've made sort of a study of that day. There's probably no one around who knows as much as I do about the details, is there, Ellie?"

"Probably not, Lonnie," she said.

Tanner's eyes narrowed. He knew that tone of voice, even if Poor Lonnie didn't. It was maternal, gentle and far too knowing. Lonnie was no threat to Tanner's plans for Ellie, no threat at all. "Anything you want to know," Lonnie said again.

"I'll take you up on that," Tanner said.

The good people of Morey's Falls had given up waiting. It was afternoon when they left the newspaper office, and there was no one in sight. They walked down the block in silence, Ellie remembering she had to limp this time, Tanner stifling his irritation as he glanced down at her. He liked her shoulders. They were thin, broad under the soft cotton shirt. Probably covered with freckles from yesterday's outing in the sun. He wished they were back up in that mountain meadow and that Charles Tanner had never lived.

No, that wouldn't do. If Charles Tanner had never lived, neither would his son. And if Charles Tanner hadn't wiped out a good portion of Morey's Falls, Ellie Lundquist would have moved away long ago, been married to a man her own age and had a couple of kids by now.

You can't change the past, no matter how much you want to. He'd learned that long ago—now was no time to be forgetting.

WHY HAD SHE LEFT her cane in the car? For that matter, why hadn't she suggested they drive to the park? To be sure, it wasn't very far away. But they were unprotected, on view, with no place to run to. She couldn't rid herself of the feeling that someone was watching them, someone with the same twisted outlook as Charles Tanner. Someone with a gun.

Don't be absurd, she warned herself. Lightning didn't strike twice in the same tiny Montana town. One crazed killer was more than their quota—coincidence couldn't be cruel enough to bring another one into their midst.

If there was another murderer around, coincidence had nothing to do with it. It had to be heredity. But the man walking beside her with that easy, loose-limbed grace wasn't the danger she was half imagining. It was someone else, watching them. But it was probably just her overwrought imagination and a sleepless night. Not to mention the upcoming anniversary. The whole town was on edge.

"This is it," she said, coming to a halt at the small patch of green on the corner of Main and Bank. She tried to see it through his eyes. It wasn't much—just an empty lot turned into a park, with benches and winding paths and a huge monolith in the center, covered with a drop cloth.

There used to be a fountain there, and Ellie still missed it. She'd liked having it there, something fresh and blue to focus her gaze one. The memorial would be nothing more than a grim reminder of something no one ever forgot.

Tanner hadn't said a word. He was moving around the structure, that distant, enigmatic expression on his face. And then he squatted down, poking at something in the dirt.

"What have you got there?" Ellie asked, moving closer. She never liked being in the park, and would have preferred to stay on the sidewalk, looking in. When it came right down to it, no one liked the park. No one spent their lunch hours on the comfortable benches, kids didn't congregate, old men didn't feed the birds. It was still haunted, fifteen years later.

Tanner rose, looking down into his hand with an odd expression on his face. "It's a cigarette butt," he said, his voice sounding peculiar.

She peered into his hand. "It doesn't look like it."

"That's because someone's crumpled it past recognition. Do you know anyone who does that to their cigarettes?"

Why was his voice sounding so strained? You'd think he'd found a bone or something equally nasty. She was about to say so, when she realized he was genuinely disturbed by the shredded bit of paper in his hand.

"No," she said finally. "But then, I don't know many smokers. Why do you ask?"

He stared down into his hand for a long, speculative moment, and then turned his palm over, letting the tiny scraps drift back onto the recently upturned dirt. He met her gaze blandly. "Just curious," he said. And she knew he lied.

CHAPTER EIGHT

Ellie Lundquist felt a sudden chill. A cloud had passed over the noonday sun, darkening the once bright day, and she shivered in her light cotton shirt.

"Where to next?" she asked in a deliberately cheery voice. "We could go out to the graveyard. Or we could see if some of the relatives would talk to us. Or we could…"

"I think I've had enough for today," Tanner said slowly. "It's after one. Let's get something to eat. What about the restaurant across the street?" He nodded in the direction of Pete's Fireside Café.

Ellie followed his gaze, looking at the faces turned out toward them. "No," she said. "That's not the place to go if you've had enough for one day."

"All right." He accepted it without question. "Got any alternatives?"

"I need to check my horses. I have them stabled out at Maude's. If we show up there she's bound to offer us lunch. Plus more advice than we could ever want."

"I'm used to advice."

"You just don't take it," she supplied.

He smiled that cold, wolfish grin. "Not if I can help it. I prefer to make my own mistakes."

"Okay, let's go to Maude's. If you want," she kept

her voice carefully diffident, "we could go for a ride up into the hills."

"On that old slug you rode yesterday?"

"Mazey's a wonderful horse," Ellie protested. "Anyway, I have three horses. You could ride Hoover. He's got a little more energy."

"I don't know if I think you're much of a judge of horseflesh." They were walking back toward the big black car, the eyes from Pete's Fireside Café following them.

"And you are?" she shot back, incensed.

He shrugged. "I know my way around a horse."

"I think you've been standing at the back end too long," she said sweetly, yanking open the car door.

His laugh was a short, rusty sound of surprise. "Ellie, you amaze me," he said, sliding in beside her. "What an image!"

She switched on the ignition, grinding the starter unnecessarily, and pulled out into the street without looking. Fortunately traffic in Morey's Falls was non-existent. It would have been extremely embarrassing to have collided with another car with Tanner as witness. Not to mention Lonnie's brooding gaze from the front window of the *Gazette* office. She had to learn not to react to Tanner's deliberate goading. She had to be cool, friendly, helpful, and let his taunts slide off her back.

It was easier said than done. For some reason she was vulnerable to the man, in ways she hadn't been vulnerable to anyone in years. Tanner saw straight through to that vulnerability and used it, and her.

She lifted her foot slightly from the accelerator and forced herself to loosen her tight grip on the leather-covered steering wheel. She plastered a pleasant smile onto her face as she headed out toward Maude's rambling ranch house. "Where do you live, Tanner? What do you do for a living? You can't walk all the time."

She didn't have to look at him to know that a cynical grin had stretched across his too-handsome face. "Welcome wagon time again, Ellie?"

She ignored the gibe. "I'm just making friendly conversation. Besides, I'm curious."

"I live in New Mexico. A little town up in the Sangre de Cristo mountains that you never would have heard of."

"What do you do there?" She allowed herself a brief glance in his direction.

His grin broadened. "I live on a horse ranch, Ellie. I'm partners with the man who should have been my father. We raise the best quarter horses known to man. And yes, I've spent more than my share of time at the back end of a horse."

"And your partner doesn't mind you taking off like this?"

It was the wrong question. His face darkened for a moment, and he reached for the pack of cigarettes in his shirt pocket with impatient fingers. "He knows when it's necessary."

"And it doesn't matter how long you're gone?" she pushed.

"It matters." He lit the cigarette and blew a long stream of smoke into the pristine interior of the judge's car.

"Then you can't very well stay here indefinitely."

"I can stay here just as long as I need to," he said in a low, rough voice. "And not a minute longer." He stared out at the scrubby landscape. "Alfred's dying."

He'd surprised himself by saying that, she could tell by the sudden grimness around his mouth. He hadn't surprised her. She had a way about her that invited confidences. People told her things they never expected to tell anyone. Usually they didn't mind when they found they'd been indiscreet. She could tell Tanner minded like hell.

"Alfred's the man who should have been your father?" she prodded gently.

He leaned forward and stubbed out the half-smoked cigarette in the ashtray, staking his claim to what had once been the judge's. "Alfred is everything Charles Tanner wasn't. My mother and I moved in with him when I was a wild teenager and Marbella had had too many of the wrong men for the wrong reasons. He gave us a home, he gave us love, he gave us a future." He leaned back against the seat. "It took him five years to talk Marbella into marrying him. She'd decided she wasn't worth the kind of love Alfred was offering her, and it took him a long time to convince her."

"So he was your father," Ellie said softly. "Your stepfather, at least."

"Marbella died in a car accident two weeks before they were set to get married," he said in a short, unemotional voice.

"But you stayed on?"

"No. I left Alfred to grieve on his own. I took off the afternoon of the accident and didn't come back for a year and a half. I wasn't even sure Alfred would let me come back. But he did."

"Where'd you walk that time?" Her voice was deliberately prosaic.

Some of the tension seemed to leave him. "I'd never seen New England. It seemed as good a direction as any. Anyplace but Montana." There was a long silence, broken only by the powerful hum of the Buick's engine.

"But now you're here."

He shrugged, and his hand strayed toward the cigarettes again, then dropped onto the seat beside her. "Alfred gave me a future when I needed it. I've got to give him the only kind of future he'll have. I've got to make sure the ranch will be safe, that it'll be in good hands."

"You've got to be sure that you won't take off again."

His eyes met hers for a brief, startled moment. "Exactly," he said. "Alfred's had two strokes, and he could have another any time now. He's holding on by the skin of his teeth, and his last months are misery, not knowing what's going to happen to everything he's worked for. I owed it to him to come up here, to the last place on earth I'd ever want to go, and make peace with the past. And why the hell am I telling you all this?" he added with sudden savagery.

"Because I'm easy to talk to?" she suggested softly.

"Because you're a nosy busybody." He lit another cigarette.

She didn't even flinch. "You know, you shouldn't smoke those things. You're not really a smoker—when you're preoccupied you forget all about needing them."

She should have known better than to have twitched the tiger's tail. He turned the full force of those cold blue eyes on hers, and she felt like shivering all over again. "And you, honey, are not really lame. You limp when you remember you're supposed to be the martyred cripple, and the rest of the time you do just fine."

The fact that she deserved it didn't help the pain slicing through her. For all the physical and emotional anguish she'd been through in her thirty years, she'd never had anyone be deliberately cruel to her. The shock of it took her breath away, and she quickly turned her face back to the road, gripping the steering wheel with shaking hands.

She could feel her eyes fill with sudden, stinging tears, and she tried to blink them away. Her mouth trembled, and she bit down on her lip, hard, as she turned down Maude's dusty driveway to the rambling little ranch house that had served the old woman as home for over eighty years.

She pulled to a stop and switched off the car. "We're here," she announced brightly, praying he wouldn't notice her absurdly childish reaction to his random cruelty. She reached for the door, hoping to get away from him, to dash the demoralizing tears from her eyes before he noticed, but he was too fast for her.

He caught her wrist, drawing her back, and her resistance was just so much wasted effort. He could see her tear-filled eyes, her trembling mouth, her stupid, babyish behavior, and color flooded her pale cheeks.

"I'm being ridiculous. I'm sorry..." she began, embarrassed, but he stopped her, his fingers touching her mouth to silence her.

His eyes were no longer cold. "You're sorry?" he echoed. He pulled back his hand, and there was a fleck of blood on his fingers. She must have cut her lip when she'd bit down. His other hand was still holding her wrist, and she felt it tighten around her, felt the infinitesimal pull, and she was ready to move with it, toward him, when he suddenly released her.

He pulled back and reached for the car door. "Maybe," he said, "I'm more like my father than I thought."

This time she stopped him, her hand catching his arm, feeling the warm flesh and bone and sinew beneath his skin. "What do you mean?"

"Taking potshots at helpless children," he said. "Maybe you should keep as far away from me as you can."

"I'm almost thirty-one, Tanner."

"That doesn't keep you from being a child in some ways. You've lived in a cocoon here in Morey's Falls. One moment of random violence and you've been protected ever since. You're not equipped to face the real world and mean, rotten men like me."

"If I'm still a child," Ellie said quietly, her tears long gone, "then it's time I grew up. And you're not a mean, rotten man, Tanner."

He leaned across the seat, and before she could realize his intent his mouth had brushed her lower lip, softly, barely touching. When she looked at him again the blood was on his mouth, not hers. "Honey," he said, "I'm one of the worst." And before she could say anything more he'd opened the door and slid out into the bright sunlight.

MAUDE GILLES was standing there, just outside the car, her dark, sprightly eyes an interested witness, no doubt, to the past few moments between her two visitors. She was shorter than Tanner remembered, and older. The merciless glare of the early-afternoon sun played up every wrinkle in her seamed, lined face, making her appear as old as time. She had to be under five feet, and her long, thick white braids hung past her tiny shoulders.

Ellie had wasted no time climbing out of her side of the car. She had the cane in her hand and a stubborn look of defiance around her mouth. "Hi, Maude. We came for lunch."

He didn't miss the look that passed between the two women. A very slight expression of inquiry passed over Maude's face, answered by an imperceptible shake of Ellie's head. He filed it in the back of his brain for further study, grimacing in annoyance as he watched Ellie limp forward, leaning heavily on the damned cane. He reached in his pocket for the crushed pack of cigarettes.

"'Bout time, too," Maude announced. "I was wondering when I was going to see the two of you. My spies tell me you've been wandering all over town."

"Who are your spies, Maude?" Tanner asked with deceptive laziness.

"Jamie, I suppose," Ellie supplied calmly, almost as if the tense moments in the front seat of the Buick hadn't happened. "He helps out around here, feeds the horses, takes Maude shopping and fills her in on all the gossip. What'd he tell you, Maude?"

"Just that the two of you were as thick as thieves. The old ladies in town are worried about you. They think Tanner here is clouding your mind."

"The spawn of the devil," Tanner said in a pleasant tone of voice. "I don't think Ellie's mind is too clouded."

"It'd take more than a good-looking young stud like you to do it," Maude said bluntly. "More's the pity. Come along in. You'll have to make do with peanut butter sandwiches, but I guess you'll both survive. I'm glad you came, Ellie. Jamie said Shaitan didn't touch his food. Of course that fool boy didn't dare get close enough to see if something was the matter. Why you have to keep a horse like that is beyond me."

"I'd better go see…."

"Ellie, he's waited this long…." Maude might just as well have been talking to herself. Ellie had taken off in the direction of the barns, limping slightly, barely using the cane. "Damn the girl," the old woman said under her breath. "What about you, Tanner? Are you going with her or are you going to help me make lunch?"

Tanner looked down, way down into those fierce little eyes. "What do you think?"

"I think you'd be a fool to spend time with an old lady when you could have a pretty young thing like Ellie. And I expect your mama didn't raise no fools."

He laughed. "You're right. But it's a close decision."

"Lunch will wait. She'll be in the stalls to the left in the big barn. You can't miss her. Watch out for Shaitan, though. If anyone's a spawn of the devil that creature is."

"I'll be careful."

The barn was dark and shadowed after the bright sunlight, and a wave of familiar smells washed over

him. Fresh straw, horseflesh, leather and saddle soap.
He stopped for a moment, letting the smells surround
him with a comforting blanket of memory. This was
solid, real, this was waiting for him in New Mexico.

He was more than used to the sudden surge of home-
sickness. He'd felt it often enough, but usually not quite
so soon. He'd be on the trail, in the midst of some wilderness or the center of a city, and a longing for home
would sweep over him. He'd start, then and there, for
New Mexico.

But he wasn't used to having it happen so soon.
He'd only been gone ten days this time. He usually
didn't feel that pull for months and months. Maybe
there was hope for him after all.

He saw Mazey's broad, bay rump in the shadowy
stall, next to a narrower, chestnut gelding. Ellie was two
stalls over, her voice a low, soothing murmur as she
talked to the biggest, blackest, meanest-looking, most
gorgeous stallion he'd ever seen in his entire life. Cove-
tousness swept over him, wiping out all previous
emotions, and he started forward.

"Don't come any closer." Ellie's voice stopped him.
She was edging out of the stall, her strong, narrow
hands running over the high, beautifully muscled back
of the black as she went. He stopped where he was, too
much of a horseman to disobey, but his hands itched to
touch that smooth back.

Ellie shut the door of the stall behind her and walked
toward him. The cane was under her arm, and she was
once more forgetting to limp.

"Shaitan doesn't like strangers," she said, gesturing
toward the barn door.

Tanner didn't move. "According to Maude, he doesn't like friends, either."

"That's right. He doesn't like anyone but me. You go near him, Tanner, and he'll savage you. What he doesn't accomplish with his teeth he'll finish with his hooves once he gets you down. He's had a bad time of it with people, and I'm the only one he trusts."

A small, cautious smile curved his mouth. "You think you'll have the same luck with me?" he said softly. She didn't reply, and he looked over her shoulder to the beautiful shape of the stallion. "He's too much horse for you, Ellie."

"You touch him," Ellie said again, "and what he doesn't do I will. I'll cut your heart out, Tanner."

"Tsk, tsk. That's not the way to earn my trust."

"The hell with your trust," she said fiercely.

"Is he all right?"

"What do you mean? Oh, you mean because he didn't eat? He was just in a mood. As soon as I showed up he chowed down. He loves me."

He stared down at her defiant face. "Just because he loves you doesn't mean he can't be very dangerous. Love doesn't always mean safety."

The barn was oddly quiet, silent but for the soft whirrup of the horses, the muffled sounds as they lipped their hay. "I know," she said, looking into his eyes with her direct, fearless gaze. "But sometimes safety's not all it's cracked up to be. Do you want some lunch?"

I want you, lying in the straw, wrapped around me, he thought, keeping his face absolutely expressionless. "Peanut butter sandwiches?" he said. "I can't wait."

SHE DIDN'T LET HIM near Shaitan again. The day clouded over, threatening rain, and Shaitan was terrified of thunderstorms. Maude kept plying the two of them with fresh-baked bread, coffee that was almost as strong as Tanner's wicked brew and anecdotes about Morey's Falls before the massacre. She never mentioned Charles Tanner—she didn't have to. Instead, she gave Tanner a feel for the town his family had come from for generations, and he listened with complete fascination.

It was one of the few pleasant things he could take away with him, Ellie thought, sitting at the table and watching him surreptitiously. Most of his search would turn up tragedy, depression and despair. At least Maude was showing him a part of his more distant past that wasn't tainted with murder.

For the time being his defenses were lowered, just enough for her to guess what he might have been like if he'd lived a normal life. Those eyes of his were no longer coldly challenging, no longer deliberately seductive. They were simply eyes, of a beautiful blue shade, and the lashes shielding them were wickedly long. His dark-blond hair was pushed back, his expression was both relaxed and intent, and his mouth was curved in a slight smile that held no threats. His skin was deeply tanned from years in the bright sun, and lines fanned out from his eyes, lines that couldn't have come from smiling.

His hands were wrapped around a mug of Maude's coffee. Ellie remembered the feel of those long, hard fingers on her wrist, touching her cut lip. She remembered the brief, tantalizing feel of his mouth on hers, and she shivered.

"I've got to be heading back," she said suddenly. "Bridge club is at my house tonight, and if I don't make tracks nothing will be ready. As it is I'll barely have time to get Tanner home."

"You don't need to 'get Tanner home,'" he drawled. "I'm perfectly capable of walking."

"Don't be silly, boy. Your family's place is on the other side of town; it must be ten miles from here," Maude said. "Besides, this is a lonely stretch of road. I don't like you being out here alone. There's too much bad feeling still simmering around here. No need to ask for trouble."

"You think someone's gonna shoot me in the back?"

"You forget, Maude knows this town and the people in it a lot better than you do," Ellie said. "And I wouldn't put it past several of them to do just that."

"I guess I'd better run for cover then." Tanner's voice was cool and remote. "I could always skulk along the side of the road and dive into the underbrush if someone came along. Except that there isn't much underbrush around here. I guess I'll have to risk it. We can't have Ellie late for her bridge game."

"Cut it out, Tanner." Ellie rose and carried her empty coffee cup over to the old iron sink. She almost picked up his, and had to force herself not to. She wasn't going to wait on him, do for him, on any level. It was too tempting, too dangerous. "It's very simple—you can drop me off home and take the car out to your place. I won't be needing it, and you can drive it tomorrow morning so that we can get an early start."

"No thanks."

Ellie sighed, leaning over to kiss Maude's withered cheek. "We'll argue about it in the car. Thanks for everything, Maude. You're a great lady."

"No," said Maude, "I'm not. You're the good one around here."

To Ellie's surprise Tanner came over and kissed Maude, too. Ellie held her breath as Maude blinked back tears of surprise and emotion. She hadn't seen Maude cry in years. Maybe she'd never seen Maude cry. "Thanks, Maude," he murmured, smiling at her, that rare, sweet smile that he'd bestowed on Addie Pritchard and no one else.

Ellie, watching that smile, felt a knife of longing twist inside her, one that she didn't dare let Tanner see. Without a word she headed out the door, letting the screen door slam shut behind her. This time she remembered to limp.

CHAPTER NINE

Ellie headed straight for the passenger's side and climbed in before Tanner could protest. "You drive," she announced. "The keys are in the ignition."

"I thought I warned you about that."

"You and I have something in common, Tanner," she growled. "We don't take kindly to advice."

They were halfway to town before he spoke. "You've got her fooled too, haven't you?"

"Who? What are you talking about?"

"Maude. She's swallowed the Saint Ellie image like everyone else."

"Don't goad me, Tanner. It just so happens that I *am* a saint. I've spent almost—" she looked at her watch "—almost nine hours with you and I haven't killed you yet. Surely that qualifies for sainthood in some parts."

He laughed, a short, sharp sound that wasn't unpleasant. "My mother would have agreed with you."

"Your mother must have been a wise woman."

"Not particularly. She had phenomenally lousy taste in men," he said calmly.

There wasn't much she could say in response to that. He was driving at a surprisingly decorous pace, and he hadn't had a cigarette in hours. She would have thought he'd be a demon behind the wheel. Right then she could have used a little bit of lead-foot. The last thing she wanted was to show up late to her own bridge club and start having to make explanations. People were going to be nosy enough.

"Is there any way I can talk you into taking the car?" She tried it one last time. "It would make things easier on both of us."

He glanced in her direction, his smoky eyes reminding her of a timber wolf. "All right," he agreed abruptly. "Though I disagree with you. Nothing is going to make things easier on either of us."

She considered, then rejected the notion of asking him exactly what he meant. She was afraid that deep in her heart she knew, and it was something she wasn't ready to face.

"I don't really like bridge." She changed the subject, her voice slightly rushed. "I just sort of fell into it. People were always looking for a fourth, and it was one thing that had nothing to do with the past. So we started meeting at people's houses, first four of us, then eight. I expect we'll make up three tables tonight. Actually, we spend more time eating than playing. And our table talk is outrageous. I hate to think what serious bridge players would think if they heard us."

Tanner made a noncommittal sound, clearly uninterested, but Ellie plowed on, no longer comfortable in silence. "Sometimes I don't think the others care that much about bridge, either. It's just a chance to get away from their husbands and kids, or an empty house with too many memories. It's a chance to let their hair down and gossip…." Her voice trailed off guiltily.

"So I imagine I'll be a major topic of conversation tonight. Over the chips and dips?"

"How about over the crudités?" she found herself saying.

Again that short, sharp laugh. "Tarnishing your image, Saint Ellie? You're supposed to turn the other cheek."

She sighed, recognizing the truth of it. She shouldn't rise to his bait, shouldn't fight back. Tanner was the one with psychic burdens weighing him down. He was suffering fully as much as his father's victims, and if she could comfort the others, why couldn't she extend comfort to Tanner?

"What are you going to do about supper? It's already after seven," she said instead.

"Why, Ellie, is that an invitation?" he mocked her. "I didn't think so. Don't worry, I won't starve to death. Pete's Fireside Café looked like a good possibility."

"No!"

"Do you want to tell me why, or should I guess?"

"Pete Forrester's daughter was killed in the massacre, and Pete took it even harder than most. He'd be one you'd want to avoid."

"Maybe. Or the one I most want to talk to."

"Don't ask for trouble, Tanner."

"I did by coming here."

"Wait until I can come with you," she said, and her voice held a note of pleading in it. "Please, Tanner."

He said nothing for a moment. They were coming into the outskirts of Morey's Falls, and the approaching storm had brought early-evening shadows down around the barren-looking buildings. "Do you want to tell me where you live?" he said, ignoring her earlier plea. "Or shall I just drive around and guess?"

"Take the next left," she said. "It's the house on the corner."

Tanner pulled into the driveway next to the judge's huge old house, and his expression was sardonic. "Very impressive," he said. "No wonder you married him."

"Don't. I don't owe you any explanations."

"True enough." He turned off the motor and opened the door.

"What are you doing?" she demanded nervously.

"Seeing you to your door. It's the least I can do. My mama did try to make me into a little gentleman. She failed, but a few things stuck." He strode around the car and opened her door with all the aplomb of a uniformed chauffeur.

Ellie looked over her shoulder nervously. The gathering shadows of the storm darkened the streets that should still have been light at that time of year, and there were lamps shining in the windows across the way. No faces there, watching the sinner and the saint. "There's no need…" she began.

"There's every need." His hand was under her elbow, guiding her up the uneven sidewalk to the back porch, moving her with such gentle force that she had no chance to limp, no chance to pull back. He paused on the porch outside the back door, releasing her, and opened the door. "You don't lock your house, either, do you?" His voice was deep with disapproval.

"It's not necessary."

"Lock your door, Ellie," he ordered. "And I'll keep away from Pete's Fireside Café."

She looked up at him. The shadows were all around them, the smell of the approaching storm thick in the air, and a sudden, waiting stillness caught at her. He was so close, and so locked away from her. His blue eyes were hooded, unreadable, and his mouth looked hard and unyielding.

It wasn't. Before she realized what he was doing he'd pulled her into his arms, out on the back porch in plain view of anyone who cared to look. His hand cupped the back of her neck, holding her in place as his mouth came down on hers.

She stood rigid in his arms, surprise and panic holding her still as his mouth moved expertly across hers. His lips were soft, warm, damp, and the knot in her stomach tightened and dropped. The long fingers behind her neck were kneading the tense muscles, lightly, erotically, as his lips tugged gently at hers.

She didn't know what to do. Half of her wanted to respond, to kiss him back, but she didn't know how. The other half wanted to shove him away from her, remove the tempting warmth of his lean, strong body. She did neither. She stood there in the circle of his arms, unmoving.

He lifted his head, his mouth leaving hers, and his eyes glittered in the shadowy half-light. "You kiss like a virgin," he said, his voice softly mocking.

She kept herself from flinching. "I wasn't kissing you," she pointed out with an attempt to sound matter-of-fact. All she sounded was shaky. "You were kissing me."

"Then let me do it properly," he whispered, and the sound played across her spine like a thousand tiny leaves. "Open your mouth."

She could no more deny him than she could have stopped her heart from beating. His hands moved up, cupping her head, as his mouth caught hers, and her mouth opened, obediently, passively.

She wasn't expecting his tongue. She jumped, but he held her still, tracing the soft contours of her lips, dipping inside, lightly at first, getting her used to the unfamiliar invasion. Her lips were damp, soft beneath his, and she began to tremble in reaction. His tongue touched hers, sliding over the rough surface, and the intimacy of it was unbearably sweet, teasing, tempting, arousing. Suddenly it was more than she could take. She twined her arms around his neck, pressed her body against his and kissed him back, desperately, inexpertly, passionately.

She could feel the hardness of him against her thighs. She could feel her nipples pressing through her cotton bra and shirt, pressing against his muscled chest. She could feel her heart race and her mind soar as she lost herself in the overpowering sensation of his mouth on hers. If she could she would have crawled into his skin. She wanted to rip off his shirt, to feel his flesh beneath her hungry hands, his body against hers, hot and hard and wanting as she was wanting.

His heart was pounding against hers and his mouth was no longer gentle; it was as hungry as hers. Her lip began to bleed again, and the small touch of pain was just one more point of arousal. She wanted to break the kiss, to pull him into the house, to lock the doors behind them and push him down on the old linoleum floor of the judge's kitchen.

The rumble of Ginger Barlow's aging Camaro

stopped her before she could make an even greater fool of herself. In sudden panic she ripped herself out of his arms, and he was too startled to try to hold her. She backed into the corner of the porch, her back against the clapboard, her breath coming in shallow gasps. She could feel the dampness on her mouth, the heat still rippling through her body. She looked at Tanner and wanted to weep. He looked watchful, patient, expectant. He didn't look as if he'd just experienced the most profoundly erotic moment of his life. He probably hadn't.

"Well," she said, her voice low and trembling, "now you know. I'm human after all."

"Yes," he said softly. "You are."

"Damn you, Tanner," she said desperately. "Don't play games with me! Leave me be!"

If she expected pity or compassion, she was getting none of it. "You've been let be for too long. Didn't the judge ever kiss you?"

Color flamed her face. "Sorry I was so inadequate," she mumbled.

"You weren't inadequate. Just…inexperienced. Why?"

"There you are, Ellie!" Ginger shouted out gaily, moving up the sidewalk with the sinuous stride she kept for susceptible males. "And Tanner, my goodness. I didn't realize you were there."

The hell you didn't, Ellie thought savagely, and then thought better of her anger. Ginger had prevented her from having to answer a very uncomfortable question. Though she suspected Tanner knew the answer. He just wanted to make her admit it.

"I'm just leaving," Tanner said. "I'm keeping Ellie from her bridge club."

"Well, I'm part of the bridge club, and it's okay with me. I tell you what—I'll give you a ride home while Ellie puts out the refreshments I brought." She was wearing too much of her current musky scent, and even out in the evening air it hung about them like a cloud.

"No thanks," Tanner said distantly. "We'll finish this tomorrow, Ellie. First thing." And with that parting threat he left them, moving down the steps to the car with a loose-limbed grace that caught Ellie in the pit of her stomach and warred with the panic that had settled there.

Ginger let out a gusty sigh as he drove away. "That is some man, I tell you," she said. "They don't grow too many of them in these parts." She turned her attention to her friend, and her wide blue eyes narrowed. "What were you two talking about when I got here? It must have been something pretty intense."

"We were talking about the massacre," Ellie lied with a skill so immediate that it astounded her.

Ginger shook her head. "That's no way to win him."

"Win him?" Ellie echoed, glad she was still standing in the shadows. "Why in the world would I want to win him?"

"Like I just told you, Ellie. Men like Tanner don't come around too often."

"Thank God," she muttered.

"You really don't want him?" Ginger demanded. "You're absolutely sure?"

Ellie looked at her old friend with knowing eyes. For a moment she wondered what Ginger would say if she told her the truth. If she said, *yes, I want him, I want him more than I've ever wanted anything in my life. Keep your hands off him, he's mine.*

Ginger wouldn't believe it. Ginger would laugh. Ginger believed what she wanted to believe, whatever was most convenient in her own self-centered life. Ginger wanted Tanner; Ellie had recognized that fact the moment she saw the two of them together, and nothing on this earth was going to shake her determination. Nothing short of Tanner's outright refusal, and much as Ellie might like to fantasize about that possibility it was highly unlikely.

If she had any sense at all she wouldn't want him herself. She'd pass him on to Ginger with her blessing and without a second thought. "I'm sure," she said in the shadows. And very carefully she wiped the dampness from her lips.

IT HAD BEEN a cool night. A sleepless night. Ellie had lain awake for hours, too tired to get up to close the window, too wide-awake to do more than lie there and worry. By six o'clock in the morning she was down in the huge old kitchen, drinking coffee in her oversize flannel nightgown, her bare feet cold on the aging linoleum as she looked around her.

If she was going to stay, she could do things about the place, she thought, not for the first time. She could paint the tall brown cabinets white, hang plants in the bay window, pull up the cracked linoleum to show the wide pine boards beneath. She could put a radio in and play country music while she baked bread. She could raise a passel of kids. It was a big house—it could hold a lot of kids. The sound of children's laughter would do a lot to lighten up this dark old place.

But children needed a father. And there wasn't a

single possibility. She wasn't going to marry Bernie Appleton or Fred Parsons with their ready-made families. And she'd long ago given up on Lonnie.

How far was Tanner going to push her when he came over this morning? She couldn't tell him the truth—she owed Lonnie that much. She owed the judge that much. Besides, it was none of his business. Her past sex life was her own concern and no one else's, and he had a lot of nerve making assumptions, asking questions, pushing her for answers.

Life was so much easier twenty, thirty years ago. Women were expected to be in a state of relative purity, and no one would have suggested otherwise.

Except, of course, if they'd been married, she reminded herself grimly. And it wasn't as if she hadn't tried.

She had never been able to pinpoint when the judge's feelings about her changed from parental to something else. Maybe they'd never been fatherly, and she'd just been too involved in her pain and loss to notice. When she'd finally realized that his possessiveness, his generosity, his heavy-handed attempts at flirtation came from unexpectedly husbandly feelings, there'd been no question in her mind what she should do. He'd given her more than any other human had, and asked nothing in return. If he wanted to have a real marriage she would give it to him.

It had been a miserable, humiliating failure. The judge was too old, too tied up with guilt and confused feelings, and Ellie was too inexperienced to overcome his emotional and physical difficulties. She was left feeling confused and ashamed, no longer knowing what she wanted.

She'd gone from bad to worse. There were plenty of reasons for her failure with the judge, reasons she could accept once the initial embarrassment had passed. As far as she knew there was no reason for her failure with Lonnie.

They'd been dating in high school, before the massacre. He'd been a shy boy, overwhelmed by his blustering father, inept at the manly sports his father had demanded of him.

But he'd been gentle and sweet with Ellie back then. And after the judge had died there'd been no one else, just Poor Lonnie, fresh from an unpleasant divorce, waiting for her.

She'd given herself time. She'd done what she could, waiting for Lonnie to make a move.

He didn't make one. She waited, and waited, and when finally curiosity and frustration grew too much for her, she took matters into her own hands. It had ended with the same futility and sense of inadequacy as her attempt with the judge. And while Lonnie had been the soul of gentleness, she knew whose fault it had to be.

Now here was Tanner, reminding her of things she'd chosen not to feel, waking her up to emotions she hadn't even come close to before. Here was Trouble, and instead of running as far and as fast as she could, she was lending him her car, her time, her mouth—and her body, if it ever came to that.

She reached down and rubbed her stiff knee. He was wrong about her knee, but maybe that was wishful thinking on his part. He wasn't wrong about her. She'd been cosseted and protected too long, out of the real world. Tanner was as solid a dose of reality as they'd had around here in a long time. Reality wasn't always pleasant, but it was better than sleeping her life away.

She wrapped her arms around her waist and hugged herself in the chilly kitchen. Two weeks. Tanner would be gone, and so would she. Maude would keep the horses, Jamie would feed them, and when she got settled she'd send for them. She'd have to come back for them—no one else would be able to get Shaitan into a horse trailer. But that would be the last time. Maude hadn't left Morey's Falls in more than twenty years, but for Ellie she'd do it. The Barlows would come to visit, wherever she ended up. But never again would she live in a living monument to death like Morey's Falls.

She didn't hear the door open. She didn't feel the eyes on her, so different from the angry, threatening gaze that seemed to haunt her, the gaze she could never trace. She was staring sightlessly out the side window, into her blank future, when Tanner spoke.

"Is that nightgown an invitation? If so, I ought to tell you that I prefer silk to flannel." And he shut the door behind him with a quiet little click before advancing on her, purpose in every line of his graceful body, his eyes intent.

CHAPTER TEN

Ellie's hand tightened around the mug of coffee for a moment before giving him her full attention. "It's too early in the morning for heavy-handed seduction, Tanner," she said calmly. "Stop stalking me and pour yourself a cup of coffee. I'm willing to bet it's a lot better than anything you've had this morning."

To her relief it worked. The predatory air left him, he strolled to the stove and helped himself. "You might lose the bet. I stopped off and had a cup with Addie Pritchard on my way over here. She makes damned good coffee." He took a tentative sip, impervious to the scalding temperature. "It's too weak."

"What else would you expect?" She wanted to button the top of her flannel nightgown, but refused to give in to the temptation. Even with Tanner's high-powered sexuality turned down to only a dim glow she was acutely aware of her state of undress.

He took the straight-backed chair across the table from her, flipped it expertly and straddled it, resting his arms on the back. "No comment. Do you always get up this early?"

"I didn't sleep well."

He grinned. She watched in fascination as it started

as a smirk, broadened, and finally reached the cool depths of his blue eyes. "Sorry."

"That's all right," she said in her mildest voice. "I expect to sleep very well in a couple of weeks." Absently she rubbed her knee through the heavy flannel nightgown.

"Once I'm gone," he supplied, his eyes watching her hand. "Think you'll last that long?"

"I've had sleepless nights before."

"I wasn't talking about sleeping."

"Tanner…" Her voice carried a very definite warning.

"I'll behave," he promised rashly, and she didn't for one moment believe him. He reached in his shirt pocket for his cigarettes and came up empty. "Damn," he said, rising. "I left my cigarettes out in the car."

"You don't really need to smoke," she protested.

He stopped where he was. "I'll tell you what, Ellie. I won't smoke if you don't limp."

Enough was enough, she thought grimly, pushing back her chair. "Come here, Tanner," she said in an even voice.

His expression was wary. "Why?"

Ellie allowed herself a determined little smile. "I'm not going to hurt you. I want to show you something." She reached down and pulled up her flannel nightgown, halfway up her thigh, exposing her knee to his reluctant gaze.

She tried to see it from his viewpoint. It was part of her body, and she'd learned to accept it. But a stranger, especially someone like Tanner, wouldn't be used to women with those kinds of scars marring them.

The scars ran from halfway down her calf to midthigh, deep, wide scars that still kept their livid color, a color that was unlikely to fade after all these years. Her leg was twisted slightly, and all the physical therapy in the world hadn't managed to straighten it completely. Ellie looked down at it and sighed.

"Pretty ugly, isn't it?" she said evenly. "I hate to tell you Tanner, but it makes me limp."

She shouldn't have done it. His mask was back in place, his eyes cool and blue and unreadable. If she'd hoped to shock him into some sort of reaction, she'd failed.

"I've seen worse," he said. "You don't seem to have any trouble riding. If you can control that black beast of yours then you can't be that messed up."

"Shaitan's very responsive," Ellie said, flaring up at the insult to her beloved horse.

"Still trying to convince me you're a cripple?"

"I'm not a cripple," she shot back. "Sometimes my knee hurts and I limp. It's that simple."

"And sometimes my nerves hurt and I smoke," Tanner said. "Another simple equation. I'll get my cigarettes, and you can get your cane. Where'd that fancy thing come from, anyway? The head of it looks like solid gold."

"It is," Ellie said. "It was a birthday present from the judge."

"It figures," he drawled. "What'd he do, give you a wheelchair for Christmas?"

"Nothing's going to shut you up, is it?"

He shook his head, unrepentant. "It takes a hell of a lot to do it."

"Get your cigarettes, Tanner," she said, pulling the heavy flannel down over her knee again. "I don't want to argue with you."

"That's a shame. I like arguing with you."

"Why?"

"Why?" he echoed. "I'm not sure. Maybe because things are safer that way." And before she could respond he'd headed back out the kitchen door, leaving it open to the early-morning chill.

THE AIR WAS COOL and crisp outside, unseasonably chilly, and he crossed the walkway to the car in long strides, taking in deep breaths of the fresh morning air. He stopped by the Buick and leaned against it for a moment, unseeing.

He began cursing, a low, steady stream of profanity. He felt sick, shaking with a rage so deep, so profound that he wanted to pound on the shiny black hood of Ellie's car.

He pushed himself back, forcing himself to take slow, calming breaths.

It had never seemed real before. Reading the newspaper accounts, seeing the survivors, even visiting the scene hadn't made it sink into his thick skull.

But those long, dark scars on Ellie Lundquist's leg were real enough. The lines around her warm brown eyes and her generous mouth were lines of remembered pain, and the limp was real. And his father was a vicious, murdering bastard.

What did that make him? What right did he have to come back here, to remind people, to remind Ellie of a past that was better left buried? Even for Alfred's sake, did he have the right to dredge up past miseries?

Except that those miseries weren't in the past, weren't safely buried. They were alive, tormenting this town, and his presence made no difference, one way or the other. The people in this town had to come to terms with that day of violence, with his father's life, just as he had. All of them, Tanner included, had put it off too long.

She was sitting where he'd left her, staring into her coffee. Her hair hung down her back in a thick chestnut tangle, her bare feet were curled on the chair rung, and her forehead was creased with thought. With worry?

As usual he felt like the world's worst bastard. As usual he wasn't going to do anything about it but make things worse. He didn't take his seat again, but began prowling around her huge, dark kitchen, opening cupboard doors, intensely aware of her troubled gaze watching his progress.

"What's on the agenda for today?" he asked, poking around the Rice Chex. "Any charnel houses we could visit? Maybe we could have a picnic in the graveyard."

She ignored his tone of voice. "I'm trying to think who would be the best person for you to talk with. Lonnie's available anytime. He has an almost ghoulish fascination with that day—he could tell you anything in terms of facts and figures, but he doesn't necessarily know about emotions. Addie wasn't around. Georgia Bellingham lost her husband and her brother, but she's just finishing teaching for the year and she'd be pretty busy. You wouldn't get anywhere with Pete Forrester, so there's no need to try the Fireside Café. Maybe George Throckton—he lost his mother and father. Or Mabel Henry. She was dating Nils-Jacob Lundquist. Or there's—"

"Please stop," he said, his voice low and bitter as he

tried to halt her cheerful litany of death. "Didn't anyone die a natural death around here?"

He could feel the warmth in her eyes—it was a tangible thing, reaching out to him, enfolding him in comfort. Determinedly he shook it off.

"Well, a few," she said. "The judge's wife, for one."

"I thought you were the judge's wife," he countered, seizing on a new topic as would a drowning man a lifeline.

If he'd hoped to shake her he'd failed. She merely shrugged. "For sixteen years of my life I'd thought of Mrs. Lundquist as the judge's wife. Just because he happened to marry me later didn't really change things. They were made for each other."

"Made for the judge, eh? I can just imagine. She must have had blue hair, an iron jaw and a massive bosom."

Ellie giggled. The sound was soft, unexpected, and it began uncoiling the knot that had twisted in his gut. "I don't suppose it takes a whole lot of E.S.P. to guess that. She also had the kindest heart around."

"What got her? Since you said it wasn't my father's rifle."

"Don't, Tanner," she protested. "Mrs. Lundquist died of a heart attack a year before the massacre."

"Lucky her."

"Tanner…"

"That reminds me," he continued, closing the door on the cereal boxes and turning to face her, leaning back against the counter. "You said someone was teaching school. How come I haven't seen any children around? Did Charles wipe out everybody of childbearing age?"

"Of course not. Most young people leave here as soon as they can. There's not much to offer a growing family. The few that stayed bus their children three towns over to the regional school. A lot of them spend the week with relatives and come home on the weekend. But you're right—there aren't too many of them."

"And you and Lonnie haven't contributed your share."

He didn't miss the tightening of her soft, generous mouth. "Clever of you to notice. Do you think I should do something about that? Maybe you could drop me off at the *Gazette* and I'll get to work on it."

She was clearly hoping to goad him. He gave her a brief smile. "Don't try sarcasm with me, Ellie. It doesn't work. Besides, I think you'd be wasting your time with Lonnie."

She lifted her chin and looked him squarely in the eye. "Got any other suggestions?"

She knew that he did, and that was enough. He didn't have to say a word, he just let his smile broaden slightly before he turned back to his perusal of her cupboards. "So which victim do we visit next?" he asked. "Unfortunately, you're the only cripple around here, but maybe we can find someone who carried emotional scars...."

"Tanner," she said, her voice low. "It's not as bad as it looks."

He knew exactly what she was talking about. So much for fooling her with his callous attitude; she'd seen right through to the very real shock and anger he was still trying to suppress. He held himself still for a moment, then turned and moved behind her. She didn't turn, didn't meet his gaze, she just waited.

He put his hand on her shoulder, lightly, feeling the tension beneath her skin, feeling the bone and heat and surprising muscle. "Thank you," he said.

She looked up then, over her shoulder, into his eyes, and her smile was breathtaking. She parted her lips, about to say something, he didn't know what, but he was leaning toward her, planning to cover her mouth with his and stop whatever words might come tumbling forth, when he heard the footsteps on the wooden porch outside.

He was six feet away from her when Doc Barlow stormed in the kitchen. He stopped short when he spied Tanner in the post-dawn shadows, for a moment his expression slipped, and Tanner saw something he wished he hadn't.

"What are you doing here?" Doc blurted out. "Jesus, Tanner, you didn't spend the night here?"

"No, he didn't spend the night here." Ellie said with a trace of asperity. "Not that it's anybody's business but mine if he did. I would have thought Ginger told you—I lent Tanner my car last night so I wouldn't be late for bridge."

"Sorry," Doc mumbled, still looking slightly dazed. "Sorry," he said again. "Of course she said something. And you're right—it's none of my damned business. I'm being an interfering old fool." The hearty tone didn't quite ring true, but Ellie was satisfied, and for the moment that was all that mattered. There was no way Doc was going to fool Tanner—not now.

"I'll grant you," Ellie said, "that seven-fifteen is a little early for visitors. Tanner thinks my coffee's too weak. Pour yourself a cup, Doc, and tell me what's got you out and about so early?"

"You make great coffee," Doc said loyally, and Tanner allowed himself an audible snort. "I'm afraid I'm just one step ahead of Dave Martin. He headed out for Tanner's place, but when he doesn't find him I expect he'll be here next."

Tanner watched with interest as Ellie's freckled face paled in the dimly lit kitchen. "Who's Dave Martin?" he asked.

"He's what passes for the law around here," Doc said, pouring himself a mug of coffee. "He's a good, strong boy and does a good enough job for what little crime we get."

"Good and strong," Ellie echoed cynically. "Muscles all over, particularly in his brain."

"Now, Ellie," Doc admonished her. "The boy's no intellectual, but he does well enough."

"Dave Martin's capabilities are beside the point. Why is he looking for me?" Tanner inquired in a carefully bland voice.

"I guess because you're the only newcomer in town," Doc said, squirming a bit.

"But what's happened?" Ellie demanded. "Why should he be looking for anyone?"

Doc squirmed even more. "You remember Mabel King's dog?"

"That nasty crossbred Doberman? The one that savaged Maude's cat? Of course. What's he got to do with anything?"

"She found him this morning with a bullet in his brain."

Ellie took a shaky breath. "Well, I'm sure he's no great loss. Someone must have thought he was running deer or something...."

"One of George Young's cattle was found the same way," Doc interrupted her. "And one of the sheep down at the Cutler ranch, and three of Marcy Laverty's chickens."

"Oh, my God," she said, and her eyes were haunted.

Tanner stood straight. "It sounds like Charles Tanner's son is the likely culprit. Who else would follow in his father's footsteps? Of course, the fact that I don't know these people or where they live is of no importance. The fact that I'd have no reason to do such a thing doesn't matter, either. Is Martin coming alone or does he have a lynch mob with him?"

"Now, son, that kind of attitude doesn't help anybody."

"I don't want to help anybody," Tanner said.

They all heard the sound of the car pulling up in back of the judge's house. Ellie rose, moving across the room to the back door with only the faintest trace of a limp. "He's alone," she announced.

"Uh, Ellie," Doc cleared his throat. "Don't you think you ought to put on something a little more, er…?"

Ellie looked down at her voluminous flannel night-gown and grinned. "If Tanner can control his lustful passions in the face of this erotic lingerie I think a happily married man like Dave Martin can. This is more covering than people usually wear."

"Yes, but it's nightclothes…." Doc's voice trailed off as Martin's sharp-knuckled rapping broke through.

Ellie opened the door and waved the burly young cop into the room. "Come on in, Dave," she said affably. "We were expecting you. Tanner, why don't you pour Dave a cup of coffee? Maybe he'll appreciate it more than you do."

Tanner had to admire Ellie. She was acting as if this was an early-morning offshoot of her bridge club, offering refreshments, polite conversation and all the social amenities. If the thick-necked young man with the humorless expression was about to bring out the handcuffs he couldn't very well do it in the face of Ellie's determined sociability.

He could try, though. "You Charles Tanner, Jr.?" he demanded gruffly.

Tanner handed him a cup of coffee, smiling sweetly. "I am."

"Where were you last night?"

Tanner knew right then and there he could play it two ways. He could be friendly, helpful, try to make the townspeople accept and understand him. Or he could spit in their eyes.

Dave Martin wouldn't respond well to friendliness and helpfulness. Neither would most of the people he'd met in Morey's Falls. Tanner smiled, the smile that never reached his eyes. "Who wants to know?" he said gently.

"Listen, boy, this is a criminal investigation." Dave Martin's face was getting redder by the minute.

"And I'm more than happy to help. I can tell you that I wasn't prowling around Morey's Falls shooting animals. I don't have a gun, and if I did it wouldn't do much good. I don't know how to use one."

Martin's expression was incredulous. "You don't hunt?"

Tanner shook his head. "I don't kill anything bigger than blackflies, Martin."

"That still doesn't answer my question."

"I'm not going to answer your question. A lady's reputation is involved."

He heard Ellie's smothered laughter. He saw Doc's expression darken for a moment and Dave Martin's face turn sullen and disbelieving. As if that weren't enough, Lonnie Olafson chose that moment to wander in from the front hall, and it was Tanner's turn to frown. *Damn it,* Ellie had to start locking her doors.

Lonnie looked the same as always, his boyish hair rumpled, his blue-and-white striped oxford shirt rolled up at the elbows, his chinos artfully creased. His running shoes were encrusted with mud—the only change from his usual yuppie perfection.

"Hello, again, Dave," he said, moving in and helping himself to the coffee. He spilled a bit, scalding himself, as Tanner looked on impassively. "Tanner, Doc, Ellie." He greeted them in turn.

"What are you doing here, Lonnie?" Ellie's irritation was obvious.

"Serving the public of Morey's Falls. This is news," he said self-righteously.

"My kitchen is news?" Ellie scoffed. "I think I'd like you all to leave. I need to get dressed. When I come downstairs it would be nice if all of you were gone."

"All of us, Ellie?" Doc questioned in a worried tone of voice.

She gave him a warmer smile than Tanner had ever seen her give another man. Certainly warmer than she'd ever given him. "All of you," she said gently. "Except Tanner." And she left the room without a backward glance.

"You better watch yourself, boy," Dave Martin said. Coming from a man a decade younger than Tanner, it sounded not so much pompous as absurd. "We don't like your type around here. The sooner you get out of Morey's Falls, the better for everyone."

Tanner didn't have to look around him to know there'd be agreement, reluctant or enthusiastic, on the faces of the other two men. "What's my type?" he asked.

Dave Martin turned even redder. "Don't sass me. You better watch your step. And don't go disappearing on me—I'm not through with you yet."

Tanner smiled, his best shark's smile. "Martin, in one breath you tell me to get out of town. In the next you tell me to stay put. Make up your mind."

There wasn't much Martin could say in response to such a reasonable statement. With a final threatening glower he stomped out the back door, slamming it behind him.

Doc's eyes were troubled, filled with something Tanner wished he'd never seen. "We'd better go, too, Lonnie. There's nothing for the papers here, and I've got patients coming in another half an hour."

"I just got here." Lonnie's high-pitched voice cracked slightly, as if he hadn't quite settled into puberty.

"You gonna go against Ellie's wishes?"

"Of course not." Lonnie set his cup down on the counter, sloshing more coffee over the sides. He headed for the door, never once looking at Tanner.

Doc followed him, pausing in the open doorway, turning to say something to Tanner, then clearly thought better of it. "For what it's worth," he said finally, "I know you didn't have anything to do with those animals."

There wasn't anything else he could say. "Thanks."

He watched as Lonnie skirted the yard and headed for his car. A BMW, Tanner noticed with a curl of his lip. Doc was driving his pickup, and as he pulled away his face settled in a look of profound trouble.

Tanner turned away. He wasn't used to having to worry about other people, other than Alfred. But already he cared about Doc, cared about what he was going through.

He moved back for more of Ellie's weak coffee, then stopped, squatting down. Thick clumps of dirt littered the floor. He'd seen that dirt on Lonnie's sneakers, but Lonnie hadn't been near one patch of the stuff. One of the other morning visitors must have brought in the same mud. He picked up a clump, rubbing it between his fingers, and then rose, stretching wearily. He didn't like the suspicions that were filtering through his mind, and he didn't like any of the alternatives. *Damn,* why couldn't things ever be easy?

CHAPTER ELEVEN

Tanner was standing in the kitchen, his back to her, when Ellie came back downstairs. He was staring out the window, out into the morning sunlight, and the faded chambray shirt stretched across his shoulders. His dark-blond hair hung below the collar of the shirt, and tension radiated through his finely muscled body. She stopped in the doorway, watching him, knowing he knew she was there, knowing he was letting her watch. And still she couldn't stop herself.

His legs were long, encased in jeans that had seen hard wear, and his hips were narrow, sexy. Everything about him was sexy, and she would be a fool to pretend otherwise. She sighed, a small, quiet sound of resignation that nevertheless traveled across the huge dark kitchen. He turned then, his blue eyes cool and assessing as they took in her appearance.

She kept her expression bland, as she'd taught herself years ago, but she wondered what he was thinking. She'd braided her hair in one thick, loose plait, and she was dressed pretty much as he was, in a denim shirt and faded jeans. She'd spent almost five minutes buttoning and unbuttoning her shirt, finally saying "The hell with it!" and leaving three buttons unfastened. If he looked closely enough he'd be able to see the remnants of the sun from her shirtless ride two days ago. Knowing Tanner, she had no doubt he'd look.

His eyes didn't linger on her chest, her hips or her face, despite all her hard work. They dropped to her feet, encased in sensible riding boots. "That's probably a better idea than riling an already riled population," he said. "Are you going to let me ride Shaitan?"

Simple and direct and easy to answer. "Forget it," she said sweetly.

If Tanner's laugh wasn't particularly mirthful, it was better than that distant, haunted expression that shadowed his eyes. "We'll see," he said. "I've worn down harder women than you."

"I'm stubborn," she said.

"So am I." And they weren't talking about horses.

They were halfway out to Maude's before he brought up the subject that hadn't been far from either of their minds. "Has this happened before?"

She turned to look at him. It was a bright, warm day, and she was wearing sunglasses, the smoked lenses giving her an infinitesimal measure of protection from Tanner's gaze that saw far too much. "What happened before?" she asked warily.

"Animals being shot. Apart, of course, from my dear departed father's nasty habits," he said, his voice low and bitter.

"Not that I know of," she mumbled unhappily.

"Great," said Tanner savagely. "What else did he do? What else have we got to look forward to? Is anyone absolutely certain he died that day? Maybe he's been lurking up in the mountains, waiting to come back."

"He died that day," Ellie said, her voice strained. "I saw his body."

He was silent for a moment. "All right," he said finally. "We can rule out the return of Charles Tanner. I suppose we can rule out ghosts. So what possibilities does that leave us with? Another madman, waiting to wreak havoc on the innocent town of Morey's Falls? Or a malicious newcomer, out to ruffle a few feathers?"

"You didn't do it."

"Thanks for that vote of confidence. I don't know if anyone else will agree with you," Tanner said evenly. "I could have done it. I had your car, and the whole night stretched in front of me with nothing to fill it. After all, you'd sent me away in favor of a bridge game."

"You don't even know where those people lived."

He shrugged. "I could have just picked random farms."

"You don't know how to use a gun." She heard her own voice sounding a little panicked. It was a game she didn't want to play; she didn't want to have to suspect him when she'd been so certain.

"I could have been lying about that," he said reasonably. "You saw how shocked your rent-a-cop was when I told him I didn't hunt. Maybe that was to throw everyone off the trail."

"Tanner, you didn't do it. I know it, and at least Doc knows it."

"So who does that leave? Come on, Ellie, it's a reasonable enough question. It needs to be asked."

"You're right. Unfortunately, I don't have any answers."

"No other lonely hermits living on the edge of town and madness? No human time bombs waiting to explode?" Tanner pushed mercilessly.

"Not that I know of. And it's a small town, Tanner. I'd know." She turned into Maude's long winding drive.

"Well, then," he said with a shrug and that charming smile that never reached his eyes, "I guess that leaves me."

And Ellie, unable to think of any way to refute it, was silent.

Maude was standing on the porch of her house, watching for them. "Are you coming in for coffee?" she called to them, her voice brittle and cracked with age, "or do you want a thermos to take with you?"

"We've already made our lunch, Maude," Ellie answered, wishing she could warn the old woman, wishing she could tell her not to look at Tanner with such sad, hungry eyes.

Maude cackled suddenly. "You two look like you've done a lot for only ten o'clock in the morning. Did you spend the night together?"

Ellie sighed. "Why does my private life have to be town business?"

"Because you decided to become the town pet," Tanner said in a cool undertone. "No, Maude," he pitched his voice louder. "She sent me home so she could play cards."

"I always said the girl had no sense," Maude said, nodding. "Jamie's already fed the horses, including that beast of Satan. Have a good time. I won't expect you till I see you."

They headed toward the horse barn, Maude still

watching them. Tanner was walking at a loose, easy pace, but Ellie still had to struggle to keep up with him. She had her cane with her, the gold-headed one that clearly grated on Tanner's nerves, and she did the best she could. She would have been boiled in oil before she asked him to slow down. He hadn't smoked a cigarette since they'd left, and if he could be forbearing so could she.

"What do you think of Maude?" She hoped she sounded as casual as she wanted to be.

If nothing else it made him slow his walk just a bit. "Maude?" he echoed, puzzled. "I like her. She's a character, for one thing, and for another, she's one of the few people who's welcomed me. Why?"

She hoped the heat in her cheekbones came from the blazing sun. "Just curious. Some people find her a bit overwhelming." She moved ahead of him, into the cool darkness of the barn. "You saddle and bridle Hoover while I take care of Shaitan. The tack's in the corner." And she walked away before he could ask any more uncomfortable questions.

By unspoken consent they headed up the path, back to the meadow where they'd first met. There were other trails, other meadows, other streams just as lovely, and for a moment Ellie had considered suggesting an alternative. Considered, then rejected the notion. The high meadow had always been her special place. Its sanctity had already been breached. If she didn't go back now with Tanner himself, she'd never feel comfortable there again.

Not that it was really an issue, she reminded herself as Shaitan picked his sure, delicate way up the narrow path. In less than two weeks she'd be gone, she'd never see that meadow again. There would be other mountains for her, other meadows.

The path widened, and Tanner brought Hoover up beside her. Shaitan sidled nervously, his eyes rolling in his head and his ears flattening as he hissed a warning. Hoover reacted with typical nerves, but Tanner had him firmly under control.

He did know his way around horses, there was no question of that. He'd saddled and bridled a strange horse in less time than it took her to ready Shaitan. To be sure, Hoover was relatively docile, and Shaitan was high-strung. But there was no gainsaying the fact that he had a way with him. Hoover was responding almost as well as his overbred stablemate, moving with the slightest pressure from Tanner's long legs, arching his head and almost prancing. Tanner looked as if he'd been born in the saddle.

But he wasn't. He had been born in that cabin, with no one but Charles Tanner and Maude to help Marbella that night so long ago. She wondered if he knew.

"So why don't you tell me," Tanner drawled softly, "why you spend your life doing nothing in a hick town like Morey's Falls?"

She looked over at him. He'd pitched his voice low, and Shaitan's ears had come up again, accepting the interloper. Which just went to prove that Shaitan had no taste in human beings. He'd tried to bite Poor Lonnie's hand off the last time she'd made the mistake of inviting anyone to go riding with her.

"Why do you think?" she countered.

"Well, if the judge didn't leave you money you'd

have to work, and I haven't seen any signs of that. Just your Lady Bountiful act for the peasants. But if he left you money I'd think you'd be long gone."

"I'm intending to be long gone," she said, stifling the irritation Tanner always managed to call forth. She was getting used to that annoyance, getting almost to like it. At least it proved that she was alive. "I don't work because this is a very poor town. Any job I took would be taking food away from some family who needs it."

"Did you go to college?"

"For a semester. The traveling got to be too much. I went to a branch of the University of Montana in Bozeman, and the drive was more than two hundred miles each way. My leg couldn't take it."

"You could have stayed there—come home during vacations."

"The judge didn't think it wise for me to be gone so long."

"You could have driven an automatic, like the monstrosity you own now."

"The judge preferred manual transmissions back then," she said calmly.

"Back when he still wanted to own you."

"He always wanted to own me," Ellie said, surprising herself. The words were out, it was too late to call them back, and she might as well continue. "He just grew surer of me as time went on. Sure enough to buy an automatic transmission, at least."

Tanner nodded. If he was startled by her sudden openness he didn't show it. There was a speculative look in the back of his eyes, a curiosity he hadn't yet put into words. Ellie could only hope he'd continue to be circumspect. She neither wanted to answer that question nor lie.

To her relief Tanner changed the subject. "It's hard to believe Morey's Falls is just a couple of miles away," he said, looking around him with dreamy approval. They'd reached the edge of the meadow, and the beauty of it drifted into their senses. "It sure would be nice to forget it existed."

Ellie made a noncommittal sound of agreement. It was even warmer than it had been two days earlier, and the wildflowers dotting the field were nodding in the soft breeze. The sky—the famed big sky of Montana—was cloudless, and the jagged peaks of the mountains surrounded them like a fairy ring. "We can stop and eat over by the waterfall," she said. "There's a pool of water there for the horses."

"All right." He was watching her, that mischievous, speculative expression on his face. "You mind if I take off my shirt? It's hot today."

She wanted to blush, to laugh, but managed to keep a calm, unruffled demeanor. "Go right ahead. Just don't expect me to do the same this time."

"Why not? There's no one around to look, and I've already seen it," he taunted lightly.

"Not up close, you haven't," she countered in a sober voice. "If you did, I'd never get rid of you."

He threw back his head and laughed out loud, and the sound was wonderful on the soft summer air. Shaitan whickered nervously, but Ellie had him in perfect control. She grinned back at Tanner, fighting the sudden knot of sorrow that had tightened in her throat. It was such a beautiful day, a beautiful place, a beautiful time. Tanner was beautiful, too, with amusement dancing in his blue eyes and his thin, sexy mouth lit with a grin. And Ellie would have loved for life to have stayed that way, just a little while.

He reached up and began to unbutton his shirt. "Maybe I'm running the same risk," he said.

"You strike me as a man who takes risks," she said.

"And you strike me as a woman who doesn't."

"I'm here, aren't I?"

He looked taken aback for a moment. He shrugged out of the shirt, tying it around his waist, and his dark skin glowed in the bright sunlight. It wasn't the tan of beaches or sunlamps; it was the color of a man who worked long hours outside in the sun. His rough, callused hands and the long, corded muscles in his arms and chest attested to that. "So you are," he said finally, and his tone was cool. "I'll race you to the pool." And before she had time to gather her bemused wits he'd taken off across the field.

Shaitan was the faster horse, but Tanner had the head start. He was already loosening Hoover's saddle when she reined in. She slid off the stallion's back and busied herself with the girth strap, all the time aware of him behind her. "Don't come any closer," she warned. "Shaitan won't like it."

Tanner stayed where he was. She didn't have to turn to know the expression on his face. It would be calm, patient and slightly predatory. He could afford to wait. For a moment Ellie rested her head against Shaitan's warm, black side, accepting his strength and comfort. And then she turned to face Tanner.

She didn't know what she'd expected, she thought

several hours later as they rode back down the narrow trail. Some sort of pass, perhaps. Maybe a full-fledged seduction attempt that would have been difficult, perhaps impossible to fight off. At least some sort of verbal come-on.

But once more Tanner had confounded her. He hadn't so much as touched her, when part of her was longing to be touched. He'd smiled sweetly enough, and occasionally his cold blue eyes would smile, too. He'd drawn her out, in subtle ways she'd recognized only afterward, so that he knew her far better than she knew him. She told him of herself, he told her of things.

One of those things was the horse ranch, high up in the Sangre de Cristo mountains, where the sky was almost as big and blue as it was in Montana, where the piñon pines grew scrubby and the land rolled in a warm red color. He told her about the horses, about Orfeo and Hammer and Magda and Gypsy, of the foals with their long, spindly legs and the yearlings with their incredible grace. He told her of the rambling adobe ranch house and the people who lived there, of Melora and Red and Jimmy and Rafael. And he'd told her of Alfred, and for the first time Ellie heard love in his voice.

She hadn't wanted to go back, so of course she'd been the one to suggest it. Tanner had agreed readily enough, so readily that paranoia began to mount in the back of her brain. It was a new and evil emotion, one she had no experience in fighting, and as they rode down the mountain she toyed with it, prodding herself with little jabs of self-inflicted torture.

He'd been turned off by the scars. Well, of course he had. She'd shown him on purpose, to try to force a little compassion from him. And he'd been horrified, for all he tried to hide it.

He'd kissed her the night before, kissed her as no one had ever kissed her in all her life. Given the perfect opportunity to follow up on that kiss, he'd made no move at all.

Maybe her obvious lack of experience had turned him off. Combine that with the scars and maybe he'd thought better of his pursuit. Maybe she'd misunderstood that pursuit; perhaps it had only been a reflex. The man was a tease, there was no question of that. Every woman who met him melted a little bit under those seductive eyes and that practiced smile. Because no one had ever dared flirt with her before, she'd probably just overreacted.

Ginger had left early the previous evening. Had she gone out to the cabin and assuaged Tanner's loneliness? It would be just the sort of thing Ginger would do, but if so, why would Tanner have showed up so early that morning? And wouldn't she have been able to tell?

She was getting neurotic in her old age. So Tanner had kissed her. Just because a man kissed her didn't mean he wanted her. If Ginger had told him about her abortive love life, then he was simply being kind....

"What are you torturing yourself about?" he drawled, coming up beside her as the path widened once more.

She blushed again. "Just thinking."

"Well, whatever it is you're thinking about, stop it. It's got to be something unpleasant."

She sighed. "It's not that easy."

"No, I suppose it isn't," Tanner said, looking straight ahead.

Maude's ranch was already in sight, their time together was ending, and frustration and despair raced around in Ellie's heart. She wanted to reach out and put her hand on Tanner's, wanted to pluck at the sleeve of his recently donned shirt. She wanted to turn in the saddle and ask him to ride away with her, back up to the meadow, across the mountains and never come back again.

"It's late," she said instead. "And we've wasted the day."

"Have we?"

"We didn't get any further on your quest. You don't know anything more about this town and who the people are," she pointed out.

"I know more about you. That's something."

She opened her mouth to refute his claim, then shut it again. She was being gloomy and emotional. She needed a good dose of sensible Maude to cheer her up.

Maude was waiting on the porch. "Doc's been trying to find you," she called out as soon as they were within hearing distance. "You'd best come in here and call him as soon as you can."

The knot in her chest tightened further. Without a word she dismounted, leading Shaitan into his stall in the cool, dark stable and loosening his girth. She shut the door behind him and raced across the yard, feeling that doom was lurking over her head like a thundercloud. Weren't things bad enough today, with the dead animals? What could Doc want?

TANNER WATCHED HER RUN. She managed pretty well without the cane. Before he left he was going to break the damned thing. All it did was remind her that she needed it. If she weren't reminded, she wouldn't need it—another simple equation.

He worked swiftly, efficiently, unsaddling Hoover, giving him a small drink of water and brushing the sweat from his coat. Shaitan was standing in his stall, deceptively docile, awaiting his beloved mistress. Tanner could see the sweat staining his beautiful black coat.

"Sorry, old boy," he said softly, and Shaitan's ears went back in alarm. "Your mistress would cut my heart out if I touched you."

Shaitan snorted, a derisive sort of sound, and Tanner gave Hoover one last affectionate pat on the rump before leaving the stall. He stood outside Shaitan's box, staring at the beautiful stallion, and a frown creased his face. "What would you do, boy?" he murmured in a low, beguiling voice that had magicked more than one restive stallion. "Would you take those nasty hooves of yours and try to trample me? I'm an old hand at dodging hooves. I bet you couldn't do it."

Shaitan's ears had lifted slightly, but his eyes were still threatening. "Of course," Tanner continued softly, "you've still got that nasty-tasting bridle in your mouth. And even if your mistress loosened your girth, that saddle must be hot and heavy. I could take that blanket off you and brush you down, and you'd feel wonderful. Besides, what have I got to lose? I think she's already cut my heart out." It was a low, seductive litany, and as always it was working. He opened the stall door and slipped in beside the stallion. Shaitan shied nervously for a moment, and his ears went back, but Tanner just continued his soft, soothing croon.

If they weren't exactly friends when he finished, they were at least tolerant of each other. He stepped out of the stall, carrying the leathers and saddle with him, and shut the door behind him. "We'll put you out to pasture later, old boy. In the meantime…"

"In the meantime," said Ellie, her voice as cold as ice, "you can tell me what the hell you were doing with my horse."

CHAPTER TWELVE

There was nothing he could say. He just stood there, watching her, his face blank, the saddle and bridle unnoticed burdens in his arms.

She was quivering with rage, a rage he couldn't begin to understand. Her face was pinched and white, her mouth a slash of pain, and he could tell that she was controlling herself with an effort.

"I told you not to touch Shaitan," she said, her voice low, hurried, furious. "I told you to keep your hands off him. He's had a hard time and he doesn't like strangers messing with him. He needs to be left alone…."

"Are you talking about your horse," he interrupted coolly, "or yourself?"

It was a good thing her hands were empty. If she'd been carrying her cane she would have gone for him, he knew it as surely as he knew his own name. But she wouldn't hit him with her hands; she didn't want to touch him. Instead she turned and ran, her limp barely noticeable, to her car. He stood in the doorway of the barn, watching as she wheeled out of the yard and tore off down the narrow driveway at top speed. She skidded as she pulled onto the main road, nearly losing control, but at the last minute the car responded, and he watched her race off down the highway.

Maude was waiting for him when he finished soaping the leathers and walked back out into the late-afternoon shadows. "You look like a man who could use a drink" was all she said.

He smiled at her. "You're an observant woman, Maude," he said. "Anything short of turpentine will do."

"Maybe a cup of hemlock?" She was mounting the shallow steps of her front porch.

"I don't feel that guilty. Ellie needs some shaking up every now and then," he said.

"I don't believe you." She headed straight for one of the cupboards and pulled out a bottle of Jack Daniel's. "Not about Ellie needing shaking up. Any fool would know that. But I think you're feeling guilty as hell." She poured a generous splash into two glasses and turned to face him, her beady little eyes knowing. "Water or ice?"

"I like my hemlock straight." He took the glass and perched on one of the stools. "Think she'll be back?"

"It depends on what you did. If you made a pass at her she'll forgive you. If you insulted her it'll be over in a few minutes and she'll be turning right around. If you were nasty she'll be back even sooner."

"I groomed Shaitan for her."

"She won't be back," Maude said flatly. "The girl's not exactly sensible when it comes to that animal. I don't know why, and I don't get anywhere when I ask. When she brought him here he was a real mess, scarred and bleeding. He'd savaged his owner and they were going to put him down when Ellie interfered. That's Ellie for you, always going for the underdog."

Underdogs like me, Tanner thought savagely, taking a deep, burning gulp of the whiskey. *Another of her charity cases.* "You'd think she'd be grateful I took care of him if she loves him so much."

"Nope," Maude said. "She's been convinced that no one could touch Shaitan, even be around him without being hurt. You just wrecked that belief."

Tanner shook his head. "Sometimes we have to learn things we'd rather not," he said woodenly.

"And Ellie has. She'll keep on, too. But it'll take her some time to get over this one." Maude drained her whiskey. "You want me to find you a ride back to your place? I don't drive, but I could give Jamie a call. Or you could take my old car. I'm sure it still runs."

"I can walk. I think I'd prefer to. I need some time to think. But I appreciate the offer and the hospitality, Maude." He smiled at his hostess, noticing with surprise the sudden dampness around her eyes. What the hell would Maude have to cry about?

"Tanner," she began, her voice low and hurried, "I need to tell you something."

He braced himself for something unpleasant, but the revelation never came. They both heard the sound of the car pull up in front of the house, and Maude's dark eyes widened with surprise.

Tanner kept the satisfaction from showing on his face as he waited for Ellie to walk in and apologize. He'd accept it graciously; he wouldn't even tease her. He leaned back, feeling expansive, and then sat back up. He smelled the scent of musk moments before the door opened, and his face was impassive, hiding the twist of something deeper than disappointment in his gut.

Ginger Barlow was the last person he wanted to see. Maude didn't look too welcoming, either. Ginger was as out of place in Maude's homey kitchen as a peacock at a barbecue. Her blond hair tumbled in heavy curls over her shoulder, she was wearing tight jeans and a hot-pink jersey that clung to her impressive breasts, and she wasn't wearing a bra. Her pink lips were wreathed in a smile of welcome, and her eyes were on the make.

More than one woman had told him he had bedroom eyes. He looked at Ginger Barlow sashaying up to him and knew for sure that she had the female equivalent.

"Hi, there," she said, her voice soft and breathy.

"What are you doing here?" Maude demanded, making no move to offer her a drink.

Ginger didn't look affronted, clearly used to Maude's rudeness. "I just passed Ellie a few miles back, driving hell-for-leather into town, and I thought I'd come out and see what had her in tears."

"Tears?" Tanner echoed, the twist of pain tightening.

"Yup," Ginger said cheerfully. "And Ellie doesn't cry much. What'd you do to her?"

"Does your daddy know you're parading around dressed like that?" Maude interrupted. "You ought to be ashamed of yourself."

"My daddy saw me walk out the door, Maude, and he didn't say a word. Why don't you call him up and commiserate with him on my shameless behavior while I give Tanner a ride home?"

"Tanner doesn't want a ride home," Maude said fiercely. "He wants to walk."

"In case you haven't noticed," Ginger said sweetly, "there's a storm coming, and the Tanner ranch is more than ten miles from here."

"He's walked in the rain before." Maude's voice was stubborn.

Tanner had had enough of this. Right now he wanted to be home, alone, and the fastest way to get there was to take a ride with Ginger. He had no doubts about his ability to get rid of her. He just had to make sure that that was what he wanted to do. He'd be a fool not to take what she was offering so blatantly, but then, sometimes that was exactly what he was.

"I'd appreciate a ride," he said, his voice lazy.

"But what if Ellie comes back?" Maude protested.

"Then you can tell her I found another ride," Tanner said. He looked over at Ginger, positively quivering with eagerness. "You ready?"

"Any time you are, Tanner," she purred.

ELLIE STOPPED CRYING when she reached the town limits. Too many people were curious already—she wanted her face to be calm and pale when she stalked into her back door and slammed it. She pulled into her driveway, shoved the car into park and reached for the key to turn it off.

She let her hand drop as calm finally began to return. What was she so mad about? He did a kindness for an animal, and she threw a temper tantrum. Had she gone completely crazy?

There were reasons, of course. She'd been frustrated

and on edge all day, waiting for the follow-up to the past night's kiss, ready to combat it, and she'd never had the chance to practice her carefully prepared and tactful rejection. Doc's phone call hadn't made her feel any better. More animals had been found on some of the outlying farms, and several people had reported a Peeping Tom lurking outside their windows.

It was Charles Tanner all over again. But it wasn't his son. If she was sure of anything in this life, she was sure of that. She'd been worried how she was going to tell him of the latest development, suffering from the accumulated stresses of the day, and seeing him able to win Shaitan over so easily had been the final straw. Of course he was absolutely right in doing it. But she couldn't ignore one inescapable conclusion. If Shaitan, who was so murderously distrustful of everyone but Ellie, fell under Tanner's spell, how could she resist the man herself?

There was a distant rumble of thunder, breaking through her abstraction, and she looked out the window into the darkening sky. They were in for a hell of a storm, and she'd left him out at Maude's with no choice but to walk home. There was no getting around it—she owed him an apology.

Maybe she could call Doc and send him out in her place. She had a wicked headache right now and her knee was aching. She would have loved to have crawled first into a hot shower, then a warm bed, with a cold glass of wine.

But she'd always prided herself on being fair. It had been her fault that afternoon, not Tanner's, and it was up to her to make amends.

Her pace back to Maude's place was more decorous, now that her rage had vanished, leaving only guilt and embarrassment in its place. The sky was almost black, wind was whipping through the thick grasses, and in the distance she could see the forked lightning snake to the ground.

She recognized Ginger's Camaro from a long ways off, and she felt a sudden tightening in her chest as she drew closer. They didn't even see her. Ginger was laughing, her heavily made-up eyes flashing, and Tanner was Tanner, smoking, lids half-closed over his sleepy, sexy eyes. Ginger probably wouldn't notice that those eyes were as cold as the north wind.

She stomped down on the accelerator, speeding past them in an immediate return of emotions too tangled to sort out. It was for the best, she told herself self-righteously, grinding her teeth and speeding. Ginger and Tanner were made for each other. Not that Ginger would like that narrow, lumpy little cot or a cabin with no doors and windows. Still, they'd probably manage just fine. Damn them, damn them, damn them.

THE SCENT of Ginger's perfume was overpowering in the closed car. Tanner lit a cigarette in self-defense and opened the window a crack, trying to keep the bored expression from his face as Ginger flirted archly. He saw the big black car coming, and he knew who it was. So much for Maude's supposition.

Ellie had recognized the car, and she didn't like what she saw. It didn't take a genius to figure that out. She drove by so fast, her face averted, that it would have been hard to recognize her if some instinctive part of him hadn't known. She'd forgiven him his transgression with Shaitan. He wondered how she'd feel about Ginger.

"That was Ellie," he said, stubbing out the cigarette, interrupting Ginger in midspate.

"Where?"

"The car that just drove past."

"Did she see us?"

Was that guilt in her voice? Or vicarious excitement? "I expect so," he said, controlling his need for another cigarette, controlling his need to tell her to hurry.

A small, satisfied smile lit Ginger's face so swiftly that he might almost have imagined it. So it wasn't guilt. "That's too bad," she lied. "Ellie won't like it that I drove you home."

"Why not?"

Ginger laughed, a throaty chuckle that was meant to be enticing. "Oh, I know Ellie very well. We've been best friends since childhood, and I know when she has her eye on someone. She finds you very attractive, Tanner. As do I."

He swallowed his sigh of irritation. He knew he should express some sort of gratification, but right then all he wanted to do was get out of the car and wait for Ellie to come back down that road that led to nowhere. He didn't even mind standing out in the middle of a thunderstorm. Anything was preferable to Ginger's arch desperation. He'd had too many women like Ginger, too many empty nights filled with more emptiness, and he didn't want the same hollow feeling. The town of Morey's Falls already made him feel rotten enough.

Ginger Barlow's tender ministrations wouldn't provide any sort of comfort, no matter how tempted he might be to believe so.

"You don't need to drive me all the way home," he said. "You can drop me off in town…."

"Heavens, I wouldn't dream of it!" Ginger protested. "As a matter of fact, I wondered whether you were all that eager to get back to that depressing little shack. I know a place that has decent food and lots of privacy, out on Route 43."

He'd seen the place. A motel and a diner—not his idea of romance. "Some other time," he said. "I've got things to do."

"Can't they wait?"

"No."

"Wouldn't you like some company?" she asked, still trying to entice him, her artificially sexy voice like fingernails on a blackboard.

"No."

She pouted the rest of the way home. Someone must have told her it was attractive, long ago. Maybe then it was. Right now it gave her a double chin, and her china-blue eyes were flat and opaque. He could see the little wheels turning behind them as she pulled up in front of the cabin, wondering how she was going to get what she wanted. The rain had started, fat, angry drops splattering the windshield of the Camaro.

"Aren't you going to ask me in for a drink?" she said. "After all, I did drive you all the way out here. Come on, Tanner, you owe me something. And I'm lonely and bored and sick of everyone around."

"Sorry," he said, his voice cool. "I don't have anything

to drink." It was a lie—he'd bought another bottle of whiskey that he'd barely touched the night before.

Ginger's determined smile wavered somewhat. "Well, what about a cup of coffee?"

"Ginger," he said, tempering the cruelty of his words, "I don't have anything to offer you."

"I wouldn't say that."

"I would. Thanks for the ride." He opened the door and slid out into the rainy evening.

Ginger jumped out of the car after him, and his sigh of irritation was swallowed by the sound of the rain. "Wait just a minute," she said, striding after him. "I'm not used to being turned down."

"Well, life is full of new experiences." He stood there in the rain, feeling it soak into his cotton shirt and run down his face. It had soaked Ginger's pink T-shirt, clinging to her erect nipples, and he stared at her, feeling like a eunuch.

"Is it Ellie?" Her voice was raw, jealous, not the voice of a best friend at all. "You're a fool, Tanner. You won't get to first base with her. No one does, and certainly not the son of the murderer who crippled her for life. You're wasting your time. Saint Ellie is going to die the way she was born, untouched, inviolate, and you…"

He didn't want to hear any more. He crossed the small patch of ground that was rapidly turning into mud, caught Ginger's wrist in a painful grip and dragged her back to her car. Opening the door, he stuffed her in, slamming it behind her, just barely missing her leg.

"Get the hell out of here, Ginger," he said. "Or I'll

see if I can find one of my father's guns." His voice was low, deadly, and he managed to convince her. The tires spun in the mud for a moment, and then she was gone, tearing off into the darkening evening.

Two women storming away from him in one day, he thought, staring after her. What had happened to his usual expertise? He ran a hand through his wet hair and sighed. He was soaked to the skin, but at least it was a warm summer rain. Maybe he'd take advantage of nature's shower and go find some soap. No one else was going to come after him—he'd alienated Ellie for good. He could only hope he'd done the same with the too-eager Ginger.

And what had she meant by those cracks about Ellie? Untouched, inviolate? Just how untouched was she? Hell, the woman was in her early thirties, she'd been married. She wasn't wildly experienced, but she couldn't be…

"No," he said out loud, dismissing the notion as completely absurd. He was willing to believe a lot of strange things, but the notion of Ellie Lundquist as a thirty-year-old virgin was too much to contemplate. Instead he headed for clean clothes, resigning himself to a quiet night with too much to think about.

ELLIE COULDN'T EAT anything that night. She could barely bring herself to turn on the lights. Instead she curled up in bed, willing the night to close down over her and shut out the pain and anger and confusion that were tearing her apart.

It worked for a few hours. When she woke it was past eleven. She felt hot, sticky and unutterably depressed.

The rain was still falling outside, a steady, relentless downpour that should have been soothing, and the house felt cold and damp.

The shower she took did little to warm her. She picked at her food, took a desultory sip of white wine before pushing it away, then she sat in the kitchen and tried to think of excuses to call Doc.

She'd be a fool to do so. Ginger wouldn't be there. Ginger didn't take no for an answer, even if Tanner was the sort of man to give that answer. They'd be together, while Ellie sat alone and miserable in her mausoleum of a house.

Why did she stay? She didn't really have to wait until the Fourth of July. She could pack her bags and go now, right now. She didn't have cash, but she had credit cards, and the tiny bank in Morey's Falls had a bigger branch in Bozeman where she could draw enough money for her needs. Then she'd never have to see Tanner again, never have to deal with Ginger's gloating.

She was being stupid and childish. She'd promised herself she'd stay till the dedication, and stay she would. She wasn't going to let Ginger's sexual desperation or Tanner's disturbing presence stop her from doing exactly what she'd planned to do.

She took another sip of her wine, but it tasted vinegary. Maybe she wouldn't feel so bad if she knew what she was missing. The books she'd read made love-making seem miraculous, splendid, the center of the universe. The attempted reality had been hideously uncomfortable and embarrassing. It was probably somewhere in between. One probably just ignored the less pleasant aspects and enjoyed the snuggling part of it.

But damn, it had been so long since someone had held her. Longer than she could remember.

Well, let Tanner and Ginger enjoy each other. If the only men Ellie had ever tried to make love with had failed to perform, it had to be a lack in her, not them. And she absolutely couldn't bear to see the look in Tanner's blue eyes when he discovered it.

She watched the hands move slowly, inexorably around the electric clock in the kitchen. She listened to the somber, depressing tones of the grandfather clock in the hall chime each quarter hour. She didn't realize till half past twelve that she wasn't going to sleep until she found out for certain.

All the houses around her were dark when she climbed into the Buick. She crept along the empty streets, heading out toward Doc's house, feeling like an immature teenager. She was halfway there when she changed her mind. The Barlow house was one of the few in town that boasted a two-car garage. She'd have to get out of the car, creep over and peer in the window, and that was sinking too low, even for her.

She was halfway out Route 5 before she realized what she was doing. She told herself she should turn back, but kept on driving. Route 5 went nowhere— there was no way she could pretend she just happened to be driving out that way. It didn't go much past Tanner's place—she'd have to turn around within hearing distance of the cabin. If he left the bed and Ginger and looked out the hole where the front door had been he'd see her driving by like the neurotic female she was.

But she no longer cared. She was chilly, even in her

thick cotton sweater and baggy jeans. She was exhausted, and her head still ached. But whether it was a rational, mature act or not, she had to find out if Ginger was spending the night with Tanner.

At first the cabin seemed dark as she slowly approached it. She was about to drive past when she saw the pale glow of lantern light through the windowless opening. There was no Camaro parked outside.

Ginger could have already left, she warned herself, pulling in and turning off the motor. Tanner had every right to be furious with her—he'd probably order her off his land. He might very well be relaxing after his exertions with Ginger, and her presence would be at best embarrassing, at worst, an unforgivable intrusion. She didn't care.

The ground was muddy beneath her feet, and the rain was a steady, warm drizzle. She barely noticed it—her hair was still half-damp from her shower and hanging around her shoulders. She ignored the pounding of her heart, the twisting of her insides, the nervous dampness of her palms. Holding her breath, she walked slowly toward the warm glow of what had once been the front door of Charles Tanner's cabin.

CHAPTER THIRTEEN

He was lying on the narrow cot, wearing faded jeans and a blue flannel shirt unbuttoned around his tanned chest. His feet were bare, his hair damp, and there was a glass of whiskey on the floor beside him. She couldn't see his eyes in the shadows, but she could recognize the tension in his body as he watched her step inside the meager shelter of the cabin.

And then the tension in him vanished, leaving only a slight wariness. "Thank God," he said. "I was afraid you were Ginger."

If she hadn't still been feeling guilty she would have turned and left at that remark. "Why were you afraid?"

"Because she's damned hard to get rid of," he said frankly. "I underestimated my powers of attraction."

If she hadn't hurt so much she would have smiled. "When did you get rid of her?" she asked, not caring if she was giving away too much of what she'd rather keep hidden.

Thank heaven, he didn't smirk. He didn't even smile. "I didn't let her in the cabin."

"That doesn't mean anything. You could have done it in the car." Now she was shocking herself by her outspoken misery.

"Ellie," he said, "she drove me home and I sent her away. Immediately."

"Did she want to go?"

"Not particularly." He pulled himself into a sitting position, leaning against the rough wall. "But she went. Does it matter?"

She didn't move. Her heart was pounding, a heavy slamming against her ribs, and she felt cold and hot at the same time. She was on the precipice, at the edge of a momentous decision, and if she had any sense at all she'd turn around and run, rather than take that final step.

She'd been sensible all her life. "Yes," she said. "It matters."

His sigh was a quiet sound in the cabin, a strange, whispery counterpoint to the steady beat of the rain on the tin roof. It was a sound of sorrow and resignation, of acceptance and delight.

"You're complicating things," he said.

"I know."

"Things are already complicated enough."

"I know," she said. "Should I leave?"

He considered it for a moment. "It would be better for you if you did."

It wasn't what she wanted, but she no longer knew how to tell him that. Without a word she turned to go, when his voice stopped her.

"Come here, Ellie," he said, his voice a sinuous thread of sound on the night air. She turned back, and saw that he was holding out his hand to her.

She put her doubts, her fears, her reservations in a box and shut the lid. Moving across the room, she took his hand in hers and sank to her knees beside the narrow cot.

"I'm sorry about this afternoon," she said, her voice low and hurried. "You were right and I was wrong. I'm neurotic and possessive about Shaitan, and I don't know if I can explain this properly. It's just that…" She took a deep, steadying breath. "I've always felt that I don't belong to myself, that I belong to this town, that everyone has a piece of me. The one part of my life that belonged wholly to me was Shaitan. As long as no one could touch him, no one could go near him, he was mine, a part of me no one else could have. When you were able to touch him I knew he wasn't mine anymore."

She was close enough to see his eyes in the deep shadows, but she didn't look. She was feeling too miserable and guilty to raise her gaze from the faded quilt that lay beneath him on the cot.

His hand was warm and dry and strong in hers. "He's still yours," Tanner said. "You just have to make room for me."

She smiled ruefully. "With Shaitan."

"Shaitan's already accepted me. I'm talking about you."

She looked up then, directly into his eyes. Why had she ever thought they were cold? They were the blue of the big sky of Montana, clear and bright and glorious. She didn't say a word; she didn't know what to say. She just looked at him, and after a long, silent moment he tugged at her hand, and she went willingly, into the narrow cot beside him.

His skin was warm, almost hot to her cool, damp hands. She lay there passively, letting him arrange her against his body, the two of them pressed against each other, his arms wrapped around her, her face pressed against the smooth flesh of his shoulder. The flannel shirt was soft beneath her ear, and she could feel the whisper of his breath on her damp hair, the steady beat of his heart next to hers, the subtle throb of pulses that were either his or hers.

His hands were gentle on her, pushing the thick hair out of her face, easing her against him. "Relax," he whispered. "I'm not going to do anything you don't want me to do."

She let out her pent-up breath, not even realizing she'd been holding it, and softened her body against his. "I've never done this before," she confessed, her husky voice as quiet as his. The flickering light from the kerosene lamp was fading as the wick soaked up the last traces of fuel, and the shadows that closed around them were friendly ones. For the moment the memory of Charles Tanner was gone.

He was stroking her hair, and at her shy words his hand stopped for a moment, then continued the steady caress. "You're not in the habit of climbing into bed with strange men in the middle of the night?"

She'd come to the inescapable conclusion that he was going to find out sooner or later. "I'm not in the habit of climbing into bed with anyone."

"Dear God," he said, and she didn't know whether it was a prayer or a curse. "Not even the judge?"

"Not even the judge." It was easier to talk in the semidarkness, her face hidden against his skin, his arms warm and hard and safe around her. "That wasn't supposed to be part of our marriage agreement."

He seemed to know intuitively what she was leaving out. "But he changed his mind?" he asked.

He might as well know the whole sordid truth. "Yes," she said. "But it didn't do any good. He couldn't—I mean, he didn't—" She was getting agitated, and his hands kept up their hypnotic, soothing caresses.

"I get the idea," he said wryly. "And there hasn't been anyone else?"

She never considered lies or evasions. "There was Lonnie," she confessed in a low, miserable voice.

"Well, then," he said, and then stopped. He must have felt the tension in her body. "What happened with Lonnie?"

"The same thing."

Tanner let out a sigh, and Ellie unconsciously did the same. There was nothing worse for him to know, it was all out in the open. "Poor Lonnie," he said absently, his lips brushing her forehead. "He really can't do anything right."

He smelled like the rain. Like warm male flesh, and whiskey and the faintest tang of kerosene. She closed her eyes, pressing her face against him, drinking in the scents and textures of the night. "Tanner," she whispered, "would you hold me? Just hold me tonight, and nothing more?"

His hand didn't stop its rhythmic stroking of her hair. "I'll do anything you want me to," he replied, his voice low and rumbling beneath her ear.

She believed him. She trusted him, more than she had ever trusted anyone in her life. It didn't matter that they were wedged together in a narrow cot in the deserted cabin that had seen one man's descent into madness. It didn't matter that he clearly had been through half the women west of the Rockies, and that there was no foreseeable future for them. Nothing mattered but the surprising comfort of his arms around her, the feel of his long legs entwined with hers, the heat of his body warming the chill that seemed to emanate from the very marrow of her bones. Nothing mattered but Tanner.

HE WAS AMAZED how little time it took her to fall asleep. He was amazed at how comfortable he was, how relaxed with her surprisingly delicate body in his arms, despite the narrowness of the cot, despite the very normal pulse of desire vibrating through him. He lay there, at ease, watching the light burn lower and lower in the kerosene lamp he'd unearthed from behind the cabin.

He didn't want the light to go out. He liked watching her shadowed profile resting so trustingly against his chest, he liked looking at her legs stretched out with his, he liked the sight of her hand curled up in his shirt.

The rain was slowing its relentless downpour. The lamp flickered and went out, the cabin was swathed in darkness, and instead of seeing her he could feel her, the softness of her skin and the seeming weightlessness of her body. He could smell her, the faint scent of flowers that clung to her, and he could hear her, the quiet, steady breathing of someone deeply asleep.

He waited for the familiar restlessness to wash over him. He'd long ago lost count of the number of women he'd bedded. It wasn't a fact he was proud of. And of all those countless, some of them faceless, women, he had never slept with one of them. Once the act was completed, whether it was adequate, boring or sublime, and his partner had drifted into sleep, he'd taken his leave.

He'd figured it out once, when the lady of the moment, one who'd stayed around longer than usual, had pointed out his dereliction. He knew it was like his reluctance to shake hands. Making love was something natural, mutually pleasurable and temporary. Falling asleep with someone, sleeping through the night next to her, was an act of trust and faith, one he wasn't going to make.

Ellie sighed, dropping her head lower on his chest, and her hair tickled his chin. He could get out of the bed easily, he knew it. She was deeply asleep, and it wouldn't take much of an effort to untangle himself. He had a sleeping bag he could spread out on the floor, or he could even head outside. The rain had almost stopped by now, and he wasn't unused to sleeping on the wet ground.

But the odd thing was, he didn't want to move. He didn't want to escape from Ellie Johnson Lundquist. In this narrow bed there was still room behind him, if he wanted to back away. Instead he slid his hand up inside her cotton sweater, gently cupping the soft round swell of her breast. She sighed again, pushing against him in unconscious longing, her nipple hardening instinctively against his fingers. And with that small victory he fell asleep.

Somewhere in the night the rain had stopped. Somewhere in the night the moon had risen, sending faint tendrils of light through the open doorway of the cabin. Tanner awoke, slightly disoriented, his body very still.

Ellie slept on, wrapped around him. He didn't move, he scarcely breathed as his body resettled itself against hers. He didn't wear a watch, and tonight neither had Ellie, so he had no idea what time it was. It didn't matter. There was nowhere else on earth he would rather be, day or night, dawn or dusk.

And then he heard it again. The unmistakable rustling of the bushes out back behind the cabin. The stream had swollen in the downpour, and the rushing water almost masked the sound of careful footsteps. Almost.

Tension raced through his veins like fire. Someone was outside, watching. Someone with a gun?

There were no animals here, but maybe whoever it was had already graduated to humans. There were more than enough people around who owed Charles Tanner revenge. People whose loved ones had been killed. Would it make some twisted kind of sense to kill Charles Tanner's own son, fifteen years later, a posthumous evening up of the score?

He could smell the whiff of tobacco. Tomorrow when he went out he'd find a crumpled butt outside his window. If he waited that long. If he got up right now he wouldn't have to wait to find out who was behind this macabre game of repeating history. He was used to being silent in the wilderness—he had no doubt at all that he could sneak up on his watcher before he was even aware he was being stalked in return.

But he wasn't going to do that. For one thing, he didn't know what he'd find lurking behind his cabin. Forcing a confrontation would mean involving Ellie, and he wasn't convinced of his ability to keep her safe.

For another, a tiny, twisted part of him was afraid of what he might find. Maybe his father was out there, maybe he'd never died. Or maybe no one was out there at all; maybe Tanner had gone crazy just like his father and was imagining things. Or perhaps half the town of Morey's Falls was there as a lynch mob.

But most of all, he didn't want to leave Ellie. He didn't want to risk waking her, risk having her panic and leave him. Right now he was willing to shut his eyes to the watcher in the trees, to the evil that lingered outside the cabin, and hold on to the goodness within his arms. Whether he'd regret that choice sooner or later didn't matter. The choice was made.

When he awoke again it was bright daylight, and he was alone. He sat bolt upright, instantly awake, dimly aware of a sweeping sense of desolation, of a sharp aloneness such as he'd never felt before.

"Thank heavens you're awake," Ellie said from the open doorway. "I would kill for a cup of coffee, and there was no way I could start a fire, much less figure out how you could work that contraption of yours." She gestured toward the dismantled coffee maker.

He couldn't read her mood. Or maybe he was afraid to. She was looking across at him, smiling, her hair a tangled cloud around her face—and he could see no regrets, no hesitation in her eyes.

"You could have left."

"You know, I considered that." She advanced into the room, brushing her hands against her jeans. "I thought I could drive over to Addie's and beg a thermos of coffee from her, bring it back and... Oh," she said suddenly, her eyes going blank. "You didn't mean come back."

"I don't know what I meant." This was coming out wrong, but he was wary, too wary. He swung his legs out of bed, watching her.

Color had stained her face, a soft blush spreading across her cheekbones. "I'm sorry. I suppose you want me to leave. I don't really understand the etiquette in these situations, and I mishandled…"

He'd reached her by this time, and it was the easiest, most natural thing in the world to pull her into his arms and kiss her as he'd wanted to the night before. If he'd expected opposition he found none. She slid her arms around his waist, pulling him closer, and tilted her head back, her mane of hair hanging down over his arm as he tasted the sweetness she offered so willingly.

It was beguiling, the innocence and enthusiasm in her untutored mouth. He kissed her slowly, lingeringly, giving her time to get used to the contours of his mouth, the dampness and texture, before using his tongue. He loved her little start of surprise at his intrusion, the acquiescence, the growing boldness as her tongue touched his.

Her hands tightened on his waist, digging in slightly, and if his mouth hadn't been busy he would have smiled. Instead he encouraged her, teasing her, his mouth sliding wetly over hers, lips nibbling, touching, biting, tongues dancing against each other.

A distant part of his brain wondered if she could feel how he wanted her. If, with her limited experience, she could sense his desire. She was pressed up against him, her hips rocking gently against his, and if her mind didn't know, her instincts certainly did. He groaned, deep in the back of his throat, and broke off the kiss.

"No, I didn't want you to leave," he said, his voice a ragged growl of frustrated desire. He kept his arms around her, kept her held against his fully aroused body. Her eyes were smoky and slightly dazed as they looked into his, and her mouth was damp and swollen from his kisses.

"I don't want to go." She stood then on tiptoe, her body rubbing against his, and the gentle friction was agonizingly erotic. She pressed her mouth against his, seeking him, and he was lost. Without even realizing what he was doing he scooped her up in his arms, never breaking the kiss, and started back across the cabin to the narrow bed.

Reality intruded seconds before he would have dropped her onto the cot and covered her body with his. Slowly, reluctantly his mouth left hers, slowly, reluctantly he set her down, every nerve in his body screaming with frustration. "No," he said, taking a step back from her, knowing if he kept touching her he wouldn't be able to stop.

"No?" she echoed, uncertainty clouding her eyes.

"Not here," he said gently. "Not now. I don't want to make love to you in Charles Tanner's bed, worrying whether your friends or townspeople are going to walk in on us at any moment."

It was her turn to be frustrated, and if his body hadn't been crying out in need he would have laughed at her expression. "I don't mind…."

"I do."

"But when?"

He wanted to kiss her again, but he didn't dare. He wanted to soothe the taut lines of her shoulders, but he didn't dare. "When it's right," he said, his tight voice belying his certainty.

She looked around her, at the weather-stained walls and shabby, broken furniture and sighed in reluctant acceptance. "Soon?" she inquired, like a child asking for an ice-cream cone.

This time he did laugh, breaking some of the tension that held him in thrall. "Damned soon," he said fervently, still not daring to touch her. "Come on, Ellie. We'll go out for coffee."

CHAPTER FOURTEEN

This town was having a dangerous effect on him, Tanner thought several hours later. Never in his life had he turned down what was so freely offered. There had been Ginger, warm and lush and willing, with no strings, no commitments, and he hadn't even been interested.

And that morning there had been Ellie, sweet and eager in his arms, and he'd wanted her so much that the pain of it was a raw ache in his gut. For some reason he'd decided to be noble. Normally he wouldn't have cared whether anyone had walked in the door. Normally he wouldn't have cared where or when.

But he cared with Ellie. He wanted to make it right; he wanted to make it perfect. And tumbling her on Charles Tanner's bed wasn't the way to do it, even if right then he was regretting his decision.

He slid down a bit on the wide leather seat of Ellie's Buick, squinting into the sunlight. She was taking a long time in the grocery store, but at least the good citizens of Morey's Falls hadn't noticed him lounging there. She'd parked on a side street, he didn't know whether by accident or design, and not a single pedestrian had walked by.

He looked over at the window of the *Morey's Falls Gazette*. Sunlight was reflecting off the streaked glass, but he thought he could see the figure of a man inside. Poor Lonnie, indeed. He could almost be grateful to the guy. Not that he usually cared one way or the other about virginity, but some small, irrational part of him liked the fact that he would be Ellie's first. He had every intention of being her best.

That same small, irrational part of him wanted to carry the notion one step further. To be Ellie's one and only. He knew that was a stupid fantasy. Ellie belonged to Morey's Falls; he belonged to a horse ranch in New Mexico. He could just imagine her reaction to the idea of bearing Charles Tanner's grandchildren.

What in the world was he thinking of? Never in his life had he seriously considered having children. Never in his life had he even thought about one woman and marriage and happy ever after. He sure picked the strangest times to get conventional. And with the least likely of women.

He reached in his pocket for his cigarettes. The pack was crushed—it had taken him longer than usual to smoke them, which was another strange sign. He lit one, thinking back to the night before.

He should have gotten up, risked waking her, risked everything. Outside the cabin, by the windowless hole in the rear wall, were clear, recognizable footprints. The rain had left the ground soggy enough to hold the general shape of a print. He could tell it was an average size man or a big woman, and the tread wasn't deep, probably made by some sort of running shoe. The crumpled cigarette butts lay scattered in a pile, shredded almost past recognition. There were at least three there—the watcher had stayed a long time, staring into the moonlit cabin, staring at the people in bed.

His own cigarette tasted lousy. Tanner rolled down the window and tossed it into the gutter. And then he looked up into Lonnie Olafson's pale, bespectacled gaze.

He was definitely Ellie's type, all right, Tanner thought for a fleeting moment. Those bland, yuppie good looks, the creased pants and striped oxford shirts were more her style than his own faded flannels and denims and too-long hair, and those pale-rimmed glasses made the editor look downright studious. Poor Lonnie.

"Howdy," he said, leaving the window down. Lonnie was wearing running shoes, but they were spotless, no sign of mud on them. Anyway, half the town probably wore running shoes, particularly if they were out for a night of voyeurism.

"This is Ellie's car," Lonnie said.

"Yes," said Tanner, waiting.

"Where is she?"

"In the store. Why?"

Lonnie squirmed a bit. There was no noticeable hostility in him, despite the fact that he must know Tanner was well on his way to succeeding where he had failed. "I guess you haven't heard about last night," he said.

Tanner felt his nerves tighten. "What happened last night? More animals killed?"

"No," said Lonnie. "Someone desecrated the graveyard."

Tanner's response was a short, heartfelt obscenity. "Do they have any idea who?"

"Same person who killed the animals, I expect," Lonnie said. "Dave Martin is running around like a three-legged dog with fleas, and the townspeople are pretty upset." He shrugged his shoulders. "Well, you can't blame them. It was bad enough, losing kin like that, but then to find their graves messed up is more than a lot of people are willing to accept."

"You mean only the graves of the massacre victims were touched?" Tanner asked, already knowing the answer.

"You got it. Red paint spilled over each tombstone and cross, all in the town graveyard. And none of the other graves were touched." Lonnie brushed a careless hand through his boyish mane of hair. "Except, of course, your father's grave."

Tanner stared at him in amazement. "My father's buried here?"

"Where else would he be buried? He has a corner all to himself in the town cemetery. People usually ignore it, but whoever it was didn't last night."

Tanner was getting the oddest feeling that Lonnie was enjoying all this, enjoying making Tanner squirm. Maybe it was his only form of revenge for Ellie. "What did they do to his grave?"

Lonnie smiled sweetly. "You know those plastic flowers and wreaths people use to decorate cemeteries? Davidson's Market does a big business in them right before Memorial Day. Well, every single bit of fake flowers was taken from the graves and piled on your daddy's corner. It looks like the gaudiest funeral this side of Salt Lake City. I imagine it's the first time anyone's ever put anything on your father's grave. Apart from spit."

He could see the hostility now, just dancing in the back of Lonnie's pale eyes. "Well, then," Tanner drawled with just the right note of insolence, "I guess I owe someone a debt of gratitude now, don't I?"

Lonnie nodded, accepting the open warfare. "I wouldn't be in any hurry to repay that debt if I were you," he said. "People are a mite upset right now. They're doing a good business in rope down at the hardware store. Heaven knows, there's more than enough plastic flowers to go around."

Tanner looked down at Lonnie's feet again. The running shoes were so clean they might have been freshly washed. They looked damp, but the streets of Morey's Falls were still wet from last night's downpour. While Tanner would have liked nothing more than to have pinned the latest occurrence on the man in front of him, he had no reason to. And Lonnie's history of cowardice and ineptitude didn't make him a likely possibility.

He smiled then, and Lonnie took a nervous step backward. "I think the flowers will keep," Tanner said softly. "Nice seeing you, Lonnie."

Ellie's hands were empty when she finally reappeared from the grocery store. Her limp was more pronounced, and the sunlight had gone from her eyes. She slid into the driver's seat without a word and started the engine, backing into the empty street with far more concentration than the simple act required.

"I gather we've got more trouble," he said, watching as she drove blindly out of town.

She glanced at him, startled. "How'd you know?"

"For one thing, you're acting like you've seen a

ghost. You went in to get some groceries, you came out a long time later without your purse."

"Damn."

"Apart from that," Tanner continued, reaching for his cigarettes, "I had a little visit from Lonnie Olafson while I was waiting for you."

"Double damn."

"Indeed. He says the townspeople are buying rope."

She cast him a quick, worried glance. "He's probably lying. The only one who's a little...irrational on occasion is Pete Forrester."

"Pete's Fireside Café," Tanner supplied.

"Exactly. But while people like him and feel sorry for him, they're not about to go out and form a lynch mob on his say-so."

"I hope you're right," he said. "You want to tell me where we're going at sixty-seven miles an hour?"

She looked startled, immediately slowing her pace. "I don't know. I just wanted to get away."

So did he, damn it. But he couldn't. Not yet. "I think the best place for you is your house," he said after a moment. "You haven't had anything to eat yet, you're still looking tired, and driving around with me is asking for trouble. We'll drive back to your house, I'll check the place out and make sure it's safe, and then I'll leave you to have a nap."

"Where will you go?" she asked in a forlorn little voice, already slowing to turn the car around.

"I want to go talk to Doc."

"You think he'll have some idea who might be doing this?" Ellie questioned, and for a moment he wanted to kiss her. Not for an instant had she suspected that he might be the one who was doing these things. Or if she had, she'd clearly dismissed that suspicion the moment she'd had it.

"He'll probably have as good an idea as anyone. He's just about everyone's doctor around here, isn't he? He should know who's depressed, who's been acting weird, who'd be capable of going off the deep end."

"Maybe," she said, but the doubt was clear in her voice.

"You don't think he'd know?"

"Well, people don't, do they?" she countered. "Everyone thought Charles Tanner was just a little bit eccentric. When you read about other mass murderers you hear that they appeared perfectly normal. There just doesn't seem to be a way to tell."

"There will be this time," he said grimly.

"You think there'll be a 'this time'?" she asked, her voice raw. "You think someone's going to get a gun and do what Charles Tanner did?"

He could hear the faint trace of panic in her voice. "I don't know." He wished he could comfort her, soothe her, but he didn't want to lie. "All I know is the only way to be safe is to be careful."

She shivered in the hot June sunshine. "It can't happen twice," she said. "It just can't."

He only wished he could be as certain.

THE HOUSE FELT COLD and dark and empty without him but Ellie knew that it only seemed that way to her. It was unseasonably warm outside, in the eighties, and that heat penetrated even the sullen reaches of the judge's house. Bright sunlight poured in every available window, flooding the usually dark rooms, and the house wasn't empty. There were ghosts all around her.

He'd bullied her into eating some soup. She hadn't wanted to, but he'd ignored her, heating the Campbell's Turkey Noodle on the old gas range and standing over her until she finished it. She found herself enjoying the soup, enjoying him. No one had ever looked after her, harangued her into doing something that was good for her, prodded and pushed and browbeaten her into taking care of herself.

She'd finally relaxed when he'd disappeared outside, only to come back a few minutes later with his handful of shredded cigarette butts and his eyes opaque.

"These were outside your bathroom window," he announced, dropping them on the scrubbed wood table in front of her. "Do you have any idea whose they are?"

She had stared at them as if they were dehydrated cobras, waiting to come to life and strike. "Outside my bathroom?" she echoed, aghast.

"I'm sure he would have preferred your bedroom," Tanner said, offering cold comfort. "But you sleep on the second floor, don't you?"

She'd been hoping to show him her second-floor bedroom. Looking at the shredded paper in front of her, she suddenly lost her appetite for a romantic interlude. "Yes," she said dully. She poked at the stuff. It was in varying degrees of decomposition. Clearly her watcher had spent more than one night peering in her bathroom window. She looked up into Tanner's expressionless face. "Didn't you find one of these at the base of the memorial?"

"And outside my cabin. Whoever it was was there last night, while you slept."

"Weren't you sleeping?"

"Not all the time." He seemed to hesitate. "Those cigarette butts are crumpled just the way my father used to crumple them."

She fought back the frisson of horror that swept down her backbone. "How do you know that?"

"Doc mentioned it when he saw me do the same thing. It's not uncommon. People are taught it in the army. People do it in the wilderness. It's so they don't leave a trace. I wouldn't have noticed if I hadn't been looking for it."

"You're sure it wasn't you? No, of course it wasn't." She answered the question the moment she asked it. She answered it too late.

Tanner was looking at her strangely, the warmth gone from his eyes. "I'm not sure of anything," he said. "Or anyone." He turned and headed for the back door.

"Take the car," she offered, knowing right then he wasn't going to take anything from her.

"Lock your doors," he said in response, and closed the kitchen door quietly behind him.

She got up and watched him leave. He skirted the Buick parked in her driveway, heading north toward Doc's end of town. The Barlow house was only a mile away; it wouldn't take Tanner more than twenty minutes to walk there, if that. As long as no one pulled up beside him, as long as Pete Forrester kept his distance.

She reached out to open the door, to follow him, then stopped. He wouldn't thank her. She'd already been less than tactful, and right now he needed some fresh air and time alone. She'd do as he said, she'd go upstairs and take a shower and a nap. By the time she woke up he'd be back, maybe with information, at least in a better mood, and the two of them could figure out what to do.

One thing she wasn't going to do was lock her door. It would be giving in to cowardice and terrorism, and once she started, she doubted she could stop. It had taken everything she had in her to learn to walk without peering over her shoulder, listening for the sound of a rifle being readied, looking for snipers in every flowering bush and tree. But she'd triumphed, and she wasn't going to let anyone drive her back into paranoia.

Another thing she was never going to do again was use the downstairs bathroom. She didn't have that much time left in this gloomy old house. For the days remaining she could just climb the extra flight of stairs to the second-floor bathroom. Her knee could use the exercise.

In the meantime, for no reason whatsoever, she was going to change the sheets on the big double bed upstairs, even though she'd changed them two days earlier, and see if she could find that pretty eyelet and cotton nightgown Maude had given her. And maybe Tanner would return in a better mood.

"SON," DOC SAID WEARILY, "I just don't know."

They were sitting out on his back porch, each with a cold bottle of beer, staring out into the heat-soaked landscape that stretched in a flat plain up to the foothills. Wildflowers dotted the thick grasses, and for a moment Tanner remembered that hidden meadow up in the mountains, and a woman riding bareback in the hot summer sun. He wished to God he'd never come down that mountain.

"What about Pete Forrester? It sounds like he's not completely sane," Tanner said, taking a deep gulp of the Coors.

"Oh, Pete's sane all right. He's just violent and bitter. The one thing he wouldn't do is sneak around. He might try to force a shoot-out on the main street, or get a crowd riled up enough for a lynching, but he wouldn't go peering in windows and shooting animals. Neither would most of the people I know, people who took the massacre particularly hard."

"What about someone like Lonnie?"

Doc shook his head. "I'd find that hard to believe. A boy like that, who's never had the gumption to do more than sit in his father's newspaper office, would hardly be the type to start terrorizing everybody. Besides, why now?"

Tanner set his beer down. "What about you?"

He had to give Doc credit—he took it well. He just turned and fastened those world-weary eyes on him. "Now why would I want to do a thing like that? These people are my friends and neighbors. I brought a goodly number of them into the world. Why would I want to hurt them?"

"I don't think these things are directed at the townspeople. They just started a couple of days ago, the moment I got into town. I think they're directed at me."

"Your ego's not hurting you much, is it?" Doc inquired kindly. "Must be kinda hard, carrying something that big around with you. What do you think I have against you?"

"Ellie."

The name hung between them like a tangible thing. A dozen emotions swept over Doc's face; anger, denial, embarrassment and eventually a reluctant resignation. "You see too damned much, Tanner," he said finally. "Does she know?"

"I don't think she has any idea."

He sighed, draining his beer. "Keep it that way, will you, son? It's just an old man's foolishness. She's my daughter's best friend, and she thinks of me as the sort of father she never had. I'd hate for anything to hurt that."

"I won't say anything."

"Thanks. And trust me, Tanner. There's a part of me that's jealous as hell of you, but there's another part of me that's grateful."

"Grateful?"

"Ellie's a fine woman. She's wasted here, wasted in a town where people can't stop looking backward. She needs someone like you to shake her up, get her out of here."

"I think you're jumping to a lot of conclusions."

"Maybe I am," Doc said. "Maybe that's my right. All I know is, you're good for her. And I wouldn't do anything to interfere with that, no matter how jealous I am."

Tanner leaned back in the chair, reaching for a cigarette, then thinking better of it. If he had one, Doc would want one, and he'd already started taking part in Ginger and Ellie's conspiracy to keep Doc's blood pressure down. "If it's not Pete or Lonnie or you," he said, "who is it? Are you sure my father died that day?"

A spasm of pain crossed the older man's face. "I'm sure. I signed the death certificate."

"You signed a lot of death certificates that day," Tanner said brutally. "You saw a lot of death. Are you absolutely certain?"

Doc reached over, took the cigarettes out of Tanner's breast pocket, and helped himself. "I told you, I'm certain. And I'll tell you something else, something I've never told a living soul. You're the only one who might understand. When I examined your father he had the strangest look on his face. For twenty years he'd been plagued by misery and despair, and for the first time since he came home he looked almost happy. It wasn't because he'd killed sixteen innocent people, either. It was because he was finally at rest."

Tanner took the pack back and lit Doc's cigarette and his own. He noticed absently that his hands were shaking. "All right," he said. "I believe you. He's really dead. That leaves one other possibility."

Doc blew out a long, pleasurable stream of smoke. "Who?"

Tanner grimaced. "Me."

CHAPTER FIFTEEN

Ellie knew she'd been a fool to lend her neighbor the car. Mrs. Martinez would have been willing to wait until her teenage son came home—Ellie didn't have to strand herself without transportation just to prove she was still a good person. She didn't have a thing to eat in the house, and Tanner would be hungry when he finally returned. She could always make an omelet, but Tanner didn't strike her as the sort of man who'd be content with an omelet.

The market was only a few blocks away. She seldom walked there. While the distance wasn't bad, carrying food back put too uncomfortable a strain on her leg. She preferred her walking to be recreational and therapeutic, rather than practical.

Tonight she might have no choice. It was almost five. The heat had scarcely abated, and the soft breeze blowing through the open windows of the old house stirred up memories and longings that were better left buried.

Of course, there was no guarantee that Tanner would be back that night. With Tanner there were no guarantees whatsoever, as she kept reminding herself. That lack of a safety net was beginning to matter less and less.

She moved to the tall bank of cupboards that lined

the back wall, staring into the uninspiring depths.
Maybe the two-year-old box of Bisquick might provide
something edible. She was busy perusing the back of
the package when she heard the car drive up. Mrs.
Martinez was back sooner than she'd expected. There
might just be time to get to Davidson's Market.

It wasn't Mrs. Martinez's squat bulk on her back porch,
nor the Buick in her driveway. It was Ginger Barlow,
wearing too much makeup, too much perfume, with a
defiant glitter in her pale-blue eyes. For an odd, irrational
moment Ellie wanted to slam the door in her face, lock
out whatever unpleasantness Ginger seemed determined
to bring in. But of course she didn't. Saint Ellie, she
mocked herself, holding the door open for her friend.

"Has Tanner got your car again?" Ginger asked
abruptly, in lieu of a greeting.

All Ellie's misgivings were proving true. "Mrs.
Martinez borrowed it," she said gently. "You know the
trouble she has with her old clunker…"

"I'm not here to talk about Mrs. Martinez," Ginger
said, setting her ample hips down on a kitchen chair and
fixing Ellie with a determined gaze.

Ellie sighed. "I didn't think you were. I don't suppose
it'll do any good to tell you I don't want to discuss it?"

"No good at all."

"In that case, can I get you some coffee?"

"All I want," said Ginger sternly, "is your undivided
attention. Sit down, Ellie, and I'll tell you a few things
you need to know about the man you've been spending
all this time with."

And with a sense of deep foreboding, Ellie sat
down to listen.

"DON'T BE CRAZY, SON," Doc said. "Who'd know better than you whether or not you were out killing animals and peering in people's windows?"

"It just struck me," he said slowly. "My father was crazy—you certainly can't argue that."

"I suppose not," Doc said reluctantly.

"And I'm his son. There doesn't seem to be any doubt about that, either. So what if I inherited his craziness? What if I'm going out at night, doing things and just not remembering? Maybe my father didn't remember the things he did, maybe he just thought he was sleeping. Maybe…"

"These are crazy fantasies. You didn't strike me as the neurotic type."

"I come by it honestly."

"The hell you do," Doc exploded. "Your daddy was crazy, and I don't deny it. But it wasn't hereditary, it wasn't inbred, it wasn't anything more than a sensitive man reacting to impossible circumstances. If you ever find yourself in a situation where you have to kill seventeen people, even in a wartime situation, and then live with the consequences, you might go a little crazy yourself. Then again, you might not. I'd be willing to bet you wouldn't. You've got more resilience than your daddy ever had. He couldn't bend, he couldn't accept the way things were. And people who can't bend, break." He stubbed out his cigarette and looked wistfully at Tanner's breast pocket.

Tanner ignored the unspoken plea. "I just hope you're right."

"Listen, Tanner, you have enough enemies around.

Don't add yourself to the list," Doc said earnestly. "And for heaven's sake, give me another cigarette. Who knows when Ginger'll be back and get on my case again?"

Tanner made no move for the cigarettes. "Where is Ginger?" He'd been more than grateful not to have seen her. She'd made it clear the night before that she wasn't the sort who appreciated being rejected, and while he didn't fancy any sort of confrontation, her absence made him more than a little uneasy.

"'Fraid my daughter's not too fond of you right now." Doc said easily. "Don't worry about it. I brought the girl up the best I could when her mother took off, but I'm afraid certain things just didn't stick too well. She wants what she wants, and she doesn't take no for an answer."

"Sometimes she has to."

"Well, that's true. But she doesn't have to like it. When you came in the front door she headed out the back. Said she was off to visit Ellie."

He should have known, Tanner thought. He should have listened to his own inner misgivings. "I'd better be getting back," he said abruptly, rising to his feet.

"Back where?"

"Back to Ellie's."

Doc nodded. "I thought so. Maybe I'd better give you a ride. I love my daughter, but she's got the devil of a tongue, and I wouldn't put it past her to twist it around some things that weren't strictly true."

Tanner didn't even hesitate. "Let's go."

GINGER DIDN'T SEE or hear him walk in the kitchen door. Ellie did. He moved silently, gracefully, and she could see how he could survive unnoticed in wilderness areas that boasted such unfriendly critters as wolves and grizzlies. Right now Ellie wasn't sure that Ginger was any less lethal than her four-legged kin.

"I've got bruises, Ellie," Ginger was saying. "The man was an animal, all over me. He wouldn't take no for an answer. I think he's—he's a little crazy."

The pause was good, Ellie thought cynically. Very effective. She moved her gaze from Tanner's still, opaque eyes to Ginger's wide blue ones, and shivered. The scary thing was, Ginger was beginning to believe what she was saying. Another time, another person, and Ellie would have believed her, too.

"I don't remember," she said carefully, "that you have too much practice saying no."

"Oh, I admit, I was attracted to him," Ginger said, pushing her mane of streaked blond hair back over her shoulder. "Who wouldn't be? There's that air of danger, that sexy mouth, those eyes of his. But it didn't take me long to realize that he's no good, as cruel and rotten as his father ever was. You may not realize it. He's been all sweetness and light to you and his dear old granny. But I saw…"

Ellie had groaned in sudden dismay as Tanner stiffened in the kitchen doorway. Ginger finally came out of her self-absorption long enough to realize they weren't alone, and her face froze as she took in Tanner's still figure.

"My dear old granny?" he said finally. "I didn't realize I had any kin left around here." His voice was cold and empty. "At least, none who would acknowledge me. I guess I was right about that."

"Tanner, it wasn't that she wouldn't acknowledge you," Ellie said desperately, rising from her chair and knocking it over in sudden clumsiness. "She was afraid you wouldn't forgive her for not helping your mother."

"She was right," he said coolly. "I presume we're talking about Maude?"

"She's a foolish old woman who can't see you for what you are," Ginger broke in spitefully.

Tanner smiled, his cold, gentle smile. "She sees through you clear enough." He glanced back at Ellie, who was momentarily speechless with misery. "But I'm not sure your friend does."

She opened her mouth to say something, to assure him that she hadn't believed a word of Ginger's lies, when the back door opened behind Tanner and Dave Martin bulldozed his way in, followed by Doc Barlow.

"There's been an accident," Doc announced, forestalling Martin. "I've got to get back to the house. Mrs. Martinez will need a few stitches, but it sounds as if she's okay. I could use your help, Ginger."

Ginger hesitated. "Coming," she said finally, her voice sulky. She skirted Tanner, holding her body away as if the air around him might be contaminated, managed a tiny sashay for an unappreciative Dave Martin, and headed out the door. "Remember what I told you, Ellie," she called back over her shoulder.

Tanner hadn't moved. He leaned back against the counter, his arms crossed, prepared to listen. If it hadn't been for the savage look in his eyes, Ellie might have been fool enough to think he was at ease.

"What happened to Mrs. Martinez?" she asked,

dread and despair filling her. "I lent her my car this afternoon. Is she badly hurt?"

"Your car lost its brakes," Dave announced. "With a little help from someone who knows his way around cars. Doc's right—she's okay. She was only going about twenty-five, and she just skidded off the road. Probably won't even need those stitches. What I want to know, Ellie, is when you last drove that car, and who else has been driving it? And I want to know, mister," he turned and glowered at Tanner, "where you've been all day, and whether you've got any witnesses who can swear to your alibi."

Tanner moved then, and for a moment Ellie held her breath, afraid of what he might do. But he merely headed for the door, ignoring Martin, ignoring her.

"Wait just a damned minute!" Dave was heading out after him. "Where do you think you're going?"

Tanner paused on the back porch, and Ellie thought she could see desolation and resignation in his eyes before his face once more grew impassive. "As far away from Morey's Falls," he said, "as my legs can carry me." And he headed down the steps into the early evening light.

HE'D GONE. Ellie knew that, and she couldn't blame him. She'd lied to him, or at least been party to a deception. She hadn't told him Maude was Marbella's mother. Maude had begged her not to, wanting a chance to get to know him, get close to him before he found out that she was one of the people who'd turned their backs on his mother when she was desperately in need. Ellie had helped give her that chance, and now it looked as if she'd destroyed her own in doing so.

Dave Martin had stood at her back door, shouting after Tanner's retreating figure, and there'd been no way she could thrust him out of her path and go after Tanner, to try to explain. She'd stood there, trapped in her own kitchen, and watched him walk away, as he'd walked away so many times in his life.

The sun set late in Montana in June. It was ten o'clock, and the sky still held enough light to see Morey's Ridge in the east. Ellie sat in her bed, among her clean, ruffled sheets, the cotton lace nightgown around her, and looked out into the twilit sky. How far would he make it tonight? Would he have gone back to the cabin for his pack, for food, or would he have just kept going?

If only she'd had a chance to tell him she trusted him. If only she'd had a chance to shut Ginger up, to silence Dave Martin, to run after him into the darkening shadows of the Montana night. Instead, there she was, left alone in her virgin bed, and he was somewhere up in the wilderness, moving away from her forever.

At least it was an unseasonably hot night. If he'd gone without his pack he'd be all right. But Tanner was too sensible for that—he would have gone back, packed everything up and been gone within an hour. He'd get quite a ways before it grew too dark to see. Would he reach the secret mountain meadow where they'd first met?

Ellie punched the pillow, squirming around in the bed. She could always drive out to his house to be certain. Within an hour of the accident people had called, offering her the use of their cars. The town pet was being taken care of again, she thought savagely. And they wouldn't take no for an answer.

Right now she had Addie Pritchard's ancient Ford pickup sitting in the driveway, and Merrill Talbott's son's Toyota parked in front of the house. She'd turned down half a dozen other offers, from Lonnie's aging BMW to a 1963 Studebaker that ran better than half the new models in town.

But she didn't have to drive out Route 5 to Charles Tanner's old place to know he was gone. She'd seen it in his eyes, in the line of his body, in the angle of his proud head as he walked out her door without a backward glance. He was gone, and she was left behind.

She leaned back on the soft feather pillow and shut her eyes. The moon was three-quarters full, shining in her window, gilding the tall, dark Victorian bed where she'd slept alone for almost fifteen years. The same moon was shining down on Tanner. Up in the mountains that same moon might be shining on someone else, someone evil, someone out with a gun or a bucket of red paint, someone out to spread pain and terror.

Her eyes shot open again, and a small, whimpering sound escaped the back of her throat. She didn't want to lie there while Tanner moved farther and farther away from her. She didn't want to lie alone ever again.

Throwing back the light cotton sheet, she climbed out of bed. She'd been passive for too long. She might not be able to find him, but she wasn't going to stay there in her big dark house and let him go without a fight.

She didn't bother changing—she just threw on an old pair of pants and a sweater over her nightgown while she made her plans. She would take Addie's pickup and drive out to Maude's place. She'd taken

Shaitan out for moonlight rides before, and the high-strung stallion had picked his way sure-footedly along treacherous mountain paths without a stumble. He could find his way back to that meadow, even without the bright moon pouring down.

She had to accept the fact that Tanner might not be there, might already have headed higher up the mountain, beyond her reach. She'd accept that, if she had to. And while she didn't know Alfred's last name, or the town in the Sangre de Cristo mountains where Tanner would be heading, given her usual determination she'd find out both. And sooner or later she'd find Tanner.

Shaitan greeted her appearance in the old barn with a whirrup of approval. The farmhouse had been dark, with Maude in bed, and while Mazey and Hoover expressed forlorn displeasure at being left behind, they responded gratefully to being let out to pasture.

She didn't bother with anything more than a bit and bridle. She dumped her sweater and jeans in a corner of the barn and scrambled onto Shaitan's back. Her white cotton nightgown shimmered in the moonlight, flowing over the stallion's black hide as she headed him toward the mountain trail east of Maude's property. Her chestnut hair hung down her back, and her feet were bare in the warm night air. Wiggling her toes, she started up the mountain.

MOREY'S RIDGE was still and silent above him. Darkness was descending, the late, streaky darkness of June in Montana. There was a soft, damp breeze ruffling the trees around him, smelling of yesterday's rain, tomorrow's flowers, the earth and the mountain and the clear stream at the edge of the meadow. The moon was a shimmering, fat crescent in the sky, with starlight spilling out around it, and Tanner took a deep, heady breath of the night air, letting the anger drain from him.

He'd been prepared to walk all night, up and over that mountain, moving into the wilderness, as far away from that cursed little town as his energy and stamina could carry him—as his personal devils could drive him. He'd left Ellie's house four hours before, loaded his pack and taken off with only a few grateful souls to see him on his way.

How would they feel, he thought, when animals were found slaughtered and Tanner's son was long gone? When the graves were still desecrated, the cars still sabotaged, the eyes still watching…?

That had slowed his headlong pace up the mountain. He'd left Ellie. Ellie, who had watchers peering in her window, Ellie, whose car had been tampered with. What if *she'd* been driving? What if *she'd* been zooming along at sixty-seven miles an hour, as she had earlier today?

He didn't even know if she'd believed Ginger. He didn't know if she'd listened to Dave Martin—chances were she hadn't. And he didn't blame her for not telling him about Maude. In the short time he'd known her, he knew Ellie wasn't one to break a confidence. If Maude wanted to keep her identity a secret, Ellie wasn't the one to break that secret.

He slipped the pack from his back and stretched his cramped muscles. The meadow looked different at night. Dark and mysterious, with moonlight silvering the aspens, turning the dew-damp grass to sparkling diamonds. The night was warm, waiting.

Waiting for what? It had to be close to eleven—the sun had set a little over an hour earlier. It was too late to head back down to town. He'd bed down here for the night, and the next morning he could decide.

Except that the decision had already been made. He wouldn't leave Ellie in the midst of that mess. It was as good an excuse as any, he mocked himself, untying his sleeping bag and spreading it out over the thick carpet of grass and wildflowers. He knew, deep in his heart of hearts, that that was what it was. An excuse. Just a few days had passed, and he was too far gone. He couldn't leave Ellie at all.

The pool was shallow enough to hold some heat from the long, sunny day. He stripped off his clothes and soaked his tired body, then climbed back out. It was warm enough not to wear his shirt, so he just pulled on his jeans, zipping them but not bothering with the snap. He squatted down by his pack, looking for the dried trail mix he always kept handy, when he heard the sound of her horse. And knew what he'd been waiting for.

He rose slowly, standing very still, watching her approach. She'd given Shaitan his head, and the big black stallion was picking his way carefully through the dense summer grasses. The soft breeze was blowing toward Tanner, and it wasn't until they were close that the horse picked up his scent. The ears went back, the head went up, and Tanner held his breath.

And then Shaitan let out a small, quiet whicker of greeting as he continued toward Tanner's waiting figure. Ellie was watching him, but even in the bright moonlight he couldn't read her expression. It was enough that she'd come.

She was wearing something long and white and flowing, and her thick dark hair hung down her back. Her long, pale legs hugged the barrel of the horse, and her feet were bare. Her hands were light on the reins, letting Shaitan lead her. And Shaitan led her straight to Tanner.

CHAPTER SIXTEEN

She could see Tanner standing at the edge of the meadow, near the clear mountain pool. He was watching her approach, and if the bright moonlight silvered his blond head and cast a tall, eerie moon shadow behind him, it failed to illuminate his expression. He didn't move. He simply waited.

Shaitan was apparently unaffected by her doubts. He moved ahead, trusting in the man even as Ellie still struggled with her thoughts. Maybe she was the last person he wanted to see. Maybe she'd been a fool to come searching for him. Maybe she should quickly kick Shaitan into action and race back down the mountain.

It was unseasonably warm for a late-June night. Tanner's pack was lying on the ground, his sleeping bag unzipped and spread out on the grass. She'd let Shaitan get a little closer, just close enough to read his expression. If it wasn't welcoming, she could leave.

His dark-blond hair was wet and slicked back away from his face. His mouth was a narrow line, thin and unsmiling, and his cold blue eyes were in shadow. Ellie could feel the dampness in her hands as they held the reins, feel the trembling in her knees. Somewhere in the distance an old owl hooted, and overhead a million stars warred with the bright moonlight to flood the field with light.

Shaitan reached the end of the field, reached Tanner, and stopped complacently, as Tanner lifted one strong, tanned hand to stroke the skittish stallion's sleek black neck. The man raised his head then, to look directly into her face, and his eyes glittered in the darkness.

Ellie didn't move. Fear was supposed to be a cold, hard lump in the chest. Her fear was a blaze of fire burning deep inside, much lower down. She didn't say a word, and neither did he. He merely stood there, his strong hand stroking Shaitan's neck. And then he moved closer, and his hand left the horse, reaching to catch her bare ankle in his long fingers.

His flesh was hot, hers was cool. He slid his hand up her calf, up to the ruffled hem of her lacy nightdress. Before she realized his intent he'd pushed the material away, exposing her bad knee. His mouth followed his hand, tracing the line of scars that stretched along her leg.

She heard a quick, shocked intake of breath, and vaguely realized it was her own. And then his hands were reaching up, encircling her waist, and he was lifting her down, down from Shaitan's high back, her body sliding against his, her skirts bunching up around her thighs, his warm, bare shoulders damp beneath her trembling hands.

When her bare feet at last touched the ground she was wrapped in his arms, her hips against his, her breasts beneath the thin barrier of cotton pressed up against his hard, muscled chest, her arms clinging around his neck as if to a lifeline.

He looked down at her, his blue eyes dark in the moonlight, and belatedly Ellie realized it wasn't just fear burning deep inside her. It was desire, pure, simple and overwhelming.

She opened her mouth to say something, she wasn't sure what. To tell him that she loved him, to tell him not to worry. But he gave his head an imperceptible shake, and his lips covered hers, stopping the words before they could be formed.

His mouth was warm, wet, seeking hers, heating her chilled heart, burning her lingering fears away. His hands reached up and held her head still, as his mouth brushed back and forth across her lips, dampening them, arousing them, so that unconsciously she was seeking him with her mouth, trying to catch him long enough to hold him.

And then he deepened the kiss, holding her still as his tongue plunged into the willing darkness of her mouth. He kissed her long and hard and deep, taking his time, until they were both trembling and breathless in the moonlit air.

He moved away for a moment, and she watched in sudden panic, afraid he was going to send her away after all, but instead he slipped off Shaitan's bridle, dropping it in the long grass, and slapped the big horse on the rump. Shaitan moved away, toward the fast-running stream, and began placidly to lip the long grass.

Tanner took a few steps that brought him back to her waiting side. He scooped her up in his arms, effortlessly, as his mouth once more took possession of hers. But there was a difference this time, a joyful, almost lighthearted acceptance that burned through her nerves and shattered them. Past failures were fast disappearing. She was alone in the moon-drenched meadow with the man she loved.

The sleeping bag was soft beneath her back. The night smelled of wildflowers and Montana grassland, of blue sage and June nights and Tanner. As he loomed over her she smiled up at him, a brave, tremulous smile, and reached out to pull him closer.

His fingers were deft on the row of tiny buttons that traveled down the front of her gown. He bared her breasts to the moonlight, and then, shockingly, put his mouth on one, while he cupped the other in his big hand.

She made a small, whimpering noise, half panic, half pleasure, and her hands clutched his shoulders. "Tanner," she said, her voice husky in the still moonlight, the first words to break the silence. "Wait," she pleaded. "I'm frightened."

He raised his head to look down at her. "I know," he said softly, regret and determination in his voice. "I know."

"Couldn't we just…"

"No," he said, pushing the nightgown off her shoulders and down her legs, ignoring her half-hearted attempts to stop him. She lay there naked in the moonlight, and fear was beating all around her. "We're not going to spend another night locked chastely in each other's arms," he said. "We're not going to lie here and neck until you run away. We're going to make love, here, tonight, on this mountain."

His breath was warm and sweet on her upturned face, his expression implacable. "What if I say no?" she asked. "Will you force me?"

It was a very small, very wry smile that danced around the corners of his mouth and lit the cool depths of his eyes. "I've never forced a woman in my life," he said gently, "and I'm not about to start with you. If you say no, I'll let you go. But you have approximately sixty seconds to make your choice. Once it's made you can't change your mind."

"You're pushing me," she cried.

"Damned right. I'm pushing you off your pedestal and bringing Saint Ellie down among the living," he said. "Yes or no, Ellie. The time is now."

If only he'd kiss her again, kiss her so she wouldn't have to think. But he held himself away, watching her, the warmth of his body lying alongside of her, his jeans rough against her silky skin.

A thousand doubts and questions sang in her mind. She ignored them. Slipping her arms around his neck, she pulled him over her. "Yes," she said. "Yes."

It was nothing like the books she'd read, nothing like her limited, fumbling experiences. Tanner took his time, slowly, languorously learning her body, discovering what tickled, what aroused her, learning almost by instinct just how to caress her small, sensitive breasts, learning just the right amount of pressure, enough to make her gasp and cry out, not enough to hurt. Until the pleasure became so exquisite that it was a pain of its own.

She learned him too, the shape and texture and contours of him, of places that had been a mystery to her, one that became even more awesome as it grew familiar. She learned the taste of him out of pleasure and her own desire, and learned the joy of his barely controlled response.

When the time came she was barely aware of it. He entered her, pulling back, pushing forward, gently rocking against her, until she was wet and slippery with longing. When she was ready, when he was ready, he braced his arms around her and increased the pressure, pushing all the way in till he rested, deep and tight inside her.

She lay beneath him, accustoming herself to the strangeness of it all, the tiny shivers of delight that were dancing through her body, the mild trace of pain that was rapidly receding into a haze of pleasure.

He lifted his head up to look at her, and she could see the film of sweat bead his forehead, the barely controlled passion that he was keeping in check. "Are you all right?" His voice was hoarse, strained. "Did I hurt you?"

She smiled up at him dizzily. "I'm fine," she whispered. "Just…fine…"

His answering smile was lopsided. "There's more to it," he said. "Lots more." And he began to move. His hands reached down, caught her legs and pulled them up around him, settling in against her. She'd scarcely gotten used to him when he pulled away, then pushed back again, the relentless ebb and flow of love and desire washing over her body. She began to shiver in anticipation of some distant, unapproachable delight, and she felt Tanner, slippery with sweat, tremble in her arms.

She wanted to cry, but she didn't know what for. For the moon, still shining down on the entwined lovers? For the stars, glittering in the sky beside their sister moon? Or cry for herself, lost and seeking, shivering and reaching and aching and longing?

Her head thrashed back and forth in mute negation of something she couldn't begin to understand. She wanted to tell him to stop, it was useless, it was more than she could bear. He thrust all the way into her, holding her with the pressure of his hips, and his hands caught her head, holding her still.

"Not without you," he muttered obscurely. And setting his mouth on hers, he reached down between their sweat-slick bodies and touched her.

Her body arched, convulsed around his. Her mind, her emotions shattered, like the thousand stars of the Montana night, and she was gone, lost, floating, and Tanner was with her, his strangled cry swallowed in their last, desperate kiss, his body rigid in her arms.

It was a long time before either of them could speak. Ellie lay beneath him, listening as their hearts hurtled against each other, as their breathing rasped into a labored silence, as the stray tremors danced across her moon-silvered flesh. She looked up into the vast canopy of the sky, and watched a star fall in a blaze of light. She felt the warm breeze lift Tanner's hair and toss it against her flushed face, heard the distant, peaceful sound of Shaitan drinking from the mountain stream. She wanted to lie forever beneath Tanner's strong, protecting body. But she knew there were no forevers for her. Not with Tanner.

He moved, pulling away from her, his hands still possessively on her. She started to speak, but he put his fingers against her mouth.

"Don't," he said, his voice as husky as hers. "No clever remarks, no jokes, no demands, no vows of undying love."

He looks as though he's in shock, Ellie thought.

There was little doubt she looked exactly the same. Slowly she nodded, and he moved his hand from her mouth. Not before she had a chance to kiss his fingers.

He pulled her into his arms again, rolling onto his back and bringing her with him. "Hold me," he muttered, his words an unconscious echo of her own plea the night before. "Just hold me."

And thoroughly content, Ellie held him close against her, slowly relaxing into sleep.

IT WAS the longest night she had ever spent; it passed in the wink of an eye. The moon was sinking lower in the sky when they awoke in the darkness, and they made love again, more slowly this time, drawing it out until they were both shaking and crying and shivering and dying with the wonder of it. Tanner even tried to talk her into swimming in the icy mountain pool, promising to warm her up afterward. When she was still hesitant he lifted her up and chucked her in, and when she emerged, sputtering and furious, he turned that heat and fury around, into a fiery passion that left them too stunned and weary to move.

The sun rose early, not much after four o'clock that close to the summer solstice. They lay on the rumpled sleeping bag, the smell of crushed wildflowers filtering through their dreams, and watched the color streak across the sky as one by one the stars disappeared.

"You know," she observed in a lazy, sleepy voice, "I never realized what I was missing. If I'd known, I would have done something about it earlier."

"It isn't always like this." Tanner's voice was a deep bass rumble beneath her ear. She had her head on his chest, and her hand was drawing lazy circles on his smooth, sun-darkened skin.

"Isn't it?"

"Take it from a man who knows," he murmured.

Ellie giggled. "I just did, didn't I?"

He laughed, and the sound was soft and comforting in the night air. She sighed peacefully, snuggling closer. There was just the faint trace of early-morning chill in the air, but she didn't mind. Nothing short of the legendary Montana winters would have made her put her nightgown back on. "Were you really leaving?"

"No. I changed my mind halfway up here, but I thought I'd like a night without someone watching me."

"I can always shut my eyes."

"Not you, woman," he said lightly.

"Why did you change your mind?"

"Too much unfinished business."

"Was I part of that unfinished business?" Her question was delicately phrased. She wasn't sure she wanted to hear the answer, whatever it was.

"Yes." he said.

"Am I finished now?"

He reached down and put his hand under her chin, tipping her face up to his. "I don't think I'll ever be finished with you," he said softly, and then a spasm of pain crossed his face. "Damn," he swore. "Why the hell did I say that?"

"Tanner…" She half rose, but he pushed her back down, hiding her face against his chest.

"Don't say it," he said bitterly. "I don't want to hear it. For God's sake, don't tell me that you love me."

She stayed where she was, her face pressed against

him, inhaling the rich, earthy scent of him. "Why not?" she asked quietly.

"Because I don't need your love. I don't want it, I don't want the strings and ties and responsibilities of having you love me."

She pulled away from him, sitting up, wrapping her arms around her bent knees. She was bone weary, physically and emotionally, and a part of her wanted to scream and cry at him.

But the greater part knew better. She looked down at him, at his stubborn, beautiful, beloved face, and carefully wiped all expression from her own, leaving only mild regret. "Sorry, Tanner," she said softly. "The warning comes too late."

"Ellie..."

"Shut up, Tanner," she said a little fiercely. "Stay as long as you can, walk away when you have to. In the meantime—" she took a deep breath "—there's nothing you can do about it. I love you, and there's no changing it."

"Until you look at your knee and remember whose son I am," he said, still stretched out on the ground, apparently at ease. But even in the dawn-lit shadows Ellie could see the tension threading through his strong body. "Do you realize you never refer to him as my father? He's always Charles Tanner. Well, he *was* my father, Ellie. He sired me, even brought me into the world, and he killed thirty-three people. At least seventeen while he was in the army, and another sixteen here in Montana. He ruined your life, Ellie, and I'm all he left on this earth. Do you really think you love me?"

She slid forward on her knees, leaning over him, her

chestnut hair hanging down in a curtain around their faces. "I'm afraid so, Tanner," she said. "Charles Tanner, Jr.," she added for emphasis. "And while you can try your damnedest to convince me otherwise, I've waited thirty years for you. It's going to take more than a harmless old ghost like your father to stop me."

"Harmless old ghost...?"

"That's all he is, Tanner. He's dead, long gone. Pain and evil live on, but your father's dead, his goodness and evil dead with him. Someone else is doing things, but it has no connection with you."

"Does that mean I could leave?"

She bit her lip. "You can always leave," she said evenly. "I wouldn't hold you against your will."

"And what if it's not against my will?"

"I don't think you know what you want," she said.

He reached up and brushed her cheek with one hand, sweeping it under her mane of hair. And then he was pulling her down, down to him, and his mouth was waiting for her. "Yes," he said, "I do." And right then she believed him.

THEY MADE THEIR WAY slowly down the mountain. Neither of them wore a watch, but the early-rising sun had been up a couple of hours, putting the time somewhere between six and seven. Tanner rode Shaitan astride, with Ellie draped sideways across his lap, partly for the horse's comfort, partly for her own. A long, soaking bath, she promised herself. She was sore in places she hadn't realized existed, and her face was flushed from the rough stubble that adorned Tanner's lean cheeks.

Tanner was still very quiet, as he had been since dawn. She hadn't convinced him, Ellie knew that. Nothing would convince him, nothing except time. She could only hope they had enough of that scarce commodity.

In the meantime, she swore to herself that she wouldn't push him. She wouldn't tell him again that she loved him, wouldn't throw herself at him, wouldn't make a nuisance of herself. She'd be patient, as she'd learned so well to be. She'd waited thirty years to find the right man. She could wait a while to be sure of him.

Maude's remote farm was in sight before he spoke. "Why didn't you tell me?"

"About Maude? I promised her I wouldn't. She still feels guilty about Marbella. She figured you wouldn't talk to her if you knew who she was."

"My mother hardly mentioned her, but when she did it was with love. It always sounded like it was my grandfather who was the problem."

"It's true," Ellie said. "But Maude loved him." She hesitated. "Ginger will have called her and told her, you know. She'll be in the house, waiting to see what you're going to do."

He sighed. "I know what you want me to do. You want me to go in there and tell that old woman that Marbella forgave her."

"Only if it's true. Maude will see through it if it's a lie."

"I'll go," he said. "If you promise to let me ride Shaitan."

"You are riding Shaitan," she pointed out.

"Alone. Fast. With a saddle."

"Personally, I like it this way," she murmured. "But

you've got yourself a deal. Just make sure she makes some coffee while you're having your family reunion. I need something to get me going."

"Tired, are you?" he inquired solicitously. "These busy nights."

She smiled up at him, rubbing her already abraded cheek against his chest. "I'll survive."

It was the wrong thing to say. She could feel him stiffening, and there was nothing she could do to make it better.

"I expect you will," he said in a distant voice. "You have a history of it."

"And a future," she said firmly. But deep inside, she wondered if there'd ever be a future for them. At that moment the odds didn't look too good.

CHAPTER SEVENTEEN

Ellie spent as much time as she could brushing down Shaitan's sleek coat, feeding and watering him before turning him out to pasture with his two stablemates. He spent far too much time in the barn as it was, but she didn't dare pasture him if she couldn't be sure she'd be around to get him back in during the storms that terrified him. Jamie was useless around him—it was all the teenage boy could do to feed him without fainting in terror.

Things would be better when she could find a place where she could keep the horses. While her half-formed fantasies had usually involved city life, she knew deep down inside her that she could never be happy surrounded by the noise and bustle of a big city. She needed mountains, she needed wide, open spaces, she needed big blue sky and room to breathe. Most of all, she needed Tanner.

However, dwelling on that thought would get her exactly nowhere. One day at a time, Doc had taught her when she was trying to get off the painkillers that had numbed her to life. One day at a time, and maybe, just maybe it would work out.

Her cotton nightdress was definitely the worse for

wear. She stripped it off, pulling on her faded jeans and sweater, accepting her lack of underwear with equanimity.

She crumpled up the nightgown, about to toss it into the trash, then thought better of it. Smoothing the soft, torn cotton with a gentle hand, she put it back in the bag that had held her clothes and stashed it back under the workbench.

Maude's dark, snapping eyes were rimmed with red, and the smile she gave Ellie when she walked in the door was bordering on the tremulous. Not that there was ever anything that tentative about Maude. But whatever had passed between Tanner and his grandmother had apparently been satisfactory to both parties. At least as far as Ellie could tell. Tanner had that distant look about him, his blue eyes unreadable in the morning light as he sat there sipping coffee from an enormous blue mug that was chipped and cracked and oddly familiar looking. With a start Ellie recognized it. It had belonged to Jacob, Maude's husband, and he'd used it every morning. When he died, Maude had put it away, and this was the first time Ellie had seen it in all of ten years.

"I wondered what was keeping you," Maude said in a voice slightly hoarse from tears, both shed and unshed, as she handed Ellie a cup of inky-black coffee. Ellie doubted she'd even spared her a thought. "I was telling Tanner here that you can take my old car until yours is ready. It's got to be better than that old pickup of Addie's. I'm willing to bet it runs fine. You know I don't drive anymore, and Jamie can take me out in his rattletrap if need be."

"Thank you, Maude." She could feel Tanner's eyes

sweeping over her clothes, could sense his hidden amusement. "You might tell Jamie I fed Shaitan and put him out to pasture. If he's feeling particularly brave he could try to bring him into the stall. Otherwise I'll come back out later."

"I can do it when I ride him," Tanner volunteered casually.

Maude's eyes sharpened. "She's gonna let you ride him? That hell-born baby of hers?"

"So she promised." Tanner's eyes met hers over the chipped blue mug, the faintest trace of a challenge in them, and any lingering doubts Ellie had slipped away.

"So I promised," she agreed.

"God almighty, it must be love!" cackled Maude.

Tanner choked on his coffee.

ELLIE COULDN'T HELP IT, Tanner thought as he drove toward the wide main street of Morey's Falls. Try as she might, she couldn't keep the light from her eyes. Try as she might, she couldn't keep her soft, slightly swollen lips from curving into a smile. Even his brooding silence didn't daunt her. The woman was simply, unequivocally happy.

It had been a long time since he'd had that effect on another human being. He was used to making people suspicious and miserable, resentful and frightened. When Ellie didn't think he'd notice, she looked at him as if the sun rose and set within him. It was an addictive, dangerous thing, and he knew he had to do something about it while he still could.

"Can we stop by Davidson's Market on our way home?" she asked, trying to keep a somber expression on her face and failing. "I have to get my purse, and I'm out of essentials."

"Essentials?"

"Milk, bread and soap. All the necessities of life," she said.

He should have known better. He did know better, but he drove straight on into the center of town without a word. He'd never been one to avoid a confrontation, and if one was brewing, they might as well face it. Maybe Ellie would see the light without having to be shown it.

It was just after ten o'clock on a sunny, late-June morning. The wide sidewalks of Morey's Falls were unusually crowded, and the faded, gloomy-looking people looked a little dazed by the glorious sunshine. They looked even more dazed at the sight of Tanner driving Ellie Lundquist in Maude Gilles's ancient sedan.

Ellie had her hand on the door before he'd even pulled the car to a stop, directly in front of the market. "Can I get you anything?"

"Don't you want me to come in?"

She looked startled. "Of course," she said, and he believed her.

"Never mind. Get me some more cigarettes." He handed her a crumpled wad of bills.

Her eyes danced. "I shouldn't. I gave up my cane; you can give up those coffin nails."

"Get me the cigarettes, woman," he ordered in a mock snarl, "or you'll be in real trouble."

"Maybe," she said, dancing away from him without taking the proffered money.

She practically skipped into the store, he noted

sourly. And the people on the sidewalks stared—first
after her, then back to him, sitting in the car, then back
toward Ellie. Tanner's instincts, never relaxed, started
working overtime.

He counted to one hundred, drumming his fingers on
the steering wheel. He counted, again, this time in
Spanish. Still no Ellie. The looks he was getting from
the passersby were growing more hostile, and the small
crowd, instead of thinning, was growing larger.

It was an unbelievably beautiful day. The big Montana sky was like a canopy of blue overhead, the mountains were sharply outlined in the distance, the green of
early summer making the town seem prettier than it
really was. But Tanner was beyond noticing. There
was trouble, real trouble, and Ellie was in the middle
of it.

The people scurried out of his way as he strode
across the sidewalk to the fancy glass door of
Davidson's Market, but he could hear the undercurrent
of resentment, feel the hostile eyes at his back. He
ignored them, pushing the door open, and then he
stopped still, just inside the store.

Ellie was standing up against a row of canned veg-
etables, and the light had gone from her eyes. Her hands
were clutched tightly around her purse, her mouth was
pale and set, and her face was white with strain. The
signs of his lovemaking were clear as day, to him at
least: the slight reddening of her soft skin from his
beard, the tiny bite mark on the side of her neck, that
slightly out-of-focus look she still carried despite her
defiant stance.

No one noticed him enter. He was partially obscured

by a tall shelf of baked goods, and he stood there, watching. One huge, threatening man stood directly over Ellie, but there was a semicircle of six or seven people surrounding her, baiting her. They should have torches and pitchforks, he thought for one bizarre, abstracted moment. Or at least come equipped with a large red letter *A*.

"There's a word for women like you," the big man was saying. He was so close to her he was spitting in her face with each angry word.

"There are lots of words for women like me," Ellie replied, her voice even despite the strain. "Start with human."

"I'll start with traitor," the man thundered. "And then go on to trash, cheap, no-good, murdering…"

"Your vocabulary's very nice, Pete," she said; though Tanner could hear the quaver in her voice he doubted anyone else could. "But I'm not a murderer, and neither is Tanner."

"He's the spawn of a murderer, and you turned your back on everyone that loved and cared for you all these years when you shacked up with him."

"Pete," Ellie protested.

"You betrayed us," a woman spoke up, her voice unfamiliar to Tanner. "You betrayed the judge, you betrayed your father and you betrayed yourself."

Very good, Tanner applauded silently. That was better than anything he could come up with to drive her away. Let her take a little bit more, and then he'd get her out of there and finish the job. Maybe it would be enough to get her out of this godforsaken town altogether, to someplace where she could live life without having to be a saint. To someplace where she could find a man she could really love, and not have to throw it away on a loser like him. If that thought was acid eating away at his innards, it was no more than he deserved. He never should have touched her, and now he was paying the price.

But Ellie was paying a higher price. Tanner had seen a mountain lion take down a sheep once. He'd known better than to do anything but sit there, absolutely still, until the blood lust had passed, but he'd seen the desperate, cornered look in the sheep's eyes, knowing the end was coming, too stupid to be anything but brave.

And there was Ellie, with the same, stupid courage. He should let them torment her just a little bit more, but he didn't think he could stand it.

"You've stabbed us all in the back, Ellie," another voice was saying. "We all loved you, trusted you...." And Tanner realized with sudden shock that it was Lonnie.

Tanner moved then, into sight, striding down the crowded aisle of Davidson's Market to the huddled group of angry townspeople.

Pete Forrester was a giant of a man, built like a linebacker, with massive thighs and shoulders and big meaty hands to match his red, angry face. He topped Tanner by probably half a foot and one hundred pounds, and there'd be no contest in a fair fight. Fortunately Tanner didn't fight fair.

Reaching around the burly figure, he took Ellie's stiff arm and tugged. She came readily enough, and he began leading her out the door.

The townspeople watched in sullen silence, too surprised by his sudden advent to protest. Pete finally broke the spell. "Get out of here, you murdering bastard!" he shouted. "And take her with you!"

Tanner stopped by the door. He looked at Pete, a long, measuring look, and noted without surprise that it still worked. Pete backed off, muttering something beneath his breath. It was always easy to stare down a coward and a bully, and Pete Forrester was exactly that. "If I were a bastard," Tanner said coolly, "we wouldn't have any problem here, would we?" And taking Ellie with him, he let the door close gently behind them.

They weren't through yet. The number of people on the sidewalk had swelled, and he half expected bottles and insults to be thrown. He should have known better in this town of the living dead. They just watched, surly and apathetic, as he helped a shaken Ellie into the car and pulled away, into the bright sunshine.

"We'll get your necessities of life from Addie. We need to tell her where to find her truck," he said, looking over at her. She had her arms wrapped around her, for warmth on this hot summer day.

"Could you take me home?" she asked in a very small voice.

He opened his mouth to say something, to comfort her, and then shut it again. Comfort from him would only weaken her. They drove in silence back through town. Tanner could feel the eyes watching their departure, feel the hostility fanning forth in waves of tension. Why the hell had he ever involved Ellie? He'd known from the start it would bring nothing but trouble, nothing but pain and despair.

Hadn't he had some half-crazy idea about bringing

her down to his level? He should have known it was impossible. She was sitting there beside him, hurt, aching, grieving. Yet he knew for a fact that she held nothing against Pete Forrester and his ilk. And nothing against his own worthless self.

He was about to do something about that, however. A quick, clean cut was the kindest. If he didn't drive her away now he'd never be able to let her go, and there was no future for her with Charles Tanner's son.

"Would you mind dropping me off at the cabin first?" he asked, keeping his voice cool.

She looked over at him, startled out of her misery. "I thought…I mean…" She floundered to a stop, took a deep breath and started again. "I wanted to be with you," she said.

"I don't think that's a good idea."

"Why not? Do you think I mind what those people said? I know them too well, I know the kind of pain they're going through."

"And have you forgotten who inflicted that pain?"

"No. I still need you, Tanner."

He steeled himself. He hated hunting, hated the notion of gunning down some helpless animal. He had no pleasure in what he was going to do. He just knew he had to do it.

"Don't make me say it, Ellie," he said, his voice still remote.

"Say what? That you don't need me? I don't suppose you do. You're much more self-sufficient than I am." She was trying to keep her voice light, trying and failing. "And you can't tell me you don't want me. I wouldn't believe it."

"Believe it." He kept his eyes trained on the roadway in front of him, listening to the little intake of breath that was a swallowed gasp of pain. "You may as well know, I went after you for a reason."

"You went after me?"

"Didn't you notice you were being stalked? There you were, sweet and pretty and just waiting to fall, and there I was, the spawn of a murderer. I thought I might even up the score a bit. Bring you down to my level."

She said nothing for a long time, and he didn't dare look at her, for fear he'd waver, tell her he was lying, ask her to run away with him and never set foot in Montana again.

He'd pulled up in front of the derelict cabin before she finally spoke. "So now that you've brought me down to your level," she said quietly, "what next?"

He opened the door and climbed out, leaving the motor running. She slid across the wide bench seat to the driver's side, put her hands on the steering wheel and looked up at him, her face calm, expressionless, waiting for an answer.

"What next?" he echoed. "Goodbye, Ellie." And he shut the door very carefully.

There was no sign of pain or distress on her pale face. He could see the faint dusting of golden freckles dancing across her cheekbones, glinting in the bright, cheery sunlight. "Goodbye, Tanner," she said. Putting the car in gear, she drove away, down the winding dirt road.

He waited until she was out of sight, waited until the sound of the big engine had faded in the distance. Then he started to curse, a mindless litany that did nothing to relieve his own grief and rage.

Finally the words faded into silence. He walked into the cabin, feeling as always the sense of desolation that the place engendered in him. He'd had to do it, he reminded himself. For his sake, and for Ellie's. Now all he had to do was survive the next few days, long enough to find out who or what was behind the incidents that were echoing his father's history. And then get the hell out of there.

He looked around the weather-stained walls. One thing he promised himself. Before he went, he was going to torch that place, scorch it down to the relentless clay it sat upon. And then, even if Charles Tanner, Sr. didn't find peace, his son would.

ELLIE DIDN'T CRY. There didn't seem to be any tears inside her, everything felt hot and dry and burned up. She skirted town, driving the long way around rather than having to see the angry faces watching her. She considered running to Doc for comfort, then rejected the idea. Ginger was there, Ginger who'd crow with triumph and then probably hotfoot it back out to the cabin to see if she could take up where Ellie had left off.

Tanner would probably be glad to see her. Compared to her, Ginger's expertise would be a welcome alternative. Maybe she'd just been so impossibly inept the night before that he hadn't wanted to bother with her.

No, she couldn't go crying to Doc, even if Ginger wasn't there. There were some things you couldn't talk to a man about, even if he was one of your oldest friends.

There was Maude, of course, but she didn't want to

do that, either. Maude had looked so happy when they left. She had found herself a grandson, a link with the future, and Ellie didn't want anything to get in the way of that happiness.

When it came right down to it, there was no one she could turn to. She'd spent so many years being calm, being helpful, being there for people, that there was no one to do the same for her. All she could do was go home and crawl into bed, between the fancy sheets she'd put on for Tanner. Maybe she'd strip the bed and sleep on the bare mattress.

A low moan of pain startled her. It startled her even more to realize the sound had come from her own throat. *Almost home,* she promised herself.

There was no one in sight when she pulled Maude's old car into the driveway. No one to watch as she limped painfully up the back stairs and into her unlocked kitchen. Closing the door behind her, she carefully turned the key she'd found a few days ago. She moved through the house, locking every door, pulling down the shades, unplugging the telephone. Her gold-headed cane was resting at the foot of the stairs. She picked it up, feeling the smooth metal with a sense of soothing familiarity as slowly, carefully, she climbed the long dark flight of stairs.

CHAPTER EIGHTEEN

Just when things ought to have quieted down, just when tempers began to calm, word came of another incident. One of Charles Tanner's victims was buried in Helena, and someone had desecrated that grave, pouring red paint over the headstone. Nerves tightened further still, tension rose in the tiny town. And Ellie kept her cane with her at all times.

She didn't waste time wondering whether it was psychosomatic, whether she needed the cane, needed to limp when life seemed empty and desolate. All she knew was that the throb in her knee was a constant reminder, and the angry expressions on the townspeople's faces were fading, returning to looks of kindly commiseration as she limped around town, alone, and Tanner kept his distance.

Even Pete Forrester seemed to have mellowed. He'd said good-morning to her when he'd passed her on the street the day before, and even judgmental old Sally Richmond had managed a wintry smile. At first Ellie's reaction was a startled relief that managed to penetrate the numbness that surrounded her. And then she realized what had prompted the kindliness.

They'd decided she'd been a victim again, this time of

Charles Tanner's son. She'd been led astray, seduced and abandoned, and they were willing to fold her back into their collective arms and forgive her momentary weakness.

As long as she went back to being the martyr of Morey's Falls, she thought bitterly. As long as she was willing to stay alone in that dark old house, doing good deeds, keeping herself untouched after her fall from grace.

For the time being that was easy enough. She had no interest in having anyone touch her, anyone at all. But that would pass. Tanner would leave, and as soon as he was gone she'd pull herself together and get out, too. Right now it hurt too much to make plans. But as soon as he was gone, as soon as there was no danger of running into him in the empty streets of Morey's Falls, she'd get back to being her normal, resourceful self, and get her normal, resourceful self out of there.

At least the odd, eerie incidents had almost stopped. A few more animals had been found dead, one or two people reported a Peeping Tom lurking around, and the news about the grave in Helena that had caused a flurry of concern had quickly died down. As far as she knew, Tanner had done nothing to get people excited again. He spent a lot of time with Addie Pritchard, he spent a lot of time with Maude. Doc, the bearer of that information, had even allowed that Tanner had spent a lot of time with him. Though not, he added, with Ginger, who'd found herself a divorced man in Menton, two towns over, and spent most nights away.

Ellie didn't know whether to be glad or sorry. On the one hand she was fiercely, gloriously relieved that

Ginger hadn't done her bit to fill Tanner's empty bed. On the other hand, the sooner he was completely out of reach, the sooner she'd recover.

She awoke late on the morning of July third with a sense of impending doom. It was no different from any other morning in the past two weeks, since before Tanner even arrived she'd woken with the feeling that life was about to crash around her head. She lay there beneath her heavy cotton sheets, feeling the thick, humid air closing around her, dreading the days ahead. Next afternoon she'd have to unveil that monolith in the pocket-sized park, she'd have to say all the appropriate things and dress in semimourning like the professional widow she was. If she could just get through the next forty-eight hours, Tanner would be gone, and so would she.

She didn't really know why he still hung around. It certainly wasn't to see her. She'd had no more than a glimpse of him in the last two weeks, and she wished she hadn't even had that. She'd gone out to Maude's, to thank her for the loan of her car while her own had been repaired, and had seen Tanner in the distance, astride Shaitan. He'd been absolutely beautiful, more at home on the big black stallion than she could ever be. Man and horse were made for each other, and the knowledge was acid eating into her soul. She didn't go back to Maude's without calling first.

It was Maude who'd told her he'd be leaving the next day, Maude, her dark eyes bright with concern, her voluble mouth for once silent. Apparently Tanner had warned her, and Maude had listened. While her expression was compassionate, her words were matter-of-fact. Tanner was leaving, and he wouldn't be coming back.

Ellie dragged herself out of bed, rubbing abstractedly at her knee before reaching for her cane. What she needed after such a sleepless night was a strong cup of coffee, maybe two or three. And then she needed to keep busy, keep her mind running so fast that she wouldn't have time to stop to listen for his footsteps on her back porch, for that lazy drawl of his insinuating itself into her consciousness. Forty-eight hours and he'd be gone. Surely she could last that long without breaking down?

She glanced at her reflection in the mirror before she reached for her robe. She looked pale, but then, she hadn't been riding in days. She looked weary, but sleep had been hard to come by recently. She looked miserable, but that was to be expected. How else were you supposed to look when your heart was crushed and bleeding?

She made a face at her nightgown. She should have followed her instincts, should have thrown it away at Maude's. Instead she'd gone back there, just a week earlier, found the paper bag with the crumpled nightdress and brought it back home. She'd washed it, mended it, and with an obsessive manner she didn't care to examine too closely she wore it to bed every night, wrapping her arms around her narrow body, pretending it was Tanner holding her.

Common sense told her that there'd be other men. Kinder men, gentler men, men who were willing to accept the kind of love she could offer. She knew she'd find them. She just wasn't ready to believe it.

She belted the old flannel robe around her waist and

headed down the long dark flight of stairs. One more morning, she promised herself. One more morning she'd have to walk down those stairs, limp down the hallway and make her coffee in the vast empty kitchen. One more morning…

The kitchen wasn't empty. The coffee was made. Tanner was sitting there, a half-drunk cup of coffee by his side, reading the speech she'd written for the dedication.

She clutched the cane tightly in one hand, in the other she reached up and pulled the robe more closely around her. He looked up then, his blue eyes as handsome and as unfeeling as the blue sage that grew so abundantly around there, and she shivered.

"Still got the cane, Ellie?"

"What are you doing here, Tanner?" She limped into the kitchen, exaggerating her lameness, doing it deliberately. It got the reaction she wanted. His mouth tightened, whether in dismay or irritation, she couldn't be sure. It was enough to be able to affect him at all.

"I came to say goodbye."

She managed a credible look of surprise. "Are you leaving?"

He wasn't fooled. "Maude told you yesterday," he said flatly.

"Okay." She poured herself a cup of coffee. He made it too strong, but she'd gotten used to the taste of it black. She took a sip, keeping herself from shuddering, and surprised just the faintest trace of softening in those icy-blue eyes of his. "You've leaving," she agreed. "To quote you on one memorable occasion…goodbye." She opened the back door and stood there, waiting, one hand on the doorknob, the other balancing her coffee cup and the cane.

"Close the door, Ellie. I'm not leaving yet."

"You are if I have anything to say about it," she snapped.

"You don't. Close the door and sit down. I have to talk to you."

"You could have written a letter."

"Stop being a prima donna and get over here." He was getting riled now. It gave her an obscure pleasure. Maybe she could get even more reactions out of him if she tried. "If you don't come over here," he continued, "I'll come get you. The neighbors watched me drive in, they know I've been in the house since just after six, and I'll be more than happy to give them more to gossip about if you don't move. It would be a shame, wouldn't it, just when you've gotten back in their good graces?"

She slammed the door, and some of the hot coffee splashed down her front. It soaked into the flannel wrapper, going straight through and scalding her. She let out a little yelp of pain, and a moment later Tanner was there, pulling the sodden material away from her skin.

She batted at his hands, ineffectually, with the cane getting in her way. "Stop it, Ellie. You're just going to make it worse." He yanked off the old dressing gown and tossed it on the floor. And then his hands stopped in midair as he realized what she was wearing.

"Damn it, Ellie," he said, his voice unutterably weary. "What are you doing?"

"What do you mean?"

"Why are you wearing this?"

She pulled herself away from him, moving to the table and scooping up the sheets of yellow paper. "Let's just say it reminds me of something I'd better not forget again."

"And what's that?"

"Not to believe something merely because it's what I want to believe. Not to do something when I know it'll cause me nothing but pain. To think with my head and not my heart. All those nice sorts of things that most people learn in their adolescence. I guess I'm a slow learner, but I've made real strides the last couple of weeks." She started toward the hall.

"Come back here and sit down, Ellie!"

"You can't make me."

She'd forgotten how fast he could move. He caught her by the door, scooped her up and deposited her none too gently on the hard wooden chair. Then he took her cane, that twisted length of hickory, and brought it down across his knee. It broke, splintered, and he tossed it in one dark corner of the kitchen. "I can make you do anything I want," he said flatly, taking the other chair.

She could feel the color drain from her face. She didn't look at the broken remnants of her cane, she didn't look at the man opposite her. She looked down at her hands, clasped tightly in front of her. "I expect you're right," she said quietly. "What do you want, Tanner? You've said goodbye. What else is there?"

"I came to warn you."

She allowed herself a bitter grin. "Too late, Tanner. I've already been seduced and abandoned."

"I can stop that mouth of yours." The threat was lightly spoken and completely sexual. Ellie shut up.

He took his time, draining his cup of coffee, his long fingers fiddling with the thin china cup that had been part of Mrs. Lundquist's prize set. Ellie allowed herself a brief, surreptitious glance at him. If she looked pale and tired, he didn't look much better. His dark-blond hair was slicked back, still damp from however he'd managed to bathe, he hadn't shaved, and the lines in his tanned face seemed to have deepened, scoring deep grooves between his nose and mouth, over his forehead, around his eyes. He looked like a man on the edge, and Ellie had to wonder just what had put him there.

"All right," she said finally, when she thought all danger had passed. "Warn me. Though I don't see what there is to warn me about. The incidents have stopped. No more desecrated gravestones, no more dead animals."

"Pete Forrester's prize hunting dog was found this morning," he said flatly. "His wife saw someone dressed like me lurking around the barn last night when she got up during the night."

Ellie's reaction was a quick intake of breath. "How did you find this out so early?"

"Easy enough. I was on my way over here when Dave Martin stopped me. He was more than happy to tell me all the details, in exchange for my alibi."

"Did you have one?"

"I was alone at the cabin." Tanner shrugged. "There wasn't much either of us could do about that. Anyway, that's not the problem. The problem is, the incidents aren't over. Whoever is doing these things hasn't stopped."

"Maybe not," she said, fighting the urge to look over her shoulder.

"I want you to do me a favor."

"Don't count on it."

"I don't want you to give that speech tomorrow. I don't want you to show up at the dedication."

"Why not?"

"I can't get rid of the idea that something's going to happen then. That everything's been building up to a repeat of fifteen years ago."

She stared at him, aghast. "You certainly have some sick fantasies."

"It makes a twisted kind of sense, doesn't it? Someone's going around, repeating the same weird things my father did, right before he flipped out completely. I'm just afraid someone else is going the same route."

"Who?"

He hesitated, and she could see an emotion dance briefly across his face, one she might almost have called vulnerability. "I asked Doc whether he thought it could be me."

"I beg your pardon?"

He met her gaze. "I asked him whether I could be doing it all and not remembering."

"What did he say?"

"He said no."

Ellie let out her pent-up breath. "I'm glad to hear he's got more sense than you have. Of course you haven't been doing those things. It has to be someone else."

"There aren't any other strangers in town."

"True enough," Ellie said, her animosity and nerves fading. "So if what you think is true, then it has to be someone who grew up here. Who's been here all along, seemingly normal, while he or she got sicker and sicker." A sudden thought struck her. "Maybe it's me."

"This isn't a parlor game, Ellie," he snapped, disgusted.

She shivered in the warm kitchen. "It isn't something to joke about," she agreed, in a more subdued tone.

"No, it isn't. Particularly when a tragedy might be about to happen again."

"You don't know that. You haven't even come up with any possibilities as to who might be doing it."

He held his breath, visibly controlling his irritation. "I realize that. Just humor me, will you? Don't go to that dedication tomorrow."

"Why should I do one damned thing for you?"

"Because I don't want you to run the risk of being killed if some madman decides to take a gun to Morey's Falls again."

"Why not?"

He grimaced, shoving his chair back and standing up. "Call me a sentimental fool."

She didn't even flinch. "Why not?"

He was halfway to the door. He kept moving, pulling it open, letting the bright morning sunshine flood her gloomy kitchen. He looked back at her, his eyes bleak. "I'll let you guess."

"Where are you going to be?"

"Right now? Back at the cabin, I expect. Waiting for a lynch mob, maybe."

"They won't come get you. Most people in town are afraid of your father's place, Pete Forrester included. They think it's haunted."

"Maybe it is," he said.

"Are you going to the dedication?"

"Wouldn't miss it for the world." His voice was grim.

She met his gaze. "Then I'll see you there."

He started toward her. She could see the conflicting emotions wash across his face, emotions she didn't dare hope she was seeing. She'd hoped to goad him into touching her, into making some kind of commitment. There were things she could see, roiling beneath his controlled exterior, but she couldn't be certain if they were really there or whether it was just wishful thinking on her part.

He stopped before he reached her, and the seething emotions vanished once more, leaving him cool and distant. "Suit yourself," he said. And left without looking back.

She stared after him, controlling the urge to run to the window, to savor every fleeting glimpse of him. She felt more hopeful than she had in two weeks. He wasn't immune to her—far from it. No matter what he told her, no matter what he told himself. That was more than enough to keep her going.

Even if she wanted to she couldn't back out of going to the dedication. It was the last thing she was going to do for the town, the final gesture, and then she'd be free. If she didn't go through with it, she might always feel as though she owed them something.

As for Tanner's fears, they were disturbingly contagious. But common sense told her it couldn't happen again. Lightning didn't strike twice in the same place. The tiny town of Morey's Falls couldn't produce two mass murderers.

It was probably someone out to cause trouble.

Maybe mischievous teenagers out to spook people. Maybe Pete Forrester himself, trying to frame Tanner and drive him out of town. There were endless possibilities, none of them leading up to murder.

She took a shower and got dressed, feeling more optimistic than she had in days. Her car had been repaired and brought back to her in two days flat. *More's the pity,* she'd thought. She'd had the fleeting hope that it had been totaled, but the Buick lived on. She drove the few short blocks to town, parking it outside Lonnie's office. There was no sign of life in there, which was surprising. Lonnie was usually sitting there in the mornings, reading the Helena paper, drinking coffee, waiting for the news to come to him.

The park was deserted. The monolith was still covered with a canvas dropcloth, its ends secured with tent stakes. She knew what it looked like—a cross between a headstone and an obelisk, carved in depressing Vermont granite. All the names of Charles Tanner's victims were engraved on its rough sides. She'd refused to have her name listed as the sole survivor, and the town fathers had reluctantly agreed. After all, it was her money that was paying for the thing.

She walked slowly around the monument, trying to still the uneasy feeling that washed over her. When she got to the back she noticed that one of the tent stakes was loose. Someone must have gotten too curious, she thought, moving closer. As far as she was concerned the unveiling could wait till doomsday, but apparently someone else was more impatient. She was about to move on when she noticed the granite chips lying in the dirt.

She stood for a moment, hypnotized, afraid of what she might find. Slowly she moved closer, squatting down by the edge of the monument, ignoring the pain in her knee. With one shaking hand she lifted the corner of the tarp.

They were all there. Seventeen names, carved in granite. Sixteen of them neatly chiseled in Roman lettering. And there at the bottom, hacked into the stone so crudely that she could scarcely read it was one new name. Eleanor Johnson Lundquist.

CHAPTER NINETEEN

Ellie began to shake all over. She put out a hand to steady herself, then yanked it back as if it had been burned. The last thing she wanted to touch was that horrific monument.

She stood up, so swiftly that dizziness washed over her. She looked around, but there was no one in sight. No one at all, in the middle of a hot July day, which was strange in itself. She stumbled out of the park, getting tangled in her own feet in her haste to escape. She was heading blindly for her car when she heard voices.

Pete's Fireside Café was jammed with people. For once no one was looking out the windows into the empty streets; they were all turned intently to something inside the diner. The voices, angry, muffled, were coming from that building.

As surreptitiously as she could Ellie crossed the street and edged up to the building. She needn't have worried. No one even glanced on her direction.

Pete's diner was the real McCoy—a refurbished chrome railway car set up high. Ellie could press against the shiny metal and no one would see her unless they craned their necks outside the high windows that were open to the listless breeze. No one bothered.

"Things have gotten out of hand," Pete was saying

in his most blustery voice. "Are we going to sit around and let this happen again? Are we going to risk losing our loved ones, our wives and our babies and our parents, just because we were afraid to take a stand?"

There was a rousing chorus of "Hell, no!" and "No way!" A voice rang out, one Ellie couldn't quite place. "Now, Pete, I'm sure we all agree with you." Belatedly Ellie recognized Terry, the dentist's suavely reasonable tones. "But I for one am not about to go out Route 5 to smoke him out."

"No one's asking you to, Terry," Pete replied. "None of us need to. I sure as hell don't want to—that place gives me the spooks as much as it does anyone. He'll turn up, sooner or later, and when he does we'll do something about it."

"Like what?" This was Sally Richmond speaking.

"Like escort him out of town and make sure he's in no shape to come back. The man needs to be taught a lesson. We've suffered enough around here at the hands of the Tanners. We don't need any more of them hanging around, shooting our animals, desecrating our graveyards, messing with our women."

The chorus of angry voices rose again. "What about his grandma?" someone shouted out. "And what about Ellie?"

"Hell, Ellie would probably buy the rope," Pete chortled. "As for Maude, she's too far out of town to know anything till it's over. She didn't help that trashy daughter of hers—why should she help her grandson? No, there's no one who'll lift a finger to help him. We'll take care of him, all neat and clean, and there'll be no one to blame unless you blame all of us."

Ellie would probably buy the rope. The words echoed in her head, sick, horrifying words. Was the town she'd loved so far gone that they'd contemplate lynching? She had to get out of here, fast, and warn Tanner. He had to keep out of town, out of sight of these trigger-happy idiots.

She ran across the street to her car, no longer caring if anyone saw her. They were making too much noise to hear her engine start up, and if her tires squealed as she raced out of town she was beyond caring. All that mattered was to get to Tanner before he walked into a trap.

Dust swirled up behind her car as she sped down the rutted dirt road. She skidded a few times, regaining control at the last minute, and almost plowed into the derelict cabin at the end of the road.

He wasn't there. She ran through the cabin, calling him, but there was no answer. "Damn you, Tanner," she muttered desperately, heading out around the back. She raised her voice, calling for him, and started into the dense woods that surrounded the cabin.

She didn't get very far. The skin on the back of her neck began to prickle. She had the oddest feeling someone was watching her, someone who wished her harm. She hadn't had that feeling in days, but there it was back again. She stopped where she was, looking around her, looking back at the cabin through the trees.

It did feel haunted. She could understand why the big brave bullies of Morey's Falls didn't want to venture out there to get Tanner. She didn't know whether it was the ghosts of the massacred Native American tribe or the restless shade of Charles Tanner, Sr. All she knew was that she didn't want to be alone in those woods any longer.

She wouldn't let herself run. She could hear rustlings, the stirring of the wind in the leaves, except that there wasn't much wind. She could hear the snapping of twigs underfoot, except that she hadn't stepped on any twigs. She looked down and saw with dawning horror the shredded remnants of cigarette butts. And she knew with a certainty that they weren't Tanner's.

She did run then, tripping once on the uneven terrain and sprawling in the dirt before she got to her feet and ran once more. She listened for sounds of pursuit, but her heart was pounding so loudly in her chest that she could hear nothing but the noise of her own fear. There was no one in sight when she jumped in her car and slammed and locked the door. She sat for long moments, listening to her breath come in heavy gasps, listening to her heart jerk against her rib cage. And then she turned the key and headed off to find Tanner.

She drove by Doc Barlow's house first. There was no sign of Maude's ancient car, but for a moment Ellie was tempted to stop. If anyone could talk sense into the townspeople, Doc could. Pete might listen if Doc were doing the talking.

She was about to pull over when she saw a flash of hot pink by the side door. Ginger was standing there, looking out, her face in a weary pout, her blond curls limp. She looked straight at Ellie, her face disconsolate.

Without conscious thought Ellie pressed down harder on the accelerator, tearing off into the hot afternoon. At that point she simply couldn't face Ginger,

face the self-satisfied smirk that had settled on her face
the moment Tanner had dropped her.

Besides, she couldn't afford to waste any more time.
Tanner had to be out at Maude's. She could call Doc
from there, see if he could do anything about the
madness in town. In the meantime, the safest place for
Tanner was back out Route 5. There might be ghosts
out there, but at least none of them came equipped with
a length of rope or a rifle.

But Maude hadn't seen him all day. It was getting
on toward midafternoon by then, and even though Ellie
tried to disguise the panic in her voice, Maude's eyes
darkened and her seamed face creased in worry. "You
don't think he's in trouble, do you?" she asked, standing
on her front porch and peering out over her empty acres.

"Tanner was born in trouble," Ellie said flatly. "The
townspeople, Pete Forrester in particular, are getting
riled up. I wanted to warn him to keep out of their way.
He's leaving tomorrow—all he has to do is lay low until
then."

"Did he come to say goodbye?"

Ellie felt a knife of pain spear through her. "Did you
tell him to?"

"I didn't dare. I didn't need to, either, did I?" Maude
looked obscurely pleased. "What did he say?"

"Goodbye," Ellie said flatly. "He said goodbye,
Maude." She turned back to her car. "If he shows up,
tell him what I said."

"Where are you going now?"

Home, she wanted to say. She wanted to go back to
the old house, pull down the shades and climb into
bed. Her head was throbbing, her knee was aching, and

fear was a dry taste in her mouth. "I'm going to keep looking for him."

Maude nodded. "Call me if you don't find him."

"Call me if you do."

She drove back through town, slowly, her eyes so intent that they felt dry and stinging. No sign of Maude's big black car anywhere. The crowd at Pete's had moved their field of operations to Bernie's Bar and Grill, and the noise spilling from the open door in mid-afternoon was mixed with music. It was turning into a social event, the kind Morey's Falls saw too seldom. *Typical of them to arrange it around violence to an innocent man,* Ellie thought with a twist of her mouth.

Even the *Gazette* was still deserted. She couldn't quite picture Lonnie in the midst of all that violent fantasizing, but maybe he was there for a story, rather than to participate in their vigilantism. Whatever it was, it no longer mattered. Not since he'd been part of the crowd that had cornered her in Davidson's Market, not since she'd looked into the pale-blue eyes and seen a stranger there.

She'd considered taking Shaitan and heading back up to their secluded mountain meadow, but had dismissed the idea the moment she'd had it. For one thing, she didn't think she could bear to ride up there again. For another, if he was there, he was safe.

Besides, where was Maude's car? Maybe she'd just missed him, maybe while she'd been avoiding the main streets of town he'd breezed right through, and the incipient mob hadn't even noticed.

She turned back toward Route 5, hoping and praying he'd returned. But there was no car at the cabin, and this time she didn't even bother to get out. She just skidded into reverse and tore back down the narrow road. Where in the world could he be?

She was halfway back to town when she thought of the graveyard. She had no idea whether he'd ever made it out there, but if he was saying his goodbyes it made sense that he'd say it to his father.

The Morey's Falls cemetery was on a rolling hill at the east end of town, well beyond the town limits. It had been started in the days when the founding fathers were a little more optimistic about the future of their fair town. It made quite a trek every Sunday, when Ellie and half the town carried flowers out to the victims. She hadn't gone the previous week. She told people she couldn't face the telltale signs of the red paint that had been dumped over the headstones, but she lied. What she couldn't face was one more ceremony devoted to the massacre.

The long, straight roads were empty as she drove out to the graveyard. She'd hoped she'd never have to see the place again. *One last time,* she promised herself grimly. One more visit to the place where she'd spent far too much of the last fifteen years, and then she'd never have to come back.

She saw the recognizable shape of Maude's car from a distance, parked alongside the rusting iron fence that kept cattle and varmints from rooting among the graves. As she pulled up she spotted Tanner, right where she thought she'd find him, standing in the deserted corner where his father was buried.

"What do you want?" he asked. It was an unpromising opening as she ran to the iron fence. He hadn't moved, and the afternoon shadows made his face unreadable.

She looked across the distance at Charles Tanner's grave, frowning. It was covered with a blanket of plastic flowers, the faded colors still garish in the sun. She allowed herself a brief glance around the crowded graveyard. There were no flowers, no flags on any of the other graves, when she knew for a fact that Pete Forrester bought a new plastic memorial for his daughter every month, and Sally Richmond made sure her veteran husband's grave always had an American flag beside it. The red paint still shone faintly on the tombstones, like blood that couldn't be washed away.

She turned back to Tanner. There were flags heaped on top of the flowers, every flag in the place. She knew better than to ask him if he'd been the one to rearrange the cemetery ornaments.

"Has this happened before?" Her voice came out strangled, and she had to repeat her question.

"Every time I've been here. I put them back, haphazard, but they're always back on my father's grave." His voice was distant, abstracted, and Ellie's heart twisted inside her.

"Come out of there, Tanner," she said, soft enough to be persuasive, loud enough to be heard.

"Why?"

"I think Pete Forrester's getting together what looks unpleasantly like a lynch mob. At best you can hope for tar and feathers, and the only place you'll be safe is out at the cabin. They're still afraid of ghosts—they plan to wait until you come back into town."

He was walking toward her, and she didn't like the expression on his face. It was half defiance, half determination. He was looking for a fight. "Why keep them waiting?"

"Damn it, Tanner, don't do this! If you don't care about yourself, think about them! They've suffered enough. How will they survive if your death is on their hands?"

"I don't intend to let them kill me." He stopped a few yards away. "Is that why you came looking for me? One more act as Saint Ellie, protecting your townspeople?"

"I don't want any more killing," she said hopelessly.

"I don't think you have anything to say in the matter. Nor, I expect, does most of your lynch mob. But someone around here wants more killing, and unless we find out who does, we're going to be powerless to stop it."

"You won't stop it by walking into a trap."

"Who are you worried about, Ellie? Them or me?"

"You think it's a difficult choice?" she cried. "They've loved and protected me for years. All you've done is hurt me."

"They've kept you a cloistered martyr for years," he said ruthlessly. "I brought you alive. Them or me, Ellie?"

It was no choice at all. "You, damn it. It's you I'm worried about."

A slow grin began to chase the shadows from his face. "In that case," he said, moving closer, "I'll go back to the cabin. If you'll…"

She felt it before she heard the sound. A stinging sensation in her upper arm, as if the world's biggest horsefly had chosen to take a chunk out of her. A moment later she heard the whine, the *thwuppp* and *chink* as a piece of granite flew off a headstone in front of her.

She looked down at her arm. No horsefly could bite her through the flannel shirt, but the cotton was torn, and she was bleeding. She looked over at Tanner in dismay.

"I think," she said faintly, "somebody's shot me."

TANNER DOUBTED he'd ever moved as fast in his entire life. He crossed the last few yards of cemetery, vaulted the iron fence and had her flat on the ground well before the second shot rang out. He cradled her head beneath his arm, forcing her down, covering her as he listened for the third shot.

It didn't come. He heard the noise of a car starting up, the screech of tires as it raced away, but he didn't dare move. He just lay there, his arms around her slender body, listening.

It was long minutes before he dared move. He would have waited longer still, but he had no idea how badly Ellie was hurt, and he didn't dare put off checking on it any longer.

He sat up quickly, peering around him. No one in sight, but that was no guarantee of safety. He hadn't noticed the third car earlier. Someone must have followed Ellie out there, and the two of them had been too intent on arguing to notice.

It was the kind of mistake they couldn't afford to make. He looked down at Ellie. It didn't look like much more than a graze, despite the generous amounts of blood soaking into her sleeve, but her face was dead white and her eyes were wide with shock.

"Can you make it to the car?" He had to repeat the question before she acknowledged that she heard and managed a faint nod. A moment later he was up, pulling her with him as they raced across the flat ground to the car.

She tripped once, her knee giving way beneath her, but was up again a second later. He shoved her into Maude's old car, dived after her, and had the aging vehicle on the road in seconds flat. They sped off in a cloud of dust that obscured Ellie's abandoned car, and headed back toward the outskirts of town, back toward the cabin.

He knew he shouldn't risk it. But he had to know, had to be certain. She was sitting huddled against the side of the car, clutching her arm, barely moving, but the bleeding seemed to have slowed. "Where was this lynch mob being formed?"

Her voice was slow, almost sleepy. "At the diner," she mumbled. "And at the bar."

"Typical." Before he could have second thoughts he turned the car into town, waiting for her protests, waiting for her to lash out at him. She said nothing, huddling deeper into the car seat.

The crowds were still going strong in the center of town. There were more cars parked there than he'd seen in the time he'd been in town, and the noise from the bar spilled out into the street. Obviously they were still in the planning stages.

A deep sense of satisfaction began to spread over him as he turned the car and headed back out toward the cabin. No one even noticed Maude's car and her renegade grandson—they were too busy getting worked up and liquored up to realize their quarry was in their midst.

He knew he should take her to Doc's and have a professional look at the bullet graze, but he didn't dare. Finally he had proof that someone, not his own subconscious, twisted self, was out to kill and maim. Ellie had proof in her bleeding arm, and it wasn't that pathetic semimob in town.

But he couldn't be certain that that someone wasn't Doc. At that point there was no one he could trust, not with his life, not with Ellie's. He'd have to count on his own considerable experience with first aid to handle her wound. He only hoped and prayed it was as slight as it appeared to be.

It seemed to take forever to get out to the end of Route 5. He kept glancing over at Ellie, terrified that she might slip into unconsciousness, that the wound might be far worse than he expected. But she kept herself upright, holding her arm tightly, staring sightlessly ahead. The bleeding had just about stopped, and he'd seen the granite fly off the headstone, so he knew the bullet wasn't lodged somewhere in her arm.

He skidded to a stop outside the cabin, jumped out of the car and raced around to her side. She just sat there, unmoving, passive, as he gently touched her arm.

He moved her hand away, pulling at the torn cloth, and then sighed with relief. As he'd expected, it was no more than a graze, not even that deep. The bleeding had about stopped—all he had to do was wash it clean and bandage it and it should be fine.

"It's okay, Ellie," he said gently. "It's only a scratch. We'll clean it up and you'll be all right." He put his arms around her, planning to lift her out of the car and carry her into the cabin.

That was when she started screaming.

CHAPTER TWENTY

The sound of Ellie's screams was a hideous, grating noise in the afternoon stillness. She was beating at him, flailing with her arms, trying to push him away, her eyes were black pits of despair, and her mouth was open in a desperate, endless cry of horror that erased time and memory.

He tried to capture her arms, to hold her close, but in her panic she was too strong. Her arm started bleeding again, soaking through the torn shirt, and she tried to break free of his restraining hands, slapping and clawing at him, her breath rasping in her lungs. She was like a wild animal, and he knew if she could she'd break away and run into the woods surrounding the cabin, run until she dropped, and it could take precious hours to find her if she did.

Tanner shook her, and she looked up at him, her eyes wide and unseeing. He realized that she had gone back fifteen years, reliving the horror of the massacre that she'd effectively blocked out, and all he wanted to do was to put his arms around her and wipe it out again.

But she wouldn't let him. She kicked at him, slapped at him, screaming and desperate, and he had no choice. She was going to hurt herself if she kept it up, and the longer she struggled the more she bled.

He slapped her across the face, only hard enough to shock her. The screams stopped abruptly, her eyes focused on him, and a vast shudder washed over her body. And then she collapsed against him, limp, weeping, clinging to him as if he were her only link with sanity.

This time when he scooped her up she didn't struggle. He carried her into the cabin, setting her down on the narrow cot, and when he tried to move away, to get the first aid kit he always hiked with, she wouldn't let him go.

"No," she whispered, her voice raw and strained. "Don't leave me."

"I've got to take care of your arm, love," he said gently.

She shook her head. "Don't leave me." And she pulled him down beside her on the narrow cot, burrowing against him like a tiny animal seeking shelter.

But it wasn't shelter she was seeking. Her hands were on the buttons of his shirt, pulling it apart, and then on his skin. Her legs were entwined with his, her hips pressed up against him, and he could feel his arousal growing. He told himself he was an animal, but it didn't stop his response. Suddenly he wanted her, more than he'd ever wanted anyone, he wanted to bury himself in her soft, willing body, wanted to lose himself in her, to wash away the death and horror and pain. He wanted her eyes glazed and focusing on him alone, not on some remembered tragedy. He wanted life, not death.

"Ellie," he said hoarsely, lifting his head, trying to pull away, to regain the last tiny shreds of self-control. He couldn't do this to her.

She put her hand up to his face. It was shaking, and there was blood on her fingertips. She pulled his head down to hers, and her mouth was waiting. And her choice was life, not death.

He tore at her clothes and she helped him, raising her hips so he could slide down her jeans and underwear and throw them across the room, lifting her head so he could pull off the bloody shirt and send it flying after her other clothes. Her own hands were just as eager, just as desperate, fumbling with the zipper on his jeans, digging into his shoulders as she pulled him over her, on top of her, into her, wrapping her legs around him and holding him tight.

No sooner had he slid into that delicious warmth when more shudders of reaction began to wash over her. He held himself still, reveling in her helpless response, and then he thrust deep, joining her in a white-hot blaze of heat that burned the past to ashes.

It wasn't long before sanity and second thoughts set in. He lifted his head, guilt and dismay sweeping over him. Her eyes were closed, and the faint purple shadows surrounding them gave her a bruised look. Her mouth was soft, swollen, pale, and her face was blotchy with tears.

"Ellie," he said miserably. "God, I'm sorry…"

Her eyes opened, her wonderful warm brown eyes, and they were shining up at him. She slid her hands up his back, under the shirt he still wore, and her mouth curved in a soft, tremulous smile. "Thank you," she whispered.

"'Thank you'?" he echoed. "Ellie, I should never have…your arm…"

"Thank you," she said again. She reached up, touching her mouth to his. And slowly, carefully, he deepened the kiss, until he felt the seeds of passion begin stirring within him, still within her, and felt her own rekindled response.

It was almost dark before he got around to fixing her arm. They were both weak, giddy, almost light-headed with exhaustion and relief. She sat on the side of the cot, wearing only his oversize white cotton T-shirt, and watched him attend to her wound.

"Do you know what this means?" he said, daubing her arm generously with hydrogen peroxide. She didn't even flinch.

"You aren't through with me after all?" she suggested brightly. "Ouch...don't be so rough."

"Don't be sassy," he grumbled. "It means that there really is someone out there. Your little vigilante gang was still intact—it wasn't one of them. It had to be the same person who's been playing his nasty little games with everyone in town. Which means I'm not crazy or paranoid or guilty."

"I never thought you were."

"You were a majority of one," he said flatly, surveying her graze with a professional eye. "We ought to get this looked at."

"Why?" She craned her neck to peer at the angry wound. He watched her swallow once, just managing to keep her hard-won self-control intact. "You said yourself it wasn't much more than a scrape."

"Gunshot wounds are tricky things."

"Then why don't we go see Doc? Why didn't we go straight there from the graveyard?"

He didn't answer, just busied himself wrapping gauze around her upper arm.

"You couldn't," she said quietly. "You couldn't believe Doc would be behind this?"

"He's a logical choice." Tanner still didn't meet her gaze. "He was my father's best friend, he was overseas with him, was affected by a lot of the same things, both good and bad."

"But why would he want to kill you?"

"Who says he did?"

"He shot at you."

"I don't think so, Ellie," he said gently. "It was *your* car that had the brakes tampered with. I think whoever it was, was shooting at *you*."

She sat utterly still for a moment. The cabin was warm, but a shiver ran over her body, and she tugged uselessly at the hem of the oversize shirt.

"My name," she said tonelessly. "Someone carved my name in the monument at the bottom of the list of victims."

He stared at her in shock. "When was this?"

"I found it this morning."

"What the hell were you doing in the park this morning?"

"Trying to make up my mind whether I could miss the memorial service after all."

"What did you decide?"

"I don't know." She looked up at him, her brown gaze calm. "Make me an offer I can't refuse."

He stared at her, wanting to pull her back into his arms, wanting to offer her everything. But he had nothing worth giving her, nothing but a lifetime of memories and a past that wouldn't let him go.

He stood up and moved away, packing the gauze and peroxide back in their compact container, ignoring the shadow that darkened her eyes. "For that matter I don't really think it's Doc. But I didn't feel I could take any chances. It wasn't just my life I was dealing with if I was wrong."

"Doc wouldn't hurt me," she said with calm assurance.

"And I would?" He didn't know what made him say it, but say it he did.

"Of course. You already have. You wouldn't want to, but you can't help it."

"Why can't I help it?" he demanded, leaning back against the table and watching her. She should have looked small and defenseless sitting there in his oversize T-shirt. He could see the faint line of scar tissue running up her bare leg, he could see her small, soft breasts through the thin cotton. Her chestnut hair was a witch's tangle around her narrow, freckled face, but her eyes were calm and her soft mouth curved in a rueful smile.

"You can't help it," she said quietly, "because I love you and you don't love me. And when situations like that exist, people are bound to get hurt."

He moved so fast that he didn't have time to think about what he was doing. He squatted down in front of her, gripping her arms tightly, noting her momentary grimace of pain and ignoring it. "What the hell do you expect from me?" he demanded in a low, harsh voice. "Do you want me to deny it, to get down on one knee and promise to love you forever?"

She smiled faintly. "Yes."

"Knowing who I am, knowing that I've hurt you

already, knowing that I'm entirely capable of walking away when the going gets rough?"

"Yes."

He took a deep, shuddering breath. "Knowing that my father's madness might hit me later on, that I might suddenly take a gun and wipe out everyone in sight?"

"That wouldn't happen."

"There are no guarantees in this life. Knowing that it could be hereditary, you still want me to tell you I love you?"

"Yes."

He sat back on his heels and stared at her. "Your children would be Charles Tanner's grandchildren."

"They'd learn to live with it. With parents like us they'd have to be tough," she said.

"You're serious, aren't you?" he demanded. His hands were no longer gripping her arms, they were gentle, caressing, soothing.

"Completely," she said. "But you won't have me, will you?"

"Honey, I'm a fool," he said softly. "But I'm not that big a fool." He dropped one knee on the scarred wood floor. "I'll take anything you want to give me, and I'll love you forever."

For a moment she didn't move. She just stared at him, hope and disbelief dancing across her face. And then she put her hands on either side of his face, and her fingers were cool and trembling. "Do you mean it?"

"I'm a lot of things, Ellie. But I'm not a liar. I mean it." He took a deep breath. "The best thing I could do for you would be to walk out of town and never look back. But I guess I'm just too selfish for that. Two weeks ago I might have been able to go without you. Not now."

"Oh, Tanner," she said softly, "be selfish. Take me with you. Take me." And she melted against him, tears running down her face, her mouth damp and trembling against his as he pulled her into his arms.

THERE WERE no watchers that night. Ellie didn't know why she was so certain, but as she alternately slept and woke in Tanner's arms she knew that no eyes were peering in the empty windows, no cigarettes were being furtively smoked and crumpled out in the scrubby woods beyond the cabin.

She woke to the smell of frying bacon and coffee. She had a thin cotton blanket wrapped around her and nothing else, and she felt aching, bruised and absolutely glorious.

"How do you like your eggs?" Tanner was standing over the camp stove, wearing jeans and nothing more, and water glistened in this thick blond hair and on his tanned, muscled chest.

Ellie sighed luxuriously. "Cooked. What I'd rather have is a bath."

"There's a dammed-up pool to the left of the cabin. Be my guest." He went back to humming softly under his breath as he deftly turned the bacon.

She pulled herself out of bed, her muscles groaning in protest, and wrapped the blanket around her. She edged over to him, leaning against his back, pressing against him. "I don't suppose I can talk you into joining me?"

He turned, sliding his arms around her, sliding the blanket around them both. "You're insatiable, woman," he muttered, kissing her, a slow, deep, possessive kiss. "But I've got bacon to fry and coffee to make, and if I join you in the water we'll never make it out of here."

"Where are we going?"

"New Mexico." There was the hint of a question in his voice, but Ellie merely smiled.

"Sounds good to me. Can we make it to the Montana border before the memorial service starts?"

"If you stop dawdling," he said, giving her a gentle shove.

Ellie didn't take long at all. For one thing, the water was icy cold, still chilled by the spring runoff higher up in the mountains. For another, the smell of bacon and coffee was too enticing to bear. If she'd had any hope that Tanner would give in and join her she would have waited, but the water was too cold and Tanner was too stubborn. Maybe the mountains of New Mexico would have warmer ponds.

It was lucky she'd wrapped the blanket back around her chilled, wet body. It would have been luckier still if she'd thought to take her abandoned clothes with her. They were probably still strewn all over the floor of the cabin where Tanner had tossed them. Doc's pickup truck was now parked next to Maude's old car, and some kindly soul had also driven back her own Buick. That meant two drivers, two people intruding in their all-too-brief idyll.

There was no help for it. She tossed one corner of the blanket over her shoulder, wearing it like a toga, shoved her damp hair back from her face, and walked in the door.

Tanner had that wary look on his face that she'd seen too often. She could guess what Doc had been telling him, urging him to let her go, and for a moment she was terribly afraid that Tanner might have listened.

He heard her, though she'd scarcely made a sound, and he raised his head, his eyes meeting hers. And then he smiled, a clean, beautiful smile, and Ellie's fears left her.

"My, my," Ginger said from her perch on Tanner's narrow bed. "Don't you look different!"

"They brought your car back," Tanner said unnecessarily, his voice giving nothing away as he handed her a cup of coffee. She took a grateful sip of it, controlling the urge to spit it out again. The first thing she'd do when they got to New Mexico was to teach him to make a decent cup of coffee.

"That was very kind of you," she said, shifting the blanket higher. Her clothes were still strewn all over the floor, and she waited for the familiar blush to stain her cheeks. It didn't come, and that small triumph strengthened her.

"That's not all," Doc said uneasily, looking from Tanner to Ellie. "There was more trouble last night."

"What was it this time?" Resignation and fear echoed in her voice.

"Blood," Ginger said succinctly. "Blood on people's porches when they got up this morning. Everyone who had kin murdered by this man's father had a nasty little calling card."

"It was probably cattle blood," Doc said hastily. "Dave Martin's looking into it."

"Well, then, there's nothing to worry about," Tanner said cynically. "If Morey's Falls's finest is on the case then everything's well in hand."

"Shut up, Tanner," Ellie said calmly.

"Did you still want a ride to the ceremony this afternoon, Ellie?" Doc asked. He was trying to keep disapproval out of his voice, but Ellie had known him too well and too long not to see that she'd shocked him. The knowledge saddened her, but not enough to make her regret one moment.

"I'm not going," she said quietly, wishing she could spare him, knowing she couldn't.

"Not going? Ellie, everyone's counting on you," he protested. "You know how important you are to this town, you know what you mean to everyone."

"She's not going," Tanner said. "She knows what she means to this town, and it's too much."

"I don't think I'd be wanted, Doc." She kept her voice gentle, placating.

"Because of Tanner?"

"And because of me. I just help them live in the past. They have to learn to look forward, Doc. You know that as well as I do."

Doc's face creased in frustration, and he felt in his breast pocket for the cigarettes he no longer carried. He looked toward Tanner for a moment, then back again. It was clear he wasn't going to ask Tanner for one blessed thing.

"Can we talk, Ellie?" he asked in deep concern.

"We're talking."

"I mean alone."

"No," she said.

"Yes," Tanner said at the same time.

"But I don't want…" Ellie protested.

Tanner had already pulled her to one side. "Don't you trust yourself?" he asked in an undertone.

"Of course."

"Then let them try to talk you out of it," he said. "I have to go return Maude's car and say goodbye to her. And we'll need to make arrangements for the horses. Why don't you meet me out there in about an hour? That should give them long enough to make you see reason."

"I'm not a reasonable person," she said stubbornly.

He grinned. "Don't I know it?" Leaning down, he brushed his mouth against hers, pulling back when she would have deepened the kiss. "One hour," he said, grabbing his shirt and heading for the door. He didn't say a word to his unwelcome visitors.

She stood there, listening to the sound of the car as he drove it away, and then she drained her cup of coffee. She'd known Doc and Ginger all her life, and she was about to do something they'd never forgive. But if she didn't, she'd never forgive herself. She'd lived the last fifteen years for other people—now it was time to live for herself.

With matter-of-fact grace she began to pick up her discarded clothes from the cabin floor. "Go ahead," she said. "I'll listen."

"Ellie, do you have any idea what you're doing?" Doc demanded, his voice harsh with repressed emotion. "What the hell is going on with you two?"

A small, secret smile lit Ellie's face. "You're too young to know, Doc."

He waved his hand in a gesture of disgust. "Ellie, he's no good for you. He won't offer you any future. In another few days, a few weeks at the most, he'll be gone, and you'll be left with the people you turned your back on."

"He's leaving today," Ellie said. "And I'm going with him."

She'd never realized how old Doc was until that moment. His face was gray, ashen, his features sunken, the leathery skin sagging. He looked old and tired and beaten, and a small, loving voice inside Ellie cried out in pain for him and for all he'd been and done for her.

He simply looked at her. "I guess it's settled then," he said finally. "You're not going to listen to common sense."

"No, I'm not. I've been sensible for more than thirty years, and that's more than enough for one lifetime. I'm going to do something foolish, and I bet it's going to turn out to be the smartest thing I've ever done."

"Don't count on it," Ginger drawled, still sprawled on the bed. "What do you two know about each other? Not a damned thing. Take it from an expert—hormones can only carry you so far before reality sets in and you find you're trapped."

Beneath Ginger's cynicism and jealousy Ellie could detect the hidden stirrings of real concern, and she made a final attempt to explain. "Sometimes you've got to trust your instincts, Ginger. I know this is right. There are too many things against it for it to be anything but right."

"What about Tanner?"

Ellie couldn't help the wistful smile that lit her face. "I think he's been around long enough to know what he wants. God bless him, he wants me."

The two Barlows didn't move for a long moment. Then Ginger rose, slowly, languidly crossing the room until she stood by Ellie. Suddenly she put her arms around Ellie's smaller figure, hugging her tightly. "Then take care of each other," she muttered. "And tell him if he hurts you I'll kill him."

As quickly as the moment came, it passed. She pushed Ellie away and strode out of the cabin. "I'll be waiting in the truck," she called over her shoulder.

Doc nodded absently. His eyes were so weary, so sad. "You're sure you know what you're doing, Ellie? You've meant so much to me." For some reason his voice stumbled over the words. "I hate to see you ruining your life."

Ellie nodded. "I'm not ruining it, Doc. I'm saving it."

There were no last-minute hugs from Doc. He just stood there, halfway across the room, resignation and something else in his body. "I'll tell them at the memorial service."

"Tell them I've gone with Tanner, Doc. Don't let them have any illusions."

"I'll tell them. You're not doing this as an act of rebellion…?" At Ellie's dreamy smile his words trailed off. "No, I suppose you're not."

"Be careful, Doc," she said.

"Of what?"

"I don't know," she said. The sheet was covering her bandaged arm, and only for a moment did she consider showing it to him. Tanner was right, they couldn't trust anyone. There was something about Doc she didn't understand, hadn't recognized before. She didn't think it was violence or anger, it seemed to be composed more of sorrow and disappointment, but she couldn't be sure. "Just watch out. Tanner hasn't been behind the incidents that have been plaguing Morey's Falls."

"Which means that someone else has?"

Ellie nodded. "Just keep your eye out, okay?"

The gaze behind the horn-rimmed glasses looked back into the hazy, blood-soaked past, and a shudder of remembrance shook his body. "I'll watch," he promised. "Goodbye, Ellie. God bless you."

"Aren't you going to kiss me goodbye?" she cried forlornly.

A smile crept beneath Doc's thick mustache as he shook his head. "Nope. Ask Tanner why not. Maybe he'll tell you."

And without another word he was gone.

Ellie stood in the center of the room and listened to the old pickup truck lumber off down the road. With an economy of motion she pulled on her clothes, ignoring the pain in her arm, ignoring the stiffness in her knee. If she hurried she'd have time to straighten everything up before she went to get Tanner. The first thing she'd do would be to pour out that hideous coffee, maybe even ditch the battered coffee pot that made such a bitter brew.

She didn't hear the sound of the car, but then, BMWs ran very quietly. She didn't hear the footsteps on the grass, but then, the stalker was used to moving silently. She didn't hear anything until the horrifying, familiar telltale click of the gun behind her.

She shut her eyes tightly, willing it to be a dream. But she knew it wasn't. She could feel the presence behind her, the eyes that had watched her, the creature that had hidden beneath windows and waited. Slowly she turned and looked into Lonnie Olafson's mad blue eyes.

CHAPTER TWENTY-ONE

Everything inside her crystallized into icy fear as she stared into the eyes of the man she'd once thought she might be able to love. He was wearing an old army uniform. The weapon in his hand was just as old. She didn't know much about guns; she'd deliberately avoided all knowledge of them, but even in her ignorance she recognized what was probably the same type of rifle Charles Tanner had used. She shut her eyes for a brief moment. She didn't want to die. She wanted to live, with Tanner. She didn't want to repeat the nightmare that had haunted her for fifteen years. She'd survived the first time—she doubted she'd be lucky enough to make it the second time around.

She opened her eyes, forcing a gentle smile to her stiff face. "Hi, Lonnie," she said softly.

"Hi, Ellie." His voice was the same, slightly high-pitched, but his eyes were blinking rapidly behind the clear-rimmed glasses, and the gun trembled imperceptibly in his hands. "Where's he gone to?"

She didn't waste time asking who. "Tanner's gone to Addie's for cigarettes," she said. "He'll be right back."

"You're lying, Ellie." His voice was sorrowful.

"Tanner stopped smoking two weeks ago. After he spent the night with you up on the mountain. He wouldn't have gone for cigarettes."

"But he wasn't seeing me for two weeks, either. I think I bring out the smoker in him." She was still holding the pot of coffee. If she threw it at him the hot liquid might scald him enough to make him drop the gun. It would give her a running chance to get to her car.

"Put the coffee down, Ellie," he said. "I'm not ready to shoot you yet, but I won't be picky if you don't do as I say. And don't bother thinking about running. I've gotten very good with a rifle in the last few years. People don't realize, they think I'm just Poor Lonnie, who can never do anything right. They don't know I've been practicing, for hours and hours. I can hit anything I want."

She took a deep breath and set the coffee pot down. "So why did you miss yesterday?"

He didn't bother to deny it. "I didn't want to kill you. I wanted to warn you, to give you one last chance to get away from him."

"When did you carve my name on the monument?"

He laughed, the sound soft and eerily familiar in the quiet morning air. This was Lonnie, whom she'd laughed with, joked with, grown up with, almost made love with. This was Poor Lonnie, poor mad Lonnie, and she was going to die.

"I did that more than a week ago. I wondered how long it was going to take you to find it. I was afraid you were going to miss it entirely."

"I would have seen it today when they unveiled the monument," she said.

He laughed again. "No, I don't think so. Of course, I haven't made up my mind, but I don't think I'll wait for the unveiling."

"Wait for what, Lonnie?" But she already knew the answer.

"To take my place in history," he said simply. "I'm not going to be Poor Lonnie anymore. I've watched, you know. I've watched all these years, when the most important person in this town was Charles Tanner. In a few short minutes he changed the lives of everyone around here. He'll never be forgotten. They still bring him up on the national news whenever there's a new killing. People don't forget, they sit up and take notice."

"Yes, they do," she said carefully. She was close enough to the coffee pot to grab it again. Tanner hadn't been gone more than forty-five minutes. He wouldn't start to worry for at least half an hour, maybe more. He wouldn't come in time to save her, but at least he wouldn't walk into a trap.

"Even Tanner," he continued, his voice aggrieved. "Do you think anyone would have paid any attention to him if it weren't for his father? He'd be wandering around here, being Poor Tanner, if it weren't for what his father did."

"Do you really think so?" She meant to keep the question light, to keep him talking, but his eyes narrowed and the gun swung angrily in her direction.

"I suppose you think it's because he's something special. All the women in town are panting after him. Even you couldn't wait. You had to soil your body with filth like him, when you'd been keeping yourself for me. I know you had. You would have been mine, too, years ago, if I hadn't changed my mind and decided to wait."

That wasn't the way Ellie remembered that embarrassing night. She remembered Lonnie's tears, his vain attempts, and sorrow swept through her.

"I'm sorry, Lonnie," she said gently.

"You're no better than the rest of them. You're trash, falling for a no-good drifter like Tanner, for the son of a killer…."

"I thought you admired Charles Tanner," she interrupted him, no longer able to bear the hideous words that were tumbling from his mouth. "I thought you wanted to be like him."

"I'm going to make Charles Tanner look like an amateur. When I'm finished everyone in this country will remember the name of Lonnie Olafson."

"I think they will anyway, Lonnie. You don't have to kill anyone to do it." Her voice was eminently reasonable, but Lonnie was beyond reason.

"You don't understand!" he cried, and he sounded like a petulant teenager. "I told you, I have to do it. And you're the first. I want you to move away from the stove."

"Why? You can shoot me here as well as anywhere," she said calmly.

"I don't want to. I think I want to tie you to the chair and shoot you then," he said, his voice dreamy. "Yes, that's what I want to do. When I'm finished with you I'll go on into town and wait for the ceremony to begin." He gestured with the rifle. "The chair, Ellie. I'm getting impatient."

She moved, slowly, so as not to alarm him, and sat down on the rickety seat. He set the gun down, and once more she considered trying to run for it. He followed her gaze, and giggled.

"Don't bother, Ellie. I took the keys to your car, and I'm a good shot. I don't want to shoot you in the back, but I will if I have to. Sit still and let me tie you."

She tried to struggle, but Lonnie, weak, useless Lonnie who'd never done a day's worth of manual labor in his life, was far too strong. The ropes cut into her wrists and ankles, and she was trapped, helpless.

"Now," said Lonnie, perching on the table and pouring himself a cup of Tanner's horrible coffee. "I want you to tell me about it."

She eyed him warily, still afraid to display any of the hostility that might ignite the smoldering violence lurking beneath his nervous exterior. "Tell you about what?"

"About what he did to you," he said, his voice low and excited. "I want to hear everything. Where he touched you, what he did to you. Everything."

"No, Lonnie."

"Tell me!" he screamed. "I know he had you. All I had to do was look at your face that day and know you betrayed me!" The muzzle of the gun was up against her throat. "You'll tell me," Lonnie said. "I've got plenty of time before I get in place."

"In place? Where are you going to be during the ceremony?" Knowing probably wouldn't help—it didn't seem likely that Lonnie would give her any chance to warn somebody, but she needed to ask.

He didn't move the gun. "Exactly where Charles Tanner stood. On the roof of the *Gazette* building. There's a wonderful view there, and no obstructions."

"You'll be there, waiting?"

"I'll be there. You, however, will already be dead."
He nudged her lightly with the gun. "Are you going to
make it hard or easy, Ellie? I want you to tell me what
it was like to bed Charles Tanner's son."

A blast of white-hot rage suddenly raced through
Ellie's trussed-up body. Fury washed over her as she
faced her tormentor, fury and a reckless abandon. Too
many men had taken guns to prove their manhood, and
now another one was facing her. She no longer cared
what he did to her; she had to fight back.

"All I'll tell you," she said, "is that he could do it and
you couldn't."

She was unprepared for his reaction. Lonnie burst
into tears, his handsome face turning red as his narrow
shoulders shook beneath the old army uniform. "No,"
he wept, sinking down on the floor. "No, no, no."

If only she'd put up more of a fight earlier, she
thought regretfully. He was so absorbed in his misery
that if she weren't tied to the chair she could walk right
by him and he wouldn't notice.

"Lonnie," she said gently, when the storm of
weeping had abated somewhat. "You don't want to hurt
me. Untie me. We'll get help for you."

He looked up then, the tears vanishing, and his
mouth curved in a sudden crafty smile. "You're wrong,
Ellie" he said. "I don't need help. And I do want to hurt
you. Very much."

Lonnie was staring at her, a bemused expression on
his face. Suddenly he pulled back the gun. "I've
changed my mind," he said abruptly.

"You'll untie me?"

"Oh, no. You're going to stay right here. But I'm not

going to shoot you. I'm going to let you live. Another survival, Ellie, with everyone you love dead around you. I think that would be even nicer, don't you think? I'll just leave you here to wonder if I found your lover. I think I have enough time to stop by Maude's house. Even if Tanner's not there, Maude will be. And you know I'll find the rest of the people in the town."

He leaned over and kissed her on the lips, a light, gentle touch, like that of a sixteen-year-old on his first date. His breath smelled like toothpaste, his hair like shampoo, his skin like soap and dried sweat. "Goodbye, Ellie," he said gently.

She sat there, disbelieving, as she heard his car drive away. And then she began to struggle.

He'd been much too clever for her. The ropes were so tight they cut off the circulation to her hands and feet. If she'd only had her wits about her she might have done something. She'd read enough books, seen enough movies. Weren't there ways she could have held her wrists, so that tight bonds loosened?

Well, she'd been too scared, and now wasn't the time to worry about lost opportunities. She had no idea what time it was—probably sometime around noon. The ceremony was scheduled for one o'clock, more than enough time for Lonnie to take his place on the roof of the *Gazette* building. And he was absolutely right, the worst thing he could do to her was leave her as a survivor once more. Particularly if he killed Tanner.

She looked around her in desperation, searching for something to cut her bonds. Nothing looked promising— the only possibility might be if she managed to break the heavy earthenware coffee mug on the rickety table.

He'd tied her ankles to the chair legs, twisting her knee just enough to make each move agonizingly painful. Ellie ignored it, jerking and yanking the chair after her as she edged across the room. When she got within reach of the table she set her jaw, shut her eyes, and deliberately toppled over against it.

She landed with a crash on the rough flooring, the table beneath her, the still-hot coffee drenching her, the cook stove crumpled, and the mug still intact. Ellie had no time for pain, no time for recriminations. Ignoring the searing pain in her arm from her reopened bullet graze, she hunched along the floor, the chair still an unwanted hitchhiker, and picked up the mug in her teeth.

She wasn't able to hurl it with much force, and the miserable thing bounced. No wonder Tanner carried it with him on the trail. It was completely indestructible.

But she wasn't going to give up. *Damn it*, she couldn't. It didn't matter if Lonnie had taken her car keys, she could run, she could crawl, she could make it into town if she had to drag herself. But she didn't think she could make it with the chair still clinging to her.

She allowed herself two minutes of furious, impotent tears before heading toward the mug again. She'd thrown it too far, and each scrunching, sideways move across the rough plank flooring drove splinters into her skin.

This time she heard the sound of the car down the deserted gravel road. She stopped, just within reach of the coffee mug, and held her breath. It had to be one of two people: Tanner or Lonnie.

Even though the last few minutes had seemed

eternity, Ellie knew full well that not much time had elapsed since Tanner had left for Maude's house. Not enough for him to start to worry, to come back to check on her.

That left Lonnie. He must have changed his mind, decided to use his rifle on her first. She lay there, listening for the sound of the car door opening, for footsteps on the path, and shut her eyes.

"Ellie!" It was Tanner, Tanner beside her, his hands freeing her, holding her, soothing her, his voice murmuring endearments and savage threats and words of love all tangled into an incomprehensibly reassuring monologue.

She allowed herself only a moment of comfort before she withdrew from the shelter of his arms. "We've got to stop him," she said fiercely. "He's going to kill everyone."

"Lonnie?"

"How did you know?" She rubbed her ankles briskly. In the few minutes she'd been tied the rope had burned deep scores into her pale skin, and her feet were numb.

"Part animal instinct, part logic," Tanner said, pulling her upright, holding her again when she swayed against him. "I think having me show up was the final straw for him."

"I don't know. It sounded as if he's been planning this for years. He would have cracked sooner or later."

"And this time I'm here to stop it," Tanner said grimly. "Where's he gone?"

"He said he was going to wait on the roof of the *Gazette* building and open fire during the ceremony."

"The ceremony starts at one, and it's a little after twelve-thirty. We don't have much time, Ellie."

"Let's go."

"I think you should stay here."

"Why?" she demanded.

He reached out, taking a moment to frame her face with his long, hard hands. "Because I don't know if I'll be able to stop him in time. And I don't want you to be in the line of fire, and I don't want you to have to watch anyone shot ever again."

She covered his hands with her own. "I have to, Tanner. Don't you see, if we can stop him, it will somehow balance out what happened fifteen years ago. If we can keep it from happening again then the town has a chance of recovering."

"Forget the town. It's you I'm worried about."

"There won't *be* any future for me if it happens again," she said bleakly. "Lonnie knew that—that's why he didn't bother to shoot me. If you go to stop him and fail, that means he'll kill you, too. And there's no life at all for me without you."

He stared down at her for a long moment. And then he kissed her, long and hard and deep, sweeping her into his arms and holding her.

When he released her they were both breathless. "All right," he said. "But keep down. And that goes for me, too, you know. There'd be no life for me without you."

THE TOWN OF MOREY'S FALLS was mobbed. People had come from all the neighboring towns, the state and even some of the national media were out in full force, and the smell of roasting chicken hit Ellie's stomach like a fist. Amid all the out-of-state cars it was hard to find Lonnie's BMW, and when they finally discovered it abandoned in front of Pete's Fireside Café the digital clock on the Morey's Falls Bank and Trust read twelve-fifty-three—and eighty-five degrees.

Tanner slammed Maude's old car to a halt behind the BMW. "Stay put," he ordered. "He might be nearby."

"The hell I will." She'd already reached for the door handle when he leaned over and yanked her back.

"Stay put," he said again. "Or I'll drive you out of here and let the town of Morey's Falls fend for itself."

She knew he meant it. "All right," she said. "But let me at least show you the back way up to the roof."

"There's no need. He's not up there," Tanner said flatly.

"How do you know?"

"See for yourself."

Ellie peered out the windshield at the crowded park. A stage had been set up behind the draped monument, and a row of chairs held the town dignitaries. Doc was sitting there, dressed up and uncomfortable looking. The town council was firmly in place, and her own seat was empty. Beside it sat Lonnie Olafson, a raincoat covering his army uniform, a small package on his lap.

If people thought a man wearing a raincoat on a sunny warm day was slightly strange, they had other things occupying their minds. Ellie wanted to scream at them, but no sound came. "He doesn't have the gun with him," she said hoarsely. "Whatever it is he's carrying, it's too small to be a rifle."

"An Uzi would fit very nicely in that box," Tanner said grimly.

"An Uzi?"

"A very small, very deadly machine gun. He'll make my father look like a piker if he gets a chance to set off that thing in this crowd."

"Maybe it's not…"

"You want to take any chances?" he countered.

"No," said Ellie. "What are we going to do? There's no way to sneak up behind them. If he sees you he's bound to open fire."

"I know." His voice was flat, hopeless.

Ellie shivered in the hot air. "Then he's going to have to be distracted."

"No, Ellie."

"Yes. He tried to shoot me before and he couldn't. I don't think he could now."

"I'm not willing to take that chance," said Tanner.

"If I draw his attention," she continued, ignoring him, "you could sneak up on the other side."

"No, Ellie," he said again, reaching for the ignition.

It took just the time she needed. "Yes, Tanner." And she was out of the car and heading for the park before he could grab her.

She didn't dare look behind her. If she did she might alert Lonnie that there were two of them. She crossed the street, ignoring the traffic, ignoring the squeal of tires and angry shouts of the tourists, and stepped into the crowded town park.

At first no one noticed her. The coffee had dried on her pants, the fresh blood had caked on her sleeve. She knew she looked bruised, dirty and desperate, and she didn't care. Fastening her gaze on Lonnie's abstracted face, she headed for the stage.

People began to move aside for her. She could hear the murmur of conversation, the rumble of curiosity and hostility as she made her way toward the monolith. Suddenly Lonnie looked up, straight into her eyes, and his face paled.

His hands twitched, clutching the package, as he stared at her. His mouth was dry, and he licked his lips, watching, waiting, his hands reaching into the rumpled paper bag.

Her knee was throbbing, her body covered in a cold sweat, and still she moved ahead. The crowds around her began to quiet as they sensed something was going on. Finally there was only a hum of conversation, a final, stray laugh, and then absolute silence as Ellie neared the crude wooden platform.

As if in slow motion Lonnie rose. For a moment Ellie wondered whether Tanner had followed, or whether he'd started the car and driven away, leaving the town to their no doubt well-deserved fate. She watched Lonnie move toward her as if mesmerized, the raincoat falling open and revealing the old uniform, his hands deep inside the paper bag, pulling out something compact and metal and hideously deadly….

Tanner exploded across the stage with the grace and power of a hawk diving for his prey. Lonnie went down beneath him, the wicked gun flew out of his hands and went skidding across the stage to land at Doc's feet, and the crowd erupted in noise and confusion.

She had expected more of a battle. Lonnie collapsed beneath Tanner's body, weeping, kicking his feet like an angry child, sobbing and howling with frustrated rage. His screams of impotent fury were all too clear to the watching crowd, and as the reality of what they'd just been spared sank in, horror grew.

When Dave Martin finally appeared with two state police Lonnie was no threat to anyone. Tanner rolled off him, twisting Lonnie's arm up behind his back to keep him docile, but there was no fight left in him. All he could do was weep.

Ellie stood at the edge of the stage, ignoring the noise and questions around her, ignoring the shivers that were still wracking her body, ignoring the hot, sweet dizziness of relief that threatened to collapse her legs beneath her. All she could see was Tanner.

He stood there, watching, as Dave and his men led Lonnie away. Doc was with them, talking in a low, soothing voice, and after a moment Tanner turned back, his eyes searching for her.

Pete Forrester was advancing on him, his burly arm outstretched in a welcoming handshake. Tanner didn't even spare him a glance. He leaped off the stage, pulling Ellie into his arms, sheltering her trembling body against his, pushing her face into the protection of his shoulder, holding her. They stood like that, wrapped in each other's arms, as the noise and crowds faded away, and there were only the two of them, healing each other.

"THIS TOWN HAS a heap of healing to do," said Maude. "Maybe now we can get on with it."

It was early evening. The shadows were beginning to lengthen on that endless Fourth of July, but the sun wouldn't set until after ten o'clock, and Tanner and Ellie had plenty of time left. All the time in the world.

They were sitting side by side on Maude's porch

swing, looking out over the landscape, the wide grass-lands leading to the foothills, up into the jagged mountains where they'd first met.

"You think they have a chance?" Ellie questioned.

"I think so," Maude said. "But then, I'm an optimist. I always think there's hope. Even for poor Lonnie. The state hospital's the best place for him. Someplace where he can't hurt anybody."

"If Pete Forrester can thank Tanner," Ellie murmured, "then anything can happen."

"Did he really?"

"He did," Tanner said. "He told me I was welcome in his place anytime. I told him the best thing Ellie and I could do for Morey's Falls was to get the hell out and never come back."

"Never?" Maude's voice quavered.

"Never," Ellie echoed. "You'll have to stir yourself and come visit us, Maude. Your great-grandchildren are going to grow up in New Mexico."

"So is that devil horse of yours," she snorted, looking pleased at the thought of progeny. "You sure you don't want to wait and take him yourself?"

"Rafael Maderos will do a fine job bringing the horses down to us," Tanner said. "I practically grew up with him, and I'd trust him with my life. More important, I'd trust him with my horses. Besides, he'll be the one to drive you down to visit, too; you might as well get used to him. And admit it, you're going to miss Shaitan."

"I'm going to miss you and Ellie, period," she said flatly. "Poor Lonnie," she added, for what was probably the twentieth time. "I'll go bring us some more coffee." The screen door bounced shut behind her spry figure.

"Poor Lonnie," Ellie agreed. "I guess he just wanted someone to pay attention to him."

"He's got that all right," Tanner said. "He'll get all the attention and help he needs—the kind my father could have used." There was no bitterness in his voice, only acceptance. Ellie looked over at him and smiled. The past had finally begun to release its stranglehold, on him, on her.

"You sure you're not marrying me for my horses?" she asked lightly.

"Who said anything about marriage, woman?" he mocked.

"My children are going to be named Tanner," she said firmly. "And the next time you get the urge to go walking, I'm going with you."

"What about your leg?"

She grimaced. "You know as well as I do that once I'm away from Morey's Falls I'll hardly notice it. Don't worry, I'll be able to keep up with you."

"As a matter of fact, I don't think I'm going to need to be doing too much walking in the future," he murmured, taking her hand and caressing the rope burns that still lingered on her narrow wrist. "Not if you're certain you know what you're doing." The levity was gone from his voice, and his eyes were no longer icy as the north wind, they were the soft gray-blue of the fragrant sage around them.

"I'm certain," she said. And she moved into his arms with the grace and sureness of the sun moving across the wide blue Montana sky, knowing she was home at last.

CHAPTER TWENTY-TWO

Spring came early to the Sangre de Cristo mountains. The sky, surely as big and as blue as Montana's fabled sky, was cloudless, bright and sunny, and the acres and acres of land surrounding the Walking Horse Ranch blossomed with the promise of the new season.

Ellie leaned back in the wicker rocker and propped her bare feet on the porch railing. Wiggling her toes in the early-morning sunlight, she contemplated the last ten months. Instead of the adobe house she'd expected, she'd discovered a Texas-style ranch house. Instead of a frail, dying old man she'd found Alfred, still full of vinegar, determined to fight his way back from the last debilitating stroke and welcome Tanner's new wife properly. He'd done it, and they'd had a good, happy six months as a family before he'd died, peacefully enough in his sleep on New Year's Day.

Tanner had had no need to marry her for Shaitan. His breeding stock was fully Shaitan's equal, and if neither of Tanner's stallions had a glorious black coat or quite the imposing height of Ellie's horse, their temperaments were a decided improvement.

She wished she could say the same thing for Tanner. She'd seen it coming for the past two months, the faraway look in his eyes, the abstraction, the distance she couldn't seem to bridge. Something was calling him, something she couldn't fight, and she was trying her hardest to resign herself to his going.

The ranch would be fine. Even without Alfred, the place was so well-organized that it ran like clockwork. Rafael knew as much about horses as Tanner did, and the others were equally adept. It hadn't taken Ellie long to take over the book work, and she knew she was more than capable of making any executive decisions that needed to be made while Tanner walked.

He hadn't said a word to her yet, but then, he didn't need to. She knew him well, knew the worst thing she could do was try to hold him back. If she fought it, if she tried to tie him to her, someday he'd walk away and never come back. If she let him go with loving hands, he'd always return to her.

The last thing he needed to hear at that moment was that she was going to have a baby. It would be one more thing pulling on him, one more thing holding him back. He wasn't ready for fatherhood, he'd told her at Christmas when she'd asked if they could try to have a child. He wasn't ready to face Charles Tanner's grandchild, not quite yet. Maybe never.

Would he blame her when he found out? It hadn't been her fault. They'd been in the barn, alone one evening, when he'd picked her up and tossed her into the hayloft, falling after her, dismissing her word of caution. If nothing had happened in Montana, surely they'd be safe this one last time.

They weren't. And her fault or not, she couldn't tell him. She could only touch her still-flat stomach and try to contain the strange mixture of fear and elation that swept over her at the very thought.

The tea beside her had grown cool. Apparently everyone at the ranch liked coffee that resembled paint thinner, and Ellie was almost grateful to switch. But with her stomach just the tiniest bit hesitant, she had a low tolerance even for tea.

The sun was climbing higher in the sky. Rafael's portly wife would be dishing up breakfast before long, and it was time for Ellie to stir her indolent body. She should be in giving Melora a hand, but couldn't resist stealing the last few moments of peace in her busy day. She cherished the early morning, with the men busy down at the barn, the smells of breakfast from the big ranch kitchen, the slowly brightening sky.

Tanner was walking up alone from the barn. She watched him approach, and once more felt the familiar clutching deep inside her, a bittersweet feeling of longing and resignation.

His hat was down low as he crossed the flat stretch of ground, but he knew she was there, watching him. There was something different about that rangy walk of his, a new ease and determination. And Ellie steeled herself for the worst.

The old porch creaked as he climbed the front steps. He usually went in the kitchen door with the other men, to wash up in the big sink out back, but today was different. He wasn't wearing his barn boots, either. He was wearing hiking shoes.

She couldn't bring herself to look up at him. If she did she'd cry. She looked out over the peaceful setting, the early-morning sky, and waited.

He put his hand on her shoulder, the weight of it heavy and solid, and she leaned her cheek against his hand. "When are you going?" she asked quietly.

"Now."

She couldn't help the little spasm of pain that swept through her, and his fingers tightened on her shoulder. "Okay," she said, and pressed her lips against the back of his hand.

"I'll be back, you know," His voice sounded tight, strained, as if he were the one in pain.

She looked up at him then, knowing there were tears swimming in her eyes, looked up anyway and smiled. "I know," she said.

THE END OF APRIL slipped quietly into May, and the mountains came alive with spring. Ellie passed the third month mark in her pregnancy with a sigh of relief, turning her concentration to the new generation of foals being born at the Walking Horse Ranch. Shaitan was about to become a father for the first time, and Ellie viewed the event with almost as much trepidation as she did her own upcoming parenthood. The mare, Alfred's Folly, had refused to be covered by any stallion until she'd seen Shaitan, and Rafael had doubts about her qualifications as a mother.

Ellie had no such doubts. Alfred's Folly, so named because of her refusal to breed, would be a fine mother. Whether she'd ever let another stallion near her was a different matter, and Shaitan was being absurdly possessive, but it wasn't worth worrying about for now.

May turned into June, and the days grew blazingly hot. Ellie told herself she was too busy to miss Tanner, and she knew she lied. She was tired and lonely, and she sat behind the big old mission oak desk in the ranch office and thought longingly of Montana, of the hidden meadow and the cool weather.

And then she remembered the town monument, the anger and paranoia and pain and death that had haunted the town for so long. According to Maude's letters, things were improving. The *Gazette* had been taken over by a young couple with two kids, Pete Forrester had stopped haunting the graveyard, and there was even some talk of a ski area being built less than twenty miles away. While it might hurt the land, it would bring jobs and people into the area, and Ellie could only be glad.

Even Lonnie was slowly improving. For six months he'd sat in the state hospital and spoken not a word. Now he was talking, working things out. Whether he'd ever be well enough to live a normal life was still up in the air, but Ellie, remembering the good years, remembering the real sweetness that lay beneath the anger and madness, could only hope so.

She hadn't told Maude that Tanner had left, but she knew she couldn't put it off much longer. Maude was itching to visit, demanding to know when she was going to be a great-grandmother, wanting to know what was going on in New Mexico. Morey's Falls was boring nowadays, she wrote. Even Ginger Barlow had settled down, marrying a meat salesman and becoming downright domestic. Doc hadn't been feeling too chipper lately, but there was a new widow in town, one who seemed to think she was just what he needed, and maybe there'd be another wedding before long.

There'd been no word from Tanner, but then, Ellie hadn't expected there to be. All she could do was wait and accept it.

It was another early morning on the ranch. Ellie was dressed, but just barely, carrying her coffee out onto the front porch when Rafael came charging up, panting heavily. "It's Folly," he wheezed. "She's ready. Better come quick."

Ellie set the coffee down hurriedly, ignoring the pain as the scalding liquid splashed on her hand. "Shouldn't we call a vet? I'll go..."

"No way. Foals get born in five to ten minutes—there wouldn't be time for anyone to get here."

"But what if she has trouble?" Ellie protested. For some reason Folly's pregnancy had taken on enormous importance to her, as if it were a precursor of her own.

"If she has trouble, we'll have to take care of it," Rafael said. "And we'll have to pray."

"I can manage that much," Ellie said. "Let's go."

Rafael hadn't exaggerated. Folly was already down. Ellie and Rafael knelt in the straw, near enough to reach her if needed, careful not to get in the way.

Ellie didn't know when he came in, so intent was she on the miraculous drama that was unfolding so very quickly in front of her. For a moment the light from the door was blocked out, and then it was bright again. And Tanner was beside her in the straw, not touching her, watching with the same silent intensity.

Rafael grinned over his shoulder in welcome, accustomed to Tanner's comings and goings. Ellie remained motionless wanting to scream and cry in joy, wanting to rage and hit him.

In the end it took Alfred's Folly seven and a half minutes to give birth to an impossibly long-legged colt with the ease and dispatch of a pro. Ellie scarcely breathed as it tried to struggle to its feet.

"We don't consider it a live birth until it's standing and drinking from its mother," Tanner said, his voice a deep rumble in the quiet barn.

"What if she won't let him drink?" Rafael fretted, still not trusting the recalcitrant mare.

"She will," Ellie said firmly.

It took another endless few minutes, and for a moment it looked as if Ellie's trust was misplaced, as Folly stared at her gangly offspring with suspicion.

"Come on," Ellie muttered under her breath. She reached out, knowing Tanner's hand would be there, and held it tightly. "Come on, Folly."

"Well, I'll be," Rafael breathed. "She's nursing him."

"Of course she is," Ellie said smugly, ignoring her moment of panic. "She just needed a moment or two." She turned and looked into Tanner's eyes, those distant blue eyes she hadn't seen in almost six weeks.

"Another one of your charity cases, Ellie?" he murmured. "One more walking wounded?"

"Are you mocking me?"

"No," he said. "I love you."

She managed a brief, tremulous smile before turning back to watch Folly nurse her colt. There it came again, that strange fluttering in her womb, that she'd first thought was nerves. It was the first time she'd felt her baby move. "I only hope," she said deliberately, "that I have as easy a time of it as she did."

Rafael had vanished by this time, tactful enough to

let them have their reunion in private. "When?" asked Tanner, his voice rough with an emotion she was afraid to guess at.

"December."

"You knew when I left and you didn't stop me?"

She turned to face him again. "I didn't want to hold you if you didn't want to stay. It had to be your decision, not because of duty or guilt or responsibility. I'll always let you go when you need to."

"Will you always let me come back?"

"Yes."

The tension suddenly drained from his taut shoulders. His dark-blond hair was too long, his face too tired, his body too weary. But he smiled at her, a tender, infinitely dear smile, and the last tiny bit of sorrow and hurt left her. "I won't go again."

"You don't have to promise me...."

"I'm not promising. I'm just telling you the truth. I couldn't stand it. The first night away was bad, the second was worse, the third was pure hell. I kept going, kept walking until I was sure the wanting would stop. But it never did. I just kept seeing you wherever I went, dreaming about you, missing you. A hundred times I picked up the phone to call you, a dozen times I turned around to come back."

"Why didn't you?" she cried.

"I couldn't until I was sure, Ellie. That's why I had to go one last time. I had to make certain the walking, the running was over."

"And is it?" Her voice was soft, beseeching, unable to hide her desperate hurt and longing anymore.

He reached out his long hands and cupped the sides

of her face. "Oh, Ellie," he whispered, "I know for sure now. I'll never leave you again." And he kissed her, her soft, trembling mouth, her tear-drenched eyelids, her chin, her breasts, her slightly rounded stomach, as he pulled her down into the sweet-smelling hay.

Folly, nursing her colt, looked at the foolish humans whispering in her stall and whickered softly. And Shaitan, unexpectedly docile for the first time in his life, looked over from the adjoining stall and whirruped in reply, as the bright morning sun flooded the barn with new life and joy. A new day had begun.

* * * * *

This book is dedicated to
David and Meredith Thacker,
who have found in each other
everything they have always wanted.
I couldn't be happier about your marriage.
I wish you much love and joy
in your life together.

HER BACHELOR CHALLENGE

Bestselling Author

Cathy Gillen Thacker

CATHY GILLEN THACKER

is married and a mother of three. She and her husband spent eighteen years in Texas and now reside in North Carolina. Her mysteries, romantic comedies and heartwarming family stories have made numerous appearances on bestseller lists, but her best reward, she says, is knowing one of her books made someone's day a little brighter. A popular Harlequin author for many years, she loves telling passionate stories with happy endings, and thinks nothing beats a good romance and a hot cup of tea! You can visit Cathy's Web site at www.cathygillenthacker.com for more information on her upcoming and previously published books, recipes and a list of her favorite things.

CHAPTER ONE

Chase Deveraux knew from the moment he got the summons to the Deveraux family's Meeting Street mansion that it was going to be hard as all get-out to hold on to his temper. And that was never truer than when he walked in the front door and saw his woman-stealing brother Gabe standing next to the fireplace in the drawing room.

Gabe looked at Chase with his typical do-gooding innocence and said, "I can explain."

"I'll just bet you can," Chase replied sarcastically, his temper escalating all the more. There were times he was glad he and his three younger siblings had all decided to settle permanently in Charleston, South Carolina, along with their father, instead of taking jobs at various places around the country as many of their friends had done. This wasn't one of them.

He glared at his baby brother and pushed the words through his teeth. "The only problem is, I don't want to hear it. Not after what I saw at noon today."

"Maggie called me." Gabe heeded Chase's low warning tone. "It was a medical emergency."

Chase lifted a brow in raging disbelief as he moved across the brilliant-blue carpet, embossed with gold stars. "One that required mouth-to-mouth resuscitation, no doubt."

"I'd have thought you would have had more sense than that," Mitch, the second oldest son, scolded their baby brother as he took off the jacket of his pearl-gray business suit and jerked loose the knot of his austere silver tie. "Seeing Maggie Callaway is bad enough, after what she did to this family two years ago." Mitch grimaced in disbelief as he spoke for the group assembled. "But kissing her? In front of Chase? That's low, Gabe!"

Amy, the peacemaker, as well as the youngest of the family, stepped into the breach. Maybe it was because she and Gabe were closest in age, but she was always quick to rise to Gabe's defense. "Isn't it possible that you misunderstood what you saw, Chase?" she asked anxiously as she fussed with the pink roses set out in crystal vases around the house. "After all, if it was a medical emergency—if Maggie fainted or something— maybe Gabe was just doing what had to be done. He is a doctor, for heaven's sake!"

"Is that what happened?" Chase asked as he turned back to the increasingly guilty-looking Gabe. The old bitterness and betrayal cut him like a knife as he pushed away the mental image of Gabe and Maggie staring deep into each other's eyes, even while Maggie had still been engaged to marry *Chase!* Not that it had mattered. In the end Gabe hadn't suffered any qualms about betraying his brother. Then or now. Family loyalty was something Gabe apparently just didn't have. "Did Maggie call you out to her beach house because she was feeling faint?"

Gabe said nothing.

More furious than ever, Chase continued, "Let me guess what happened next. You rushed over. She answered the door—swooned at the sight of you. And then you hauled her into your arms and laid a big one on her. All in the name of medical science, of course."

Looking guiltier and all the more uncomfortable, Gabe dragged a palm across his jaw. "She didn't faint." It was his turn to push the words through his teeth as he moved toward the floor-length sash windows that graced both ends of the elegantly appointed room.

"Then what happened?" Mitch sank down on a Duncan Phyfe chair, which was covered in the same brilliant-blue-and-gold-star pattern as the carpet.

"I can't really say," Gabe replied with a reluctant shrug. "Beyond the fact that Maggie called me and asked me to meet her at her place, pronto."

"For…?" Amy probed curiously, when Gabe didn't go on.

"That's confidential," Gabe replied stiffly as he moved beneath the portrait of Revolutionary War hero General Marshall Deveraux.

"I'll just bet it is." Deciding he'd had enough of trying to play it cool, Chase went straight for his father's whiskey and poured himself a shot.

Gabe met Chase at the bar. He helped himself to a club soda over ice. "Look, if you must know, she was talking to me about a medical matter."

Chase knew his brother had worked hard to perfect his bedside manner during med school and residency, but this was ridiculous. "Is that how you minister to all your patients?" Chase asked, deliberately goading Gabe. "By kissing them?"

"She's not my patient," Gabe said hotly. "All I was doing was listening to her and offering advice."

Chase would have liked to believe it was just that innocent. Just as he would have liked to believe that Maggie's feelings for his brother had been platonic, from the get-go. Unfortunately that wasn't true and he knew it. The minute Maggie had laid eyes on Gabe, her engagement to Chase might as well have been history. And that was a public humiliation Chase still found very hard to take, regardless of the fact that his feelings for Maggie, whatever they had been, had long ago faded to obscurity.

"Then what were you doing giving her mouth-to-mouth?" Chase demanded, trying to push the image of the two standing on Maggie's doorstep, wrapped in each other's arms, out of his mind. If that wasn't a sign of some ongoing clandestine rendezvous, he didn't know what was!

"That kiss you saw today just happened," Gabe countered hotly. "We didn't plan it. Any more than you planned to be driving by at the exact second I was saying goodbye to her."

"I see. It was an accident. Just like your stealing Maggie away from me just two days before our wedding and then dumping her the moment her wedding to me was officially off was an accident."

Gabe glared at Chase in frustration. "I couldn't get involved with her after what had happened to our family!"

Chase snorted derisively as he choked down a swallow of fine Southern whiskey. "Too bad you couldn't have decided that before you wrecked my wedding plans," he fumed.

"If anyone wrecked your wedding plans, Chase, it was you."

Chase set his glass down with a thud. He turned away from the sideboard and asked ever so slowly, "What did you say?"

Gabe's eyes gleamed with temper. "You heard me. If you'd just paid one-tenth the attention to Maggie that you pay to your work at the magazine…"

Chase flushed. Was it his fault Maggie had led him to think she was a low-maintenance woman, when the truth was she was anything but? "If she'd wanted me to sit around listening to her all the time, I would have done so!" Or at least he would have tried, Chase amended silently, knowing as well as everyone else in the room that he had a very low tolerance for chitchat.

"A woman shouldn't have to tell you that," Gabe shot back, looking even more peeved.

That wasn't Chase's experience with the fairer sex. The women he dated couldn't have cared less about scintillating conversation—they wanted passion and sex. Period. Besides, he'd never been able to read a woman's mind the way Gabe could.

"Now listen," Amy broke in, anxiously wringing her hands, "Chase and Maggie's breakup was probably bound to happen, anyway. Because of the Deveraux family legacy—"

Chase and Gabe groaned in unison. "Not that again," Chase said, shooting an exasperated look at his little sister.

"Amy might have a point," Mitch said with extreme civility. He looked at Chase sternly, acting more like the older brother. "If you and Maggie had managed to marry and live happily ever after, you would have been the first Deveraux to do so in three generations."

Chase scowled. "Our failed betrothal has nothing to do with the curse put on our great-aunt Eleanor."

"Tell that to everyone who's had their love life wrecked for no reason in the past sixty years," Amy countered. "And then tell me the curse hasn't carried over to the next Deveraux generation!"

Gabe glared at Chase, even as he addressed his remarks to his two calmer siblings. He downed the rest of his club soda in a single gulp. "I still say I had nothing to do with the breakup. If Chase and Maggie had been meant to marry, they would have. Curse or no curse. And nothing I said or did or didn't say or do would have stopped them from tying the knot."

"You just keep telling yourself that," Chase said sarcastically. He'd had some miserable days in his life, but he'd never been more hurt and humiliated than he was the day Maggie had walked out on him and their wedding. For he'd known then that it wasn't just his divorced parents or brother Mitch—who was also divorced—who were unable to find and keep wedded bliss. People just didn't stay together in this day and age. They didn't find happiness in the act of permanently joining their life with another's. Hell, nowadays they were lucky if they could even make it to the altar and say "I do." And learning that lesson the hard way had made him stop trying to find the "happily ever after." Instead, it made him look to the immediate present for his happiness, and no further.

"Moreover," Amy continued passionately as she stuck her hands in the front pockets of her pastel coveralls, which were embroidered with the name of her decorating business, "Chase needs to get over the way Maggie walked out on him and be glad she came to her senses before they entered into a marriage that most likely would have ended in divorce, anyway. And most important of all, he needs to stop trying to seek revenge for Maggie's actions on the whole female population!"

"And how am I doing that?" Chase demanded furiously, incensed to find Amy—who could usually be counted on to soothe the wounded egos of all three of her brothers—scolding him, too. It wasn't as if he promised women anything but what he could give them, which was today!

Amy gave him a droll look as she explained, "You do that by turning women into objects in your magazine and trying to nail every female in Charleston."

Chase shook his head in exasperation, knowing that the very well-paid models for *Modern Man* never complained about how beautiful they looked in the pages of his magazine. "Actually, that's old news. I've moved on—" Chase quipped, knowing even as he spoke it wasn't entirely false "—to the entire East Coast."

"That's not funny, Chase." Amy scowled.

"It's not supposed to be," Chase retorted bluntly, using this—and every other opportunity that came his way—to shamelessly plug the premise of the notoriously lighthearted and controversy-inspiring magazine he had created just for guys. "Women are here on this earth for one reason and one reason only. To make guys happy." And as far as he was concerned, guys were only there to make women happy. It was pretending otherwise, in his opinion, that made people so darn miserable.

"And that tally includes dear old Maggie," Chase continued, deliberately ignoring the warning glare Gabe gave him. "Which is undoubtedly the reason Gabe rushed out to the beach house." Chase turned to his brother and proceeded to hit Gabe where he knew it would hurt the most—Gabe's legendary sense of duty. "Maggie was lonely. She was desperate." *And like the rest of us mortals, in urgent need of some happiness to call her own.* "So she dialed the emotional equivalent of 911, and Gabe here, ever the good Samaritan, rushed right out to administer the much-needed and much-wanted, obligatory mercy—"

Chase never had the chance to finish his sentence. But then, he thought, with a certain grim satisfaction as Gabe's fist came flying up to meet him, he'd known for certain he never would.

BRIDGETT OWENS parked her Mercedes convertible at the rear of the Deveraux mansion and headed in the servants' entrance. She paused just long enough to kiss her mother's flushed cheek and ask, "What's the emergency?"

Theresa Owens grabbed a floral-print apron from the drawer and slipped it on over her uniform—a plain navy-blue dress with a white collar. Tying her apron behind her as she moved, Theresa headed swiftly for the ancient subzero refrigerator in the corner. Quickly she pulled out a package of fresh crabmeat and another of cream cheese. "Grace is coming home." Theresa checked her recipe and collected milk and horseradish from the fridge and an onion from the mesh basket on the counter. "Tom went to the airport to get her. All the children are here. And I'm short-staffed."

"Where is everyone else?" Bridgett asked. Tom Deveraux had a chauffeur and a gardener, in addition to her mother, his full-time cook and housekeeper.

Theresa brushed auburn tendrils off her face with the back of her hand. "It's their day off."

"Mom, you should have a day off," Bridgett said, wishing her mother would listen to her and give up working as a domestic. Especially now that it was no longer necessary. Theresa could retire and live with Bridgett and never have to worry about money or putting a roof over their heads again.

Theresa frowned as she measured ingredients into the casserole dish and stirred them together briskly. "Then who would cook for Tom?"

"Maybe he could order takeout?" Bridgett suggested as her mother slid the crabmeat dip into the oven to bake. "Or eat at a restaurant."

Theresa wiped her hands, then restored order to the bun on the top of her head. "I have all the time off I need whenever I need it."

Bridgett sighed, knowing she was about as likely to talk her mother into taking early retirement at fifty as she was to get her to change her hairstyle or stop wearing the "uniform" that Tom and Grace Deveraux had both told her years ago she did not have to wear. "Except you never take any time off," Bridgett reminded her mother gently.

"Honey, I don't have time to argue with you." Theresa went back to the refrigerator for salad fixings. "I'm trying to put together a dinner party for six on thirty minutes' notice. And Tom said it was crucial that everything be very nice."

Bridgett zeroed in on the concern in her mother's voice, even as she did what she had done for years, as the daughter of a Deveraux domestic—pitched in to lend a hand. "Did something happen?" Bridgett asked as she rolled up her sleeves and helped her mother make a dinner salad on the fly.

"I'm not sure." Her expression increasingly worried, Theresa got out the food processor and set it on the counter. "But he said Grace might be upset when she gets here and he wanted all the children to be in attendance so they could talk to them together."

A feeling of foreboding came over Bridgett as she watched her mother fit the slicing disk into the machine. Bridgett hadn't seen much of Grace Deveraux since Grace had gone to New York City to host the *Rise and Shine, America!* morning news program fifteen years ago, but she cared about her nonetheless. She cared about all the Deveraux, just as her mother did. "Grace isn't ill, is she?"

Theresa shrugged. "I'm not sure Tom knows what this is all about, either. But you know how it's been between the two of them since they divorced."

"They can hardly stand to be in the same room with each other."

"So if Grace called Tom and asked him to pick her up at the airport and bring her here, of all places..."

To the home the two of them had shared in happier times.

"It must be bad," Bridgett concluded, reading her mother's mind.

Theresa nodded.

And it was then, as she looked at her mother's face, that Bridgett realized the real reason her mother had called her. Not because she needed help preparing dinner or carrying a tray of canapés. But because she needed moral support in dealing with whatever the fallout of Grace and Tom's news. Theresa might insist on reminding herself daily in a million little ways that there was a huge class difference between the Owenses and the family Theresa had worked for since before Bridgett was born, but Theresa and Bridgett both loved all the Deveraux like family nevertheless. "How is Chase and everyone taking this?" Bridgett asked, knowing that Chase was likely to have a tough time with any calamity involving his parents. Maybe it was because he was the oldest, but he had taken his parents' divorce thirteen years ago especially hard.

"I'm not sure," Theresa said, jumping and grimacing at the big thud and shouting from the front of the house. Then the sound of glass breaking.

"Apparently," Bridgett said, answering her own question, "not so well."

There was another crash, even louder. Then the sound of Amy screaming.

"Oh, dear." Theresa's hand flew to her chest and she got a panicked look on her face.

"Sounds like another fight." One of many, both before and after Tom and Grace's divorce. Bridgett sighed. She put up a hand before her mother could exit the kitchen. "I'll go, Mom." She had experience breaking up fights. Why should this one be any different?

"DAMMIT, GABE, I don't want to hurt you." Ignoring the pain across his shoulder, where he'd caught the edge of the mantel, Chase staggered to his feet. He pressed one hand to the corner of his mouth, which seemed to be bleeding, and held Gabe at bay with the other palm upraised between them. "So back off!"

Gabe shook his head, his expression angry, intense, and continued coming, fists knotted at his side. "Not until you take back what you said about Maggie," he stormed.

Chase smirked, not above taunting a self-righteous Gabe. "Right. Like you plan to take back sucking face with her?"

"That does it!" Gabe leaped over the back of the sofa, grabbed Chase by the shirt and swung again, his fist arcing straight for Chase's jaw.

Chase ducked the blow and countered with a punch to Gabe's gut. As he expected, it didn't do much damage. Gabe had been ready for him, muscles tensed. Just as Chase was ready for the tumble over the upholstered Duncan Phyfe chair to the floor. Gabe landed on top of him, but not for long. Chase forced him over onto his back. He grabbed his brother by the front of his shirt, still seeing red. For the life of him, Chase didn't understand why Gabe continued to defend—and apparently desire—the woman who had come as close to two-timing Chase as any woman ever would. Especially when Gabe had to know how hurt and humiliated Chase had been, both by the events and all the sordid speculation that had followed. Not that it had been any easier for Gabe and Maggie. Both their squeaky-clean reputations had been forever tarnished, too. And for what? It wasn't as if the two of them had found any happiness, either. "Gonna give up now?" Chase demanded in frustration, wishing they could put this ugly episode behind them before it further destroyed their family.

"Not on your life." Gabe scowled back, looking ready to do even more damage.

And that was when it happened. A shrill whistle split the air and two spectacular female legs glided into view. Sexy knees peeked out beneath a short silk skirt. His glance then took in slim sexy calves, trim feminine ankles and delicate feet clad in a pair of strappy sandals. Chase knew those legs. He knew her fragrance. And he especially knew that voice. It belonged to one of the most sought-after financial advisers in Charleston, South Carolina.

"One more punch, Chase Deveraux," Bridgett Owens said sweetly, "and you're going to be dealing with me."

THE FIRST THING Chase thought was that Bridgett Owens hadn't changed since he had last seen her. Unless it was to get even better-looking than she already was. Her long auburn hair had been all one length when she'd gone off on her phenomenally successful book tour three months ago. That soft-as-silk hair still fell several inches past her shoulders, but now it was layered in long sexy strands that framed her pretty oval face. She'd done something different to her eyes, too. He couldn't say what it was exactly, though he figured it had something to do with her makeup, because her bittersweet-chocolate eyes had never looked so dark, mysterious or long-lashed. She was wearing a different color of lipstick, too. It made her lips look even more luscious against her wide, white orthodontics-perfect smile.

She was also dressing a little differently.

Maybe it was because she also ran a private financial-counseling service out of her home and hence felt the need to present a serious, businesslike image to the public that she'd worn suits that were so tailored and austere it was almost ridiculous. Today, however, she was wearing a silky pencil-slim skirt that was so soft and creamy it looked like it was made of raspberry-swirl ice cream. With it she wore a figure-hugging tank top in the palest of pinks and a matching cardigan sweater. The overall effect was sophisticated, feminine and sexy. Too sexy for Chase's comfort.

"Honestly," Bridgett continued, seeming to scold Chase a lot more than Gabe, "aren't you two a little old for such nonsense?"

Chase scowled. The last thing he wanted—from anyone—was advice on how to handle the restoration of his pride. "This is none of your business," he fumed, still holding tight to Gabe's shirt.

"The heck it's not!" Bridgett charged closer, inundating Chase with the intoxicating fragrance of her perfume. "When it's gonna be my mother explaining to your parents what happened to all the priceless furniture here!"

"No explanation needed," came a deep male voice from somewhere behind them.

Every head turned. There in the portal stood Tom Deveraux, dressed in a dark business suit, pale-blue shirt and conservative tie. Coming in right behind him was Chase's mother, Grace. As the two of them stood frozen, looking at their two brawling sons, it was almost like going back in time for Chase—before his mother had moved to New York City. Before the estrangement between his mother and father, which neither he nor his siblings really understood to this day. To the time when they had been, for whatever it was worth, a family that was united, even in times of strife. Nowadays it seemed that all they had left was the strife. And the heartache of a once-loving family that had fallen apart.

"I suppose we don't even have to ask what was the reason for this," Grace said wearily, touching a hand to her short and fluffy white-blond hair.

Chase immediately noted the strain lines around his mom's mouth, the shadows beneath her blue eyes, and his heart went out to her. Something had happened, he thought, and it was bad enough to bring his dad to her side again.

"If the two of you are fighting like this, Maggie Callaway has to have something to do with it," Tom surmised frankly, clearly disappointed in both of them.

Neither Gabe nor Chase said anything.

Bridgett offered Chase her hand. Though hardly ready—or really even willing—to end the brawl with his woman-stealing brother, Chase took the assistance Bridgett offered. And, to his mounting discomfort, found his old pal Bridgett's manicured hand just as delicate in shape, strong in grip and silky soft as it looked.

Tom continued shaking his head at everyone in the room, then settled on Mitch and Amy. "You couldn't have stopped this before they broke half the vases in the room?" he asked them.

Amy made a face and brushed her long hair, a dark brown like Tom's, from her eyes. "It's sort of a long story, Dad."

Mitch shrugged his broad shoulders. "Amy and I figured they were going to come to blows again, no matter what. Better it happen here. Where they're unlikely to get arrested or otherwise bring dishonor to the Deveraux name."

Tom looked at Chase and Gabe. His lips thinned in disapproval as he demanded, "What do you two have to say for yourselves?"

"Not a thing," Chase muttered, resenting being questioned like this at his age, even if he and Gabe did deserve it.

Gabe grimaced, looking at that moment like anything but the good Samaritan he was. "Me, neither."

Tom turned to Bridgett. "At least you were trying to break it up."

Bridgett smiled at Tom respectfully. "Someone had to. And since I have...I think I should excuse myself."

"No reason for that," Grace said, putting up a staying hand before Bridgett could so much as take a step out of the drawing room. "You're family, Bridgett, you know that. Besides, I have something to tell you all," Grace added, just as Theresa came into the room, a silver serving tray of hot crabmeat dip and crackers in hand. "Sit down, everyone." Grace waited until one and all complied, including Theresa, before she continued reluctantly, "I wanted you to hear this from me before it hits the airwaves." Grace paused, took a deep breath. "I've been fired."

CHAPTER TWO

Chase stared at his mother, barely able to believe what he was hearing. "What do you mean, you've been fired!"

"They can't fire you!" Mitch cried, incensed, as the entire Deveraux family closed rank around Grace. "You're the a.m. Sweetheart!"

Looking even more upset than their mother, Amy argued emotionally, "The American public loves you! They said so at last year's Favorite Celebrity awards!"

Grace sighed and shook her head. "It doesn't matter."

"Since when?" Chase asked, incredulous, unable to understand how his mother could remain so resigned in the face of such a professional catastrophe. For the past fifteen years, her whole world had revolved around that job. She had given up her life in Charleston, sacrificed her marriage and what little happy family life they'd had, at that point, for that job. "Amy's right, Mom. The morning news shows sink or swim on the personality of their cohosts."

Grace sat down, looking unbearably weary. Her skin was pale against her cheerful yellow tunic and matching trousers. "The show's ratings have been sinking for some time now."

Gabe picked up an overturned chair and set it to rights. He looked their mother square in the eye. "You're sure you can't do anything to change the network's decision?"

Again, Grace shook her head. "It's not just me," she said softly. "They're replacing my cohost, too. And going with a younger couple."

The family gave a collective sigh as Tom went over to the bar and fixed a tall glass of diet soda and ice. He brought it back to Grace and sat down next to her.

"When is all this going to happen?" Chase asked. He caught Bridgett's gaze and saw she was just as concerned about his mother as he was. That was no surprise. He knew Bridgett loved his mother, too.

Grace cupped the glass in both her hands and ducked her head. "The network is going to announce my replacement later today. It'll probably be on the evening news tonight. It may make the Internet before then."

"You're not going to hold a press conference?" Mitch, ever the businessman, asked.

Grace shook her head. "I'm letting my publicist handle it. We crafted a statement together before I left New York. She'll release it."

"And then what?" Gabe asked. "Will you be going back to finish up?"

"Surely the network is going to give you a big send-off," Amy said.

Grace sipped her soda. "The network wanted to make a big deal about my leaving, but I told them I didn't want it. Those things are always maudlin. I'd rather viewers remember me just as I was this morning, when I taped my last show. Besides, it's not the last time

I'll ever be on television. My agent is already fielding offers. They began coming in last month when there were rumors a change was going to be made."

Silence fell. Chase noted with no small amount of admiration that his mother seemed to be handling this catastrophe better than the rest of them. "So what are you going to do now?" he asked casually after a moment.

"Your mother is going to be staying here at the mansion," Tom said. "I'll be staying at a hotel."

Chase wasn't surprised. That had been the case ever since his parents' divorce. Whenever his mother came to Charleston, she stayed at the family mansion, and his father moved—temporarily—to the Mills House Hotel. It was the only way his mother could get any privacy, she was so well-known. She was besieged by autograph hounds if she checked into a hotel. And staying at the mansion made it easier for her to see all four of her children.

"Now, if you don't mind," Grace said, suddenly looking as if she was going to burst into tears, after all, "it's been a very long day and I think I'll go upstairs and lie down. That is, if you boys think you can stop fighting long enough to give us all some peace."

"They had better—" Tom Deveraux cast a warning look at his sons "—or they aren't half the men I thought they were."

"WELL, I GUESS he told us," Chase murmured after his father and mother had disappeared up the wide sweeping staircase.

Bridget looked at Chase. "It's not as if you didn't

deserve it," she said, clearly exasperated. "You and Gabe are far too old to be rolling around on the floor."

"I'll certainly second that!" Theresa Owens fumed, like the second mother she was to them all. "Chase, you're bleeding. And Gabe, you need some ice on that eye."

"You take care of Gabe. I'll take care of Chase," Bridgett told her mother. Before Chase could reply, Bridgett had him by the sleeve of his loose fitting linen shirt and was tugging him toward the powder room tucked beneath the stairs. She shut the door behind them, pushed him down on the closed commode and began rummaging through the medicine cabinet for supplies.

"Just like old times, huh?" Chase said. Glad Bridgett had volunteered to act as his nurse, but sorry she had witnessed his humiliation and juvenile behavior, he began unbuttoning his ripped shirt to get a look at the stinging skin underneath.

Bridgett set the antiseptic, antibiotic cream and bandages on the rim of the pedestal sink. She turned back to him, pushed up her cardigan sleeves and prepared to get to work. "You haven't punched out Gabe since the wedding that wasn't, have you?"

"No." Chase peeled off his shirt and stared at the nasty-looking scrape that ran from his left shoulder to midchest and down his arm. He was pretty sure it had happened when he slammed into the mantel and slid to the floor. "Although maybe I should have," Chase added as he touched his lip and found that it, too, was still bleeding, just a little bit. "Gabe still doesn't seem to have learned his lesson about stealing someone else's woman." Chase grimaced as he checked out a rug burn beneath his right elbow.

"He stole another of your girlfriends?" Bridgett frowned at the scrape on his forearm.

Chase scowled, recalling. "I saw him and Maggie at her beach house a few hours ago. They were kissing."

Bridgett wet a sterile pad with warm water, doused it liberally with soap, and began washing the scraped skin. "You and Maggie are back together?"

"Hell, no!" Chase clamped his teeth together. Damn, that stung! And damned if Bridgett didn't seem to enjoy making it sting, too!

"Then why does it matter if Gabe kisses her?" Bridgett added more soap and moved on to his shoulder.

Chase tried not to think about how good it felt to have her hands moving across his skin in such a gentle, womanly way. Bridgett was and had always been his friend, not an object of lust. "Because she was my woman and I was there first!" Chase hissed again as Bridgett dampened another sterile pad and rinsed away the soap on his skin.

Bridgett shrugged. "If that's your only objection, she was right not to marry you."

Chase shot her a look. He didn't care if the two of them had been as telepathic as twins since the moment they were born. He didn't like the censure in Bridgett's low tone. "What do you mean by that?" he demanded, turning toward her.

"I mean," Bridgett enunciated as if speaking to a total dunce, "I understand your not wanting him to kiss her if you were in love with her, but if you're not—"

"I'm not," Chase interrupted firmly.

"Then it shouldn't matter to you. Period."

"Well, it does." Chase bristled under her watchful gaze.

"Why?" Bridgett dabbed antibiotic cream across his shoulder.

"Because it's like pouring salt in a wound," Chase explained in frustration, wishing she would hurry up and get this over with.

"One that obviously has yet to heal," Bridgett countered, moving close enough to Chase that he could see the barest hint of cleavage revealed by the décolletage of her form-fitting sweater set. He swallowed around the knowledge that Bridgett's breasts were fuller and rounder than he had ever realized. Or wanted to realize.

"I'm over her," Chase said, struggling to keep his mind on Maggie, instead of Bridgett and what her closeness, her sheer femininity, were doing to him.

"Just not over the humiliation of being dumped by her," Bridget guessed, apparently oblivious to the discomfort she was causing him.

Chase shifted his weight to relieve the unexpected pressure at the front of his khaki beach shorts. "You got it."

Bridgett unrolled sterile gauze across his shoulder. "Well, then, I suggest you get over it," she advised, her warm hands brushing across his even warmer skin as she taped the bandage into place.

"And why would that be?" Chase asked, feeling as if he was going to explode if he had to sit there for one more second.

Bridgett looked at him sternly. "Because if Gabe was kissing her today, Chase, that can mean only one thing. Gabe still has the hots for Maggie. Even after all this time. And he doesn't care who knows it."

Chase vaulted to his feet, grabbed his shirt and shrugged it on. "I'm tired of talking about me and my unconscionable behavior. Let's talk about you and yours," he said, leaning back against the closed bathroom door.

Bridgett squared her slender shoulders and shot him a stern look. "I don't behave unconscionably."

Chase quirked a brow, wondering if she had missed seeing him as much as he had missed seeing her. And how was it the two of them had grown so far apart, anyway? Was it just because they were older with different personal and career agendas to pursue? Or was there more to it than that? "You used to get into trouble right along with me," he said softly, thinking about the fun the two of them had had during their childhood and teen years. It had only been later, after college, that they'd begun to drift apart. To the point that these days they rarely saw each other at all. And then, only by chance.

The picture of efficiency, Bridgett put the first-aid kit back in the medicine cabinet. "I've grown up," she told him plainly.

Too much, Chase thought, wondering when it was, exactly, that Bridgett had gotten so serious. "So I see." he shot her a teasing leer, meant to make her laugh.

"Cut it out, Chase," she ordered. Frowning, she gathered up the paper bandage wrappers and excess bits of tape and tossed them into the trash.

Chase could see he had offended her, when that was the last thing he'd wanted. "You used to have a sense of humor."

Bridgett shrugged and continued to avoid looking at him. "I used to be immature."

"And now you're not."

"No." Bridgett lifted her head and looked at him coolly. "I'm not."

Silence fell between them. Chase knew she was ready to leave the intimate confines of the guest bath, but he didn't want to let her go. Not yet. Not with the mood between them so unexpectedly tense and distant. He folded his arms in front of him and asked seriously, "How was your book tour? I assume you just got back."

Finally the sun broke out across her face. "Last night," Bridgett confirmed happily. "And the experience was wonderful, if grueling, and very satisfying, economically and personally. Just the way every three-month book tour should be."

Chase found himself warming to the deep satisfaction he saw on her face. He had always wanted the very best for her. Always known she would get it. "Did you really cover every region across the country?"

Bridgett nodded, the depth of her devotion to her work apparent. "And I helped more women than I can say," she confided, leaning back against the sink.

Maybe it was because he had grown up wealthy as sin and knew firsthand how little real joy a hefty bank account could bring a person, but it bothered Chase to know that Bridgett valued money more than just about anything these days. She used to treasure more than that. She used to treasure her friends—especially him. "Just what this world needs." Chase sighed, ready to goad her back to sanity, if need be. "Even more women who think money is the route to happiness."

Bridgett scowled at the sarcastic note in his low tone. "It is." She crossed her arms beneath her breasts defiantly.

Chase kept his eyes on hers. "If you say so." He inclined his head indifferently.

The fire in Bridgett's eyes sparked all the hotter. "Don't belittle what I do for a living, Chase."

"Why not?" Chase pushed away from the closed door and stood straight, legs braced apart, once again. "You certainly belittle what I do," he reminded her as he narrowed the distance between them to just a few inches.

Bridgett straightened, too. "That's because your magazine—"

"Modern Man," Chase helpfully supplied the publication's name, in case she'd forgotten.

"—does nothing but teach guys how to get what they want from women!"

"What's wrong with that?" Chase demanded. Clueless for as long as he could remember about what women really wanted or needed in this life, he had started his magazine as a way of collecting data from other men, about what worked and what didn't with the women in their lives. As far as Chase was concerned, he was providing a public service, making both men and women a little happier, while doing his part to tamp down the battle of the sexes and reduce the number of unhappy relationships overall.

"I'll tell you what's wrong with that." Bridgett planted her hands on her hips. "It makes guys think that women are 'a problem to be handled' and that there is something fundamentally wrong with marriage."

"There *is* something fundamentally wrong with marriage," Chase shot back flatly, not about to sugarcoat his opinion on the subject on her account. "Or hadn't you noticed the soaring divorce rate in this country?"

Bridgett released a long slow breath. She looked as if she was fighting for patience. "Lately the divorce rate has actually been going down. No thanks to you!"

Chase brought his brows together in consternation. "You don't know that," he argued back. He was tired of taking the blame for things that were way beyond his control. "Maybe I'm the one to credit for that." He knew for a fact, from reader mail, that there were a lot of guys who had really appreciated his series on how to get their women not to just tolerate, but love the sports they followed. The same went for his series on cooking in, instead of eating out.

Bridgett rolled her eyes. She stared at him, making no effort to hide her exasperation. "And how do you figure that?" she asked drolly.

"Because," Chase said, thinking how much he had always enjoyed a spirited argument with Bridgett and how much he had missed having them with her since she'd been away, "I also run articles that convince guys not to get married when they're not ready."

Bridgett's eyes turned even stormier. And worse, looked hurt. "Exactly."

Too late Chase realized he had hit a real sore point with Bridgett. The fact that her own parents had never married, even when Theresa Owens had gotten pregnant. "I'm sorry," he said swiftly, seriously. "I know your, uh—"

"Illegitimacy?" she provided when he seemed unable to blurt it out.

"—is a real sticking point with you," Chase continued, with some difficulty. It was, he knew, probably the biggest hurt of her childhood, though she rarely talked about it.

Bridgett waved him off, already done talking about it, and ready to move on. "I just think you're doing a disservice to men with that whole marriage-isn't-really-all-that-necessary attitude you and your magazine perpetuate."

"Yeah, well, I think I'm helping my readers," Chase said stubbornly. He was making them see that marriage was a serious step. And if they weren't serious about a lifetime commitment, or the women they were chasing weren't serious about the same, marriage was not the path to take. He certainly didn't want them to end up a public laughingstock, the way he had, when his bride had ditched him just days before they were to marry.

"Whatever." Bridgett tugged the sleeves of her elegant silk-and-cotton cardigan down to cover her wrists. "It doesn't matter to me."

Like hell it didn't, Chase thought, studying the wealth of emotion on her face.

"I'm late, anyway," Bridgett continued.

"For what?" Chase asked curiously. And that was when he saw it. The big fat emerald ring.

CHAPTER THREE

Bridgett thought she was past the third degree when it came to Chase and her beaux. Apparently not. He still felt—wrongly so—that he had the right to comment on the men she chose to date. Not to mention the gifts they might have or have not chosen to give her.

"What," Chase demanded, his handsome features sharpening in disapproval as he looked down at the emerald ring glittering on the ring finger of her right hand, "is that?"

Bridgett had an idea what he was going to say. She didn't want to hear it. Deliberately misunderstanding where he was trying to go with this, she lifted her shoulders in an indifferent shrug. "I can't buy myself a ring?"

Chase's sexy slate-blue eyes narrowed even more. He took a step closer and said, very low, "I know you, Bridgett. You invest in real estate, growth stocks, a car that will go a couple hundred thousand miles before it quits. You don't spend thousands of your hard-earned cash on baubles. Someone gave you that very pricey emerald-and-platinum ring."

Someone he apparently already didn't like, even though he had yet to find out who it was. "So what if it was a gift?" Bridgett shot back just as contentiously.

Expensive as the ring was, she knew that to a man like Martin, it was just like penny change. Martin never did anything in a small or inconsequential way. When they dined out, it was at the very best restaurants. They drank the rarest, most expensive wines. He didn't just send her roses. He gave her vases of the most exquisite orchids or lilies. Once, he'd flown her to Europe for the weekend, simply because he wanted her to see Paris in the springtime. Initially, of course, she'd tried to discourage such lavish gifts. Now she knew that was just the way Martin and everyone else in his family lived.

Chase braced a hand on the wall just beside her head. "I want to know who gave you that ring."

Bridgett refused to let him intimidate her with his I'm-in-charge-here body language. Honestly, she didn't know how Chase did it! She had been back in Charleston less than twenty-four hours and already Chase—the bad boy of the Deveraux clan—was already under her skin. Big-time.

She angled her chin at him defiantly "I don't have to answer you."

"Darn it, Bridgett. You know how much I care about you."

Cared, Bridgett thought, but didn't love. Would never love. At least not in the way she had once wanted desperately for Chase to love her. Now she knew better, of course. Chase might have once considered her his very best buddy and partner in mischief, but when it had come to dating, he had always chosen others. At first she had thought— wrongly—it was just because he was romancing women from his own social class. That theory had been blown out of the water when he became engaged to Maggie Callaway, who was from the same working class background as Bridgett. Then she had known that social status was not the reason Chase didn't pursue her. He simply wasn't attracted to her. Not in that way. So she had put any lingering hope of a romance between them aside and kept her distance from Chase as much as possible. She had known then what she had to remind herself of now. Chase protected her and watched out for her in a familial sort of way. There was nothing the least bit romantic in his feelings toward her—and never would be.

Silence fell between them. "Your mother didn't tell me you were engaged," Chase said finally when she didn't respond to him.

"That's because I'm not yet," Bridgett explained with a great deal more patience than she felt.

He dropped his arm, stepped back until he was once again leaning against the opposite wall of the first-floor powder room, his six-foot-two-inch frame dwarfing her own five-foot-seven one a little less. "But you're close," Chase asserted unhappily, still studying her face.

"I think we're definitely headed that way. Yes."

Abruptly Chase looked as if he had received a sucker punch to the gut. Again Bridgett warned herself not to take his reaction personally. Chase was probably just suffering the pangs any "brother" would have about seeing his "sister" married off.

"Who's the lucky guy?" Chase asked finally in a rusty-sounding voice.

Bridgett tried not to notice how handsome Chase looked in the soft lighting of the room. After all, it wasn't as if she wasn't used to his stunning good looks. She had grown up looking into those long-lashed, slate-blue eyes of his and knew full well they were the color of the ocean on a stormy day. She had committed to heart the rugged planes of his face, the square jaw, the high cheekbones and wickedly sexy smile. Okay, maybe his shoulders did look a little broader and stronger, his abdomen a little flatter, since the last time she had seen him. Maybe he was a little more tan and rough around the edges. But the ensemble of pleated khaki shorts, loose-fitting short-sleeved shirt and sneakers was the same. Chase wanted people to see him as a slacker when she knew full well he was anything but. Deep down he was as ambitious and determined to succeed in business as she was, if not more so.

"The guy?" Chase prodded again when Bridgett failed to answer his query. "The ring giver does have a name, doesn't he?"

Bridgett flushed. "Martin Morganstern."

Chase shook his head and looked all the more disappointed and distressed. "Not the art-gallery guy over on King Street," he said, groaning.

"One and the same," Bridgett confirmed, unable to help the haughty edge that came into her voice. "And you needn't speak of him with such derision."

Chase rolled his eyes. "Man, Bridgett! That guy is old enough to be your father!"

Bridgett forced a droll smile as she allowed, "Only if I were sired when he was thirteen."

"Which makes him…?"

Bridgett pushed aside her own lingering uneasiness that there was something just not right about her and

Martin, despite the fact that on paper, anyway, when it came to all the relevant facts, they looked very good as a couple. "He's forty-five."

"To your thirty-two." Chase blew out a gusty breath and slammed his hands on his hips. "The guy's too old for you. Way too old."

Bridgett shrugged. She didn't know why, exactly, but Chase was making her want to punch him. "You're welcome to your opinion," she told him icily. "Fortunately," she said as she tried to step past him once again, "I don't have to abide by it."

Chase smiled as if he had an ace up his sleeve and once again stepped to block her way. "What does your mother think about that ring?" he asked smugly.

Another alarm bell went off in Bridgett's head. Ignoring the probing nature of Chase's gaze, she said stiffly, "She hasn't noticed it yet." She'd been too busy in the kitchen.

Chase immediately had an "Aha!" look on his face.

Bridgett grimaced all the more. "I was about to show her when you and Gabe started brawling."

Chase smirked. "Likely story."

Not for the first time in her life, Bridgett wished Chase didn't know her so well. "I'll do it later," she said.

Chase ran a hand along the light stubble on his jaw and continued to regard her smugly. "I think you're stalling."

Bridgett squared her shoulders as if for battle. "I am not."

Chase lifted his dark brow in silent dissension. "Your mom won't approve of you accepting such a lavish gift from him," he predicted matter-of-factly.

Unfortunately Bridgett was pretty sure Chase was

right about that, since to date Theresa hadn't approved of much of anything Martin had done.

"In fact," Chase predicted, leaning even closer, "I bet she doesn't like you dating Martin any more than I do, does she?"

"Fortunately for me," Bridgett parried, ignoring the warmth emanating from Chase's tall strong body, "it's not up to my mother whom I should or should not spend time with."

Chase's brows drew together like twin thunderclouds. "You should listen to her, Bridgett. Your mother has always had a lot of sense."

"In most matters." Bridgett felt her hackles go up as she delineated precisely, "Not this."

"You need to give that ring back, Bridgett."

"Really." Taking exception to the tone of his voice, Bridgett folded her arms beneath her breasts contentiously and glared at him. "And why would that be?"

Because that ring is the kind of gift a man gives to announce a woman is his. And his alone. And I just can't see you with a smooth talker like Morganstern, Chase thought. Aware she was waiting for an answer and fuming while she did so, Chase did his best to conjure up an answer. "Because you're too young to get that serious about someone," he said finally.

"I'm thirty-two," Bridgett shot back, temper sparking her beautiful brown eyes. "If I want to have a family of my own—"

"You've got plenty of time for that."

Again she looked down her nose at him, as if he just didn't get it. "I'm ready to get married and settle down now," she explained as if to a moron.

Chase frowned, and unable to help himself, blurted out in frustration, "At least find someone who can make you happy while you do it!"

Bridgett propped her hands on her hips. "What makes you think Martin won't make me happy?"

Because I just know, Chase thought, uneasiness sifting through him. Aware how lame that would sound, he remained silent.

Bridgett stared at him as if she had never seen him before and had no clue who he was. "Like I said, I've got to go." She ducked around behind him and exited the powder room without another word.

CHASE WAS DISAPPOINTED he hadn't been able to make Bridgett see what a mistake she was making even dating Mr. Wrong. But that didn't mean he was giving up. He figured it would take time—and persistence—to make Bridgett see the error of her ways. But he figured she'd be grateful to him in the end. He didn't want her suffering the way he had when he'd been betrothed to the wrong person.

In the meantime he needed to check on his mother. He found Grace upstairs in the guest room where she always stayed. She had changed out of her travel clothes and into a slim apple-green dress that only seemed to emphasize her recent weight loss. The strain lines on her face seemed all the more pronounced in the late-afternoon sunlight streaming in through the windows. "Are you going to be okay?" He didn't know why, but she seemed more vulnerable now than when she had first arrived and told them she'd been fired. He wasn't used to his take-charge, kick-butt mother being weak.

"Of course I'll be all right," Grace said in the firm parental voice she had used on him and his siblings. She looked at him sternly. "I don't want you worrying about me."

"Can't help it." Chase sauntered into the bedroom and shut the door behind him, so they could talk privately. "In the first place, I'm the oldest son."

"Which does not make you responsible for me."

Maybe that would've been true had there been someone else—like a husband around all the time—to protect her. But there wasn't. "Even so, in your place, I'd be reeling," Chase told her frankly.

Grace opened the first of several suitcases with a beleaguered sigh. "I've suffered setbacks before, Chase."

Chase knew she had. First and foremost among them had been her legal separation from his father, a year after she had moved to New York City to work on *Rise and Shine, America!* Another year after that, there'd been the finalization of the divorce. None of which Chase understood to this day. Oh, he knew marriages didn't last anymore. And maybe they never should have lasted for decades even in years past, when that was the norm. Most of the married couples he knew did not seem all that happy once the wedding rings were on their fingers, the shackles around their ankles.

"Plus, I work in television," Grace continued, as she took out a stack of clothes and put them neatly in a dresser drawer. "Being hired and fired is all part of the routine business cycle."

"It still must hurt," Chase persisted, taking a seat on the ivory chaise in the corner.

Just as the divorce had hurt. Not that Grace and Tom

had ever let their kids see them quarrel. It had been their strict policy not to let their four children be privy to anything going on in their marriage, especially anything bad. The idea, of course, had been to protect Chase and his siblings from any unpleasantness. And so all their kids had thought everything was fine when it was not, and had ended up feeling baffled and distressed when Grace and Tom—for no reason any of their children could fathom—suddenly stopped speaking to each other and began living separate lives. Chase had often wondered what the breaking point had been. Had one of them been unfaithful or done something equally unforgivable? And if so, why? Was the love between a man and a woman something that could just end without warning or reason? Frustratingly these weren't the kinds of questions his parents fielded. All he knew for certain was, after they'd split, the anger and bitterness between Grace and Tom had been fierce and unrelenting. And that tension had gotten worse, before it had ever gotten better. These days, of course, the two were able to be cordial to each other—at least on the surface. But deep down, Chase still felt there were problems that remained unresolved to this day. Divorce or no divorce.

"I admit my pride is wounded," Grace said in a way that reminded Chase that this was the first time his mother had been fired from a job. Previously whenever Grace had left a television show, it was to take a better position at another show.

Grace took out several pairs of shoes and carried them to the shelf in the closet. "It hurts having the failure of the show blamed on me and my cohost. But that's just the way it is in the business." Grace returned to her suitcase for her toiletry bag. "Whoever is out in front takes the credit or the blame, and in this case it was blame that needed to be apportioned out to appease the sponsors."

Restless, Chase got up to help. "Something better will come along. Before you know it, you'll be back in New York on another network," he assured his mother as he unzipped the first of her two garment bags.

Grace smiled ruefully as she lifted out the clothes already on hangers and carried them to the closet. "I'm not sure I want to work in early-morning television again. Getting up at three-thirty every morning did not do much for my social life. I was going to bed for the night when everyone I knew was just getting off work for the day."

"Then something that airs later in the day," Chase persisted, pushing away the disturbing thought of his mother wanting to keep company with any men besides his father. It had been bad enough occasionally coming face-to-face with his father when he was squiring other, usually much younger, women around. Now he'd probably be seeing his mother going out on dates, too. "An afternoon talk show, maybe," Chase suggested.

Grace made a face as she set out her hairbrushes and combs on the old-fashioned vanity. "Right now that sounds like even more of a grind. No. What I want to do right now is spend more time with you and your brothers and sister, Chase. I've missed that."

Chase warmed at the idea of being able to see and talk to his mother whenever he wanted again and still live and work in the city he had grown up in and come to love like no other. "We've missed you, too, Mom." More than she would ever know. It was their dirty little secret, but without Grace around, the Deveraux did not seem like much of a family. Not the way they once had been, anyway.

Grace enveloped Chase in a warm hug. "And besides, I've always wanted to learn how to cook."

"I THOUGHT YOU'D BE happy for me," Bridgett told her mother emotionally. She had just shown her the emerald ring Martin had given her after picking her up at the airport and taking her to dinner the evening before. "I thought you wanted me to be happy." And frankly she was hurt that her mother wasn't more enthusiastic about the serious turn her relationship with Martin was about to take.

"I do want you to be happy," Theresa explained gently. "Which is why I want you to spend time with someone whose background is similar to yours."

"Not to mention," a deep male voice said from the doorway, "someone your own age."

Theresa beamed at Chase the way she always did whenever he entered a room. "See, he agrees with me," Theresa said as Chase kissed her cheek.

"Chase just doesn't want to see anyone get serious," Bridgett said, more irritated than ever to have Chase putting his two cents in about her personal life. She stopped folding napkins for her mother long enough to glare at Chase. "Chase does not believe in monogamy, never mind marriage."

Chase plucked a carrot from the salad Theresa was making. He shrugged his broad shoulders without apology as he turned back to Bridgett. "I certainly don't believe you should yoke yourself to some hoity-toity art dealer."

"Hoity-toity?" Bridgett echoed in amazement, unable to believe Chase had actually used such a term.

"Haughty, arrogant, condescending." Chase pulled up a stool and joined them at the butcher block, where they were preparing dinner.

"I know what it means," Bridgett countered irritably, wishing Chase would just go away. She put the last of the fan-shaped napkins into a basket for her mother. "I write for a living, too, you know."

"Martin's old money, darling," Theresa warned. "Very old money. And you know what they always say…"

"The rich are different," Bridgett repeated wearily. She had heard that old saw from her mother a thousand times.

"Not all of us." Chase helped himself to a tomato wedge. "Some of us old money fellas are down to earth. Just not ol' Martin Morganstern of the Morganstern Gallery of Charleston. Martin is as blue-blooded and luxury-loving as they come."

Bridgett found herself defending her soon-to-be fiancé hotly. "He's very nice."

Chase raised a dissenting brow as he added salt to the tomato wedge.

Theresa sighed as she continued to whip up a vinegar-and-oil dressing. "All men are nice when they're trying to…to…"

"Get into my bed?" Bridgett guessed, saying what her mother seemed unable to articulate.

Theresa flushed with embarrassment but did not

back down as she poured dressing on the salad and tossed it. "You're the daughter of a domestic servant, Bridgett. You may want to forget that. But ten to one, in the end, Martin Morganstern and his very old and very proper family won't."

REALIZING IF SHE DIDN'T get a move on, she was going to be late, Bridgett said goodbye to her mother and headed out the back door. To her dismay, Chase followed her. "Your mom is right," he said as he shadowed Bridgett out to her Mercedes. "What you have is new money. To a guy like Martin Morganstern, there's one heck of a difference. To a guy like me, well, cash is cash."

Bridgett unlocked her car and tossed her purse inside. "Thank you ever so much for enlightening me." Hot air poured out of the sedan's interior through the open door.

"I don't care if you have any money or not," Chase continued while Bridgett waited for her car to cool down before she got in. "I am and will always be your friend, regardless of your financial circumstances." Chase folded his arms on the top of the door and continued to regard her with a cheeky seriousness that really got under her skin. "Can you really say the same about Martin Morganstern?"

Realizing she would be too hot with her cardigan on, Bridgett slipped it off, and tossed it on the seat beside her purse. She ignored the way Chase's gaze slid over her bare arms and shoulders. "You've been listening to my mother for too long!"

Chase grabbed her wrist before she could slide in,

his fingers warm on her skin. "Your mother is just trying to keep you from getting hurt," he said seriously.

"And what's your excuse for butting into my life?" Bridgett turned away from the stormy gray-blue of his eyes and put up a hand to stop any further diatribes. "Don't answer. I really don't want to know."

Afraid she would lose it if they said anything else to each other on the subject, she started her car and drove off.

MARTIN WAS WAITING for Bridgett in the Barbados Room in the Mills House Hotel. He was wearing a sage-green suit with a tie and white shirt. His black hair was neatly brushed away from his handsome face, his gray eyes alert and interested. As always, he looked thrilled to see her approaching him. Just being with Martin made her feel calm inside, not all fired up and agitated the way she was when she was with Chase Deveraux.

As she neared, he stood and helped her with her chair. "I ordered you a glass of wine."

Bridgett smiled gratefully, appreciating his gentlemanly manners. "Thank you."

"What's wrong?" Martin studied her silently. His glance fell to her right hand, before returning to her eyes. "Don't tell me. Your mother thinks you shouldn't have accepted the ring I gave you."

Bridgett didn't have the heart to tell Martin how upset her mother had been about the gift and what it might mean when he had been so excited about giving it to her. So she said only, "My mother's very old-fashioned when it comes to a lot of things."

Martin frowned. "You should have let me come with you when you went to see her today."

That would have only made things worse, Bridgett thought, because there was no telling what her plain-spoken mother would have said to upset a quiet cultured man like Martin. "It'll be fine," Bridgett insisted, glancing at the menu.

Martin studied her. "I hope so. I really want your mother to like me. That's rather hard to manage when she never spends any time with me."

Bridgett swallowed. She had tried to get her mother to have an open mind about her relationship with Martin—to no avail. Her mother thought people should get married only if they were wildly in love and of similar backgrounds. She and Martin flunked that litmus test. Their backgrounds were as different as night and day, and as for their feelings for each other, well, those were more of a tranquil nature. Steady and reliable. Without the ups and downs of passion. What no one seemed to understand, Bridgett thought, was that this was what she wanted. A relationship that was as safe and dependable as municipal bonds. She didn't want to be worried about being abandoned by the man she loved, the way her own mother had. Nor did she want to worry about getting divorced, the way Tom and Grace had. It was so much better, she thought, to enter into a lifelong relationship with someone with a cool head and a sensible attitude.

Martin continued to watch Bridgett, waiting.

"My mother is going to need a little time," Bridgett said finally, thinking that a guaranteed low-yield invest-ment was better than the ups and downs of a high-risk annuity any day.

"I have been patient, darling," Martin said gently, covering her hand with his.

Bridgett swallowed and tried not to think how heavy and almost uncomfortable the emerald-and-platinum ring felt on her right hand. She looked into Martin's eyes. "I know you have," she said softly.

"I waited for you throughout the long months of your book tour."

And he had never complained about her absence, Bridgett thought in her soon-to-be fiancé's defense. Not once.

"But my patience," Martin continued, "is almost gone."

HOURS LATER, Bridgett's mind was still reeling with all Martin had demanded of her as he walked her to the front door of her newly acquired "single house" in the historic district of Charleston. Like all town homes of the early 1800s, the single-pile redbrick Georgian had been turned sideways on the narrow city lot. A two-story piazza, or covered porch, had been built along the length of the building to provide outdoor living space for each floor, as well as shade on the windowed facade. On the first floor the street-front room was her office, where she worked on her books and advised clients on financial matters. The single room behind it was an eat-in kitchen. On the second floor, she had a combination master bedroom and bath at the front of the house and at the rear a cozy sitting room, where she relaxed, read, watched television and entertained. It was small but perfect, and as soon as Bridgett had purchased it, she had known she had really made it. No longer was she merely the daughter of the housekeeper of a well-heeled Charleston family. Now she was one of the elite that kept the city humming.

"You'll call me in the morning to let me know what you've decided?" Martin said as he ever so tenderly increased his grip on her hand.

Bridgett nodded as she looked into his eyes. "Absolutely."

"Sleep well, my precious." Martin brushed his lips across her temple. He turned and headed down the sidewalk to the car at the curb. Bridgett waited, enjoying the splendor of the cool spring evening, until he'd driven away before she turned to let herself inside. And that was when she saw him, relaxing in the shadows, of her first-floor piazza.

CHAPTER FOUR

"My precious!" Chase echoed. "Who says something like that? Oh, right." He snapped his fingers. "Someone from the *previous* generation."

Bridgett told herself she was not in the least bit glad to see him as she unlocked her front door. "What are you doing here?" She tried to behave as if she wasn't perturbed by the fact that Chase had been not just waiting for her to come home from her date, but had declined to make his presence known right away, spying on her and Martin, as well.

"Isn't it obvious?" Chase strolled around to join her and followed her into the house. "I came to talk to you."

Bridgett shut the door behind them. "It's after midnight, Chase."

"I know." Chase made himself at home on the red damask settee.

Bridgett noted he was still in the casual clothes he'd had on earlier, with one exception. He'd taken off the shirt he'd torn in the brawl with Gabe and put on a plain blue oxford-cloth dress shirt that looked as though it might have belonged to his dad. He'd left the shirttails out and rolled the sleeves to his elbow. "You changed your shirt," she said.

"Had to." He sat back amiably and propped an ankle on his knee. "Dinner with the folks."

Deciding the room was much too cozy with only one lamp burning, Bridgett walked around the room and turned on a few more lights. "How'd that go?"

Chase's eyes turned serious as she came back to join him in the small sitting area of her home office. "It was exceptionally quiet. Gabe got called back to the hospital halfway through. Amy was her usual worried self. And Mitch seemed preoccupied—something to do with the family shipping business. I wasn't really paying attention."

"What about your parents?"

"They were pretty quiet, too. I had the feeling they wanted to spend some time alone, talking about Mom's situation, I'm sure. They were just going through the motions of a family dinner to reassure us everything would still be okay, despite the very public firing."

"Once a parent, always a parent, I suppose."

"I guess." Chase surveyed her midnight-blue silk chiffon sheath, with the handkerchief hem and matching chiffon shawl. He regarded her in a way that reminded her just how well he knew her. "What are you doing out so late on a weeknight, anyway? Don't you have to work tomorrow?"

Knowing he was right—normally she would be in bed a lot earlier on a weeknight so she could be up bright and early the next morning to write or meet with the clients she was advising on financial matters— Bridgett sat down in a straight-backed chair opposite from him. "I'm taking a few weeks off before I start my next project," she said. "And I have no client appointments scheduled for the next week, either."

"Good. Glad to hear it." Chase leaned forward earnestly, hands clasped between his spread knees. "Because I need your help. Professionally speaking."

"I'm not writing anything for *Modern Man*," she told him flatly.

"Sure now?" Chase flashed her a sexy grin. "We could use a woman's perspective on money matters. You wouldn't even have to write anything. We'd conduct it interview-style. And I'll put it all together in an article about you and your success."

Bridgett knew that where Chase was concerned, nothing was this simple. If he wanted to do something, it was because he knew his readers would benefit in ways specifically aligned with his way of thinking. She had to think for a minute to figure out how Chase would probably spin it. "So you can tell your readers how to get women to do what they want in a financial sense," Bridgett guessed. *While still avoiding marriage like the plague.*

Chase flattened a palm against his rock-solid chest and regarded her with mock hurt. "You sound like you've been listening to my critics."

"I've been reading your magazine," Bridgett said.

"And...?"

"If you really want to know, I think you're so off base in your assessment of the current battle between the sexes, it's ridiculous."

"Come on, Bridgett." Chase gave her a look that begged for understanding. "Most of the stuff you're referring to is meant solely to amuse."

"You and I know that." Bridgett crossed her legs

demurely at the ankle and continued to regard Chase seriously. "I'm not sure most of the male population under thirty does. I think they take all your advice about how to thrive as bachelors very seriously even the stuff that is clearly over the top."

Chase regarded her with lazy indifference. "Maybe that's because my readers don't want the wife, the house and the two kids in the suburbs. When they do start wanting that stuff, they stop reading *Modern Man* and move on to whatever it is married guys with kids read."

Chase had always been fun-loving and reckless to a fault, but in the wake of his own broken engagement and his parents' divorce, he had also become a lot bitterer than she figured even he realized, and her heart went out to him. She looked at him and said with as much gentleness as she could muster, "You're going to find another woman, Chase."

Chase scowled as if the last thing he wanted was Bridgett's pity. His jaw set as he vaulted from the sofa and paced her home office. "I didn't come for advice on my love life."

"I figured that," Bridgett retorted. It didn't mean she wouldn't give it. Particularly when he'd been so free to comment on *her* love life.

"But there are a couple of matters I do want to discuss." Chase shoved his hands in the front pockets of his khaki shorts.

"Okay."

His manner abruptly serious, he continued, "First I want you to talk to my mother for me. About her finances. I want to make sure she's all set, despite this firing."

Bridgett hedged, aware Chase was once again treading where he shouldn't. "I'm sure your mother already has excellent financial advisers."

His eyebrows assumed a troubled arch. "I'm not so sure about that. She's never had much interest in financial matters. To tell the truth, she made so much money with *Rise and Shine, America!* and has been so slow about spending it that she never felt it mattered. Now, with a sudden drastic reduction in her income, it may matter a lot. You've had a great deal of experience in getting women who don't want to deal with their finances to face the music. I just thought if the two of us took my mother to lunch tomorrow, we could talk about your work and how successful you've been for yourself and your clients in your private financial-counseling service. And then see if we can get my mother to ask for your advice or at least accept it and read one of your books. That last one was particularly on the money, in my opinion."

"You've been reading my books?" Bridgett tried not to make anything of the fact that he was as up on her work as she was on his.

Chase shrugged. "I wanted to see if you knew what you were talking about," he admitted with partially disguised pride. "You do."

Despite her annoyance with him, his respect meant a lot to her. As did the fact that he had come to her, instead of one of his own financial advisers, with this request. "I'd be happy to help you, Chase."

"Good." He breathed a sigh of relief.

"But I have to warn you," Bridgett continued, "I think you better be prepared to be very subtle with your mother. If you come on like gangbusters, in the wake of the humiliation she has already suffered in being fired…"

Chase lifted a palm as if being sworn in. "I'll be the soul of discretion, I promise."

Bridgett moved gracefully to her feet, knowing she really needed to get him out of her house before the mood between them became too intimate. She didn't want to feel this close to him, as if they were still and always would be the very best of friends. Not when she was getting ready to say yes to a marriage proposal from another man. "Well, if that's all…" she said politely, dropping her chiffon shawl on the chair.

"Actually it's not." Chase blocked her way to the door. Ignoring the impatient expression on her face, he said, "I want to know if there's any real passion between you and Marvin."

Leave it to Chase to get right back to that, Bridgett thought on a beleaguered sigh. Leave it to him to make her have to explain. "His name is Martin, Chase. Not Marvin. And we have passion," Bridgett declared, hating the defensive note that had crept back into her voice.

"Oh, yeah, I could see that." Chase rolled his eyes and shook his head as he recounted, "The guy brought you home and didn't even give you a proper good-night kiss! If that's what it's like now, what is it going to be like for the two of you after you get married and things really cool off?"

A flush climbed from Bridgett's neck to her face. She hated Chase's ability to follow the track of her thoughts—and concerns—so easily. "Martin respects me," she countered testily, pushing her own nagging doubts about what she was doing aside.

"You mean he treats you like a porcelain figurine he doesn't want to damage," Chase corrected. "You're not going to be happy sitting on a shelf in some rich man's house, Bridgett."

Bridgett marched past him and grabbed the door handle. "Get out." She forced the words through her teeth.

Chase caught up with her and flattened his hand against the wood next to her head, holding the door shut. "Not until I've had my say," he said.

The air was coming in and out of Bridgett's lungs with difficulty.

"I don't want to see you hurt," he said next.

Tears of frustration welled in Bridgett's eyes. "*You're* hurting me."

"What can I say?" Chase countered, his expression as stern and unrelenting as the words he tossed at her. "Sometimes the truth knocks you on your butt. Only, I care about you too much to stand by while you throw your life away."

Bridgett wished that was true. When they were growing up, she would have given anything for Chase to notice her and want to protect her like this. But he hadn't. He had treated her like his best pal—and that was all. Eventually she'd had to face the fact that he didn't desire her in the way she desired him and never would. She'd been devastated. So devastated, in fact, that she had done her level best to avoid being alone with him like this ever since. They'd been together in groups, but never absolutely alone. Never like this.

"Why are you looking at me like that?" he asked softly, brushing the hair from her face.

Because I want you to see me as a woman, Bridgett thought, desire welling up inside her with the force of a tidal wave. *Because just once I want you to haul me into your arms and kiss* me *like there's no tomorrow.* Not about to tell him that, however, she angled her chin stubbornly, glared at him for a long pulse-throbbing moment, then turned away and said, "Because I want you to stop interfering in my life and telling me what to do."

"Is that right?" Chase challenged. He caught her by the shoulder and brought her gently but determinedly back around to face him.

"It's absolutely positively right!" Bridgett shot right back.

And the next thing she knew, she was in Chase's arms and he was lowering his mouth to hers. Their lips met in an explosion of softness and heat, pleasure and need. Bridgett murmured a quiet "Oh!" of surprise and another helpless whisper of breath. His tongue touched hers, lightly at first, then with growing ardor, his passion igniting her own. Longing shifted through her, more powerful and wonderful than anything she had ever felt—or dared imagine. She whimpered again, more helplessly still, against the sensual pressure of his lips. "Bridgett," Chase whispered as his arms brought her closer still, until her breasts were pressed against the hardness of his chest and their bodies were almost one. Lower still, she felt the flatness of his abs and stomach, the hard demanding evidence of his desire, the strength in the arms around her. She melted against him, threading her hands through his hair, completely caught up in the liquid mating of their lips and tongues. She had always known if he kissed her, it would be like this.

Chase hadn't come over there to kiss her, hadn't ever let himself consider the possibility of the two of them being anything but friends. But now that they were kissing, he found he couldn't stop the feelings pouring out of him. Bridgett felt so right in his arms. So sweet and giving. She made him want to be lost in her, in this. But even as he thought it, he knew he couldn't allow their embrace to go any farther. Not before he got a few things straight, anyway.

Reluctantly he lifted his head, stepped back. He swore silently at the regret and confusion already in Bridgett's dark-brown eyes. He could tell she was already wishing they hadn't crossed this bridge in their relationship. And that disappointed him more than he could say.

"What was that all about?" Bridgett demanded, glaring at him as if the searing embrace was all his fault and she hadn't kissed him back at all.

Angry that she had shifted the blame to him, Chase shrugged. And as always, when he felt his happiness or status quo threatened, he fell back on his customary devil-may-care attitude. "I'll be damned if I know," he said.

CHAPTER FIVE

"You can't just come in here and kiss me like that and then tell me you don't know why you did it!" Bridgett stormed. Just then her phone rang.

The problem was, Chase thought, as Bridgett's phone continued ringing, he did know why he did it. He'd been seeing red ever since he had seen the ring on her right hand earlier that day and known she was about to make the mistake of her life. That feeling had only intensified when he had seen Martin leave her at her door without so much as a real good-night kiss. Bridgett deserved more, he thought furiously. A helluva lot more. But unable to tell her that—when clearly all she wanted him for was a pal and a sort of unofficial brother—he shrugged. "I wanted to show you what you'd be missing if you hitched yourself to that old geezer."

Bridgett gave him a look that revved up his motor even more, then asked with so much feigned sweetness he wanted to haul her into his arms and kiss her all over again, "Meaning, if I don't marry him, you'll keep supplying me with passionate kisses?"

"Do you want me to keep supplying you with kisses?" Chase asked, as Bridgett's prerecorded message on her answering machine finally ended. A beep sounded, signaling it was time for the caller to leave a message, and then a familiar female voice filled the room.

"Bridgett, darling, it's happened again!" Chase's aunt, Winnifred Deveraux-Smith said. "I've seen Eleanor! And I can't find anyone to help me witness it—Chase, Amy, Gabe, Mitch, Grace and Tom are all out! So call or come over if you can!" The machine clicked as the message ended.

Chase groaned and slapped the heel of his hand against his forehead. "Not again," he grumbled. "Two mentions of that ghost in one day are all I can take." First Amy had suggested that the curse put on Eleanor—and by association the whole family—was the real reason his engagement to Maggie had ended. And now Aunt Winnie—the only member of the family who had ever actually encountered the ghost of the long-since-departed Eleanor—had experienced another ghostly encounter.

Bridgett plucked her evening bag and keys off the table. "Well, I'm going over there." She wrapped her shawl around her shoulders.

Chase frowned. "Not by yourself, you're not."

Bridgett glided past him as he held the door for her. "Now why would you want to go over there, Chase? You don't believe in ghosts."

"Exactly." Chase waited for Bridgett to lock up, then escorted her to his Jeep. "Someone has to talk some sense into Aunt Winnifred and put all this nonsense to rest before you and Amy and everyone else in the family starts believing it, too!"

Bridgett watched Chase circle around the front of the vehicle and climb into the driver's side. "There have been some unexplained phenomena. Besides, it doesn't matter if you or I or Amy or anyone else believes in this ghost. Your aunt Winnifred does. And as long as she thinks there's a curse on the members of your family, preventing anyone and everyone from living happily ever after, she will never remarry."

Chase frowned as he drove the short distance to his aunt's residence on East Battery. The three-story pink-stucco mansion overlooked the eastern side of the Charleston peninsula and had a magnificent view of the bay. The Greek-revival mansion also had a piazza on all three stories, as well as a parapet on the roof that bore the family coat of arms. When his aunt gave big parties, as she was inclined to do on a regular basis, people spilled out onto the porches, the lawn and sometimes even the roof and had a wonderful time.

Chase noted from the way the place was lit up that it looked like his aunt had thrown a party that very night. He led Bridgett through the front gate of the tall black wrought-iron fence that surrounded the house on all sides and up the elegantly landscaped walk to the front door.

"Aunt Winnie might never remarry, anyway. Mom and Dad both said she was devastated when her husband was killed in that training mission on his first year of active duty with the military." It had been nearly twenty-seven years, and Winnie showed no signs of being completely over her loss.

Bridgett exchanged concerned looks with Chase. "Thank goodness Winnifred has Harry."

Chase knew exactly what Bridgett meant. Winnifred's butler was more than just a family employee, he was Winnifred's right hand. There'd been a bit of a scandal when Aunt Winnie hired Harry, of course. Her husband had barely been dead a year, and the very British Harry was far too handsome and close to Winnifred in age for people not to wonder if it was wise for them both to be living—more or less alone most of the time—under the same roof. But the gossip had faded over time when Harry had remained Winnifred's trusted loyal servant and closest confidante and nothing more.

Harry answered the door. His pale-blond hair was slicked away from his face, and he was wearing black tie, tails and gloves. Looking resplendent in a shimmering evening gown, the fifty-year-old Winnifred was right behind him. "Oh, Chase, thank goodness you're here, too!"

"Why?" Chase asked as he followed Bridgett inside. He noted that Winnifred's cheeks were awfully pink.

"Because it was you Eleanor was warning me about!"

"What'd she do?" Chase quipped, becoming more amused by the minute. "Repeatedly call my name?" If he didn't know better, he'd think his aunt was matchmaking.

"Of course not," Winnifred said as she lifted the skirt of her party gown and made her way up the sweeping circular staircase to the second-floor sitting room. "Eleanor made a lot of noise in the attic, which was what drew me up there, and when I got there, she was sitting on the trunk that contains all the toys you used to play with when you were a child. So I know it's you she's concerned about this time."

Chase looked beyond Winnifred to Harry. "How much champagne has she had this evening, anyway?"

"Not enough to imagine that," Winnifred said sternly, looking at Chase in a way that left no doubt in anyone's mind she was sober as a rock. "If you don't believe me, you can—" She stopped midsentence as they heard light rustling sounds on the floor above. "You see!" Winnifred cried joyously. "There she goes again. Calling us up there!" Winnifred rushed toward the attic door. "Hang on, Eleanor, we're coming!" she shouted. Harry was right behind her, flashlight in hand.

"Did you see the ghost, too?" Chase asked Harry as he tucked Bridgett's hand in his and pulled her along beside him.

Harry shook his head as Winnifred yanked open the door to the attic and all four of them were assaulted with a blast of remarkably frigid air. "I was downstairs paying the caterers," Harry said.

Winnifred hit the light switch as she ascended the stairs to the third floor. Noticing Bridgett was shivering in her thin evening dress, Chase tugged her close and wrapped an arm around her shoulders.

Chase wasn't surprised to see the attic still remained just the way he recalled it. Big steamer trunks of family belongings fought for space with the odd piece of furniture and a dressmaker's dummy from years past. "Show me where you saw Eleanor," Chase said.

Frowning—probably because there was no ghostly apparition anywhere in sight and all the noise had stopped, too—Winnifred picked her way across the crowded attic floor and stopped just short of an antique oval mirror. "Right over there," she pointed to the trunk just in front of the mirror. "I saw her sitting right there when I rushed up the stairs."

Maybe because Eleanor Deveraux was considered a "friendly" ghost, Winnifred wasn't the least bit afraid of the apparition she'd seen.

Chase frowned as he tried to figure out a logical explanation for what his aunt had seen. "Are you sure you didn't just catch sight of yourself in the mirror?" he said. "If you were excited about seeing Eleanor again…" Sightings of the ghost were infrequent at best, usually tied to some family romantic calamity. In this case, Chase felt, the calamity would have had nothing to do with him or with Bridgett. In this case, the calamity would have been his mother returning to Charleston—the city where her ex-husband/Winnifred's brother still lived—and Winnifred's ever-present hope that Grace and Tom would finally patch up their differences and reconcile so that at least someone in the Devearaux family would defy the legacy and be happily married at long last.

"I think I can tell the difference between gold-and-white silk brocade—which was what Eleanor was wearing this evening—and my own red-silk evening gown, Chase. Furthermore—"

Feeling a lecture he did not want to hear coming on, Chase interrupted and held up a staying palm. "Look," he said with a great deal more patience than he really felt, "I didn't mean to imply—"

Without warning, the lights in the attic flickered and went out, leaving them in total darkness.

"See?" Winnifred cried. Harry switched on his flashlight and swung the illuminating beam around. "You've ticked her off, Chase."

"It's probably just a fuse," Chase said.

Bridgett tensed. Able to feel her trembling, Chase tightened his arm around her. Harry handed Chase the flashlight. "I'm going down to the root cellar to check the fuse box. If there's nothing wrong there, I'll bring up some lightbulbs. Maybe they just all need to be replaced."

"I'll go with you," Winnifred said, trembling, too. She pointed at Chase and Bridget and commanded, "You stay here and wait for the ghost."

Chase focused the flashlight on the path Harry and Winnifred needed to take to make it safely down the attic stairs. When they were gone, he turned back to Bridgett. "Sorry about all this," he said, although in truth he wasn't sorry at all. This latest disaster-in-the-making was giving him an excuse to be close to Bridgett again, physically, as well as emotionally.

"You can't help what your aunt believes." Bridgett shivered and snuggled more closely in the protective curve of his arm.

Chase drank in the fragrance of her perfume. "The question is, what do you believe?" he asked softly, studying the pretty contours of her upturned face. "Do you think there's a ghost up here?"

Another gust of chill air descended on them, causing Bridgett to shiver all the harder.

"I don't know what to think," Bridgett whispered as nervously as if they'd been overheard. "Intellectually, of course, I know there are no such things as ghosts." She wrapped her arm around Chase's waist. "And yet, people all over Charleston have claimed to have seen any number of ghosts over the years. We've had books written about them."

Chase grinned. "Not to mention created some very lucrative tourist traps," he added in amusement.

"And then there's Winnifred. If she says she saw Eleanor here tonight—" Bridgett broke off at the rustling sound in the darkness behind them, close to the trunk and the antique mirror.

"Maybe it's just a mouse," Chase said.

Bridgett moaned at the thought of that and wrapped her other arm around Chase's waist. Chase would have liked to stay that way forever, with Bridgett clinging to him. Unfortunately they had a mystery that needed to be solved. Determined to see what had been making the racket, Chase extricated Bridgett from his arms. Then he positioned himself in front of her and ever so carefully, ever so slowly, leaned forward, until he could just about see over the trunk to the floor between trunk and mirror. Bridgett was right behind him, hanging on to his waist for dear life, her body shielded completely by his.

Like him, barely daring to breathe, she poked her head around, stood on tiptoe and ventured a look. And that was when it happened, when something small and furry leaped up and flew right past her face.

Bridgett's scream was loud enough to wake the dead. Chase bit down on a thousand curses, too vile to mutter in a lady's presence. And then, whatever it was, headed straight back for them.

Bridgett screamed again and wrapped herself even more tightly around Chase—arms, legs, every possible inch of her was pressed tightly, desperately against every inch of the front of him. "Do something!" she cried as Chase dropped the flashlight, and the furry thing zoomed right past their faces. Bridgett, who wasn't about to let go of Chase even when he bent down to get his flashlight, screamed again before all went quiet.

Trembling, near tears, Bridgett looked up at Chase. He wanted nothing more than to kiss her again. But knowing that would have to wait until he'd gotten her safely out of the attic and away from whatever it was they had disturbed, Chase turned the beam toward the stairs. "Do you think you can walk?" She was so frightened she seemed damn near frozen in his arms.

She nodded and kept clinging. "Just get me out of here," she gasped.

Chase hugged her close and complied. As soon as they reached the bottom of the stairs, the lights in the attic came back on. Chase left them on in hopes of quieting or scaring away whatever was still up there and led a still-shaking Bridgett out of the attic.

Harry and Aunt Winnifred met up with them on the landing between the first and second floors. Winnifred took one look at Bridgett's pale face and the way she was clinging to Chase and said, "You saw Eleanor's ghost, too, didn't you?"

"WE ONLY WISH," Chase said as he ushered Bridgett into the closest sitting room, the second-floor library, and settled her on the antique cream sofa in front of the fireplace. "I'm sorry to tell you, Aunt Winnie," he continued as he gathered up a cashmere throw and slid it around Bridgett. "But you've got some kind of vermin up there."

Winnifred's jaw dropped in stunned amazement.

"I don't think it was a bat, but whatever it was," Chase continued, "it was definitely flying."

Winnifred pressed a hand to her throat. "Are you serious?"

Chase nodded. "You're going to need to call Clyde's Critter Removal Services first thing in the morning and get him out here to take care of whatever is up there."

"I guess that means you didn't see Eleanor?" Winnifred looked disappointed as Harry returned with a snifter of brandy. He poured four glasses, then passed them out, one by one.

"Not even a glimmer of our dear family ghost," Chase confirmed. "Sorry."

"I wonder, though," Aunt Winnifred said thoughtfully, "if it was all some kind of sign...?"

"What are you getting at?" Chase asked impatiently.

"I thought Eleanor had appeared tonight because she was worried about you. But maybe that's not it at all." Winnifred looked at Chase and Bridgett thoughtfully. "Maybe what Eleanor really wants is for you and Bridgett to be together," she said.

CHAPTER SIX

Bridgett stared at Winnifred, wondering how her evening could get any more bizarre. "You can't be serious," she said.

"Oh, I am. Quite. Eleanor, you see, never does anything without a darn good reason. And if she got you and Chase here tonight, then she must want you two to be together."

Bridgett looked at Chase helplessly. He knew as well as she did that Chase's being at her place when Winnifred's call came was pure accident. His desire to tag along with her was also a whim that had nothing to do with the wishes of any ghost!

Chase held up his hands in surrender. "Don't ask me for explanations," he said, clearly amused. "I never claimed to know anything about ghosts, never mind be privy to their secret agendas and wishes."

"I've always thought the two of you belonged together, anyway," Winnifred continued as she settled into a chair across from Harry and sipped her brandy. "Isn't that right, Harry? From the time I saw Bridgett and Chase playing together as kids, I said, 'Those two are going to grow up and marry each other one day.'"

"Only one problem with that, Winnifred," Bridgett

said, tongue in cheek. "I am currently dating someone else."

Chase braced an arm along the back of the sofa and leaned over her. "Exclusively?" Chase cut in, the flexed muscles of his thigh nudging the softer ones of hers. "Or casually?"

Bridgett turned her gaze away from Chase's and moved slightly forward so they were no longer touching. "I don't know what you mean," she said.

Chase caught her wrist before she could stand. Not about to let her off easily, he regarded her with a probing smile. "Have you promised not to date anyone else?"

Trying not to notice how her wrist was tingling beneath the warmth of his grip, Bridgett drew the cashmere throw more closely around her shoulders. "There's been no formal agreement between us." Chase arched his brow skeptically, prompting Bridgett to add, "I mean, we're not in high school, for goodness' sake."

Chase released his hold on her and sat back against the cushions of the sofa. "So you've been dating others?"

"No. I've been too busy doing interviews and personal appearances on my book tour."

The hint of a satisfied smile played around the edges of Chase's lips. "What about him?"

Bridgett warned herself not to react to Chase's smug tone and know-it-all attitude. "Martin called me several times a week."

Chase looked unimpressed as he folded his arms across his powerful chest. "Did he ever visit you?"

"Twice." Bridgett tried but failed to contain a self-conscious blush. "But he knew I was working…"

"So he was content to just wait out your return," Chase guessed.

Anticipating where this line of questioning was heading, Bridgett gritted her teeth. "Obviously."

"What about before you left?" Chase pressed, relentless as ever. "How often did the two of you see each other then?"

Bridgett shrugged. "Once or twice a week or whenever our schedules allowed."

Chase did a double take that would have been comical had it not been so irritating. "That's all?"

Bridgett regarded him steadily. "Martin and I are both very busy with our careers."

Chase inclined his head in wonderment. "That's a pretty sophisticated attitude to take."

Bridgett stiffened her spine and refused to let Chase get to her. "Martin's maturity is one of the things I like about him," she said with a smile.

Chase made no effort to contain a snort. "Is that what it is—maturity?" he said, nudging her ever closer to losing her composure.

Bridgett drew a calming breath. "Just what are you implying?" she murmured icily.

Chase looked her square in the eye. "Every reader survey we've ever done confirms that the initial courtship phase of a relationship is the most intense. And if that's as 'intense' as it's going to get between the two of you, maybe there's a reason there has been no formal agreement of exclusivity between you. Maybe things aren't as set between the two of you as you'd like to think."

Bridgett began to fume. So what if Martin had never said he loved her? Actions spoke louder than words.

And he'd been courting her steadily and patiently for more than a year. "You're wrong about that," Bridgett told Chase, the distinctly male satisfaction on his face inching her temper ever higher.

"We'll see if I am or not," Chase told her in a determined voice that sent a shiver of awareness shimmering down her spine. "But I can tell you right now that until you have a bona fide marriage proposal—or in any other way link yourself exclusively to the old geezer—as far as I or any other male is concerned, the field is still wide open."

For what? Bridgett wondered, incensed. "You make it sound like a race," she said.

"Maybe it is."

"And maybe it isn't," Bridgett snapped right back.

Chase merely smiled, more seductively and knowingly than ever.

Bridgett glared at him. She was not going to let him do this to her. She had gotten over whatever small crush she'd had on Chase long ago. She wasn't going to resurrect those feelings or get into a relationship with someone where her feelings might eventually be unrequited.

Harry cleared his throat loudly enough to break up the staring match between Bridgett and Chase. He looked at Winnifred. Whatever Harry and Winnifred were thinking, Bridgett noted, they were in distinct agreement.

"As long as we're talking about commitments, Bridgett," Aunt Winnifred said smoothly, breaking the uncomfortable silence, "that ring you're wearing is absolutely exquisite."

"Thank you." Bridgett breathed a sigh of relief,

happy to talk about anything but Chase's sudden and unexpected pursuit of her. It wasn't like Chase to be so hot-blooded, at least not where she was concerned. She wasn't quite sure what to make of it.

"I'm guessing Martin Morganstern gave it to you?" Winnifred continued.

Bridget ignored Chase's frown. She smiled at Winnifred. "You're guessing right."

"It's not an engagement ring, though," Winnifred continued, suddenly looking just as concerned as Chase.

"More like a welcome-home present. But Martin's been hinting that a diamond engagement ring is going to follow soon," Bridgett said with some satisfaction before turning and glaring at Chase, letting him know that this was yet another goal she'd made for herself and would soon achieve. Before she knew it, her future would be secure on all counts. She had a successful career, lots of money in various investments and a gentle deferential man who adored her and wanted to build a life with her. Whether Chase Deveraux wanted to accept it or not, her life was almost set.

"What does your mother think of all this?" Winnifred asked.

Still trying to ignore the fiercely scowling Chase, Bridgett continued to speak with Winnifred. "My mom isn't exactly happy about my choice of beau."

"Because…?" Winnifred inquired as Chase got up to pace.

"My mother thinks old money and new money don't mix any better than old money and no money."

"A wise woman, your mother, and a wonderful cook,

but she is dead wrong about this," Winnifred said firmly as she fingered the ruby necklace around her neck. "Money doesn't have anything to do with marrying someone. The only thing required for a happy marriage is love. So, Bridgett...do you love Martin Morganstern the way you should?"

CHASE LEANED against the mantel and waited for Bridgett's answer. It wasn't long in coming, nor was the embarrassed blush in her cheeks. "I really don't think I should be discussing my private feelings about Martin with anyone but Martin," Bridgett said stiffly.

Which meant she didn't love Martin Morganstern, after all, Chase thought. Otherwise, she wouldn't be having such a hard time saying so.

"Perhaps you're right. You shouldn't be discussing that with me," Aunt Winnie said. "But you can discuss things like the need for a formal engagement party to announce your betrothal, when the time comes. I'd love to help you and your mother with that in any way I can. In fact, we could even have your wedding and your engagement party here, if you like."

"That would be lovely, but—" Bridgett looked all the more flushed and uncertain "—Martin doesn't really want a big wedding."

"You've discussed this already?" Chase interrupted, feeling more put out than ever at the way Bridgett was about to ruin her life.

"Of course," Bridgett said before turning back to Winnifred. "And...Martin and I have decided that... given the way my mother feels about my marrying Martin, maybe the two of us should just elope."

"Nonsense. There's no way you should allow that beau of yours to talk you out of having the wedding of your dreams," Winnifred said.

"I agree." Chase gave his opinion even though he doubted Bridgett would listen to him. "I've been waiting a lifetime to see you all gussied up in a wedding dress, and I don't think I and everyone else who loves you should be deprived of that."

"Somehow I knew your concern would be about you," Bridgett retorted drily, giving him the kind of look that told him she thought she understood him better than anyone ever had or ever would.

The trouble was, Chase thought to himself on a troubled sigh, she didn't. She only thought she did. Because if she knew what was really in his heart and had been for a very long time now—he had just been too stubborn, too locked into the buddy relationship they'd had as kids and long since grown out of—to admit it. He hadn't wanted things to change.

Hadn't wanted to take a risk of ruining the closeness they had.

Now, realizing she was on the verge of making *the* mistake of her life, he had no such qualms. He had to do whatever was necessary to help her come to her senses. Even if it made her furious with him in the short run.

"You're wrong," he told Bridgett softly. "My main concern here isn't my needs. It's you. I want you to be happy. And toward that end, I think you should take Aunt Winnie up on her offer to have both your engagement party and your wedding here in this venerable old house just as soon as possible."

"Is SATURDAY EVENING all right with you?" Winnifred asked Bridgett.

Bridgett blinked. She didn't know what had come over everyone. She wasn't sure she wanted to know! "This Saturday—four days from now?"

"Yes. Given the fact that you and Martin have already privately agreed the two of you should be married, I think you should make your relationship permanent as soon as possible via a formal engagement party. Just so there will be no misunderstandings of what Martin's true intentions toward you are."

"You know, with people like me," Chase helped his aunt explain, "who might be wondering why the old geezer has been taking so long to claim you as his and his alone."

Bridgett glared at him. Chase really was doing his level best to make her life difficult right now. And enjoying himself, to boot. If she didn't know better, she'd think he was jealous!

"And don't worry about your mother, dear. I'll drop by and talk to her sometime tomorrow. Between the two of us, I know we can get a party put together for you and Martin by Saturday."

"Whoa, whoa, whoa!" Bridgett held up a hand. "We're really getting ahead of ourselves here." Bridgett turned to Winnifred. "And besides, I thought you and Eleanor wanted me to be with Chase."

"We do, darling," Winnifred replied fondly. "But we also want you to realize *your* dreams. And if Martin is a part of them…"

"What's the matter, Bridgett? Think Martin might be afraid to formally commit to you?" Chase taunted.

"Actually," Bridgett replied testily, "Martin's become very impatient as of late." Uncharacteristically so, Bridgett added silently, thinking of the ultimatum her usually quite deferential beau had issued earlier in the evening during dinner.

"Well, not to worry," Chase drawled as he thrust his hands into the pockets of his shorts. "I'm sure if Marvin's the accommodating romantic you say he is, you'll have no trouble getting him to buy you a diamond and pop the question before Saturday evening."

"It's Martin, Chase, as you very well know, and the decision of when to buy a ring and pop the question should be his and his alone."

"I thought this was an equal partnership," Chase said.

"It is."

"Then if this is really what you want—" Chase looked at Bridgett determinedly "—what's holding you back? Why don't you ask him to marry you, instead of waiting for it to happen the other way around?"

Good question, Bridgett thought. It wasn't like her to be so passive. Usually she went after what she wanted with everything she had and then succeeded in getting it. But with Martin she had always been so passive. So content to let things happen at a snail's pace.

Now that she was back in Charleston near her mother and Chase and the rest of the Deveraux family, even that was starting to change.

She couldn't understand it. She had planned this so carefully. Thought about it for months now. Listed all the reasons Martin was the man for her. Why, then, was she suddenly getting cold feet now that the time was upon her to make a real commitment? Why, then, was she suddenly wondering if maybe Martin was too old for her when all along his maturity, the way he never challenged or pushed her or made her examine her motives and feelings the way Chase did, was what had appealed to her?

Aware Chase was waiting for her answer, she zeroed in on a reservation she could talk about. "Look, I'm not sure how much my mother will want to be involved in any party celebrating my betrothal to a man she doesn't think is right for me. And I don't want to put her on the spot."

"Nonsense," Winnifred said. "You're her only daughter. Of course she'll want to be involved. She's just nervous for you, the way all mothers are nervous for their daughters."

"With good reason in this case," Chase muttered just loud enough for Bridgett to hear as he strolled back over to the sofa where she was sitting.

Bridgett tilted up her chin and gave him a dark warning look. Chase quieted promptly, but to Bridgett's irritation did not look the least bit sorry he'd said what he had as he sat back down beside her.

Bridgett shifted slightly away from Chase. "Thank you," she told Winnifred finally. Deciding she was being silly, backtracking now, she pushed on resolutely. "To tell you the truth, Winnifred, I could use your help bringing my mother around. I really don't want to get engaged to Martin without her blessing."

"Then I'll help you," Winnifred promised with a broad smile. She reached over and took both of

Bridgett's hands in hers. "And I think the first step would be for the three of us—no make that five—let's include Grace and Amy, too, since this is an all-women soiree—should sit down tomorrow afternoon and discuss the merits of your relationship with your beau."

"I could join in, too," Chase offered.

"Yeah, right," Bridgett said.

"I'm serious," Chase said stubbornly as Harry poured more brandy all around. "This doesn't have to be a chicks-only thing."

"Well, it is," Bridgett said, giving Chase a look that let him know just how unwelcome his interference in this matter was.

"YOU'RE OVER HERE awfully early," Winnifred observed the next morning as Chase let himself in the back gate and joined her on the sun-drenched first-floor piazza. She put down the newspaper and looked at him over the rim of her reading glasses. "Conscience bothering you?"

"Now, Aunt Winnifred," Chase drawled, pulling up a chair at the white cast-iron-and-glass table. "Why would my conscience be bothering me?"

"Oh, I don't know. Maybe because of the way you were trying to sew seeds of doubt in Bridgett about her beau. I would have thought after the way Gabe came between you and Maggie, that would be the last thing you'd ever do to someone else."

The irony of the situation was not lost on Chase. He'd been up half the night ruminating about it and was more than a little ashamed of the nosy and intrusive way he had behaved. And yet, even knowing that, if he had the chance to do it all over again, he'd do exactly the same thing. Because watching Bridgett tie herself to Martin Morganstern was like watching an express train speed toward a break in the tracks. As much as he wanted to remain cool and detached, he couldn't stop trying to prevent Bridgett from making a mistake that would haunt her the rest of her life. Was this how Gabe had felt when he had seen Chase and Maggie? Knowing all the while that the way Maggie looked at Gabe was the way Maggie should have been looking at Chase?

"I thought you wanted to see me and Bridgett together," Chase remarked as he recalled the thinly veiled matchmaking his aunt had attempted the evening before.

"I do." Winnifred smiled at Harry as he brought Chase a cup of tea and a plate of fresh fruit and raspberry-jam-and-cream-cheese sandwiches, and just as discreetly disappeared. Winnie turned back to Chase and gave him a stern look. "I'm just not sure this is the way to go about it."

Chase knew that, too. There was a chance that if he continued on this path, Bridgett would never forgive him.

Fortunately Chase was spared further discussion of the subject by the arrival of Clyde and his Critter Removal Services truck. Chase and Harry went up to the attic of the pink-stucco mansion with Clyde to fill him in on what had gone on the night before. Clyde looked around, explaining what he was doing and why to Chase and Harry as he went, then they all headed back downstairs to give the report to Winnifred.

"You've got flying squirrels up there," Clyde told Winnifred.

"How do you know they're flying squirrels?" Winnifred asked.

"Couple reasons," Clyde said as he pocketed his flashlight and wiped his hands on the rag sticking out of his belt. "One, we've been having a lot of trouble with them this year—seems like they sneaked into just about every attic in the area over the winter. And two, they left tracks in the colony's feeding area."

"What do you mean, colony?" Winnifred asked, visibly distressed.

Clyde accepted a cup of tea, but waved off the sandwiches and fresh fruit Harry offered. "Flying squirrels nest in groups of five to seven or thereabouts. So if you've got one, you've got at least a few more."

"Oh, dear," Winnifred said.

"They've been coming in through a hole next to the chimney," Clyde continued. "I can patch that up and any other weak places, but before we do that we're going to have to set some traps."

"Do whatever you have to do." Winnifred shuddered. "Just get rid of them!"

Clyde drank the rest of his tea, then set to work. Harry disappeared, too. Chase knew he and Winnie hadn't quite finished the conversation they'd started earlier. He looked at her tenderly. Whether she liked it or not, this had to be said. "I know you mean well, Aunt Winnie, but I'm not sure we should be encouraging Bridgett to marry Martin Morganstern." He wasn't sure why he had goaded her into solidifying her commitment, either—except that he had hoped it would help Bridgett realize her relationship was a huge mistake.

Winnie arched one well-plucked brow. "It seems to be what Bridgett wants."

Chase shifted restlessly in his chair, irritated to find his conscience bothering him again. "Look, it's obvious she's marrying him to take the place of the father she never had."

"Their age difference really bothers you, doesn't it," Winnie murmured.

Chase scowled. "Doesn't it bother you to see her out and about with a man who is so clearly a father figure?"

"Not if she loves him."

"That's just it," Chase protested, wondering why he was the only one besides Bridgett's mother concerned about this obviously ill-fated match. "I don't think Bridgett does love that guy." Bridgett was smarter than that. The problem was, she had never gotten over not having a dad as a kid. Having someone old enough to be her father pay attention to her, well, it probably filled some void in her life. And while Chase wanted Bridgett to be happy, he didn't want her hooking up with the wrong guy for all the wrong reasons. Which was obviously what she was doing. Plus, he had a bad feeling about Morganstern. Oh, he knew the guy was an old-fashioned gentleman who said all the right things at all the right times, but on a gut level, Chase had never quite trusted him. And he didn't think Bridgett should, either. It took more than fine manners and generations-old social connections to make a man.

"If you feel that way," Harry broke in as he cleared away the empty teacups. He gave Chase a man-to-man look. "You should do something about it."

Deciding Harry was right and his Aunt Winnifred wasn't, Chase headed over to his father's office at

Deveraux Shipping. He caught him just before Tom headed into a meeting. "Sorry to interrupt like this," Chase told his father, "but I've got a problem and I really need to speak to you privately."

Tom ushered Chase into his office, his look openly concerned. "Your mother's okay, isn't she?"

Chase had always thought his parents still loved each other. The protective look on his father's face confirmed it. Chase shrugged. "As far as I know she is— all things considered, anyway. I'm supposed to have lunch with her and Bridgett out at the beach in a little while."

"Good." Tom relaxed visibly as he sat behind his desk. "She needs our support."

"No kidding. That job was her life."

Tom frowned in a way that reminded Chase how much his father had always resented his mother's devotion to her broadcasting career. His lips thinning, Tom sorted through the papers on his massive mahogany desk. "What can I do for you, Chase?" he asked brusquely, knowing Chase would never have stopped by in the middle of a workday unless it was something very important.

Chase met his father's glance equably. "I need the name of a private investigator who can work quickly and quietly."

Tom stopped what he was doing. "Are you in trouble?"

"No," Chase said seriously, "but a friend of mine is."

Tom studied Chase a moment longer. Finally he said, "Talk to Jack Granger. He handles those kinds of matters for me. He'll know who you should call."

Chase thanked his dad and walked down the hall to Jack's office.

The grandson of one of their longtime employees, Jack had started working for the company when he was fourteen. He'd begun as a runner, moved to the docks and then co-op work in the executive offices. When Jack graduated from law school and passed the bar, Tom hired Jack as company counsel. It had been a good move. Jack was a quick study who already knew the shipping business and had the respect of the dock workers. And having their own lawyer had saved the company a bundle on legal fees.

There was also a bond between Tom and Jack, an understanding that seemed to go beyond work. A kinship and trust born of what, exactly, Chase didn't know. Like Tom, Jack Granger played his cards very close to his vest. Jack seemed to be the kind of guy who saw so much of what was going on behind the scenes that he knew instinctively where all the bones were buried....

And it was that kind of help, Chase thought, he was needing now.

Jack was just hanging up the phone as Chase walked in. "Your father said you needed a PI?"

Unable to help but note the Charleston newspaper spread all over Jack's desk, Chase nodded. He looked down at the photo that topped that day's gossip column. "Since when did you start reading the society page?" Chase asked curiously.

Jack flipped the page so that the Lifestyle section was closed and the photo of the beautiful blond Daisy Templeton was hidden from view. "Since I was looking for any mention of your mother being back in town," he said mildly.

Chase had the feeling Jack was hiding something. What, he didn't know. "And was there any mention?" he asked.

"Not this morning," Jack allowed with a grimace. "But with the network's announcement of your mother's firing, you can bet there will be something there tomorrow morning."

Chase sighed, knowing how his mother felt about being the object of pity or gossip, as she had been during the divorce from his dad. "You're probably right about that."

Jack thumbed through his Rolodex, then scribbled down a name and number. He handed it to Chase. "This man's expensive. But he's good."

Again Chase had the feeling Jack was wary about revealing too much—even if Chase was Tom's son. "You've used him before?"

Jack Granger hesitated, then said, "Yes," and offered nothing more.

Telling himself it was none of his business whom his father might have wanted investigated, Chase gestured at the closed newspaper section. "What did the article say about Daisy Templeton?"

Jack shrugged as if the subject hardly mattered to him. "Something about Daisy taking the spring semester off…"

"Which no doubt means she got kicked out of yet another college," Chase said. Daisy was the bad girl of Charleston society. Not promiscuous, just wild. Always in some sort of trouble.

Jack frowned, looking suddenly protective of the

wayward socialite. "You'd think they would have better things to write about."

"I don't know," Chase retorted mildly. "Seven pricey colleges in five years. Isn't that some kind of record?"

Jack's frown deepened. For the briefest moment he looked concerned. Which was odd, Chase thought, since Jack had no connection with the Templetons or Daisy that he knew of, anyway.

Jack tossed the paper into the trash, turned back to Chase. "You let me know if you have any problems with the PI."

"I will," Chase promised. But he didn't expect he would. If Jack Granger recommended the man, he had to be topnotch.

CHAPTER SEVEN

"Grace said you might be by and that you'd probably be peeved when you got here," Theresa observed drolly an hour and a half later when Chase strode into his parents' home. "Looks like your mother was right on both counts."

As far as he was concerned, Chase thought, he had a right to be peeved after what Bridgett had pulled. Not that he planned to discuss the matter with either his mother— or Bridgett's. No, this was between Bridgett and him.

Chase thrust his hands into the pockets of his olive-green cargo shorts. He met Theresa's eyes and forced his best what-the-hell smile. "I need to talk to Bridgett," he stated. He knew she was here. He'd seen her car parked behind the tall wrought-iron gates of his family's mansion when he drove up.

Theresa eyed Chase with the knowledge of a woman who had cared for him—and about him—since birth. Finally she returned just as quietly, "She's with Grace and Paulo in the solarium."

Great, Chase thought. Not only had he been stood up by both women, he'd been stood up for another man. "Who's Paulo?" he bit out with as much indifference as he could muster.

Theresa gave Chase another long thoughtful look, then sprayed the hall table with a generous amount of furniture polish. "Paulo is the hottest yoga instructor in Charleston."

Chase's father had always been into sports—golf, tennis, waterskiing, racquetball. So had Bridgett. Not his mother. You had to twist Grace's arm to get her on the treadmill. And Grace had only done that to stay trim for TV. "Since when has my mother taken up yoga?" Chase asked.

Theresa gave her full attention to the table she was cleaning. "Since Bridgett talked her into having a lesson."

This, he had to see. He strode out of the kitchen and down the hall that ran across the back of the house. Even before he reached the solarium, he heard their fluttering voices. He rounded the corner. Walked in. And took in the twenty-something stud responsible for both women's amusement.

With his long flowing golden-brown hair, streaming well past his brawny shoulders, Paulo looked like the hero on the cover of a romance novel. He dressed like a male cover model, too—in a revealing tank top and snug-fitting gray pants.

"You may be sore tomorrow," Paulo warned Grace as he continued to knead her shoulders with an intimacy Chase found both disrespectful and totally unwarranted. "But I promise you, if you keep it up, it will all be worth it in the end."

Grace, who was still sitting cross-legged on the mat, beamed up at Paulo. "I'm sure you're right, Paulo! I feel so-o-o much better already!"

And so did Bridgett, Chase noted. *She* was practically glowing, she looked so happy and relaxed.

"Thanks for the lesson, Paulo," Bridgett said cheerfully as she mopped her face with the end of the beach towel she held in front of her. Ignoring Chase altogether, she turned and left the room.

"Are you out of your mind, hooking my mother up with that gigolo?" Chase hissed as he followed Bridgett out of the solarium and down the hall. Needing to talk to her privately, he took her by the elbow, pushed open the French doors.

Giving her no chance to protest, he steered her outside into the immaculately maintained flower garden. Sun streamed down on them, warming their bodies. The scent of flowers and saltwater—just a half a block away—teased their senses.

"No, but apparently you are out of yours." Bridgett retorted in exasperation as she pivoted to face him and dropped the towel she had been holding in front of her like a shield.

For the first time since arriving at the mansion, Chase got a good look at what Bridgett was wearing for her workout with her instructor. It was a long-sleeved pale-pink yoga top with matching pants—a combo that was sexy as all get-out. The clinging fabric covered her from neck to ankle, emphasizing the fullness of her breasts, the nip of her waist, the inviting curves of her hips and equally enticing slenderness of her thighs. Just looking at her made Chase's mouth go dry and his lower half pulse to life. Which was, he thought, exactly what he didn't need. An aching awareness of Bridgett as a woman, as well as a friend.

"Where do you get off, striding in there with disapproval written all over your face?" Bridgett countered indignantly as she plucked her sweat-soaked shirt away from the generous curves of her breasts. "And furthermore, you have no right to call Paulo a gigolo. He is anything but!"

Chase decided to reserve judgment on that. "Damn it, Bridgett, I don't want my mother hurt. Bad enough the network fired her after she sacrificed everything, including her marriage, for them!"

"Paulo won't hurt her," Bridgett insisted.

Chase wished he could be that sure. But if Paulo was anything like the opportunistic Romeo he appeared...

"So if that's all you wanted," Bridgett continued haughtily, starting to step past him.

"Actually it's not." Chase moved to block her way to the door. He stood with legs braced apart, arms folded in front of him, and regarded her every bit as contentiously as she regarded him. "Why did you blow off lunch with me?" he demanded. It wasn't like Bridgett. She hadn't even called him to let him know she was canceling. He'd only found out about it when he had showed up at the restaurant they'd agreed upon and discovered—via a message from his office, no less!—that neither his mother nor Bridgett were coming after all.

Briefly guilt glittered in Bridgett's eyes, telling Chase she knew damn well how she had humiliated and angered him. "Look, I promised you I would meet with your mother about her financial situation, and I did— over breakfast this morning," she said, defending herself with difficulty. "Beyond that..." Bridgett shrugged and her voice trailed off.

Chase passed on the opportunity to remind her that she could just as easily have called him at home or on his cell phone as she had many times over the course of their friendship. There had to be a reason she hadn't done so now, and he was pretty sure it was the same reason she had declined to share a meal with him today. He stepped closer, more aware than ever of his inability to understand women and what drove them. No matter how hard he tried, what they felt, what they wanted, were complete mysteries to him. Take last night, for instance. He'd been certain that Bridgett had wanted him to make a move on her. And that feeling had been borne out by the way she'd clung to him and kissed him back. But this afternoon she was looking at him as if she didn't know whether to slug him or forget him. So naturally he had to ask, "Did you tell Martin about the kiss?"

"No." Bridgett's teeth raked her lusciously soft lower lip. She tilted her head up to give him an even more withering glare. "And you better not, either," she warned, stepping even closer.

"Why not?" Chase taunted lightly, enjoying the way they were squaring off, toe-to-toe, as much as he always had. "Think lover boy wouldn't understand?" When Chase had been in a similar situation with Gabe and Maggie, he had been livid. Chase expected Martin to react with equal fury and jealously.

Twin spots of color appeared in her cheeks. She straightened her slender shoulders. "I think he'd be hurt if he heard something like that from you and I don't want to hurt him. Besides—" Bridgett paused and drew a deep breath as she looked him directly in the eye

"—it's not as if it's going to happen again. You made your point," she concluded icily.

It was Chase's turn to be confused. He had never quite understood Bridgett and the way, as they got older, she ran so hot and cold with him. One minute acting as if he was her very best friend in the whole wide world, and the next as if she never wanted to see him again. "Which was what, exactly?" he prodded, wondering what she was getting at now.

Bridgett swallowed hard and looked both hurt and distressed. "That you'd pursue everything in a skirt, if it soothed your wounded ego, and that includes me."

"You think that's why I kissed you—to put another notch on my belt?" Chase stared at her in amazement, realizing Bridgett was no closer to understanding him than he was to her.

Bridgett's chin set mutinously. "What other reason could there have been," she lobbed back emotionally, "except for the fact that you saw your brother kissing your ex-fiancée yesterday and had to kiss someone just as 'inappropriate' yourself!"

What was inappropriate about him kissing her? Chase wondered, especially since she and Martin weren't officially "exclusive." And, Chase was willing to bet, weren't anywhere close to being in love with each other, either. Of course, if she'd actually been engaged, she would have been off-limits and he would've had to find another way to make her see reason. But she wasn't engaged or pledged only to Martin, so he was free to use any means of persuading her he found necessary. Except maybe for the fact that they were, and had always been, friends. He drew in a long calming breath. "My kissing you had nothing to do with Gabe's kissing Maggie," he explained patiently.

"Really." Bridget sized him up furiously. She moved forward until they stood nose to nose. "Then why did you kiss me, Chase?"

That was just it, Chase thought uncomfortably, he didn't know. It wasn't his style to kiss a woman friend. And Bridgett was his oldest and dearest woman friend.

Aware she was waiting for an apology, he ran a hand through his hair. "You're right," he said finally. "I was out of line kissing you that way." It didn't necessarily mean he regretted it. Kissing her like that, holding her close, had made him see her in a whole new light. It had opened up possibilities that he had never really let himself consider before, but wanted very much to consider now. He had the idea Bridgett felt the same way deep down, but was too stubborn, or maybe just too afraid, to admit it. Because if they went down that road and things didn't work out just right, they could sacrifice their friendship in the process. And their friendship meant as much to him as anything in this life.

"You're darn right you were out of line last night," Bridgett agreed, and started to brush by him again.

Chase caught her arm. Determined to make amends, he said, "Look, I'm sorry if you got the wrong idea about why I did what I did."

"Are you now." Bridgett didn't look the least bit convinced that was true.

"But I want you to be happy," Chase continued sincerely.

"Then do me a favor," Bridgett said softly, wresting her arm from his grip. She looked at him with complete and utter loathing. "And don't ever—ever—kiss me again."

BRIDGETT RUSHED upstairs to change. She'd no sooner shut the guest-room door behind her, than she crossed to the bed and sank onto it, trembling. The truth was, she was just as confused about the kiss they had shared the night before as Chase obviously was. She wasn't sure why she had let him kiss her. And she sure as heck didn't know why she had kissed him back the way she had. At first it had been just shock that had kept her immobile. But then pleasure had taken over. She'd been so wowed by the soft insistence of his lips, the warmth of his hands, the sweet urgency of his tongue that she hadn't been able to resist. The truth was, she'd never felt anything like that before. Never felt passion. Never wanted so desperately for anything to continue as she had that kiss.

Oh, she had seen the fire in Chase. She had known for years what a sensual, passionate, pleasure-loving man he had grown up to be. Just as she had known he had never had, nor ever would have, any sexual or romantic interest in her. He saw her as a sister. Just as she had seen him as a brother.

Until now.

Until he had held her in his arms and showed her how wonderful the physical side of love could be.

Bridget couldn't stop thinking about the kiss.

Couldn't stop wanting another.

But that way lay folly, she knew.

Chase didn't want to marry her. Martin did. Chase

didn't want to fall in love with her. He didn't want children, marriage and an enduring future with her.

Martin was ready to commit to just that—and more.

So the choice was simple.

She knew what she wanted. And she knew what Chase didn't.

"SO, WHAT IS THIS WOMAN to you, anyway?" Harlan Decker asked later that same afternoon, as soon as Chase had arrived for his appointment and explained what he wanted Harlan to do.

Chase folded his arms and regarded the burly, gray-haired man in the rumpled Hawaiian shirt and knee-length cutoffs on the other side of the desk. Harlan might come highly recommended, but he looked more like the riffraff he collared than the Charleston cop he'd once been.

"She's a friend," Chase said, knowing even as he spoke that that didn't begin to cover it. Bridgett was and always had been a big part of his life. He wasn't willing to let her go. Not when his gut told him she wasn't going to be happy marrying a blue blood who didn't know the first thing about cutting loose and having fun. Bridgett had been a mischief-loving tomboy growing up. Even though she didn't act or dress like it these days, he bet she still was, deep down. Unfortunately a society stiff like Morganstern would never appreciate that part of her. And Bridgett, Chase thought on a wistful sigh, was a woman who deserved to be appreciated.

"I'll be blunt with you, kid." Harlan removed the digital camera he'd had slung around his neck and put it next to the straw tourist hat he'd been wearing when he walked in. He gave Chase another stern warning look.

"I'm not sure this is what friends do for friends. Unless of course—" Harlan peered at Chase skeptically as he brought a cigar out of his pocket and rubbed it between his thumb and index finger "—you and this gal are more than that."

Chase shifted in his chair, wishing this meeting were already over. He hated being put on the defensive. But with time short and Harlan Decker the best there was, he didn't have much choice. "I've known her a long time, okay?" Chase said irritably. "I want to make sure she's all right."

Harlan plucked the city tour map out of his breast pocket and dropped it onto the cluttered surface of his desk. Slowly and with great care he lit the end of his cigar. He took a long drag on it and blew the smoke up in the air. "Did she ask you to do this for her?"

Fighting back an unexpected wave of guilt, Chase stared at the sunburn on Harlan's face and neck. Once again, Chase wondered if this was how Gabe had felt when he'd interfered in Chase and Maggie's walk down the aisle. Because whether Chase wanted to admit it or not, Gabe had been correct about one very important thing. Chase and Maggie never should have gotten engaged. Wanting the same things in life, wanting to be married, to start a family of your own, was simply not reason enough to hitch your future to someone else's for all eternity. Aware Harlan Decker was still waiting for an answer, Chase said tightly, "No, she didn't."

"Then you might want to reconsider before going down this path," Harlan said genially as he offered Chase a cigar.

Chase took one, wondering why Harlan was trying

to make him feel remorseful. He was being gallant here, going all out to save and protect his childhood friend from making the same mistake he nearly had. "Why?" he asked as he tore the wrapper off the cigar.

"Because if the little lady finds out what you've done, she's going to resent the hell out of you," Harlan warned. "That could mean the end of your—" Harlan paused "—friendship."

Chase didn't even want to consider that. It had been tough enough as it was, losing touch with Bridgett the past few years as their careers took off and their free time dwindled to nothing. "Or, she could be grateful to me for caring enough to make sure she's all right," Chase said, envisioning how relieved Bridgett would be once she'd come to terms with the fact that his gut instinct was right and Martin Morganstern was not the man for her. Not at all.

"Beggin' your pardon, son," Harlan stated between puffs on his cigar, "but I've seen that little lady on TV promoting her book and talking investment strategy. She doesn't strike me as the type anyone, no matter how smooth, could easily bamboozle."

"Generally that's true," Chase agreed as he lit the end of his cigar. "But that was before her marriage alarm clock, or whatever the heck it is, went off and she decided it was time to settle down, pronto, even if she hadn't found the right guy yet."

"You think Morganstern wants her for her money?"

Chase shrugged and took a leisurely puff on his own cigar. "Who the heck knows? He wouldn't be the first blue blood to run his family fortune into the ground, and I've been in that art gallery of his over on King Street and seen some of the paintings he's been peddling. I can't believe he's making anywhere near what it looks like he's been spending. Bridgett, on the other hand, is rich as can be these days. And pretty and talented and sexy, to boot. So it's easy to figure out what he sees in her."

Not so easy, Chase thought, to figure out what attracted Bridgett to Morganstern. Sure, the guy was handsome enough in that impeccably dressed pretty-boy way. Probably held doors open for her. Complimented her all the time, even when he didn't really mean it. And he certainly gave her lavish gifts and spared no expense when it came to entertaining her. But did that prove he could make her happy? The Bridgett he remembered, the Bridgett who'd spent her youth hanging out with him and having fun with him, would be bored to tears by a guy like Morganstern in a year. Two, tops. And then she'd have to divorce him, even though Bridgett had always said she didn't believe in divorce. Once two people had decided to get married and made that leap of faith, she believed they should stay married.

As uncomfortable as Chase was pursuing a woman who was tied, however informally, to another guy, he couldn't just back off and let whatever happened, happen. Bridgett's heart—heck, her whole life!—was at stake. He had to protect her. Had to shake some sense into her. Make her see that Martin Morganstern was not the man for her and would only hurt her in the end. What he couldn't do was stand idly by and let her make a mistake of this magnitude.

"Okay," Harlan said. "I'll check it out. What you do with the information when I get it is up to you."

CHAPTER EIGHT

"Winnifred is here. She and Grace are talking to your mother. And I've got to tell you, you're living dangerously, letting that tea party start without you," Tom Deveraux said when he encountered Bridgett in the east-wing hall.

"What do you mean?" Bridgett asked warily, setting her athletic bag full of sweaty workout clothes on the floor next to her feet. Amy had been invited, too—but hadn't been able to come because she had a decorating job.

"I think the three of them are about to plan an engagement party for you, with or without your permission," Tom said.

"Winnifred and Grace have talked my mother into that already?" Bridgett asked, stunned.

Tom's handsome face took on a wry grin as he allowed kindly, "Well, let's just say they're giving it their best shot. And you know how persuasive my sister and my ex-wife can be when they get their minds set on something and tackle it together."

Bridgett did indeed. Tom and Grace might have divorced more than a decade ago, but Grace remained as close to Tom's sister Winnifred as if the breakup had never occurred.

Tom paused, looking down at Bridgett with paternal concern. "Tell me the truth, Bridgett. Are you really serious about Morganstern?"

Two days ago Bridgett would have answered with a resounding yes. Now, in the wake of Chase's sudden intense interest in her and their impulsive kiss the night before, she didn't know. She kept trying to tell herself that she and the kiss did not mean anything to a playboy like Chase. She even believed it—until she recalled the tenderness of his lips and the possessiveness of his arms. And then all bets were off. She was fantasizing that there might really be something there on his part, too. Something special and wonderful and utterly romantic.

Tom led Bridgett to the seat beneath the windows at the top of the stairs so the two of them could talk privately for a moment. Together they sat down on the red velvet cushion. "Look, I know I'm not your father, but I've always tried to look out for you, anyway."

"And you've done a great job at it," Bridgett said sincerely, knowing she would never find a way to adequately express her gratitude for all Tom and Grace and indeed the entire Deveraux clan had done for her over the years. "Paying for my schooling, cheering me on at every endeavor…consoling me when I'm down."

"Like now," Tom said gently, his love for her as evident as the wings of gray in his dark-brown hair. "I can look at your face and see something's the matter."

"I'm just confused about this whole marriage thing," Bridgett confessed as she clasped her hands tightly in her lap. "I mean, I thought I had it figured out. You pick someone who's right for you, you start dating him and then you get engaged, and before you know it you have a whole life together." It was all so simple. Or at least, Bridgett thought it should be.

"Are you engaged?" Tom nodded at the emerald ring on Bridgett's right hand.

"I could be today if I wanted to be," Bridgett said. What was it Martin had said to her the night before during dinner? *It's time for us to stop putting our careers first and concentrate on our personal lives, and have that family we have both always wanted.*

"But you're not sure you want to be engaged, is that it?" Tom studied her.

Bridgett bit her lip. She knew she could tell Tom whatever was in her heart and he would understand. "I don't want to make a mistake."

Understanding filled Tom's eyes. "There's nothing wrong with taking your time," he assured her.

"But what if that's not what I'm doing?" Bridgett asked nervously. She jumped to her feet and began to pace. "What if I'm just stalling because I'm afraid it won't work out, that he'll ditch me before we ever get to the altar, like my father ditched my mother. Or worse, we'll get married despite my reservations and then end up getting divorced."

"I guess we grown-ups haven't set a very good example for you, have we," Tom said sadly.

"You all have done fine," Bridgett said firmly, wishing she had never brought up the subject of divorce to Tom.

"I wish I thought so." For a moment Tom looked sad, like he had often since his divorce from Grace.

Again Bridgett wished she had never started this discussion. She didn't want to hurt Tom or Grace or her mom. Her real father, damn his deserting soul, was another matter. "Look, sometimes these things just happen. Sometimes things just don't work out. It doesn't have to be anyone's fault."

"You just wish you knew how to tell in advance what's going to work out and what isn't," Tom guessed sympathetically.

Bridgett nodded.

"Unfortunately there's no crystal ball we can look into that will predict the future," Tom said, comforting her. He stood and patted her on the shoulder with parental affection. "What you can rely on is your gut instinct. Or, as you ladies like to say, your intuition. It'll tell you what to do when the time comes. All you have to do is listen to it."

TWO HOURS LATER, Bridgett was still trying to figure out how Grace and Winnifred had managed to turn her mother's attitude around so quickly when she ambled outside and saw Chase leaning against her car. He had his back to her, his cell phone pressed to his ear.

Like a bad penny—or was it a bad boy? she wondered wryly—he just kept turning up. And she had the feeling that until she either married Martin or broke up with him, it was going to keep happening.

"I saw some of the photos at the exhibit, and I have to tell you, Daisy, I really liked them." Looking as handsome and carefree as ever, with the sun glinting off his hair, Chase grinned at something Daisy apparently said. "Of course I've got an ulterior motive. Don't I always?" Chase laughed, then caught sight of Bridgett. "Listen, I've got to go. I'll call you back in a few minutes, okay?" He cut the connection and slid his cell phone back in his pocket. "That was Daisy Templeton," he said in answer to Bridgett's wordless query.

Bridgett knew of the twenty-three-year-old heiress, even though they were nearly nine years apart in age. They'd grown up in the same neighborhood of pricey historic homes. Bridgett, a daughter of the servant class, Daisy, an unwilling member of the elite.

Bridgett moved past Chase to unlock her trunk. "A little young for you, isn't she?" she said, unable to quell the jealousy welling up in her as she tossed her athletic gear into her trunk.

Chase shrugged and made no effort to get out of Bridgett's way. "Daisy would be a tad young if I *were* interested in dating her." He held Bridgett's gaze. "I'm not."

"Either way," Bridgett returned, telling herself that was not relief she felt, not at all, "it's none of my business."

"Actually it is," Chase said genially, "since I want her to take some action photos of you and me."

Forgetting for a moment her hurry to get out of there, Bridgett asked, "Why on earth would you want her to do that?"

Chase's expression turned serious. "Because a photo op of the real you would make a great sidebar for the review I'm going to do of your new book. You know, it will show how even a buttoned-up financial counselor like you can have fun during her leisure time."

Bridgett ignored the teasing undertone in his voice, along with the hint that in her quest to become a financial and career success, she had become a stick-in-the-mud. "Why would you want to do a review of my book for women in your magazine?" she asked suspiciously.

"Because, whether you like it or not or even want to admit it or not, Bridge, your advice is not for women only. Men can and should benefit from your considerable expertise, too."

Privately Bridgett had been giving a lot of thought of expanding her series of financial-advice books to include a book geared specifically toward young newlyweds. A feature article in *Modern Man* magazine might reach these guys on yet another plane. Hence, at least on a purely business level, she was happy about his offer to help expand her readership in a fairly serious way. His timing and motivation, however, were suspect. She tilted her head at him, wondering if she would ever figure out what drove him. "You're doing this to make up to me, aren't you," she guessed eventually.

"Maybe a little," Chase allowed with a sexy grin as he reached up and shut her trunk for her. "But mostly I'm doing it because I'm a great businessperson, and I know having your picture in a flash on the cover of my magazine would sell a lot of copies."

Bridgett rolled her eyes. Leave it to a self-professed ladies' man like Chase to figure out a way to exploit the good looks she'd inherited from her mother into a business opportunity for him.

"Of course, in keeping with the theme of my magazine," Chase continued with a salacious wink, "we'd want to show you're a gal who really knows how to have fun, too."

Bridgett did her best to quash an answering grin. "I am *not* dancing on a table with a lampshade on my head." Although she knew, under the right circumstances, Chase could probably convince her to do just that.

Chase mugged comically. "I had in mind something a little tamer."

Bridgett tried and failed to slow her suddenly thudding heart. "Such as?" she asked.

Chase's slate-blue eyes turned sentimental. "Remember when we used to go sea kayaking together when we were in college?"

Without warning, Bridgett was filled with nostalgia, too. "Over to Fort Sumter."

"Yeah." Chase gazed deeply into her eyes. He looked serious now. Hopeful. "Want to do it again?" he asked softly.

BRIDGETT WAS ABOUT to throw caution to the wind and just say yes when the back door opened and Tom Deveraux came out of the house, carrying a suitcase in one hand, a garment bag in the other. Grace followed a second later, her delicate hand upraised. "Tom!" she called after him. "Wait!"

Her face still glowing from the aftereffects of her yoga session, Grace dashed outside and caught up with Tom at the car. "I've been thinking. There's no reason for you to go back to the hotel," Grace said.

"We went over this yesterday," Tom said gravely, not caring anymore than his wife that Chase and Bridgett could see and hear every word they were saying. "I won't have you staying in a place where you can be harassed by reporters and tourists. Besides—" Tom's expression gentled protectively, as he gazed down at his ex-wife "—you know it's easier for you to see the kids if you're here."

Looking disinclined to argue with Tom on either

point, Grace said, just as courteously, "Normally when I'm here for just a few days, that's fine. But now that I'm here for good, it doesn't seem fair for me to be booting you out of your home."

"What do you suggest we do?" he asked.

"Well, why don't we both stay here?"

Beside Bridgett, Chase tensed. Bridgett knew how he felt. For all his parents' current civility in the wake of Grace's crisis, there were still times when they were just as bitter and contentious as they had been when they split, for no reason any of their children, or Bridgett or Theresa, could figure out. Hence, having them both under the same roof for an extended period of time could resurrect the bad feelings between them. Meanwhile, Tom looked just as stunned by his ex-wife's suggestion as Bridgett and Chase were.

"I don't want to feel that I'm putting you or anyone else out," Grace continued. "Realistically it's going to take at least several weeks to find a place of my own here, and probably even longer to get whatever I do eventually buy in move-in shape. So…"

"You're sure you're okay with this?" Tom said.

Grace nodded. She linked her arm through his, already steering him back toward the door, suitcases and all. "Absolutely. I want to know you're comfortable, too," she said as she led him back into the house.

Silence fell between Bridgett and Chase. Eventually Bridgett said, "Do you think there might be a chance, even a small one, that your mother's being without a job will bring your parents back together?" Bridgett had lived on the property with her mom at the time Chase's parents had split up, and she was as aware as Chase that his parents hadn't always been able to be cordial to each other since the divorce. Eventually things had calmed down between Tom and Grace, of course, but for a while there had been a lot of tension. No one, though, had ever found out what, exactly, caused their divorce, since neither Grace nor Tom would say. All anyone knew, including their own children, was that they had differences that simply couldn't be resolved. Period.

"I wouldn't even want to speculate about that," Chase said, his expression turning grim again. He turned back to Bridgett, forced a smile. "And speaking of unknowns, you never did tell me how that tea party went."

Now it was Bridgett's turn to grimace. "Your aunt and both our mothers have joined forces to throw a party here on Saturday evening. Martin and I are the guests of honor."

"Well," Chase said after a moment, looking just as unhappy as she felt, "that's what you wanted."

Was it? *Be careful what you wish for—you just might get it.* "Maybe," Bridgett allowed, doing her best to keep her conflicted emotions in check, "if I didn't feel like I were such a victim of reverse psychology, at least on my mother's part."

"You think she's not sincere about wishing you and Martin well in your...whatever it is," Chase said.

Bridgett shrugged, knowing if anyone could understand this, it was Chase. "I think deep down my mother doesn't feel, because of our different backgrounds, that Martin will ever marry me. But Winnie and your mom have talked her into at least giving Martin a chance to prove his devotion to me and just see what happens.

Your mother, in particular, thinks a happy marriage is worth the risk. She convinced my mother to just step back and let me follow my heart, knowing that whatever I eventually decide, my mom will be in my corner, backing me up and cheering me on."

Chase swallowed. Emotion crept into his voice, tenderness into his eyes. "My mom said that?"

"Yeah." Bridgett sighed, feeling quite nonplussed. She turned her face up to Chase. "Strange, isn't it, to have her so clearly pro marriage, especially as she divorced your dad over his initially pretty vehement protestations."

Chase nodded in a way that reminded Bridgett how hard he, too, had fought against his parents' divorce, both at the time and later, in the years immediately following the breakup. To no avail. Once the divorce decree was issued, Tom and Grace never made any move to reconcile or explain why they had done what they had. "What about Aunt Winnifred?" Chase asked. "What persuasive argument did she give to change your mother's mind?"

"Exactly what you'd expect from anyone who was widowed after just a year of marriage to the love of her life. She thinks time—for any two people in love—is simply too short. And that I should savor whatever it is I've found with Martin or anyone else, because before I know it, it could all be taken away from me."

Chase sighed. "Poor Aunt Winnie. She's never gotten over losing her husband."

"I know," Bridgett murmured.

A companionable silence fell between them, reminding Bridgett of all she and Chase had once shared.

There'd been a time when they could talk about anything. Was it possible they could get that closeness back? And if they did, how would that affect her relationship with Martin? Although he'd never been the jealous type, she wasn't sure Martin would appreciate or approve of any renewed intimacy between Bridgett and Chase.

"So what does Martin think of all this?" Chase asked, abruptly looking as pensive and sentimental as she felt.

"I don't know." Bridgett felt herself tense again and she turned away from Chase's probing gaze. She felt suddenly disloyal to Martin for having talked to Chase about the party first. "I haven't told him yet."

"WHY LEAVE IT at just a gala in our honor?" Martin said, when Bridgett told him. "Why not make it something really special by announcing our wedding date that night?"

Bridgett sucked in a breath. No doubt about it. Her world, which for years had chugged along at a snail's pace, was suddenly moving way too fast. "Because we're not engaged yet," she said calmly, wondering when these precommitment jitters would go away. Were she and Martin meant to marry? Or would they be better off as friends? Bridgett was too nervous to know. Martin, however, had no such qualms.

"All you have to do is let me buy you a diamond, and we will be." Martin took Bridgett into his arms. Before he could kiss her or even attempt to, Bridgett found herself turning her head. Another first for her. Martin's expressions of affection hadn't been all that frequent, but she'd never rebuffed them—until now.

Then again, she'd never kissed anyone else since she and Martin had started dating each other—except for Chase. Guilt flooded Bridgett as she extricated herself from Martin's tender embrace. She had been putting off telling him about the kiss, but she knew she couldn't do it any longer. As the man who wanted to marry her, he deserved to be told the truth about her mistake. She put several feet of space between them, folded her arms tightly in front of her and struggled for the courage she needed. "There are things you don't know about me, Martin," she told him softly.

Martin smiled and sat on the edge of his desk in the Morganstern Gallery office, looking as relaxed and genial as ever. "I know everything I need to know. You're smart and pretty and kind and loving, successful in your own right. You're everything I ever wanted in a woman, everything I thought I'd never find. I know people have been filling your head with doubt because I waited so long to marry. But there's no reason for you to be upset about that," he told her firmly and straightforwardly. "The thirteen-year difference in our ages is not going to be a problem. I promise you, I'll see to it you always have what you need, in every respect."

Bridgett looked at Martin, trying to find strength in his cool self-assured presence. "I know you will." She smiled back at him, still struggling with her conscience. Martin had been so good to her. The last thing she ever wanted to do was hurt or betray him.

Martin took her hand and led her to the sofa, where they both sat down. "Then meet me at King Street Jeweler's tomorrow morning. And help me pick out a ring."

Once again Chase disrupted her ability to make plans with Martin.

"I can't," Bridgett admitted reluctantly. "I promised Chase Deveraux I'd do this sea-kayaking photo shoot for his magazine." Briefly Bridgett explained Chase's plans to review and further publicize her latest best-seller.

Instead of being jealous or the least bit put out, Martin smiled. "That sounds like a great publicity opportunity for you," he said, his approval evident. "It should really help sales of your new book."

Shouldn't her soon-to-be fiancé be jealous that she was ditching him for Chase? Bridgett wondered silently. Especially when Martin was trying at long last to formalize their relationship by buying her a ring? Shouldn't he at least sense something amiss, especially when Bridgett was so sick with guilt over the forbidden kiss that she could barely stand it? Then again, maybe she was the one making too much of things. As Chase had pointed out to her, she and Martin had no formal commitment to each other just yet. No promise of exclusivity had been made, even though Bridgett had more or less been adhering to that ever since Martin and she had started dating. She assumed Martin had done the same, but the truth was, she didn't really know what he'd done during the three months she had been off promoting her book. And she hadn't been curious enough to ask.

As for her unexpected interlude with Chase the night before...well, she was smart enough to know that kiss, sensual as it had been, had meant no more to Chase than any other pass he'd made at any other woman. And she had made it very clear to Chase that he wasn't to put the moves on her again. So the likelihood was, nothing else of a romantic nature would happen tomorrow when they went sea kayaking together, particularly since they were going to have Charleston Wild Child Daisy Templeton as their twenty-three-year-old chaperone.

And if it didn't happen again, what would be the point of telling Martin, especially as it was bound to hurt him?

"Do you think you'll be free late tomorrow afternoon, say, around four-thirty?" Martin continued, oblivious to her conflicted thoughts.

Keep your eye on the future. On the man who wants you and will marry you. Bridgett looked at Martin and forced a smile. She couldn't let Chase lure her into a mistake, the way he had once seduced her into mischief, just because wicked fun or rollicking good times lay ahead. She was too old for that. Too focused on what she needed and wanted, which was marriage, stability, family and a future happiness that would last. Martin was offering her all those things. Chase wasn't.

"I'm sure we'll be finished long before then," she said.

"Then we'll meet at the jeweler's tomorrow," Martin said firmly. "And make this relationship of ours official."

CHAPTER NINE

Bridgett couldn't believe it. Chase wasn't even dressed. In fact, Bridgett noted with growing pique, he looked as if he had just that moment stumbled out of bed. Which was odd, because Chase could usually be counted on to be prompt. Bridgett's brows drew together. "Did I get the time wrong?" she asked.

"Nope." Chase consulted the clock on the wall behind him. "You were supposed to be here at seven-thirty and it's…seven twenty-nine."

"Then how come," Bridgett questioned as he ushered her inside his beachhouse, "you're still wearing your pajamas?" Actually, it was just a pair of incredibly sexy pajama bottoms, with a drawstring waist that rode just below his navel and seductively showcased his lean hips and long legs.

"Daisy's idea." Chase yawned as he lifted his arms and lazily raked his fingers through the mussed waves of his dark-brown hair. Apparently he had no compunction at all about shifting the blame. "She wanted me to look as if I was just waking up when she took the photos of me that are going to appear on the introductory page, along with my monthly letter to the readers."

Bridgett glared at him. She had gotten up at the crack

of dawn after a late night out with Martin socializing, rushed to shower and do her hair, endured a wardrobe crisis that sent her into a tizzy, and then driven all the way out to the beach at top speed, only to find Chase still in bed! And from the looks of his rumpled hair, drowsy eyes, unshaven jaw and the time he had taken to greet her, he had still been sleeping soundly when she rang the bell. "You should have told me you weren't going to be ready at seven-thirty," Bridgett said. "Then I could have arrived later."

"We needed you here." Daisy Templeton bounded up on the deck of Chase's beachhouse and over to where Chase and Bridgett were standing. "We're going to photograph you waking Chase up, tugging off the covers and pulling him out of bed. Sort of fits with the theme of his magazine, don't you think?"

"The theme of impossibly irritating men?" Bridgett said.

Daisy grinned. At twenty-three the dazzling blonde was evidently young enough not to mind Chase's playboy image. Or the way he constantly pushed women's buttons.

"Come on." Daisy took Chase by the hand and led him through a living space that included a den with a fireplace and sofa, kitchen and dining area all in one, to the loft upstairs. "Let's get you back under those covers before you wake up any more. Bridgett, you come, too."

Bridgett sighed, set down her shoulder bag and car keys, and marched up the stairs after them. By the time she got up there, Chase was lying facedown on the bed, the covers draped artfully over his legs. His arms were folded beneath his pillow. He had his head turned slightly to the side. His back and shoulders were beautifully bare, all sculpted muscle and smooth suntanned skin. Just seeing him that way made Bridgett's mouth go dry.

"What do you think, Chase?" Daisy said, as she snapped pictures. "Should we have her stretch out beside you?"

Bridgett's insides fluttered at the thought of being on the bed with him. The last thing she wanted to do was roll around under the covers with Chase. Nearly engaged or not, it might give him ideas. Heck, it might give *her* ideas!

Chase grinned, opened one eye and trained it on Bridgett. "Ol' Marvin might object to that," he drawled.

"It's Martin." Bridgett pushed the words through clenched teeth. "And he would have every right to object." She grabbed the sheet beneath Chase's middle and tugged it free. Knowing even as she did so that it was less about her following the directions of Chase and his college-kid photographer than getting Chase up and out of that bed of his.

Daisy stopped snapping long enough to turn her incredulous gaze to Bridgett. "You're not dating Martin Morganstern, are you?"

"Yes," Bridgett said, as her temper burned ever hotter. "Why?"

"Because he's—" Daisy hedged uncomfortably, her camera still cradled in her hands "—I was going to say…ancient."

The heat of her embarrassment crept into Bridgett's cheeks. Ignoring Chase's I-told-you-so smirk, Bridgett turned back to Daisy. "Martin is not that old," she said stiffly before the notoriously reckless Daisy could blurt out anything even more insulting.

"I think he is," Chase said, rolling onto his side. The covers slid down even more as he stretched his long legs. He eyed Bridgett in a goading manner. "I think he's way too old for you. And a stick-in-the-mud, as well."

Bridgett propped her hands on her hips. Compared to Chase, Martin did seem old. But then, wasn't that the point—for her to marry someone dependable and mature? Someone she could count on not to run out on her the way a sexy young guy like Chase might?

"Are we going sea kayaking or not?" she demanded as Daisy went back to snapping away what would likely turn out to be a highly amusing photo essay.

"Sure," Chase said. He checked Bridgett out in a leisurely male fashion that made her pulse pound. His smile widened even more. "Right away."

"HOW LONG IS THIS going to take?" Bridgett asked as they fastened their bright-yellow safety vests, pushed their kayaks out into the channel between Sullivan's Island and Fort Sumter and climbed in.

"The usual, I suspect," Chase said as Daisy continued to take action photos of them from the beach. "About half an hour to kayak over to Fort Sumter, a while to mess around once we're there and half an hour or so back here."

"Fine," Bridgett said, aware it was already after nine and all they'd managed to do was get her so riled up she wanted to scream. She set her jaw and tried to have a good time as she settled comfortably in the seat of her kayak. "Just as long as we're done by three-thirty." In the distance, Daisy climbed into the speedboat that would follow the two of them from a distance and allow her to take photos of them as they crossed to the man-made island in Charleston Harbor upon which Fort Sumter had been built.

Chase paused long enough to give Daisy and her hired-boat pilot a salutary wave, then turned back to Bridgett. "What happens at three-thirty?" he asked curiously.

Bridgett dipped one end of her oar in the water, then the other, beginning the practiced rhythm that soon had her gliding through the water with ease. "I need to go home and get a shower," she told Chase as the spring sun beat down on them. "I'm meeting Martin down-town at four-thirty."

"Getting the Senior Citizen Special for dinner, huh?"

Bridgett accidentally-on-purpose used her oar to splash water on him. "Very funny," she said. "And no, we are not planning to eat dinner that early."

The muscles in his brawny shoulders rippling smoothly, Chase paddled hard enough to take the lead. "Going to help him pick out a pair of orthopedic dress shoes?" he said as he sent an arc of water across her face and chest.

Bridgett paddled harder and faster. She kept her eyes straight ahead as she drew even with Chase again. "Wrong again, bucko," she told him with a great deal more satisfaction than was warranted. "We're going to pick out my engagement ring."

Chase stopped paddling and slanted her an as-tounded look. "He asked you to marry him last night?"

"Not exactly." Bridgett slowed down, too, as she blinked the water from her eyes.

"If he didn't propose—" Chase narrowed his glance at her as he paced his paddling to stay exactly even with her "—then why are you picking out a ring?"

Bridgett concentrated on the soothing rhythm of their oars hitting the water.

"Because it's time," Bridgett said stubbornly, refusing to let Chase goad her into feeling let down by the matter-of-fact way events were unfolding.

"Well, that's an amazingly pragmatic attitude to have," Chase said grimly as they drew ever nearer to the small beach.

"What do you mean by that?" Bridgett discovered she was gritting her teeth again as she watched a tour boat, crowded with people, pull up next to the burned-out ruins of Fort Sumter.

Chase shrugged. "I just figured you'd have wanted some highly romantic proposal, you know, some great big deal when Marvin actually asked you to marry him. I expected him to surprise you with a ring, not just set an appointment and take you to pick out one."

Bridgett knew she didn't have to defend herself to Chase and probably shouldn't even try. But before she realized it, the know-it-all look on Chase's face had her opening her mouth again. "Look, there was no reason for Martin to get down on bended knee when we both know what we want."

"I'd think, if he wants to marry you so much, that's exactly what he'd do," Chase said, looking disappointed for her.

"Is that what you did for Maggie?" she challenged as she paddled right up onto the beach.

"No." Chase sighed. "Although," he allowed as he

dragged his kayak up onto the sand out of harm's way, "maybe if I'd made more of a fool of myself over her, she wouldn't have dumped me for my brother."

"And maybe," Bridgett said as she braced both her hands on the lip of her kayak and levered her way out, "your marriage to her just wasn't meant to be, after all."

Chase reached over and helped Bridgett pull her kayak out of the water and up onto the narrow beach beside his. Silence fell between them as he looked at her appraisingly. Then he grinned at her in the way he always did when trouble was coming. "And maybe neither you nor I are really the marrying kind," he asserted just as strongly.

Bridgett flushed self-consciously. "What's that supposed to mean?" she demanded as she reached for the water bottle in her pack.

"Well, think about it." Chase pulled a bottle of a popular sports drink from his pack, too. "Except for my mistake with Maggie and yours with Morganstern—"

"My relationship with Martin is not a mistake," Bridgett snapped. Her temper had begun to flare.

"—neither of us has ever been close to tying the knot." Chase inclined his head at her. As his gaze drifted over her face, his eyes warmed even more. "Don't you think that should tell us something?"

Bridgett planted her bare feet even more firmly in the sand. "Like we're cautious?"

"Ah, but we're not cautious, Bridgett, either of us." Chase kept his eyes on the flushed contours of her face. "'Cause if we were, we would have selected safe and easy career paths. Instead, we both struck out on our own, risked everything we had and built two very successful businesses out of nothing but our own desire in a few years' time."

Bridgett dropped her water bottle back into her bag and plucked out a pair of sneakers. She brushed the sand off her feet and slipped them on. "Just because I take some pretty big risks in my professional life doesn't mean I take them in my personal life," she said pointedly. "Now come on. Let's have some fun."

CHASE WASN'T SURE why he'd started this, other than to distract Bridgett and keep her from doing anything rash like accepting a marriage proposal from Martin. He knew that everything he was saying was pure bull. But when she looked at him like that and went toe-to-toe with him, challenging everything he said and did, Chase couldn't help but get into the banter. He'd missed matching wits with Bridgett. Missed her—more than he'd known. The question was, how was he going to keep her from slipping out of his life as easily as she had slipped back in?

"What?" Bridgett said once she'd finished tying her shoes and straightened up to square off with him again. "No smart remark?"

Chase tore his eyes from the bare silky skin of her slender shoulders and the sexy indentation of her collarbone. "I'm thinking." He lifted the plastic bottle to his lips and drank deeply of the chilled liquid.

"About...?" Bridgett prodded.

"The two of us," Chase slipped back into the banter that was as comforting as it was familiar. "And why we're just not suited for marriage," Chase said in response, liking the angry sparkle in her eyes. There was nothing more alluring, in his opinion, than Bridgett, out to prove a point.

"Back to that again," Bridgett said, giving him her full attention.

Chase brought out a pair of nicely broken-in deck shoes and slipped them on. "We're cut out for fun, Bridgett."

"So?" Bridgett rolled her eyes in exasperation as he recapped his bottle and tossed it back into his pack.

Enjoying the feel of the spring breeze on his body, Chase braced his hands on his waist. He looked at Bridgett seriously. "So, marriage is all rules and responsibility, obligations and expectations."

Bridgett raked her lower lip with the edge of her teeth. "And the single life is…?"

Chase picked up the oars and set them in the wells of their kayaks. "Full of excitement and adventure."

"And a lot of lonely nights," Bridgett added, frowning as she rubbed her index finger across her lips.

"Doesn't have to be that way," Chase disagreed. "Not anymore. You can always call me."

"And then what?" Bridgett rummaged in her pack and finally plucked out a tube of lip balm.

Chase swallowed as he watched her slowly stroke it on her lips, then offer it to him. "Oh, I'm sure we could find some mischief to get into," he added drily as he put the tube to his mouth and ran it over his lips much more swiftly than she had done.

"I'm sure we could," Bridgett agreed sagely. "I'm just not sure we should."

"You've got to cut loose again and set yourself free," Chase advised her cavalierly, aware his lips now tasted like a combination of wintergreen-flavored balm and Bridgett. He pressed the tube back into the palm of her hand and frowned as the heat of her skin sent an even more potent charge barreling through him.

Bridgett narrowed her eyes at him, then continued in a soft low tone, "Tell me something. Does this speech work on most women, Chase? 'Cause it's not working on me."

Chase laid a hand over his heart and regarded her with mock pain. "I'm hurt," he said with only a twinge of guilt. Because the truth of the matter was, he was beginning to think he'd do literally anything to get her away from tying herself to Martin.

"I want to settle down with a nice guy and never have to worry about a dateless Saturday night again."

Chase shrugged. "I'm a nice guy."

"With a very short attention span when it comes to the fairer sex." Bridgett dug the toe of her sneaker into the sand and turned her attention back to the water lapping at the shore. She brushed the hair from her eyes and frowned back at him. "How many women have you dated, anyway?"

"I don't know." Chase shrugged uncaringly. "Fifty."

Bridgett's brow arched in cool disbelief.

"A hundred," Chase amended.

Her brow climbed even higher. "Try a couple of hundred," she corrected drily.

Chase refused to feel guilty about that. Sure, he'd had a lot of evenings with a lot of other women, but his dates with those women were as forgettable as they had been superficial. Women wanted to be with him because he was successful. Whereas he had been looking to fill lonely hours. He smiled at Bridgett and continued truthfully, "Which just goes to show that I'll take out just about anyone who's in need of a little diversion."

"Providing, of course, she's beautiful and sexy, to boot."

Chase opened his mouth to disagree, then shut it again. He'd never really thought about it and certainly a woman's looks weren't the basis for any friendship he'd ever had, but he supposed Bridgett had a point. "Actually," he allowed with a disarming shrug, "it's really a woman's personality I'm interested in."

Bridgett threw back her head and laughed.

"It just doesn't matter if she looks great, too," Chase continued easily, figuring there was no reason to fudge about it. He did prefer the company of a beautiful woman. And in his estimation, there was no woman on earth more beautiful than Bridgett Owens. He leaned closer and looked down his nose at her. "Not that I've seen you dating anyone who was missing the handsome gene, either."

"Oh, really, and what kind of men do I date, since you're such an expert on me?" Bridgett scoffed.

"The handsome, successful, exceedingly reliable and responsible type. The type who wouldn't know how to have fun if it stared 'em in the face." The type, Chase thought, who set his teeth on edge, they were so completely wrong for her.

Bridgett smiled at him slyly. "I think you'd be surprised at some of the fun I've had."

Jealousy struck like a craw in his gut. The thought of Bridgett having the time of her life with someone else was curiously almost more than he could bear. Suddenly struggling with completely unwarranted feelings of protectiveness, coupled with the urge to take Bridgett in his arms, say to heck with everything he was trying to accomplish here—namely, bringing her to her senses—and just kiss her madly, Chase turned back to the water to search out Daisy and the blessed distraction and chaperoning presence she offered.

She was still some distance away, perched comfortably in the boat she'd hired, snapping photos. In desperate need of immediate diversion, Chase waved her in.

"YOU'RE AWFULLY SOLEMN," Bridgett observed short minutes later as they joined the other tourists streaming toward the park ranger standing in the grassy center of the former parade grounds, located inside what was left of the five-foot-thick walls of the old brick fort.

Probably because I just realized my feelings for you aren't as simple and uncomplicated as I thought they were, Chase thought as he tipped his head down at her. *And I'm not sure if you're ready to deal with that any more than I am.* "It's a solemn place," he said with a shrug as they surveyed the ruins of the former military installation. Daisy followed a discreet distance behind them, taking photos.

Mindful of the unevenness of the terrain beneath their feet, Chase reached over and took Bridgett's arm. He swallowed hard against the building knot of sentiment in his throat, more aware than ever of all that was at stake. "The first battle of the Civil War was fought here, you know."

"Somehow I think it's more than that," Bridgett persisted with a flicker of concern in her deep-brown eyes.

Bridgett always had been able to read him, more than anyone else, Chase thought. He took her by the hand and led her away from the park ranger, who was telling how the fort had been built to protect the harbor. "I was just thinking how much I've missed hanging out with you," he said honestly as they checked out the three cannons and the mortar on the parade ground, as well as the projectiles imbedded in the wall in front of the guns. When they were teenagers, they had kayaked over here frequently, spent countless hours on the beach. They knew all the history, as well as every nook and cranny of the old fort.

"We did have a lot of fun when we were growing up," Bridgett admitted with a wistfulness that warmed his soul as they toured the ruins of the officers' quarters.

Chase turned to face her. She had never looked more beautiful than she did at that moment, standing there in a clinging pink swimsuit and black nylon shorts. Her cheeks were ripe with color, her lips soft and bare. The seabreeze ruffled her auburn hair, pulling tendrils from the neat French braid onto her face and the nape of her neck.

He moved a strand of hair from her face and tucked it behind her ear. His mood suddenly as pensive and wistful as hers, he asked, "How did we lose touch with each other?"

Bridgett shrugged and headed up the stairs to the observation deck that overlooked the bay. The set of her lips turned as melancholy as her voice. "Our lives went in different directions."

"It's more than that."

"Is it?" Bridgett turned so her back was to the metal railing. Like him, she seemed to be struggling with her feelings, both about what their relationship had been and what it might or might not become. "You were starting a magazine from scratch. And you had a very active social life, to say the least."

Chase grinned at the note of jealousy in her voice. He'd known her a lot of years. He'd never seen her look at him quite that way.

"The point is," Bridgett continued, "you were so darned busy it didn't leave much time for the two of us to pal around."

Chase supposed that was true. In the aftermath of his called-off wedding, he had been avoiding anyone who was close to him and might want to "talk." No one had been closer to him, no one had known his moods better, than Bridgett. Not about to take all the blame, however, he pointed out softly, "You're at fault for the lapse in our friendship, too."

Bridgett's expression grew even more introspective. "You're right. I have let my career take up all my time and energy, too." She was silent as she looked out over the water, first toward the beach on Sullivan's Island, where his house was located, and then toward the many beautiful mansions along the Battery, where his Aunt Winnifred lived. "We have to face it, Chase, even if we don't want to." Bridgett pivoted slightly away from him and studied the place where the Ashley and Cooper rivers came together. "You and I have both changed."

"Maybe not as much as you think." Chase put his hands on her shoulders and turned her so that she had to face him. When their eyes met, he continued pragmatically, telling her what he was pretty sure she already knew. "That guy in my magazine—the ultimate bachelor all the papers write about—isn't the real me."

Bridgett searched his face. "Then why do you portray yourself that way?"

Chase shrugged and reluctantly let his hands fall back to his sides. "For exactly the reason you portray yourself as the ultimate female investor. Because dedicated perfection, in any venue, appeals to the buying public."

Bridgett's lips came together in a delicate scowl. "But my advice to people helps them, Chase."

Not about to let her get away with that false assumption, Chase grinned and chided, "I printed a knockout recipe for grilled hot wings just last month. As well as a guide for getting girlfriends to enjoy sports as much as guys do. Now if those two things together won't bring about world peace, I don't know what will."

Bridgett rolled her eyes. "You always did have a way of twisting things around to your advantage."

"And you always had a way of worrying way too much," Chase said, thinking he had never wanted to haul a woman into his arms and kiss her senseless as much as he wanted to kiss Bridgett at that very moment.

Bridgett's eyes widened. Her lips parted. She swayed toward him, chin tilted up to his. Chase brought his hands to her shoulders. And damn it all if he wouldn't have said to heck with her cautions not to ever kiss her again had they not suddenly been invaded by a noisy group of fourth-graders.

Bridgett jerked away, blushing furiously.

Chase dropped his hands and stepped back even as he silently and vehemently condemned the interruption.

Before they had a chance to catch their breaths, Daisy joined them once again. "Stay right where you are!" she shouted above the cacophony of two hundred schoolchildren on a field trip. "I love these action shots!"

Chase would have settled for a little less action. He would have settled for having Bridgett in his arms again. Her mouth against his—soft, warm and pliant. But wasn't that just the way…

"YOUR NOSE IS sunburned," Martin said when Bridgett joined him at King Street Jeweler's later that afternoon.

So were numerous other parts of her body, Bridgett thought, already beginning to feel the sting. She had no doubt she would be in agony by the end of the evening. But not wanting to ruin what should be a very exciting moment of her betrothal, she said in explanation, "I think my sunblock wore off in a couple places." Like her chest, back and legs. "The sea-kayaking photo shoot took a little longer than I thought it would."

"How'd that go, anyway?" Martin held out a straight-backed velvet chair.

Bridgett slid into it gracefully, tucking her skirt around her legs. "It was great, except for the two hundred fourth-graders that overran the place at the end." She smiled, remembering the pandemonium. "Chase and Daisy and I about got trampled in the stampede."

"I can't wait until we have a fourth-grader of our own," Martin said.

A week ago Bridgett would have been delighted at

the thought of having children with Martin. Now…all she could think about was what they'd have to do together to make a baby. Deciding there was no reason for her to be worrying about *that* now, Bridgett hastily changed the subject, as well as the direction of her thoughts. "Did you find any rings you liked?"

"Yes, as a matter of fact." Martin pointed out a pear-shaped four-carat ring. "What do you think?"

Bridgett studied it with a critical eye, knowing that Chase would never in a million years pick out something that ostentatious. Finally she said honestly, "Too cumbersome."

Martin scaled it down to a three-carat marquis.

Bridgett wondered how Martin could be so out of touch with her taste after a year of courting. Again she shook her head, admitting quietly, "I just don't like the shape."

They tried a square, an oval. Large. Small. Platinum and gold. Nothing appealed to Bridgett, even though they were all exquisitely beautiful rings. Eventually Martin turned to her in frustration.

"You're not going to like anything today, are you," he guessed.

"They just don't seem right." *We just don't seem right,* Bridgett thought uneasily and then immediately wondered what was happening to her. Until Chase had come back into her life, she'd been certain she and Martin would marry. They'd both have fulfilling careers and settle right here in Charleston. They'd have two children, a girl and a boy, a beautiful home in the city and another smaller, cozier place at the beach. Their life together was going to be serene and perfect and scandal-free. Her children would be neither illegitimate nor the victims of a divorce. Her children would be safe and protected from all that pain and embarrassment. So why, suddenly, was her vision of the future so murky? Why was she filled with doubts?

Martin studied her. "You want to be surprised, don't you," he said thoughtfully after a moment. "In fact, you should be surprised. Buying you a ring this way is too… unromantic."

Which was, Bridgett thought uneasily, exactly what Chase had said.

CHAPTER TEN

"You kissed Chase," Amy Deveraux repeated incredulously at seven that evening when she'd come by to finish up a spring redecorating project Bridgett had commissioned before she left for her book tour.

"Chase kissed me," Bridgett corrected as she and Amy searched for a place to hang the brilliantly colored seascape Amy had found. "Then I kissed him back."

"And…?" Amy looked as if she could barely believe what she was hearing.

"And nothing," Bridgett said, trying not to feel disappointed as she took down the framed poster that had been hanging above her piano and replaced it with the painting. "We both said it was a mistake."

"Chase said that?" Amy regarded Bridgett skeptically.

"Well, I said it," Bridgett admitted as she put her poster aside for use in another room, "and he had no choice but to agree, because I'm going to marry Martin."

"Right." Amy rolled out a rug of sage-green, pale yellow and cream in the center of Bridgett's second-floor living room.

Bridgett sighed in exasperation as she helped return

the coffee table and two wing chairs to their positions. "Not you, too!"

Amy shot her a sisterly glance as she moved a large vase of sea oats closer to the black-marble fireplace. "Martin is awfully old for you, Bridgett."

"Thirteen years is not that much older," Bridgett said stiffly. And Bridgett was getting tired of making the argument.

Amy lifted a dissenting brow, at that moment looking very much like she sided with her brother Chase. "Maybe not for some couples, if one person is slow to mature and the other is exceptionally fast," Amy allowed cautiously, "but Martin seems like he's from a completely different generation!"

Which was, Bridgett thought, sighing inwardly, like saying he was old enough to be her father. Something else she had heard again and again. Bridgett brushed the hair off her forehead, then deciding she needed to get it off her face altogether, she slipped into her bedroom and pulled her hair up into a ponytail. "Our life experiences have been different. But our fundamental values are the same."

"Don't get me wrong. I'm not knocking good values. I think every prospective beau should have them." Amy paused in the doorway to Bridgett's bedroom, her shoulder against the frame. "But don't you want a lot more in a beau than shared values?"

Bridgett blotted the perspiration from her brow with the back of her hand and walked back out into the living room to join Amy. "I can count on Martin, Amy. I love your brother—I love all you guys." The Deverauxs were as much her family as her mother. "But I don't think I could ever count on Chase," Bridgett continued, wishing the opposite were true. "Not the way I'd need to, anyway." He might hang out with her for a while if she stopped seeing Martin, but the next time a pretty girl came along, off he'd go. And then she'd be alone again, pining after someone who was destined to be her friend and nothing more.

Amy looked unhappy, but much to Bridgett's disappointment, she didn't disagree with Bridgett's harsh assessment of Chase and his notoriously short attention span when it came women. "What does Martin say about all this? Have you told him what happened between you and Chase?" Amy asked gently, bringing out a vase of dried flowers and sea grasses and placing it on the piano.

A warm flush climbed from Bridgett's throat to her face as she helped Amy take off the wintry red-velvet slipcovers on Bridgett's furniture and replace them with slipcovers in a springlike fabric. Guilt warred with her need to keep her life running smoothly and without conflict. "I tried," she admitted, exasperated, "but he kept interrupting. Finally—" Bridgett let out a shaky breath and crossed her arms "—it just…it didn't seem like the right time. But I know I have to come clean with him." And she knew, for all their sakes, that she had to do it soon.

Amy slanted her a worried glance. Her turquoise-blue eyes probed Bridgett's face relentlessly. "Sure about that?"

"Amy, I can't accept an engagement ring from him with a secret like that between us. It would be dishonest." Which was, Bridgett admitted to herself unhappily as she rolled up her old slipcovers and put them aside for cleaning, the real reason she hadn't been able to pick out a ring that afternoon at the jeweler's. Martin thought she was just being picky, that she'd been disappointed because he hadn't been more romantic, but she knew it was more than that. Much more. Her reservations about making a commitment to Martin—any kind of a commitment—were beginning to feel overwhelming. She wanted to think it was just an early case of prewedding jitters, but she had a sneaking suspicion it was more than that. And if that was the case, then it meant everyone else was right and she was wrong.

Amy shrugged as if Bridgett's kiss with Chase was not the big deal Bridgett kept telling herself it had been. "Well, I don't see why you have to tell Martin about a kiss that didn't mean anything, anyway," Amy said, continuing to regard Bridgett sternly. "You said it's never going to happen again." Amy ripped off the tags and added coordinating throw pillows to Bridgett's newly covered sofa.

"It won't happen again," Bridgett said bluntly. "Chase understands that." He knew as well as she did that if they ventured down that road, it could destroy their friendship. She was certain Chase didn't want that any more than she did, especially now that they were beginning to get close again.

Amy stopped what she was doing and propped her hands on her hips. "Then what would telling Martin accomplish, besides hurting him? I mean, it's not like anyone else knows about this, is it?"

"No one but you." And Bridgett even felt bad about that, but she had known she had to confide in someone about the guilt and confusion she had been feeling, or she would go nuts. And Amy had been the logical choice for a couple of reasons. One, she was the closest thing to a sister Bridgett had, since the two of them had more or less grown up together. Two, Amy was someone she could trust to protect both her and Chase. And three, Amy had weathered some romantic setbacks of her own.

"Do you want me to talk to Chase for you?" Amy asked as she made a final check of the room and found everything in order. "Tell him to back off?"

"No. I can handle it," Bridgett said as she wrote out a check to Amy's redecorating business. *I can handle him, as long as he doesn't try to kiss me again.* Because if he did and she responded, with even one-tenth the passion she had the last time, and they were somewhere they wouldn't be interrupted when it happened, there was no telling what might occur next.

Amy smiled as she accepted the check and stuffed it into the front pockets of her pants. "Okay, well, I hope things work out for you."

"You are coming to my party Saturday night, aren't you?" Bridgett asked as she walked Amy to the door.

Amy hugged her warmly. "I wouldn't miss it for the world."

As soon as Amy had left, Bridgett went back upstairs to get ready for bed. She had just stripped and was liberally applying aloe lotion to her sunburn when the doorbell rang. Bridgett groaned at the interruption and went to the window. Her heartbeat picked up when she saw Chase's Jeep sitting at the curb.

IT TOOK FOREVER for Bridgett to answer the door. Chase even had the idea she was hoping he'd just give up and come back another time. And had Morganstern's Bentley been anywhere around, he probably would have. But since Morganstern didn't seem to be around and it was only nine o'clock, he decided to stick it out and wait for her to answer the doorbell.

Finally she opened the door, and he had to admit it was worth the wait. She looked gorgeous in a crop top and wide-legged pants that dipped just below her navel. She'd swept her hair off her neck in an untidy knot at the back of her head, but silky wisps escaped to brush her temples, the curve of her cheek and jaw.

"Chase, it's late," she said.

Chase might have felt bad for intruding had he not known that Bridgett was a night owl when she wasn't working, same as he. It would be hours before she went to bed. Deciding not to wait for a formal invitation that might not come, he walked on in as happily as if invited. "I just want to show you the proofs from today."

Bridgett turned sideways to let him pass. As he did so he was inundated with the delicate feminine fragrance of her skin and hair, and a wave of longing swept through him. She smiled at him blissfully, clearly intrigued. "You've got them already?"

"Yeah." Struggling to contain his awareness of her, Chase studied the rosy flush of excess sun across her face and shoulders. Suddenly, his coming by so late did not seem like such a great idea. But he couldn't back away now, because then she'd know something was up with him. Something he wasn't entirely certain either one of them could handle. "Daisy works with a digital camera." Chase swallowed hard around the sudden tightness in his throat as she shut the door behind them, and then ventured even farther into the room. "She downloaded the pictures onto her computer and e-mailed me the proofs this afternoon." Aware he had at last gotten Bridgett's full attention, Chase smiled. "We're a long way from picking the final pictures that will accompany the questions and answers in the magazine, but I thought I'd get your impressions right away. That way if you had any favorite photos, I could make sure we include them," he said kindly. "Before we get to that, though, I wanted to go ahead and do a pre-liminary draft of our interview. I'll ask the questions. You answer. I'll have a hard copy printed up, and we can edit from that."

Abruptly Bridgett looked a lot less cooperative. Maybe because she'd just realized how long all this was going to take. She folded her arms and arched her brow at him skeptically. "You want to do this now?"

Chase nodded, realizing all over again how beautiful and sexy she looked. He shifted his weight to ease the pressure at the front of his slacks. "Unless you've got something better to do."

About a dozen responses flickered in her eyes. To his disappointment, since he was sure they were of the tart-tongued amusing variety, she said none of them aloud. She merely nodded, said, "Fine, then. Let's go upstairs to my private quarters. We'll be more comfortable there than down here in my office."

Still mulling over her reluctance to engage in repartee with him—because of where a battle of wits and words might lead?—Chase followed Bridgett as she led him through her first-floor office and up the stairs to the second-floor living room. As they walked into the room, Chase blinked in surprise. It looked completely different from the last time he had seen it. "What happened here?"

"Amy redid it for me."

No doubt about it, his sister was a decorating genius. And together, Bridgett and Amy had great taste. "With stuff you already had?"

Bridgett nodded. "For the most part, although we added a few things."

"Looks nice," Chase said. Cozy. Warm. Pulled together. And yet unpretentious, all at the same time. Very much like Bridgett.

"Thanks." Bridgett smiled as she curled up in a corner of the sofa. "I think your sister did a great job, too."

He sat down in the wing chair closest to her, unzipped his backpack and got out his tape recorder and notebook. Determined to get their very real business out of the way first before anything of a personal nature, he asked, "So what's the first step for anyone trying to get his financial affairs in order?"

"The reader needs to do a complete inventory of all his debts and assets and put it down on paper."

Chase made an unenthusiastic face. "That sounds like a lot of work."

Bridgett shrugged her slender shoulders, the movement of her breasts beneath the soft cotton top telling him she wasn't wearing a bra. "How else are you going to know where you stand—financially, I mean."

"True." Chase tore his eyes from the silky bare skin of her midriff, which was now, thanks to the one-piece swimsuit she'd had on earlier, slightly less tanned than much of the rest of her. No need for him to be thinking just how easy it would be to slide his hands up and underneath that pale pink cropped top of hers. He shifted uncomfortably on the sofa and returned his eyes to her face. He had to stop thinking about making love to her. Going down that road could ruin their friendship. "What do you do when you compile all that information?"

Bridgett looked at him, complete confidence shimmering in her dark-brown eyes, and explained patiently, "You develop a budget that includes both debt repayment and saving, as well as day-to-day expenses."

Chase worked to keep the hoarseness out of his voice. "That sounds even more time-consuming."

Bridgett smirked and shook her head at him. "Are you helping or hindering here?" she asked drily.

It was Chase's turn to shrug. "I wanted my readers to have something easy."

Bridgett leaned forward earnestly, her belly button—which was a very sexy "inny"—tucking in slightly as she moved. "Saving and investing money can be easy," she told Chase passionately, "but first you have to get organized."

Chase decided if he was going to have even the slightest chance of success here, he needed to get his mind out of the bedroom. Pronto. He swallowed hard and rummaged around in his backpack for some more paper. "Maybe we should make up some charts to help the readers along in the process. Although," he admitted frankly, "I've got to tell you, even though I'd like my readers to save enough of their earnings to be able to afford a place as nice as yours, I don't necessarily think every penny of anyone's paycheck should be accounted for. I think there should be liberal amounts of money for bumming around every month built in to any budget."

Bridgett regarded him skeptically. "Like how much?" she said as she kicked off her sandals and tucked her bare feet beneath her.

"I don't know." Chase shrugged, enjoying their easy banter as much as her decidedly feminine company. He felt his arousal grow as he got another whiff of her perfume. "Twenty-five, fifty percent?" What was the matter with him, anyway? He'd lived in the same house with Bridgett. He'd seen her in sleepwear for years. He'd seen her in a lot less. In bikinis that barely covered the essentials. It had never really bothered him before. Then, he'd barely given her a second look. Now, he couldn't stop looking. Thinking. Considering the *what ifs* and the *why shouldn't wes*...

Oblivious to the sexual nature of his thoughts, Bridgett frowned at Chase and leaned toward him impatiently. "Chase, come on. If you advise your readers to blow twenty-five percent of their income on pleasure every month, your readers will never save anything or be able to afford a downpayment on a place of their own."

Chase tore his gaze from the soft movement of her breasts beneath her cotton top. "I'm not saying my readers shouldn't save anything. I think my readers should save something. And I want them to have their own place at the beach or luxury condo or whatever it is they want to own. They just shouldn't put so much money away for the future that they have no funds to have fun in the present."

Bridgett gave him an admonishing look. "You can have fun without spending a lot of money. Take today, for instance. That sea-kayaking expedition didn't cost us anything. And it was a lot of fun."

It had been a lot of fun, Chase admitted. But the idea that it hadn't cost them anything was false. After spending most of the morning and half the afternoon with Bridgett, his peace of mind had gone right out the window. "That's because I owned the kayaks," he murmured, wondering even as he kept up the argument if Bridgett had any idea—even the slightest clue—how very sexy she was. Or did she think men viewed her in the same buttoned-up, way-too-proper way she viewed herself?

"Even if we'd had to rent them—" Bridgett smiled at Chase patiently, once again giving him her full attention "—our expedition to Fort Sumter wouldn't have been all that expensive. Not compared to a dinner at one of the finer restaurants in town, for instance. Which brings me to my next point. As a general principle of ongoing financial savvy, anything that can be done at home, free of charge, like laundry and cleaning and cooking, should be done by the reader. You can save big bucks that way."

Chase stretched his legs out in front of him and leaned back against the sofa cushions, enjoying their give and take more than he'd enjoyed anything in a long time. "That's easy for you to say, you're a girl," he shot back lazily. "My readers are guys. They don't like to do stuff like that."

Bridgett's lips pressed together in a contentious moue. "They should learn," she said emphatically.

"Or get girlfriends or sisters or moms to do it for them," Chase countered mildly.

Bridgett studied him, taking in his short-sleeved madras shirt and olive-green khaki slacks before returning her gaze to his face. "Do the females in your life do your domestic chores?"

Chase knew a loaded question when he heard one. "No," he admitted frankly, studying the blush of too much sun on Bridgett's face and the unabashed interest in her eyes. "But that's just because I don't want them underfoot."

"So you do them," Bridgett said, a new edge in her voice.

Chase wondered if he was ever going to figure out a way to impress her to the degree he suddenly wanted to impress her, while still being himself. "I keep my place neat enough, but I draw the line at laundry."

She shook her head, still holding his gaze. Chase felt his pulse kick up another notch. "Let me guess. You don't approve of me sending my clothes out?"

"Honestly? I think you're wasting money, big time."

Chase inclined his head slightly to the side and narrowed his eyes at her. "I suppose you do all yours?" For some reason that seemed sexy to him, too. In fact, there wasn't anything he could think of about her right now that didn't seem sexy.

"I used to." Bridgett leaned back and stretched, abruptly looking and acting as physically restless as he felt. "Now, most of what I wear has to be dry-cleaned."

"Then our laundry bills are probably the same, 'cause all my stuff is wash-and-wear."

She conceded his point, reluctantly, and they spent

the next fifteen minutes talking about various investment strategies, going over the difference between stocks and mutual funds, municipals bonds and the various types of individual retirement accounts. Chase was impressed but not surprised that she not only knew her stuff, but could explain it in down-to-earth terms. By the time they had finished and he had tailored her advice just for guys, he knew his readers were going to get a lot out of the article.

"That was easy enough," she said, looking as relieved as he was that business was over.

"This will be, too," Chase promised as he got his laptop out of his backpack and, for lack of a better place, put it on the coffee table in front of the sofa. He opened it up, turned it on and accessed the photos. Bridgett moved close enough to see the screen. He picked up the laptop and situated the computer so it was half on his thigh, half on hers. "Here's where we started," he said, already wondering if Bridgett was going to get the same kick in the gut he had when he had first viewed the pictures of the morning's outing.

He scrolled through the hundred or so photos Daisy had taken. Bridgett looked at them in silence, one after another, gazing at the raw intimacy Daisy had managed to capture on film. An intimacy that went way beyond two old childhood friends and seemed to indicate a blossoming—forbidden—love affair. Finally, when she'd come to the end of them, Bridgett shook her head and sighed her displeasure. "We can't use any of these photos, Chase," she said crisply.

Chase looked at her in stunned amazement. "Why the heck not?"

"Because," Bridgett said before vaulting up and off the sofa, "those photos of us look like…"

"What?" Chase demanded when she didn't finish.

"Well, they're misleading." Arms folded tightly in front of her, Bridgett began to pace.

"Misleading how?" Chase asked, holding her gaze and playing dumb. He wanted to hear her say it.

"The way we're looking at each other here…" Bridgett sat back down beside him, took the laptop computer entirely onto her lap and scrolled back to the series of photos taken on the observation deck at Fort Sumter, just before they'd been inundated with school-children on a field trip. "We don't look like friends here," she pointed out unhappily.

Chase looked at the enamored expressions on their faces, recalling full well how they had been about to kiss and would have, had they not been interrupted. "We look like lovers," he said softly, wanting her to face what was happening between them, too.

"But we're not lovers," Bridgett protested hotly. She shoved the computer at him and vaulted from the sofa again.

But we want to be, unless I am misreading all the signals you are sending me, Chase thought as he watched her resume pacing the small room in agitation. For the first time he allowed himself to wonder if they could be lovers *and* friends. Not just for a while, but for the long haul. Knowing he had never enjoyed a woman's company more, Chase set his laptop computer carefully on the coffee table out of harm's way. "The camera doesn't lie, Bridgett," Chase said quietly.

"In this case, I think it does." Her shoulders tensing

even more, Bridgett walked to the French doors and opened them onto the piazza.

"Are you sure about that?" Chase stood, too. He crossed to her side and forced her to face him. "Because I think what's in those pictures is already in your heart. And mine. Face it, Bridgett. There's no way in hell you should be looking at me like that if you're going to marry Morganstern." There was no way they could continue to pretend the chemistry between them didn't exist.

Bridgett pushed him away and stalked out onto the moonlit piazza, where the scent of honeysuckle and magnolia blossoms filled the night air. "Then what should I do?" she cried as she crossed to the edge of the covered porch and put her arm around one of the thick white pillars that supported the roof above her. "Have a fling with you? Because that's all it would ever be, Chase. A fling."

He noticed she had stopped denying she desired him. That was a start, anyway, to dealing honestly with whatever this was between them. "Flings end. I don't see this ending."

"Did you see your relationship with Maggie ending when you got involved with her?" Bridgett asked in a low serious voice.

Chase stared at Bridgett in frustration. She was deliberately misconstruing events and she knew it. "That was different," he stated firmly.

Bridgett turned to face him and stood with her back to the round white column. "Different, how?"

"Because I thought at that time that I wanted to get married and settle down, and I was looking for a wife. Maggie seemed to be everything I wanted in a spouse— sweet, kind, undemanding, supportive."

"Your basic helpmate."

"I guess."

Silence fell between them as Bridgett moved back toward the yellow light spilling from the doorway of her living room. Disappointment glimmered in her eyes as she turned and regarded him quietly. "Did you love her?"

"In retrospect, probably not," Chase admitted, disillusionment filling his heart. "But at the time, it felt perfect."

"Only, it couldn't have been." Bridgett tilted her chin at him stubbornly. "She couldn't have loved you, either. Otherwise, your relationship with Maggie never would have ended the way it did."

"Maggie said she loved me, but for me it was only infatuation, the thrill of the hunt. Once we were ready to walk down the aisle, my infatuation with her ended. She said I was never meant to get married, that I only wanted the challenge of getting a woman to say yes."

Bridgett shot him an ominous look. "Is that true?"

"To a point, yeah," Chase conceded reasonably. "Marriage scares the hell out of me. The thought of making promises I might not be able to keep, well…" He paused, shook his head. "It's just not something I really want to do."

Bridgett's eyes widened. "Ever?" she questioned, aghast.

Chase shrugged helplessly, caring about Bridgett too much to lie to her. "I'm just not sure marriage is a workable institution. Maybe people are just supposed to be together as long as they make each other happy. Maybe the idea of being together for a lifetime is just not a workable concept in this day and age."

Bridgett sighed and folded her arms. "How do you figure that?"

Chase lifted both hands, palms up. "Look at our own families. Any distress your mother had was caused by wanting your biological father to marry her. When that yearning stopped, so did her suffering. My aunt Winnifred still hasn't recovered from being widowed a year after saying her vows. The hurt my parents inflicted on each other in their divorce is legendary. The same goes for my brother Mitch's situation—his divorce was so ugly people are still talking about it."

"Next you'll be talking about the Deveraux curse," Bridgett muttered disparagingly.

"No," Chase said, not about to let Bridgett bully him into taking back his sentiments on the subject. "The hurt marriage can dish out is much more far-reaching than that. The hurt marriage inflicts on people involves everyone who even tries it."

Bridgett studied Chase, her expression suddenly becoming closed and unreadable again. "How did Gabe figure in what happened between you and Maggie?" she asked casually, leading the way back into her living room.

"I don't know." Chase followed her, taking in the graceful sway of her hips. "I never gave him a chance to explain."

Bridgett whirled to face him. "Why not?" she demanded impatiently.

Because I didn't want to hear it. "I caught my fiancée looking at my brother like he just hung the moon. And when I asked her if she was attracted to him, she didn't even try to deny it. What else was there to say?" Chase challenged.

Bridgett released an exasperated breath. "Plenty, maybe, if you'd ever given Gabe a chance," she said.

Chase paused. He studied the flushed contours of her upturned face. "You think I should hear his side of things, do you?"

Bridgett nodded, her dark eyes lasering into his in a way that let him know she had always thought that. "For the sake of family unity," she said quietly, "yes, Chase, I do."

CHASE FOUND GABE at the hospital in the doctor's lounge. He didn't look any happier to see Chase than Chase was to see him. "If you're here to punch me out again," Gabe said drily, "beware. The hospital has a policy against biting the hands that heal."

Chase released a long breath and jammed his hands on his waist. He was glad he'd been able to track Gabe down so quickly and they had the chance to talk alone. Bridgett was right—this had been a long time coming. "I don't intend to hit you," he said.

Gabe dropped onto one of the sofas in the room and sent Chase a grin that brought forth memories of other brawls the two of them had gotten into while growing up. Punching hadn't always been involved, true, but the two of them had usually ended up rolling around on the floor or breaking something, anyway, during the scuffle. "That's good," Gabe said, "'cause then I'd have to slug you back. And hospital security would be in here in no time flat to haul us both away."

Recalling what Bridgett had said to him about giving his brother a chance to tell his side of the story, Chase shoved his hands into the pockets of his slacks and said, "I never gave you a chance to explain what happened."

"Are you willing to listen now?" Gabe's voice turned contentious.

Chase shrugged, even as he warned himself to hang on to his temper. "That's why I'm here," he said.

Gabe continued to regard Chase with stony resolve a moment longer, then said, "The week of the wedding, I saw that Maggie had some doubts."

"About marrying me," Chase guessed, knowing that of all the guys he knew, Gabe was the most intuitive when it came to women. He seemed to understand them in a way most men didn't. Chase envied him that ability, even as he resented what Gabe had done.

Gabe nodded reluctantly. "At first, I took her aside and tried to talk her out of it. I told her what a great husband you'd make, but she said the closer the two of you got to the wedding, the more distant and distracted you'd become, to the point you barely seemed to know she was alive. She wanted out, but you know how she is."

Chase remembered. "She's not the kind of woman to make waves."

"And her father had already spent a fortune trying to put on a wedding they could ill afford, and most of the deposits were nonrefundable."

Chase scowled. "I would have paid those."

"Her father never would have allowed it. And she knew it."

Chase paused. He was beginning to feel as if he should forgive Gabe, even though he didn't want to. "She told me she had feelings for you," he said.

Gabe shrugged. "I don't deny there was some chemistry." He looked Chase straight in the eye. "But I never slept with her."

Chase believed him—about that. "What about the other day at the beach house?" he demanded gruffly, suddenly wanting this unpleasantness to be over between him and Gabe.

"She needed a favor from me on a medical matter. I turned her down. I told her things were still dicey enough between you and me already without making them worse."

Made sense, Chase admitted reluctantly, since Maggie had always trusted Gabe's judgment on medical matters implicitly, even when Gabe had still been a resident physician undergoing training. "And the kiss I saw?" Chase barked.

"Was simply goodbye," Gabe said.

Which meant one thing, Chase thought. Bridgett had been right all along.

CHAPTER ELEVEN

Chase was halfway out the door to his beach house the next morning when his brother Mitch drove up. Looking as impeccably groomed and buttoned-up as always in his suit and tie, Mitch climbed out of his Jaguar and said, "Mom asked me to tell you we're having a family dinner tonight at the house. She's cooking and she wants us all there."

"Mom's cooking?" Chase was stunned. Everyone knew his mother didn't know how to cook. Not at all. And she certainly hadn't had time to take those lessons she'd been wanting.

Mitch nodded. "Mom gave Theresa the night off so Theresa could plan the party for Bridgett."

Chase swore. This was all he needed. His mother trying gaily to pretend nothing was wrong when something clearly was. His father on edge—probably because he hadn't yet figured out how to behave at family affairs in the wake of the divorce he had never wanted. And he and Gabe still not exactly friends.

Mitch read his mind and warned, "Just show up and be nice. I don't care what Gabe and Maggie Callaway have been up to, then or now. No more fights with Gabe."

Chase finished locking up and walked down the steps. "You don't have to worry about that," he said serenely. "Gabe and I made our peace."

Mitch's jaw dropped in stunned amazement. "When?"

"Last night." Briefly Chase explained. "So if that's all…" He continued past Mitch, in a hurry to get to Harlan Decker's office.

"It's not."

Chase turned and waited.

Mitch's frown deepened. "Amy told me you've been putting the moves on Bridgett."

Chase tensed. He should have known he couldn't keep anything secret from his family. "How does she know that?" he bit out.

"So you're not denying it," Mitch surmised unhappily.

Chase took exception to the censure in his brother's low voice. "What happened or didn't happen is between Bridgett and me," he stated heatedly.

"Listen to me, Chase." Mitch put on his sunglasses and clamped his lips together. "I don't want to see Bridgett hurt. Neither does Amy."

"I'm not going to hurt Bridgett!" Chase snapped, losing his cool. She was his best friend in the whole world. He would lay down his life for her! "Besides, Amy doesn't want Bridgett to marry Martin any more than I do."

"Amy also knows, just as I do, that it's not our decision to make. It's Bridgett's."

Chase knew his brother was a genius when it came to the shipping business that had supported the

Deveraux clan in style for nearly two hundred years, but Mitch was hardly an expert on women and love. Mitch's extremely unpleasant divorce two years back had proved that. "Martin Morganstern won't make her happy," Chase reiterated bluntly, aware he and his brother Gabe were equally bad at dealing with the opposite sex. Gabe could get a woman to turn to him for help and Chase could attract them, but none of them could hold onto a woman for any length of time or forge a real and lasting relationship. "And frankly, I can't understand why Bridgett thinks, even for one minute, that he will. The man has no real passion for anything but the good life and the art in his gallery."

"Yeah, well, you see, there's your problem," Mitch parried, adopting a lighter but no less goading tone. "Passion will get you in trouble every time."

Chase knew Mitch felt that everything, including a person's personal life, should be run with the efficiency of the Deveraux finance department. But business didn't keep a person warm at night. Business could only satisfy a person so far. Chase wanted more out of life. So should Mitch. And Bridgett.

Chase slipped on his sunglasses, too. "Passion," Chase corrected, "is the only thing worth living for." To exist without it, well…he didn't want even to contemplate that. And neither should Bridgett.

"SO WHAT HAVE YOU got on Morganstern?" Chase asked the moment he was in the private investigator's office door.

"Nothing that will cause this gal to call off the wedding," Harlan said. "He's squeaky clean."

Chase forced himself to remain calm as he eased into a chair in front of Harlan's desk. "He can't be." Chase had a pretty good gut instinct about these things. That instinct was telling him that ol' Martin was not the right guy for Bridgett, for reasons that weren't easily visible to the naked eye. He had been counting on Decker to uncover what precisely those flaws were.

"Sorry, kid. At least, according to the facts, he is above reproach. His art gallery isn't making a ton of money, thanks to the number of up-and-coming artists he sponsors, but it is revered throughout the Southeast. He invests judiciously, so the family fortune is intact—which means there's no reason for him to be marrying that gal for the money she's made with her writing."

Chase gripped the arms of the chair he was sitting in. "What about his history with women?" he demanded.

Harlan shrugged. "He's dated a number of women through the years, but the scuttlebutt around the garden clubs in town is that the woman always broke off the relationship. Mainly because he wasn't interested in marriage."

"Until now," Chase concluded grimly.

"With that gal friend of yours, yeah." Harlan pulled out a cigar and lit the end of it. "He wants kids now, though, so that's probably what's changed his mind about heading down the aisle."

Bridgett wanted kids, too.

The PI sat back in his chair and blew smoke rings above his head. "That happens to a lot of confirmed bachelors when they hit their forties. They realize time is getting away from them. And it's a now-or-never proposition."

Chase sighed. He had been so sure Harlan would find something he could use. He looked the street-smart detective square in the eye. "There's nothing I could tell Bridgett that might change her mind about marrying Morganstern?" he asked, more aware than ever that time was running out.

Harlan shook his head, "The guy has never gotten so much as a traffic ticket. And he really knows how to treat a lady."

"There's more to life than good manners," Chase argued. Good manners alone were not going to make Bridgett happy for the rest of her life.

"That may be, but the ladies really go for his charm and sophistication." Harlan regarded Chase sympathetically. Apparently not about to pull any punches, he continued, "I think you're out of luck."

Not necessarily, Chase thought, his mind already leaping ahead to the next possibility. He wasn't giving up until the last dog died. "What about her father?" he asked impatiently, knowing he still had one ace left up his sleeve. "Were you able to locate him?"

Harlan nodded. He scribbled down an address and phone number and slid them over to Chase. "He still owns the textile mill in Greenville he inherited years ago from his folks."

"THERE'S NO WAY on this green earth that I'm going to let you extort money out of me," Simon Oglethorpe told Chase the moment he was ushered into the well-appointed library at his country estate just outside of Greenville. "And to make sure of that, I've asked my lawyer to be here with us for this meeting."

Chase had no idea what kind of man Simon had been in his youth, but he could see what the man was now. He was a suspicious, nasty blue blood with none of the warmth or love in him that a woman like Bridgett deserved from a parent.

"Furthermore—" Simon narrowed his icy eyes at Chase through the lenses of his small gold-framed glasses "—I categorically deny being that young woman's father!"

Chase took in the man's jodhpurs, silk shirt and ascot and wondered if he thought he was living in colonial Africa, instead of at the foot of the Blue Ridge Mountains. "Theresa Owens wouldn't lie."

"Well, apparently Theresa has." Simon stalked the length of the library in his knee-high boots. He paused beneath a stuffed shark, displayed above the mantel. "And I told that to her daughter the last time she was here."

This was something Harlan Decker hadn't uncovered. Chase inhaled slowly. "Bridgett was here to see you?"

Simon nodded. He stalked back to his desk and sat down in the imposing leather chair behind it. "Ten years ago, on her twenty-second birthday. I told her then her mother had obviously misled her and I asked her not to ever bother me again."

"You said that to her face," Chase ascertained, struggling to remain in his chair. He was getting a powerful urge to punch the guy.

"Yes." Simon gave Chase a tight-lipped smile and pushed his glasses closer to his eyes. "Fortunately she believed me and left. Which, by the way, is exactly what you should do."

Chase ignored the hint. For the life of him he couldn't see one decent thing in this guy who had sired Bridgett, but for her sake, he had to try to get through the defenses to the kinder, gentler person he hoped was somewhere beneath the haughty disdain and mega-attitude. "How can you do this to Bridgett?" Chase asked in the same low, conscience-prodding tone his own parents had used on him many times. "How can you hurt her that way?"

Simon Oglethorpe looked at his lawyer. The lawyer nodded. Simon turned back to Chase and stood, signaling the meeting was over, whether Chase liked it or not. "Look, son, I have a family. Children. That's all I need."

And Bridgett, her mother and what they had been through because of this man's selfish irresponsibility be damned, Chase added silently.

"I don't want trouble here," Simon continued as he showed Chase the door. "But I promise you, if you or that young woman ever come and darken my doorstep again," Simon concluded grimly, "it's trouble you're going to get."

CHASE HEARD his mother's soft melodious laugh floating out through the open kitchen windows. Wondering what had prompted her amusement, he opened the door and walked in, then blinked in shock at what he saw. His mother standing very close to his father. The pair of them talking in hushed tones—hushed *flirtatious* tones. And it looked to him as if his father wanted very much to kiss his mother, and vice versa.

Chase felt a flare of hope, then warned himself not to jump to conclusions. He had wanted his parents to reconcile for a long time, even though it had never looked as if this would happen. Yes, his father had agreed to stay at the mansion along with his mother this time, instead of bunking at a hotel as usual. But that was only because his mother was planning to be at the house for several weeks, instead of the usual day or so. The two were bedding down at opposite ends of the upstairs hall, leading their own very separate lives. Still, there was something going on here. Something new. Different. And he hated to interrupt.

He was about to retreat and go out in as unnoticed a manner as he had come in when Grace turned and saw him. "Chase!" Grace blushed and backed away from Tom immediately, and went back to stirring whatever it was she was cooking on the stove. "You're the first to arrive." She stirred so hard sauce glopped up over the side of the pan.

Hoping they wouldn't notice how bummed out he was about not being able to reunite Bridgett with her father and hence, put a stop to whatever plans she had to spend the rest of her life with a man who was nothing but a father figure, Chase merely smiled and asked, "What's for dinner?"

"Garlic-roasted chicken and scalloped potatoes, peas and salad." Grace tried to wipe up the excess mess around one of the burners, and the end of her dish towel nearly caught on fire. "I'm making the white sauce now," she said as she hastily carried the smoking cloth to the sink to dampen under running water. "And your father has graciously agreed to peel the potatoes for me."

Chase looked at his dad in astonishment. He'd never

known his father to do anything in the kitchen, period. But here he was, tie off, shirtsleeves rolled up above his elbows, slowly and clumsily wielding a knife. His mother must have exercised some influence. Either that, or Tom was simply working hard to get in Grace's favor.

"I tried to catch you at your office earlier," Tom said. "They said you were out until Monday."

Chase had an idea how that played with his never-missed-a-day-of-work-if-I-could-help-it-and-I-usually-could father. He went to the refrigerator and helped himself to an ice-cold beer. Bypassing the opportunity to explain how he always took a few days off after putting a month of his magazine to bed, Chase merely shrugged and said, "I had something important to do."

Grace slanted him an inquisitive glance, but as always was too discreet to pry.

Chase knew he could say nothing more and neither parent would press the issue. But he also figured he needed to confide in someone who'd had children, who could help him make sense of what he'd uncovered. "I went to see Bridgett's father."

Tom put down his knife and stared at Chase. "That's why you wanted the name of a PI," he said.

Chase nodded. "I figured maybe if Bridgett had a relationship with her dad, she wouldn't be so hell-bent on marrying that geezer. But it didn't work out the way I had hoped." Briefly Chase filled his parents in on the details, then said, "I just can't understand why Simon Oglethorpe would refuse to acknowledge Bridgett."

"He told you," Tom said patiently, "that he already has a wife and family to tend to."

A vaguely irked expression on her face, Grace began tearing the lettuce into bite-size pieces.

"He has a responsibility to Bridgett, too," Chase argued back as he uncapped his beer and took a swig.

Tom shrugged and began slicing the potato he'd just peeled. "Maybe he's meeting it in other ways," he said.

"Such as...?" Chase was surprised his dad would take Simon Oglethorpe's side on this, when his dad had always been so devoted to his own children. "We know he never supported Bridgett financially. If he won't acknowledge her personally or be there for her emotionally, what other ways are there?"

Tom clamped his lips together in obvious frustration. "Look, it's just not always as simple as it seems. I'm sure Simon has his reasons. And who knows, maybe Bridgett is better off without Simon Oglethorpe in her life."

"I don't know how you can say that when she's about to throw her life away by marrying some old geezer," Chase retorted heatedly.

Again his mother remained silent. Chase watched her tear the lettuce angrily. "What do you think about this?" Chase asked her finally. It wasn't like her not to weigh in when it came to family dilemmas, and Theresa and Bridgett were both considered family.

Grace stared grimly at the tile back-splash above the stove. "I think men who have families shouldn't sire children with women other than their wives, that's what I think!" she said vehemently.

Chase knew his mother cared about Bridgett and Theresa—all the Deveraux did. But her protectiveness seemed to go beyond that. "So what do you think I should do?" Chase asked his mother cautiously after a moment.

In the end, it was Tom who answered him. "Leave well enough alone, son," Tom advised sternly.

Grace gave the simmering white sauce another stir. "So what else have you been up to?" she asked Chase in her best let's-change-the-subject-for-all-our-sakes tone.

Deciding maybe his mother was right, Chase leaned against the counter and took another swig of his beer. "I talked Bridgett into letting me feature her in *Modern Man*. I did an interview with her last night, and we also did a photo essay yesterday." Briefly Chase explained about the sea-kayaking expedition to Fort Sumter. "I asked Daisy Templeton to take the pictures."

Looking tenser than ever, Grace consulted a recipe and began layering potato slices in the bottom of a buttered casserole dish. "I thought Daisy was still a college student."

"She got kicked out of Wellesley a few weeks ago, so she's back in Charleston again. To tell you the truth, I don't know if she'll ever graduate, but she's one heck of a photographer. She takes photos that are just incredible in their truth," Chase said, thinking of the way Daisy'd captured Bridgett looking at him on film—as if Bridgett wanted him in her life, and in her bed.

"I'm not sure Daisy's family would want you taking advantage of her that way," Tom said as the white sauce on the stove bubbled up higher.

"Hey, I'm paying her exactly what I pay every photographer I hire for my magazine," Chase said in his own defense. Though what it was to his father, he didn't know, since—to his observation, anyway—the Templetons and the Deveraux weren't all that close.

Grace's cheeks took on a pink tint. "I think what your father is trying to say is that your giving Daisy a job now might prevent her from being motivated to go back to college and finish." Grace looked at Chase sternly. "I wouldn't want you to be responsible for ruining Daisy's life. She's obviously had a very hard time as it is."

Now Tom looked angry. Why, Chase couldn't figure.

"I think we should drop this whole subject," Tom said curtly, turning to Chase as a peculiar unappetizing flavor rose from the saucepan on the stove. "Let Bridgett handle her own life and make her own decisions," he said. "And for pity's sake, don't mention anything about this to Theresa!"

"I agree," Grace said tensely as the unpleasant smell in the room grew stronger and stronger. She shook a spoon covered with gloppy white stuff at Chase. "Once something's done, it's done, and whether you like it or not, you can't go back and change Bridgett's paternity. All you can do by bringing it up is embarrass Bridgett and her mother, and I will not have either Bridgett or Theresa humiliated that way!"

Chase wrinkled his nose. "Is it my imagination or is something burning?" he asked.

Grace rushed back to the stove. The white sauce had turned a funny brown color and was bubbling almost over the top of the pan. She cried out in dismay and turned off the element.

UNFORTUNATELY FOR THEM ALL, dinner went the way of the white sauce and was, if not totally inedible, not very tasty. Worse, his mother and father were barely speaking to each other, for reasons Chase couldn't fathom.

Not that this was the first time the two of them had gone from warm to cold in a matter of minutes. They'd been like that a lot both before and after their divorce. Chase could tell his mother resented the heck out of his father and still blamed him for something he'd done or hadn't done. And his dad was equally frustrated with his mother. Chase figured it all went back to the mysterious reasons for their divorce.

Hence, Chase got out of there as soon as he could. And the minute he got back to his beach house that night, he reached for the bicarbonate of soda. He had just fixed himself a tall glass of the soothing concoction when he heard a car engine outside. He glanced out the window and felt a mixture of anticipation and dread as he saw Bridgett charging across the sand and up the steps. She was furious, he noted. And from the looks of it, probably with him.

CHAPTER TWELVE

Chase wondered if Bridgett had any idea how beautiful she looked charging toward him in the moonlight, the waves crashing against the sandy white beach forming a romantic backdrop. His immediate neighbors had already gone to bed, and the only real light where he was standing was the soft glow of the lanterns on the perimeter of his deck.

"I don't believe you!" Bridgett said as she stormed up the wide wooden steps to confront him. Her auburn hair tumbled over her shoulders in loose flowing curls. She was dressed in a snug black cocktail dress that outlined her every curve to a tantalizing degree and at the same time comically restricted her stride to little more than baby steps. High-heeled black sandals and sheer black stockings made the most of her sensational legs.

Watching her, Chase couldn't help but grin, even as his lower half sprang to life. Who would have thought Bridgett would be doing the sexpot walk? He bet she hadn't considered how hard it would be to march anywhere quickly in that narrow-hemmed dress when she'd purchased it.

"Who told you that you could meddle in my life!"

Bridgett said as she closed the remaining distance between them with short, hip-swiveling steps.

Chase tore his eyes from the sexy fit of her dress around her slender thighs and cute-as-buttons knees and concentrated on the very big trouble he was definitely in. He supposed this was what he got for trying to help his very best friend in the whole world. Slowly he let his gaze rove her upturned face, lingering on the pert tilt of her nose and the softness of her lips before returning to her eyes. "How'd you find out?" he asked, already wondering just what it was going to take to get her to forgive him.

"I read this!" Bridgett slapped a piece of paper in his hand.

Chase studied the fax transmission. It was from Simon Oglethorpe's lawyer and had been sent to Bridgett's home. The letter warned her she would be facing harassment charges if she or Chase ever bothered him again.

Chase stared at it in frustration. The last thing he had wanted was to cause more grief for Bridgett, who in his estimation, had been hurt more than enough by her father's abandonment. Chase felt his gut tighten. Sorrow inundated his low voice as he looked at her again and reluctantly explained, "I was trying to help."

Without warning, moisture shimmered in her eyes. Bridgett looked as if she wanted to punch something—namely, him. Her lower lip trembled as she demanded emotionally, "By going behind my back?"

"By bringing your father back into your life," Chase corrected as he caught and held her gaze, beginning to get upset at how quick she was to try and convict him.

He set the paper onto the stylish wrought-iron table beside him and put an unlit citronella candle on top of it so it wouldn't blow away in the evening breeze. He turned back to her and took another step toward her, wanting the new tension between them to disappear as quickly as it had sprung up. "I had no idea you'd ever been to see him." Unable to quell his hurt, he tightened his lips with a mixture of hurt and displeasure. "You never said anything to me."

The tears she had been holding back rolled down her cheeks. Bridgett dashed them away with the back of her hand. "I never said anything to anyone about what happened that day, not even my mother," she replied in a strangled voice.

Chase thought about what a hard secret that must have been to keep. Once again he wished he could have been there for her in the way she had obviously needed him to be. "So your mom doesn't know you met Simon Oglethorpe," Chase said softly.

"I didn't want to hurt her." Strain reverberated in the low note of her voice. "It was bad enough, the way the louse rejected her after she got pregnant."

Deciding she needed to sit down, Chase took her hand and led her to a chaise. When she was sitting back against the thick green-and-white-striped cushions, he sat down in another right beside her, facing her, still holding one of her hands in both of his. "Do you know what happened between them?"

Bridgett drew a deep trembling breath. Suddenly, it seemed, she needed to confide in him, every bit as much as he needed to hear it.

"They met when my mom was nineteen. She was

waiting tables at a place out on the beach." Bitterness and hurt crept into Bridgett's low tone as some of the tension left her shoulders and she turned her hand palm up to mesh her fingers with his. "Oglethorpe was there with his family." She dropped her gaze to her lap. "He romanced her like she'd never been romanced before, made her believe he was in love with her and would marry her as soon as he'd finished college. She believed him."

Chase sighed. He wished he could erase all the unhappiness of the past. Let everyone live happily ever after without all this heartbreak and angst. "Until your mother got pregnant and found out otherwise," he guessed.

Bridgett nodded, her lower lip trembling once again with the effort it was costing her to hold back her emotions and continue in a flat, matter-of-fact tone. "He wanted her to terminate the pregnancy. When my mom wouldn't, well, that was it."

What a bastard, Chase thought. No wonder Theresa was worried about her daughter. No wonder Bridgett also found it so hard to trust.

Chase studied Bridgett's face. "Why didn't your mother go after him for child support?" he asked, trying to understand how Theresa, who was also a very strong woman in her own right, let Simon ignore his financial responsibilities to his child.

Bridgett stood, restless again, and paced away from him to the waist-high wooden railing that edged the deck. She leaned against it, her hands clasped in front of her, elbows resting on the rail, auburn hair blowing in the wind. Wanting only to be as close to her as it was possible to get, Chase got up and followed her wordlessly.

Bridgett turned to face him, one forearm still on the railing. She looked up into his eyes. "He said if my mother tried—if she forced him to pay—there'd be a custody fight over me and he'd win. With his family connections and money, my mother knew he'd probably get at least partial custody and she was afraid of what being put in an environment where I would be resented, instead of loved, might do to me. So she told him what he wanted to hear—that I wasn't his baby, after all, and they never saw each other or had any contact again."

Chase moved closer to her. He breathed in the jonquil and vanilla fragrance of her skin and hair. "I'm sorry," he said sadly, wishing he could do something to erase all the unhappiness she had suffered and was still dealing with. "I wish things had been different for you, growing up."

Bridgett stiffened. The don't-you-dare-pity-me look was back in her eyes. "I had a fine childhood, Chase."

Chase had never admired her spunk, her inner toughness, more than he did at that moment. "In a lot of ways, yeah, you did," Chase agreed as he caught the strand of hair blowing across her face and gently tucked it behind her ear. Whether she wanted to or not, he figured it was time they talked about this openly and honestly. He looked deeply into her eyes. "But you also missed having a dad."

Bridgett shrugged indifferently and cut him off with a defiant glance. "Fortunately," she said, the softness in her low voice at odds with the terrier-toughness in her attitude, "I had your dad watching out for me."

Chase regarded her with more tenderness than he

had ever thought himself capable of. "Unfortunately it wasn't enough," Chase said. "Otherwise…"

Bridgett's soft lower lip shot out in a truculent manner before he could finish. Chase knew that look. It was the look that said she wasn't going to let anyone close to her. "Otherwise what?" she demanded impatiently.

"Otherwise, you wouldn't be about to make the mistake of your life, by entering into what you and I and everyone else in Charleston know is going to be a loveless marriage!" Chase shot right back.

Bridgett glared at him and stepped back a pace. She folded her arms beneath her breasts, the action pushing the uppermost curves out of the sexy V neckline of her dress. "And you, Mr. Bachelor-of-the-decade, think you're qualified to judge," she taunted.

"I know I am," Chase said hotly.

Her pretty chin went up a notch and fire ignited in her eyes. "On what basis?"

On the only one that mattered, Chase thought. "On the basis I care about you," he said, closing the distance between them in one swift determined stride.

"Care?" Bridgett echoed hoarsely as he pulled her into his arms.

"Yes, care!" Chase declared.

He told himself it was just to shut her up, but even as he brought her closer yet, so they were touching the full length of their bodies and his lips found hers, he knew it was a heck of a lot more than that. He had wanted Bridgett forever. In his arms. Kissing him. Just like this. He rubbed his lips across hers, gently at first, then with growing intensity. He let his hand slide through her hair to the back of her neck, and the way she melted against him then, all soft and wanting, made his heart pound. He wanted her, just like this. And though he knew there would be hell to pay later for what he was about to do, right now he didn't care.

She groaned as his tongue found its way into her mouth and tangled with hers. "Chase..."

He knew all the reasons they shouldn't be together, even as he felt the desire pouring from them both. He also knew none of those reasons mattered anymore, if indeed they ever had.

Determined to make Bridgett see what she would be missing if she pledged herself to another man, a man who was all wrong for her, Chase tucked his thumbs beneath her chin and angled her mouth, for better access. Her lips were soft and hot and yielding beneath his, and so was her body. Pouring everything he felt, everything he wanted and needed into the embrace, he kissed her again and again, until whatever reservations she might have had fled and she was kissing him back with all the fervor she possessed. His body throbbed and heated and demanded more. Much more. But it wasn't going to be out here on the deck, he thought fiercely. It was going to be upstairs. In his bed.

Still kissing her, he danced her backward toward the door, one hot passionate caress melting into another. When they stepped inside, his impatience to make her his won out over the pressing need to have her lips beneath his. Aware he was already hard as a rock and they hadn't even caressed each other yet, he kept one arm around her shoulders and slid the other beneath her knees. She had a dazed yearning look in her eyes as he carried her up the stairs to his loft.

He put her down next to the bed. Her eyes widened. She looked wary again. Caution had gotten the better of them for too long. Too much caution was what had led them both to nearly marry the wrong person. No more, Chase thought as he brushed his thumb across her lower lip. Not when they had the chance to discover what it was they really wanted, needed. He brought her other hand to his mouth and pressed a kiss to the back of her knuckles. The kiss was both harder and sweeter than he'd intended. He wanted Bridgett to feel as overwhelmed as he did by what was happening between them. He wanted her to feel the power of their attraction for each other, the need. He wanted her to throw caution to the wind and make love with him.

His satisfaction deepened as Bridgett released a sigh and wrapped both her hands around his neck. He felt the soft surrender of her body pressing against his, the hot sweetness of her lips. This, Chase realized belatedly, was all he had ever wanted. Bridgett was all he had ever wanted.

Still holding her close, Chase kissed her until she arched against him and her breaths were as short and shallow as his. For so long he had been restless, filled with yearning. Now, at last, he knew why. The two of them were destined to be together. To make love together and feel and experience everything possible.

Needing, wanting, more, he slipped his hand inside the neckline of her dress and smoothed his hand from the silk of her shoulder to the silk of her breast, spilling out of her bra. She trembled in response, her flesh swelling to fill his palm. He pushed the fabric aside until he could cup the full weight of her breast in his palm. Bridgett gasped and swayed as his lips traced the path his hand had taken. Her nipple budded in his mouth, even as his hands slid beneath the hem of her dress, along the soft insides of her thighs. "Chase..."

Her whimpered plea was all the encouragement he needed to take their lovemaking another step. The dress had to come off, he thought as he unzipped the garment, feathered kisses down her neck, across the top of her breasts. He pushed the fabric down her hips, let it fall to the floor in a circle around her feet. Then he unhooked the lacy black bra and tugged everything else off. She was even more beautiful than he had imagined. He gently caressed the mounds of creamy flesh with his palms, savoring the silky warmth and softness of her skin, then bent his head and took a rosy nipple into his mouth, sucking lightly on the tender bud. Bridgett drew in a quick urgent breath, then wove her hands through his hair, holding him close. He loved her with his mouth and hands and tongue until her back arched and her knees faltered and he had no choice but to lower her to the bed.

"Oh, Chase," she whispered, bringing him closer yet as he shucked his own clothes and stretched out beside her. She looked at him, her eyes glowing with desire. "If this is what it's going to be like between us, I don't want to wait."

"Neither do I," Chase murmured back, his heart filling with wonder that she was really here with him like this, in his bed. "Neither do I." As he felt the increasing hunger in her body, everything blurred and all rational thought flew from his mind. The jonquil and vanilla scent of her filling his senses, Chase kissed his way across the tan lines, past her sexy navel and the perfection of her abdomen, to the warm moistness beneath. She stretched sinuously and melted against him, her hands curling around his shoulders as he found his way to the silken core of her. She tasted as sweet and delicate as he had hoped, and she moaned soft and low in her throat and arched her head back even more. Her passionate response, coupled with the urgent press of her hands on his shoulders, sent need throbbing to his groin. "Now, Chase," she said. She grabbed his upper arms, her fingers digging into his biceps and urged him back up the length of her body.

Needing to taste her again, to possess her again the way he only could with an honest-to-goodness, mouth-to-mouth, tongue-to-tongue kiss, Chase captured and caressed her lips. Folding her against him, breast to chest, he let her know just how wild she was making him, how hungry. Growling low in his throat, Chase parted her knees and slipped between them, increasingly aware of a need only she could ease. The V of her thighs cradled his hardness and he throbbed against her surrendering softness. They hadn't begun to explore each other—not the way he wanted—but he knew there would be time for that later, and like her he just couldn't wait, didn't want to wait….

As he continued to kiss and caress her, Bridgett trembled as wildly as Chase. So this wasn't what she'd expected, what she'd planned, when she had come here tonight. So what if it wasn't an investment likely to amount to much of anything? She had to have him.

Had to be loved, possessed, taken like this. She had to be a part of Chase, at least once in her life. And heaven knew the opportunity might never come again.

So she kissed him back and surged against him, wrapping her legs and arms around him. And when the tip of his manhood pressed against her delicate folds, she moved to receive him, forgetting for a moment the pain, the discomfort, the shock of being one, and gave herself over to the pleasure of loving him with all the passion she possessed. Chase might not love her, she might not ever be loved, but she would have this, Bridgett thought as he drove into her, taking them both to paradise and beyond. And for the moment, for now, it was enough.

BRIDGETT HAD BARELY had time to catch her breath when Chase extricated his body ever so carefully from hers and said, "We have to talk about this."

The matter-of-fact timbre of his tone, coupled with the stunned look on his face, was like being splashed with a bucket of cold water. Chase had wanted her; he just hadn't wanted her to be a virgin. And that, she concluded unhappily, said more about his true feelings for her—or perhaps lack of them—than she really wanted to know.

Not that she should be surprised, Bridgett told herself, unable to help feeling both disappointed and disillusioned by Chase's unhappiness. Hadn't she known that a guy like Chase was only in something like this for a good time? That lovemaking came with a complete lack of responsibility? Except when bedding a virgin, she feared. But there was no way she'd allow that in her case, Bridgett decided, determined to salvage her pride.

"No, we don't," Bridgett told Chase with an insouciance she didn't begin to feel.

To her frustration, Chase caught her and pinned her beneath him before she could leave the bed. Not about to let her off that easily apparently, he regarded her in a way that made her blush. "Why didn't you tell me you were a virgin?" he demanded, looking both regretful and annoyed.

Because I knew you would stop if I did. And I didn't want you to stop, Bridgett thought, her heart inundated with a crazy mixture of wonder, confusion and contrition. She had wanted Chase to feel elated that he had been her first. Not be guilty and remorseful.

When she didn't answer him right away, Chase said, "For pity's sake." He sat up in bed, dragging the covers with him to his waist. He reached over and covered her, too. Practically all the way to her chin. His frown deepened as he slanted her a dark accusing look. "You have to know that I would have—"

"Come to your senses and not made love to me at all?" Bridgett interrupted in the most carefree voice she could manage. Really, this remorse of his, on the heels of what had been a truly remarkable lovemaking session, was almost more than she could handle!

Chase leaned back against the headboard and folded his arms in front of him. Was that her imagination, Bridgett wondered, her glance sliding down the sheet drawn across his waist, or was he aroused again?

Aware her throat was suddenly very dry, somewhere else was very wet, and she was beginning to tremble in anticipation of something that probably wasn't going to happen, Bridgett sat up.

Chase cleared his throat. Abruptly his look became one of sadness as he told her gently and sorrowfully, "It's just…I would have done it a little differently if I'd known it was your introduction to lovemaking. I would have gone slower, began more gentle and careful."

What Chase had done, Bridgett thought on a wistful sigh, had been just fine. He had more than met her expectations. He had fulfilled every romantic and sensual dream she had ever had. And therein lay the problem. She was already taking their roll in the rumpled covers of his bed much more seriously than he ever would.

Whereas he was now feeling guilt and anxiety over his behavior, she was head over heels in love.

If that wasn't an out-and-out prescription for a broken heart, Bridgett didn't know what was.

"And you haven't answered my question," Chase continued as Bridgett's misery built to an untenable degree. Chase's blue-gray eyes narrowed in speculation, the guilt he felt about deflowering her still on his face. "How is it possible that you and Martin haven't…" Chase paused as if struggling for the right words. "You were going to marry the guy, Bridgett!"

Well, you're right about one thing, Bridgett thought, feeling pretty darn guilty and upset about her actions, too. *Clearly any thought of accepting a proposal from Martin now is off. There's no way I can marry him now. Not after this. Because this never would have happened if I loved Martin the way I should.*

Aware Chase was still waiting for an answer, and she had one thing left—her pride—Bridgett vaulted out of his bed and tossed back haughtily, "Martin and I didn't make love because Martin didn't try and pressure me into sex, a fact I very much appreciated."

Chase blinked, his confusion building, instead of lessening. His gaze flicked over her as he stood, too. "Why the hell not?" Chase demanded. "When he's supposed to be in love with you!"

Bridgett's face turned hot with shame as she struggled into her bra and panties. She wished Chase would put on some clothes, too, before they ended up back in bed, making love again. "Because Martin doesn't think that way."

"Well, he darn well should," Chase stated vehemently, finally reaching for his pants.

Bridgett tried not to feel disappointed as Chase covered his beautiful—and yes, aroused—body from her view. It wasn't hers to admire. Or love. Or want. As much as she might want that to be the case.

"Martin respects me." Bridgett stepped into her dress and pulled it up over her hips. And until now, anyway, she thought as she put her arms through the armholes, Martin's hands-off policy had been a good thing. Now, for the first time in her life having made love with a man who truly desired her, Bridgett had to wonder if Martin's disinterest in her sexually was a good thing, after all.

Chase snorted derisively as Bridgett scrambled around looking for her evening sandals. He found them first and handed them to her, then stood back and watched her put them on.

"I respect you, too, Bridgett." Chase stepped behind her and helped her with her zipper. "But that doesn't keep me from wanting to take you to bed. It makes me want to pleasure you all the more."

Just the sound of that and the erotic mental images it conjured up made Bridgett want to make love with Chase all over again. Aware her breath was coming hard and fast—her nipples had already tightened, her middle gone all soft and hot—Bridgett straightened. She did not need to be thinking about how it felt when Chase was deep inside her, driving her toward sweet oblivion. She didn't need to think about the tenderness of his kisses or the wonderful magic of his hands. Or the even more astounding reaction of her body.

Doing her best to appear unaffected by all the frank talk and open declarations of his desire, she squared off with him, chiding, "You're impossible! You know that, don't you?" Suddenly, inexplicably, her throat was clogged with tears. Maybe because she knew this wasn't going to last—Chase's desire for any one woman never did.

"Why?" Chase taunted impatiently, refusing to back down or move away from her. He cupped her shoulders lightly, possessively, the warmth of his palms sending even more sensual messages radiating through her. "Because I'm honest about wanting you?"

Bridgett stared at him despairingly, hardly able to believe she had gotten herself in such a quandary. She was certainly old enough to know better. Just because something felt right didn't make it right.

"Sex and love are not the same thing," she informed him hoarsely. Her mother had told her that over and over again. And Bridgett had lived long enough, and seen enough of her girlfriends bedded and then abandoned, to know that was true. There were a lot of guys out there who would say and do anything to get a woman into the sack. And until tonight, until he had made love to her as if she was the only woman on earth for him, until she realized that Chase was the only man on earth for her, she had thought Chase was one of them.

Now, because of what she was feeling, Bridgett wasn't one hundred percent certain that was true. Unfortunately she wasn't sure it wasn't true, either. She knew Chase cared about her and always had. But were caring and love the same thing? Or was she just supposed to accept the sex as a new part of their "friendship," and nothing more? The only thing she knew for certain was that she couldn't go on pretending nothing had changed between them, because for her, it had.

"You're right. Sex and love aren't the same," Chase shot back passionately, giving her a look that let her know she was making this unnecessarily hard on them both. "But sex with love is even better," he continued practically. "And caring about someone without taking it to the next level is crazy."

Bridgett studied him warily, weighing everything he said and did. She was almost afraid to hope, and her heart pounded like a wild thing in her chest. "What are you saying, Chase?" she whispered tremulously.

Chase gazed down at her, his eyes misty, as he spoke the words she wanted so very much to hear. "That I want us to be together, Bridgett. And I know now that I always have."

CHAPTER THIRTEEN

"You can't mean that," Bridgett said. Her voice was overflowing with feeling and her eyes were filled with tears.

"The heck I don't," Chase shot back just as emotionally. He cupped her chin in his hand and gently tilted her face up to his. "It took you almost marrying someone else to make me see it," he said, "but I want to be with you, Bridgett. I've wanted that for a very long time. I just wouldn't admit it to myself."

Happiness swept through Bridgett with the force of a tidal wave. "Oh, Chase," she cried, rising on tiptoe and bringing her lips to his, "I want to be with you, too." She kissed him with all the passion and tenderness she possessed. For so long now she had wanted him to yearn for her the way she yearned for him. And yet, as much as she enjoyed the feel of his lips on hers, Bridgett knew they had to pull apart. And talk about this very difficult situation they were in, before their affection for each other went any further. Bridgett splayed her hands across Chase's chest. Like it or not, she knew she and Chase wouldn't be happy until they had cleared the way for the two of them to be together for more than just tonight.

"But that still doesn't mean what we've done here tonight is okay," Bridgett said, determined to make things right. She might not have been engaged to Martin just yet, and she and Martin might not have quite gotten around to making a formal commitment to each other or any promises of exclusivity, but they had been very close to doing all of that. And probably would have, had Bridgett's feelings for Chase not gotten in the way. And so now she was left feeling very upset and guilty. Because she knew now she should have realized Martin wasn't the right man for her and stopped seeing him a long time ago.

Instead, because Martin had offered her the kind of settled married future she wanted, the kind most of the men her own age still didn't, she had kept seeing him. Fooling both of them into thinking that the two of them had a future together that would one day include marriage and children.

And that had been wrong, Bridgett realized, even if she hadn't done any of it deliberately or understood quite what was happening at the time. Or been in something of a blind panic because she was thirty-two and still nowhere near marriage and the children she had always wanted. Because somewhere deep down, she must have known she didn't care about Martin the way she should. Even if she couldn't admit it to herself. Just as she knew she was the marrying kind. And Chase was the kind who would never marry. What was it Chase had said to her? she thought uneasily. *The thought of marriage scares the heck out of me. The thought of making promises I might not be able to keep, well, it's not something I want to do.*

Chase's expression was grim, his concern about the situation evident, too, as he smoothed the hair from her face. "I'm sorry we made love before you had a chance to tell Morganstern you can't and won't see him anymore," Chase told her quietly, then paused and searched her face. "I know that must feel disloyal. But surely you know now that you don't love him and never did. Because if you did, you never would have made love with me tonight."

Bridgett knew that was true. Funny that she hadn't noticed until tonight that she and Martin had never once professed their love for each other. She had just assumed that getting along with and liking each other was enough. She saw now it wasn't.

Hopefully Martin would see things that way, too.

Chase tightened his arms around Bridgett possessively. "You have to tell him the marriage is off."

Bridgett planned to do just that as soon as possible. The problem was how to do it without hurting Martin. Bridgett didn't want to be cruel, and she didn't want to invade her privacy with Chase, either. She swallowed hard and looked up at Chase. "He's going to want an explanation," she warned.

Chase shrugged, less concerned about Martin than he was about her. "Then tell him the truth," Chase advised. "That you and I realized we have feelings for each other, have had them for a long time, and you can't marry him under those conditions. He won't like it," Chase predicted, his eyes narrowing seriously, "but if Martin's half the man you say he is, he'll accept it. And he'll be grateful to you for telling him the truth."

Bridgett's heart pounded in her chest as she faced the

uncertainty of her future. "And then what?" she asked warily, very aware that although Chase had made love to her with all the passion and tenderness he possessed, he hadn't actually said he loved her.

Chase tensed. After a moment he dropped his hands, stepped away. "I don't know," he said, still holding her gaze. "I don't usually think that far ahead. But I'm sure we can figure out the best way to handle this," he hastened to assure her.

Her mother was right, Bridgett thought wearily as she studied the conflicting emotions on Chase's face. Love and sex weren't the same thing. Not at all. And she still wasn't the type of woman who could run around having flings and keep her heart intact. Desperation filled her as she took another drink and set her soda can aside. "Listen, I've really got to go." Determined to end the evening now, before the situation deteriorated any further, she brushed by him.

"Now?" Chase followed her out onto the deck.

Bridgett gathered what was left of her dignity and wrapped it around her like a cloak. Love and friendship weren't enough for her. And never would be. Whereas with Chase, well, that was all he wanted. All he probably would ever want. Given that, it was best to end this now, she told herself logically, before their friendship suffered even more irreparable damage. It was going to be hard enough to look him in the eye without remembering all they had done and said. She swallowed around the knot in her throat. "I don't think this should happen again," she said, telling herself it really was for the best.

Chase stared at her as if he had no idea who she was

or what she wanted out of life. "You're telling me that's it?" he asked in a low incredulous voice.

Bridgett nodded. And then, unable to say more without bursting into tears, she slipped out the door and made a dash for her car.

BRIDGETT MET MARTIN at the gallery the next morning before it opened.

As soon as he ushered her inside, she said, "I've got something to tell you."

He studied her, taking in her somber navy-blue sheath and upswept hair. "Before you do, I think you should make sure it's something I want to hear."

Her heart pounding uneasily, Bridgett fingered the long strand of pearls around her neck. "What do you mean?"

"We're not children anymore, Bridgett." He took her by the elbow and steered her toward his private office at the rear of the building. As soon as they were inside, he shut the door behind them. "And I'm not as clueless as I sometimes appear."

Bridgett drew a steadying breath, but finding her legs would no longer support her, she dropped down onto the sleek white leather sofa. "You know…" She hesitated.

"That Chase Deveraux has been pursuing you?" Martin shrugged. He poured them both a cup of English tea and brought hers to her. He sat down beside her and swiveled toward her. "I'd have to be a fool not to have seen that," he said as politely and unemotionally as if they'd been discussing the weather.

Bridgett moved back slightly, so that his bent knee

was no longer touching her thigh. She looked down at the fine wool of his impeccably tailored suit, still struggling to understand Martin's total lack of emotion about such a serious subject. "Then why didn't you say anything?" she asked.

Martin looked at her even more tranquilly. "Because I didn't think it was necessary."

Bridgett blinked in confusion. She had expected a jealous angry scene, not this cool reaction. "But if...?" She knew Martin was mature, especially in contrast to men her own age. That was one of the things she had always liked about him. But still, she did expect him to be more emotional about the subject of another man.

Martin sipped his tea and gave her a look that was almost pitying. "I don't care if he's made a pass at you, Bridgett," Martin explained matter-of-factly. "I don't care if you've accepted it. I simply don't want to know about it."

The sheer audacity of his view left her momentarily speechless. "You could overlook something like that?" she asked eventually, not sure if she was more disillusioned or disappointed in his lack of true feelings for her.

Martin set his cup aside slowly and deliberately. He unbuttoned his suit coat and leaned back on the sofa once again. "I think if we're going to be married and have children together and stay married, there may be moments when we have to overlook such things. They don't mean anything. I would just expect you to be discreet, as I would be, if the situation ever arose."

"That's a very sophisticated attitude to have," Bridgett said finally.

Martin smiled. "How else do you think the people in my family have managed to stay married and keep their fortunes intact all these years?"

Feeling increasingly foolish because it turned out Chase had been right about Martin, after all, Bridgett stood and began to pace the elegantly appointed room. "You never said anything about this," she murmured, upset. Because if Martin had, she would have stopped seeing him months ago. Before she had wasted all that time. And made such a fool of herself defending him to others, like her mother and Chase, who had sensed all along that there was something just too good to be true about Martin Morganstern. That there was some reason no other woman had deigned to marry him or even get engaged to the forty-five-year-old bachelor.

Martin lifted his hands and let them fall back to his lap. "To be frank, I didn't think it would be a problem. You didn't seem all that passionate a person to me...."

At least until Chase Deveraux came along to show her otherwise, Bridgett amended silently.

"And frankly, I'm not, either," Martin continued pragmatically. He gazed at her with the tenderness and kindness she had once so revered. "And I'm happy about that. I think not being so physical makes life a lot easier. Companionship and understanding are what I'm looking for."

What he was describing was fine in a friend. Just not enough in a spouse.

"Unfortunately I'm not all that understanding," Bridgett stated as she opened her purse. Deciding it was time to call an end to this farce once and for all, she handed Martin a velvet box containing the emerald ring he had given her. "Because I do want fidelity, on both sides. I can't imagine being married without it."

CHASE HADN'T WANTED to let Bridgett go after they'd made love. He had wanted to keep her there with him all night and move her in with him the next morning. But he had sacrificed his own desire because he had known Bridgett was right about one thing: she had to end it with Martin before her relationship with him went any farther. And she had needed to do it alone. So he had put aside his own irritation at the inexplicable way she had gone so hot and cold on him again and reluctantly let her go with their own future unresolved. That hadn't stopped him from worrying, however. And when she hadn't contacted him by noon the following day or returned any of his calls, he went in search of her. First he wanted to make sure she was okay and that she had broken it off with Martin as she had promised. And second he wanted to understand why she had decided, without consulting him, they shouldn't make love again. He intended to change her mind about that. But first, he had to understand her reasons. And bitter experience told him that was not going to be an easy task.

He found her jogging in Battery Park. Hurriedly he finished stretching and joined her on the path by the seawall. Deciding nothing would be gained by beating around the bush, he plunged right in. "You've been avoiding me."

"And I'm going to keep right on avoiding you," Bridgett said, confirming his earlier assumption that he would never understand women and what they wanted, no matter how hard he tried. Bridgett was even more of an enigma to him. But she wouldn't stay an enigma, Chase decided firmly. Not if he had his way.

"And why is that?" he asked easily.

She turned and regarded him then, the look in her eyes so melancholy he was afraid they'd never be friends again, never mind lovers. "You know why," she said softly, and picked up her pace.

Which was, Chase thought, the hell of it. Because now that he was with her again, he did know why. He had handled last night—heck, his whole relationship with her—all wrong! Bridgett deserved romance. Courting. Dates and flowers and surprises. Intimate walks on the beach. Wonderful dinners. And all the courtship rituals that showed a woman she meant something to a man. Instead, what Bridgett had gotten was a roll in the hay. And as passionate and tender as their lovemaking had been, it wasn't enough. Not for her. Unfortunately Chase couldn't take it back. He couldn't give her a better introduction to lovemaking, more suitable to the innocent woman she was, rather than the sophisticate he'd thought her to be. All they could do was move forward. He was more than ready to do that, if she'd only give him a chance.

"I'm sorry about last night," he said eventually, wishing she'd give him at least half a chance to make it up to her. "If I'd known—"

The flush in Bridgett's cheeks deepened attractively. "Don't apologize," she said quickly. And the impersonal way she looked at him then made him realize he'd do whatever he had to do to keep her from easing out of his life again. "We might not have planned it." Her voice sounded hoarse. Stressed. "But we're both adults," she continued, almost too casually. "We can handle it."

Could they? Chase wondered, noting the hurt in her eyes. He disagreed. "We can't keep avoiding each other."

"Don't you think a little time-out is warranted?" she asked, picking up her speed even more. "I mean, it's not as if talking about it will help anything."

"It would help me," Chase said, beginning to get angry.

"Too bad." She frowned at him. "Because all it's doing is annoying me."

Giving him no chance to answer, Bridgett raced ahead as if trying to leave him way behind. Not about to be pushed away that easily again, Chase picked up his own pace until they were once again running side by side. It didn't matter whether she went faster or slower, he stayed with her. Predictably, bright spots of color that had nothing whatsoever to do with the exertion she was expending, soon appeared in her cheeks.

After a while, figuring his point had been made, Chase turned his glance her way and prepared to resume their conversation. If Bridgett didn't want to talk about the two of them, they'd talk about the rest of her romantic life. He made no effort to disguise his relief as he observed casually, "I heard you and Martin called it quits."

Bridgett's lips tightened as they skirted past a group of professionals enjoying the beautiful spring weather on their lunch break, then went back to running side by side. "Who told you that?" She kept her gaze straight ahead.

Chase slanted her another glance, taking in her Charleston Harbor T-shirt and sunshine-yellow running shorts. "Your mother. She was happy about it."

"Yes—" Bridgett kept her eyes on the cargo ship entering the harbor as if it was the most interesting thing in the world "—I know."

Chase ducked behind Bridgett as they ran past another group of joggers coming the opposite way. "She said she thought you were relieved."

"I am." Bridgett turned off the path abruptly and stopped beneath the shade of a tall palmetto tree. "It turns out you were right about him, after all." She brushed the damp hair from her forehead. "He's not the man for me." Briefly she explained Martin's sophisticated views on infidelity. Views she didn't begin to share. Victory spilled through Chase, followed swiftly by soul-deep satisfaction.

"I knew he had ice water in his veins," Chase stated smugly. Turned out his gut instincts had been right on target, after all.

"So you're off the hook, Chase." Bridgett bent over at the waist, still looking as if she had lost her best friend in the whole world as she worked to catch her breath. She wiped the perspiration from her brow and looked at him meaningfully. "You don't have to feel guilty about breaking the two of us up any longer. You did me a favor." She straightened and spun around, ready to jog off again.

This time Chase grabbed her by the shoulders and prevented her flight. Figuring she'd run far enough, he forced her head up to face him. "I don't feel guilty," he told her flatly, still wishing fervently that their first bout of lovemaking had come about some other way and some other time, when she already believed how very much he cared about her. "And I don't consider what happened between us a favor."

Instead, it had been a revelation. For both of them. And there had been a brief time, just after it had happened, before reality'd had time to sink in and she had panicked and run out on him, when Bridgett had known it and felt it, too.

"Maybe you should consider it another one of those things friends do for each other." Bridgett shrugged out of his light grasp.

"Why?" Chase demanded, tamping down his hurt, aware it was all he could do not to haul her close and kiss her senseless.

"Because," Bridgett countered just as stubbornly, "you and I both know that it didn't mean anything and it's not going to happen again."

The defiance in her voice was unmistakable. "You can't mean that," Chase said, stunned. His inability to understand women or how they thought, what they felt, had never seemed more pronounced.

Bridgett looked at him as if he didn't know her at all. "Yes," she said softly, and raced off. "I do!"

CHASE FINISHED his run—alone—then went to the one place he figured he could enlist some help, if not with talking sense into Bridgett, at least with understanding her. Because right now the romantic heart of her was as much a mystery to him as ever. And he didn't think he could endure the way she went hot and cold on him for seemingly no reason much longer.

His mother was the first person he saw upon arrival, and she was knee-deep in a rainbow of spring flowers. Grace looked up at him as he walked in and promptly scowled at the sweaty state of his running clothes. She paused, crystal vase in hand. "Don't you dare track dirt in on that floor, Chase Deveraux! If you do, Theresa will have your hide."

"Nice to see you, too, Mom." Chase left his grimy running shoes outside on the back porch and walked on in, blotting his face with the towel he'd slung around his neck. Knowing better than to perch on any of the beautiful wicker furniture in the sunroom in his present state, he headed into the kitchen for a bottle of water from the refrigerator and a wooden chair, and brought them both back to the sunroom. He put the chair down back to front next to his mother and sat. "What are you doing?"

Grace gave him a look that told him he should have had a shower before coming over. "I'm arranging flowers for Bridgett's party tonight."

Chase folded his arms over the chairback and took another long thirsty swallow of water. "You heard she and Martin broke up."

"Yes." Grace snipped the ends off a handful of daffodils, then put one each in the dozen or so vases she had lined up on the folding table, erected for the purpose. Finished, she reached for a handful of buttercups. "Consequently Martin won't be attending this evening."

"A shame," Chase said.

Grace looked up from her snipping. She regarded him steadily. "You don't seem to think so," she remarked drily.

Chase shrugged, refusing to pretend otherwise. "I never liked the guy," he said flatly.

"From what I've seen, he's a very nice man. Handsome. Polite. Prosperous."

Obviously, Chase thought, Bridgett hadn't told *his* mother Martin's views on marital fidelity. Knowing Bridgett, she probably hadn't said anything to her own mother, either.

"It takes more than handsome, polite and prosperous to make a good husband," Chase said. It took the kind of love only he could give her. Not that he'd ever get Bridgett to admit that.

"Still, from everything I've heard, Martin really seemed to care for Bridgett," Grace said carefully after a moment.

If you want a husband with ice water running through his veins, Chase conceded sarcastically to himself, Martin probably would be a good choice. He studied his mother, wondering just what it was about women and marriage. From what he could tell, the young ones, who had yet to be married, wanted desperately to be hitched. This feeling intensified, the older they got. Hence, Bridgett's attachment to Martin. The ones like his mother who had suffered through a divorce and gone on to build a life alone seemed totally disinterested in tying the knot again or even being that serious about any one man. Deciding to delve into the reasons for that, he asked his mother casually, "Do you think you'll ever get married again?"

Grace looked up, stunned. "To someone other than your father?"

Of course, Chase thought. Unless... Deciding not to beat around the bush, he asked, "Are you considering remarrying Dad?"

Twin spots of color appeared in Grace's cheeks. "No, of course not," she replied hastily. Finished with the buttercups, she reached for the pink roses.

"How come?" Chase shot back, deciding to use this opportunity to try to find out why his parents had divorced.

"Because I've been there, done that," Grace said briskly.

"What about with someone else, then?" Chase asked.

Grace continued to avert her gaze. "I don't think so, no."

Why not, Chase wondered. "Don't you believe in marriage?" Because, he realized belatedly, he was sure beginning to.

"Yes. Of course I do." Grace stuffed lilies into the mix.

Chase took another swig of water. "Then...?" Chase prodded, sensing there was more.

Grace paused, her beautiful face masked in disillusionment. "If it didn't work out with your father, I don't think it will work out with anyone."

Chase knew what it was like to feel that kind of pain—he was feeling it now with Bridgett. He couldn't really see himself ever marrying anyone else, either. "You really loved Dad, didn't you?" he said after a moment.

Sorrow appeared in his mother's eyes as she readily admitted, "Yes, I did...."

"And Dad loved…loves you," Chase said carefully.

"I believe so, despite our differences." Grace paused and searched Chase's face.

"What would have made you stay with Dad, instead of getting a divorce?"

That, it seemed, was easy.

Grace looked Chase straight in the eye. "If I'd known I was the most important person in his life, above all else—our careers, any difficulties we had, everything. If I'd just known I could count on him to love me the way I needed and wanted to be loved, I would have stayed."

CHAPTER FOURTEEN

Bridgett wasn't exactly in a party mood, but given all the trouble her mother and Grace and Winnifred had gone to, to welcome her back to Charleston, there was no way she could avoid the party. So she got herself ready, taking as much care as she would have had she actually been going to see Chase that evening.

Her mother, it seemed, approved of Bridgett's attire, too. "Oh, honey, you look gorgeous!" Theresa enthused when Bridgett stopped by her mother's apartment on the third floor of the Deveraux mansion.

"So do you, Mom," Bridgett returned, the emotional catch in her voice mirroring Theresa's. For once Theresa was going to be a guest at one of Grace and Tom's parties, instead of the housekeeper running things behind the scene. Bridgett had never been prouder of her mother than she was at that moment. Theresa might have had a hard life as a single mother and domestic, but tonight, in a beaded sapphire-blue dress and matching shoes, her red hair swept up in an elegant twist, Theresa looked young and vital and ready for a romance of her own.

Theresa studied Bridgett's reflection in the mirror, knowing, as always, when Bridgett was upset. "Are you worried about people talking about your breakup with Martin?" Theresa asked, concerned.

"No," Bridgett said. And it was true. That kind of gossip she could deal with. It was the damage to her friendship with Chase that had her feeling so sad and uncertain. Because she honestly didn't know where they went from here. Was she right to try to go back to being just friends before any further hurt or disillusionment was inflicted on either of them? Or should she chance it and hope for the best, knowing all the while, because of her background and the fact that she had grown up illegitimate, that she had never been the kind of woman made for casual flings?

"Are you worried about never getting married?" Theresa persisted.

I'm worried about making the same mistakes you made. I'm worried I'm going to give my heart to a man who can't or won't love me back, and then spend the rest of my life regretting my foolishness, Bridgett thought. But not wanting to hurt her mother's feelings, she swallowed and sat down on the edge of Theresa's bed. She smoothed the damask coverlet with her fingertips and chose her words carefully. "I know it's silly. Childish of me, really. But I always thought, growing up, that there was going to be this one man out there for me whom I would love above all else. And that he would come along and sweep me off my feet and make me his bride, and we'd have children together and live happily ever after." She'd thought—even more foolishly—that her knight would be Chase. And worse, now that she had crossed that bridge and made love with him, she knew she would never care for any man the way she cared for Chase.

"I know how you feel, honey." Theresa moved around the end of the four-poster to sit down beside Bridgett. "I had the same dream."

"Only, it didn't come true for you." Bridgett swallowed around the lump in her throat, for the first time understanding the pain her mother must have suffered when her love affair ended. She must have been devastated. "Simon Oglethorpe left you."

"And you," Theresa reminded Bridgett gently, taking her hand in both of hers. "And I have to worry if that didn't scar you, just a bit, despite everything I tried to do to protect you."

Bridgett had always appreciated her mother's honesty and efforts to do right by her. "You told me the way it was," she countered stubbornly, tightly clasping her mother's work-worn hand.

Theresa sighed heavily. "And in the process left you looking for someone mature and reliable who was never going to make you as truly happy as you deserved to be, instead of that one true passionate love of your life." She stood and moved away, her heels clicking on the wood floor. Then she turned back to Bridgett, sorrow in her eyes. "I fear I did you a disservice, asking you to judge a man's trustworthiness by his bank account or lack thereof and warning you away from romance." Regret colored her low voice. "There's no reason we both should be paying for my mistake in choosing the wrong man, who just happened to be self-centered and wealthy, because that's exactly what you've been doing, Bridgett. Putting too much weight on the facts of a man's life that we can all see and admire, and not enough store in your own feelings."

Bridgett studied the love in her mother's eyes. "You're telling me to take more chances, aren't you," she asked softly.

Theresa nodded. "I'm telling you to follow your heart, honey."

And Bridgett knew what her heart was telling her to do.

HE WAS LATE. And he was never late. Bridgett walked over to Gabe, aware the party had been going on for a full three hours now and Chase had yet to appear. This was not a good sign. She smiled at his handsome younger brother. "Did you hear from Chase today?" Bridgett asked. She hoped the two of them hadn't had another argument, one that would preclude Chase's coming to the party tonight.

"No." Gabe looked at Bridgett, taking in her stunning dress and elegantly upswept hair. "You?"

Bridgett sipped a little of her champagne, but passed on the canapés being circulated by white-coated waiters from the catering company. She turned back to Gabe. "I saw him earlier jogging in the park," Bridgett admitted.

"I gather he didn't say anything then about skipping the party," Gabe said.

"No." But she'd made it pretty clear to Chase that he was no longer welcome in her life, Bridgett recalled ruefully. What a fool she had been. Pushing Chase away when all he had wanted was to be close to her.

"Sorry about you and Morganstern," Gabe continued.

"That's okay. It was for the best," Bridgett said, and

meant it. She felt nothing but relief. And gratitude to Chase for forcing her to see what she would rather not have admitted—that she was with Martin out of fear and desperation, rather than love. And those were not reasons anyone should marry, have children and try to build a life together.

"You'll find the right man someday," Gabe said.

I already have, Bridgett thought as a hush fell over the crowd. Bridgett and Gabe turned toward the door. Chase walked in, his former fiancée, Maggie Callaway, on his arm. And Bridgett felt her heart sink clear to the floor.

CHASE COULD SEE Bridgett was taking this the wrong way. But given the fact that all eyes were now upon them, he had no choice but to take Maggie all the way over to Gabe.

"Maybe this wasn't such a good idea," Maggie Callaway whispered to Chase.

"Trust me, it's a great idea," Chase said, holding on to Maggie more tightly and refusing to let her drag her feet. He should have done this two years ago. Think of all the heartbreak and humiliation, not to mention family tensions, he would have avoided if he had just bothered to own up to his own shortcomings and talk to Gabe. Chase and Maggie stopped just short of Gabe and Bridgett. Not surprisingly, Gabe looked fit to be tied and jealous as all get-out. "I believe you owe this lady a dance," Chase told Gabe, inclining his head to the moonlit garden beyond.

Bridgett looked at Chase as if he was crazy. "There's no music outside," she protested.

"So they'll make some," Chase said. He took Bridgett's arm in his, as a visibly stunned Gabe and a trembling Maggie wandered off outside, looking as if they had a lot to say to each other, as well.

Bridgett looked incredibly beautiful in some sort of shimmery gold gown with a halter top and close-fitting bodice, and a skirt that fluffed out at her waist before falling in a whisper-soft circle to her knees. The fabric was very soft, and so was all the exposed skin on her back, shoulders and in the V neckline, Chase thought. She'd swept up her hair into a loose tumble of auburn curls and put on a gold necklace and earrings that perfectly accented the dress. Chase didn't need to edit a magazine to know she had taken an extraordinary amount of time dressing for the evening. As had he.

"I didn't think you were coming," Bridgett said in a low voice.

"Then you have a lot to learn about me and how relentless I can be when I want something," Chase said. And right now he wanted Bridgett more than anything he'd ever wanted in his life. He could only hope that by the time morning came, she'd feel the same. If not, he'd just have to work harder at bringing her around. "I've decided we're going to refocus our priorities."

Bridgett's gaze trailed slowly over his black tux before returning slowly and deliberately to his face. Too late, Chase recalled she had never liked being told what to do or how to behave. "And if I don't agree?" she murmured mischievously, giving him a saucy look. "Then what?"

Chase inclined his head at her. "Then we'll keep talking until you do," he said.

A challenging light sparkled in her eyes and a smug smile curved her lips. "Confident, aren't you?"

"Resolute," Chase said, knowing this was one battle of the sexes he would win. "And with good reason." An awful lot was at stake. And this time he wasn't going to screw things up. This time he was going to hang in there and do whatever it took to make sure he understood Bridgett, heart and soul. No more chalking up their differences to the mysteries of the female psyche and walking away. From now on, his first order of business was making sure he met all the needs of the woman in his life.

Impatiently he looked toward the foyer again, wondering what was taking so long. A second later his aunt Winnifred moved away from the window and bustled toward the door. She opened it as previously planned, revealing a Rolls-Royce limousine idling at the curb. "That's our ride." Chase plucked the champagne glass from Bridgett's hand.

"What do you mean, 'our ride'?" Bridgett asked.

"You'll see." Grinning, Chase put an arm beneath her knees and scooped her up in his arms. The guests laughed and clapped while Bridgett flushed from head to toe.

"For heaven's sake! Put me down," Bridgett demanded as Chase strode with her down the walk to the waiting car.

"Okay." But Chase waited until a tuxedo-clad Harry, Winnifred's butler, had opened the limo door before he set Bridgett on the plush leather seat and pushed his way in after her. The butler closed the car door behind them and then circled around to climb behind the wheel.

Bridgett settled back against the seat opposite Chase and folded her arms in front of her. "I don't know what you think you're doing!" she said breathlessly as the car pulled away from the curb and headed for the prearranged destination. "Carting me off, caveman-style!"

Chase grinned at Bridgett, loving the passion in her voice and eyes—it was something he planned to see every day for the rest of their lives. "Yes, you do," he replied smugly.

"You just let everyone at that party know that we...that we're..." Bridgett sputtered irately.

"Yeah," Chase said with satisfaction as he slid across to sit beside her. For as long as he lived, he would remember the look in her eyes as she realized he had come to claim her as his. "I sure did. And you know what? You loved every romantic second of it."

Bridgett opened her mouth to disagree, then clamped it shut again. "Since when did you get so demonstrative?" she demanded after a moment.

Deciding she was still too far away, Chase pulled her over onto his lap. "Since you came back into my life in a very different but very important way."

Bridgett splayed her hands across his chest and looked deep into his eyes. "You're planning to make love to me tonight, aren't you?" she asked softly.

Chase's pulse kicked into overdrive as he thought about the upcoming evening. "And then some," he said.

CHAPTER FIFTEEN

Bridgett would have preferred an immediate seduction, one that gave her no time to think. She should have known that wasn't Chase's plan. Whatever happened between them was not going to be ill thought out this time. He wanted to know if they could be lovers and still be friends. He wanted a decision from her about their future. Finality. No impetuous decisions that would wrench them apart again. Bridgett knew what her decision was. Was it too much to hope that Chase's decision was identical?

His expression as serious as her thoughts, Chase nodded at the window. "Here we are."

Bridgett turned and saw they had arrived at the marina and had parked in front of the boat slip that held the *Endeavor,* the sleek Deveraux yacht. Harry opened the door, Chase took Bridgett by the hand and led her toward the gangway. "Everything's all set for you," Harry said.

"Thanks," Chase said.

Bridgett didn't even have to ask if Chase could pilot the vessel. He and all his siblings had learned to navigate all matter of watercraft from the time they were teens. Inside, the yacht was lit with candles and decorated with pastel roses. Chase led her to the helm and then took his place behind the wheel.

"You'll have to give me a minute to get out of here," he said, his attention momentarily diverted as he started the yacht.

"And then what?" Bridgett asked.

"Then we'll talk," Chase promised.

It took a good twenty minutes to get out into the ocean and drop anchor. As soon as they did, Chase cut the engine, took her by the hand and led her to the stateroom, where a bottle of champagne on ice and a sumptuous meal were waiting. Chase's expression was serious as he took her wrist and clasped it warmly. "I know I've never lived this way, Bridgett, but I can give you this kind of life. Between my trust fund and what I earn at the magazine, we could have a dozen homes and as many different kinds of watercraft and cars as you want."

"Oh, Chase." Bridgett sighed, realizing Chase thought a big part of what had attracted her to Martin Morganstern had been his enormous family wealth and elegant lifestyle. "Money was never what I wanted from you. You could live out at the beach at your place and I could live in town at mine, and I'd still be perfectly happy." *As long as I knew you loved me and always would. As long as I knew the two of us would always and forever be there for each other.*

"I don't think that would work for me, the two of us living in two different places. I'm going to be very demanding," Chase told her soberly. "I'm going to want the two of us under one roof. And I'm not about to ask us both to look the other way while we each have our discreet little affairs. There's only going to be one man in your bed, and that's going to be me."

The possessiveness in his blue-gray eyes stole her breath away. "It sounds like you're staking a claim," Bridgett murmured. A pretty long-term claim.

"You better believe I am."

The next thing Bridgett knew, she was in his arms again and he was kissing her with all the tenderness and passion she had ever wanted. She shifted closer, wrapped her arms around his neck and kissed him back with all the love she had in her heart.

Finally, when she was breathless and aching, he scooped her up in his arms and carried her to a bedroom that looked as if it had had no preparation at all, save the usual cleaning. "You didn't turn down the bed?" Bridgett teased as he set her down next to it.

"No way was I hedging my bets." Chase slipped off his tuxedo jacket, his cummerbund and tie. "Besides, I'm not in a hurry tonight."

Her mouth dry, Bridgett watched as he unfastened the first two buttons of his shirt, kicked off his shoes.

"You're very beautiful," he murmured as he took her back in his arms and kissed his way down her neck. "Have I told you that?"

Bridgett's heart pounded with anticipation of the lovemaking to come. "So are you." He felt so good against her, so warm and strong and solid.

"And soft. Especially here." He unclasped the back of her dress and slipped his hand beneath the halter top and bra, gently cupping and caressing her breast. He rubbed his hands across her nipples until she sucked in her breath. He covered her breasts with both palms and massaged them until she trembled. Then he fit his lips around the tip of one breast and suckled lightly until she strained against him. Wanting more. Wanting everything. Bridgett threaded her hands through his hair, holding him close, wanting his slow sensual possession of her never to stop.

He came back up to kiss her thoroughly, taking her mouth in a slow mating dance. He kissed her until she, too, was treating each kiss like a beginning and an end in itself, until she was so aroused she could barely breathe. She moved her hips, rubbing against him. She was so empty inside. So tired of being without him.

"And soft...here..." His other hand lifted her skirt and moved to the inside of her thigh.

Bridgett swayed as he slipped his palm inside her panties. And found her, silky wet. Aware they had just begun to make love to each other and she was already on the brink, she slid a hand inside the waist of his trousers and touched him, too. "And you're...not!"

Rather, he was hard as a rock, hot and velvety smooth. Just touching him that way made her want him deep inside her. But he wasn't to be rushed, she realized, as Chase stayed her hand and drew both her wrists behind her. Unfastened her earrings and set them aside.

He kissed both lobes and then made his way leisurely down the slope of her neck, feathering kisses, taking his time, making sure she understood they were going to do this his way, in his time. "I meant what I said about slowing things down, giving you the kind of loving you should have had the first time," Chase murmured as he unbuttoned and opened his shirt with his free hand, then rubbed his chest across her bared breasts, tantalizing her budding nipples with the silky mat of chest hair and hard muscle beneath.

"How about fast now and slow later?" she whispered back, bringing her lips back to his for another slow, sensual, searing kiss.

He eased her back onto the bed, even as she trembled fervently. His smile was wickedly determined and full of the need to please. "I don't think so."

"Chase…" Sensations hammered at her.

He undressed her slowly, kissing each newly bared expanse of skin. She arched against him as he lingered over her breasts and her thighs and every sweet inch in between. "We've got all night. And this time," he murmured as he clasped her hips in his hands and held her steady, "I won't be rushed." And with that, he set about showing her just how thorough he could be. She offered him whatever he wanted from her, whatever he needed, and she took, too, even as she surged toward the outer limits of her control and beyond.

"I love you, Bridgett," he whispered as she undressed and loved him, too, until he was trembling and just as feverish as she.

"I love you, too, Chase," she whispered back. More than she had ever dreamed possible. Then he was pushing her thighs apart with his knees, lifting her hips and sliding a pillow beneath them. She was shaking with a fierce unquenchable ache. She rocked against him, every part of her wanting every part of him. He kissed her in ways that revealed his soul. He kissed her until she was lost in him, in this. And then he was stroking her gently again with his hands, finding the soft feminine center of her, easing the way. She moaned, wanting to feel connected to him, all the way, not just physically, but heart and soul. And then, at long last, they were one. Moving together, surely, sensually. And he was letting her know, with every deep passionate thrust, that he wanted her every bit as wildly as she wanted him.

Her heart soaring at the love and the intimacy and pleasure she'd found, Bridgett wrapped her arms and legs around him, brought him closer and arching her back, pulled him deeper still. And then there was no more holding back. They were soaring. Shaking. He was so deeply buried in her that they were one, free-falling into ecstasy.

BRIDGETT WASN'T SURE how long it took them to come back down to earth and regain their breaths. She only knew she felt so cozy and right lying there wrapped in his arms that she never wanted to move again. But eventually, of course, they did. Chase eased his weight off her and rolled onto his side. He slid a hand beneath her back, hooked a leg over both of hers and looked down at her, all the love she had ever wanted to see in his eyes.

"I know we talked about marriage," Chase said, taking her hand in his.

Bridgett silenced him with a finger to his lips, wary of anything that might spoil this special moment. "We don't have to talk about that, Chase," she told him seriously, meaning the words with every fiber of her being. "Not anymore. Because I've changed my mind." She was ready now to make some sacrifices, too. "I don't need a ring on my finger or a legal document telling me how you feel." All she had to do was look in his eyes, feel the way he loved her, to know how much he cared for her and always would. "All I need is for us to be together, whenever, however we can be together." The details of which she was sure they would work out over time.

Chase studied her, amazed and pleased. "You mean that, don't you," he murmured.

Bridgett nodded. "With all my heart." To prove it, she kissed him again, sweetly and tenderly, surrendering fully to the love that was in her soul, the love that now bound them together. She had never really trusted a man until now. And the way she trusted Chase, with her future and her happiness, left her feeling wonderful and free of the burden of fear she had carried for so long. She didn't know exactly how things would work out. She just knew that they would.

Chase regarded her affectionately as he threaded a hand through her hair. "There's only one problem with that, Bridgett," he told her. A sentimental smile curved his lips. "I don't want us to simply live together. And I sure as heck don't want us living apart. So that means—" he untangled their bodies and reached over to get something from the bedside-table drawer "—we're going to have to make it official as soon as possible." He folded a velvet ring box into her palm and kissed the back of her hand. "Marry me, Bridgett, and make me the happiest man on this whole planet."

Bridgett's eyes filled with tears and a wave of tenderness washed over her. She'd never felt so happy in her life or so full of hope for their future. "Of course I'll marry you," she said as Chase fit the beautiful diamond ring on the ring finger of her left hand. And their futures pledged, their hearts full of love and wonder, they set about making love all over again.

EPILOGUE

A week later the whole family and guests gathered on the deck of the *Endeavor*. They took the yacht out into the harbor and dropped anchor just off Fort Sumter, with Chase's beach house in view. There, beneath the brilliant South Carolina sun, Chase and Bridgett joined hands beneath an arbor of pastel roses, looked deep into each other's eyes and made the love they shared official.

"I, Bridgett, take thee Chase…"

"To have and to hold…from this day forward…"

"In sickness and in health…as long as we both shall live…"

The minister beamed down at them. "You may kiss the bride."

Chase wrapped her in his arms and kissed her with all the love he had in his heart. Bridgett kissed him back just as passionately. As they drew apart, the guests erupted in cheers and applause. "How does it feel to be Mrs. Chase Deveraux?" Chase teased.

"Every bit as good as it does for you to be my husband." Bridgett winked.

"How about a picture of the entire family?" Daisy Templeton asked, camera in hand.

Chase wrapped his arm around Bridgett's shoulders.

As everyone lined up, he couldn't help but note that Maggie Callaway was talking a lot to Gabe, although they still didn't look as if they were together. But his parents, strangely enough, were hardly talking at all. In fact, in their unguarded moments, he couldn't ever remember seeing them so tense. Which was pretty strange, since this was a very happy occasion and he knew they both approved wholeheartedly of his marriage, as they'd told him so repeatedly in the past few days. Which meant it had to be something else causing the tension between Tom and Grace.

"Everything okay?" Chase asked his mother when they had a moment alone.

Grace smiled. "Of course. I'm very happy for you and Bridgett."

"But...?" Chase prodded.

Grace merely squeezed his arm and moved away. Subject closed.

Frustrated to find his parents still not able to completely work out their differences, whatever the heck they were, Chase turned to his dad. "Did you and Mom have a fight?"

"Fight?" Tom blinked, stunned by both the premise and the question. "No."

"Then what's going on between you two?" Chase persisted.

Tom was silent a moment as he stared down at his champagne. Finally he confided, "Weddings have been hard for us since our divorce. I guess they remind us of our own failure. But your mother and I are happy for you and Bridgett, Chase. Very happy."

Chase could see that, just as he could see something

else was going on. Something neither of his parents wanted him to know.

He also knew, whatever the answer, the mystery would not be solved tonight. So he put it aside, accepted his father's good wishes and moved across the deck. Maybe his parents would get back together yet. But whatever happened, Chase knew it was going to take time. His heart full of hope for the future, he returned to his new bride. Bridgett was seated next to Mitch and laughing at something his sister, Amy, said. As Chase reflected on the events leading up to the wedding, he realized that Amy had seemed pretty happy, if a little wistful at times. Which made sense. She had never made a secret of wanting a family of her own. She just hadn't found the right guy. But Mitch had not seemed happy at all. Maybe it was because Mitch had recently been through a bitter divorce. Or maybe, Chase thought, something else was bringing Mitch's spirits down. Like a problem at work. Chase knew Mitch wanted a more important role in the family shipping company than simply being one of the vice presidents on his father's executive staff. But with Tom still so young and vital and immersed in the business, it wasn't likely to happen soon. Tom probably wouldn't hand over the reins of the family company to Mitch for another ten or fifteen years, at the earliest.

"You don't have to pity me," Mitch said to Chase as he stood to let Chase sit down at the table.

"I wasn't—"

"Yeah, you were," Mitch said, looking Chase straight in the eye. He touched his shoulder. "And it's not necessary. I'm fine. You just pay attention to your new bride."

"What was that about?" Bridgett said when Chase sat down and Mitch moved off.

Chase grinned. "Some guy thing. Not to worry. He'll work it out." And he knew Mitch would, too, because Mitch had Deveraux blood in him, and the Deveraux were one hardy, resilient bunch.

After dinner the yacht motored back to shore. The guests disembarked, and then Chase and Bridgett took the yacht back out to sea and dropped anchor. "Alone at last," Chase teased as he took Bridgett in his arms.

"And not a moment too soon." Bridgett stood on tiptoe, wreathed her arms about his neck and kissed him tenderly. "I love you, Chase Deveraux," she whispered softly.

"And I love you, Bridgett. With all my heart."

They kissed again, and then hand in hand, turned to go below.

Their wedding-night lovemaking was as tender and passionate as Bridgett could ever have wished. Arm in arm, they went aloft to watch the dawn. There, in the mists hovering above the water, was the specter of a beautiful young woman in white. She was unmistakably a Deveraux. And her ghostly image disappeared almost as soon as it appeared.

"Eleanor," Chase said.

"I'd say it was our imagination if not for this." Bridgett picked up one of a dozen or more red rose petals scattered across the deck of the yacht and a faded card, with the words "A Love that Lasts Forever" written across its front. Inside the card was one word— "Mitch."

"What do you think this means?" Bridgett asked

Chase as a chill breeze moved across the deck and sent her into his arms.

Chase held Bridgett close. "I don't know," he said, studying the beautifully penned script with a frown. "Unless…"

"What?" Bridgett asked, her heart pounding as she clung to Chase.

Chase shrugged and guessed, "Mitch is next."

* * * * *

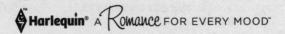

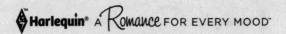

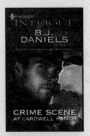